DAVID DRAKE

"Drake has distinguished himself as the master of the mercenary science fiction novel."
—R*A*V*E Reviews

"One of the most gifted users of military raw material at work today in science fiction."
—Chicago Sun-Times

"David Drake is one of those rare authors who seems capable of switching from one mode of writing to another, hard science to near-future political thriller to high fantasy, with a smooth meshing of gears."
—Science Fiction Chronicle

"Another first-class story of picked mercenaries . . . reflects Drake's interest in classical mythology."
—Booklist

"Top-quality military action and a generous dose of political intrigue . . . Drake's talent for detailing military hardware and battle scenes results in a satisfying blend of gritty realism and human drama."
—Library Journal

"Very well done exciting stuff."
—Interzone

Tor Books by David Drake

THE
VOYAGE

David Drake

A TOM DOHERTY ASSOCIATES BOOK
NEW YORK

This is a work of fiction. All the characters and events portrayed in this book are either fictitious, or are used fictitiously.

THE VOYAGE

Cover art by Donato

A Tor Book
Published by Tom Doherty Associates, Inc.
175 Fifth Avenue
New York, N.Y. 10010

Tor® is a registered trademark of Tom Doherty Associates, Inc.

ISBN 0-812-51340-1
Library of Congress Card Catalog Number: 93-33506

First edition: January 1994
First mass market edition: September 1995

Printed in the United States of America

0 9 8 7 6 5 4 3 2 1

To Clyde and Carlie Howard
Because they're friends—and in hope that it was
worth the wait.

ACKNOWLEDGMENTS

It's amazing the number of people who helped me on this one. As I edited my manuscript, I kept noticing places where a friend had been of direct assistance (and there were others that I don't recall, I'm sure).

Among the folks I owe on this one are Dan Breen, Sandra Miesel, John Rieber and Kent Williams, Mark Van Name, Allyn Vogel, Clyde and Carlie Howard, and my wife Jo. As I said, there were others as well.

I owe a particular debt to Tom Doherty. Not because he bought the book (which I appreciate, but somebody was going to buy it) but rather because he saved me from myself when the size of the project became clear to me.

It's good to have friends.

Contents

Telaria

—⁂—

A S NED SLADE walked toward the dockyard building
with the HEADQUARTERS—PANCAHTE EXPEDITION sign
on the door, a line of six human males and a squat, shaggy
alien from Racontis jogged past.

"You wonder why I'm a private," the leader sang.

"And why I sleep in the ditch," sang-wheezed the remaining joggers in several keys. The Racontid had a clear, carrying
voice which would better have suited an angel than a creature
which could pull a strong man apart with its bare hands.

A metal saw shrilled within the starship in the adjacent
frames, overwhelming the song. Ned's mind supplied the
words anyway: *"It's not because I'm stupid, but I just don't
want to be rich . . ."*

The door was ajar. Ned knocked, but he couldn't hear the
rap of his own knuckles over the saw, so he let himself in.

"Shut the curst thing!" ordered the man at the electronic
desk, cupping a palm over his telephone handset. He was
paunchy and at least sixty standard years old. "I can't hear
myself think!"

As he spoke, the sawblade coasted back to silence. The fellow at the desk returned to his call. The rangy, somewhat younger man leaning against the office wall prevented Ned from swinging the door to. "Leave it, kid," the man said. "I like the ventilation."

Ned looked from one stranger to the other. Neither of them paid him any attention. "No," the older man said into his handset, "I'm Adjutant Tadziki, but it will *not* help if you call back when Captain Doormann is here. She's already made her decision on a supplier."

Tadziki looked like a bureaucrat. The other fellow wore a stone-pattern camouflaged jumpsuit with WARSON, T over the left breast pocket. Ned didn't recognize the uniform, but Warson was as obviously a soldier as the men and the Racontid jogging around the starship outside were. Warson continued to gaze out the window, singing under his breath, *"I could've been a general and send out folks to die . . ."*

"No," said the adjutant, "since she'll be eating the rations herself, your offer of saving three-hundredths per kilo isn't very important to her—and it *bloody* well isn't important to me!"

"But the sort of things a general does," Ned murmured, watching the soldier, *"they make me want to cry."*

Warson turned sharply. "You know the song?" he asked.

Tadziki slammed down the handset. "Fucking idiot!" he said.

"Yeah, but in an armored unit it's *'You ask why I'm a trooper,'* " Ned said. "That's the way I learned it."

"Where?" Tadziki asked. "And for that matter, who the hell are you?"

"On Nieuw Friesland," Ned said. "In the Frisian Defense Forces. I'm Reserve Ensign Slade, but I'm from Tethys originally."

"Slade?" Warson said in amazement. "You're *Don* Slade? Via, you can't be!"

Ned's lips tightened. "You're thinking of my uncle," he said stiffly. "I'm not Don Slade, no."

The voices of the jogging troops became faintly louder.

They were making circuits around the vessel under construction. Warson nodded disdainfully toward the window and said, "Herne Lordling's got us doing an hour's run each day to shape us up. They're singing that to piss him off."

"Lordling's a general?" Ned asked.

"He was a colonel," Warson said. "He's a pissant, is what he really is. Sure you want to join a rinkydink outfit being run by a pissant, kid?"

"Lordling isn't running anything," Tadziki said sharply. "Captain Doormann gave the order, and she gives all the orders."

He suddenly smiled. "Via, Toll," he added, patting his gut. "I'm twenty years older than you and I'd never run across a *room* before this stuff started. It's still a good idea."

"I could have been a colonel," the joggers chorused, *"but there it is again . . ."*

"I want to join the Pancahte Expedition, yeah," Ned said, handing an identification chip across the desk to the adjutant. "Whoever's running it."

"We're pretty full up," Warson said without emotion. He could have been commenting on the color of the Telarian sky, pale white with faint gray streaks.

"The plush seats colonels sit on, they tickle my sensitive skin . . ."

"The captain makes all those decisions, Toll," said the adjutant as he watched the data his desk summoned from Ned's ID. "Especially those decisions."

"I never met your uncle," Toll Warson said, eyeing Ned with quiet speculation. His look was that of a man who had absolutely nothing to prove—but who would be willing to prove it any way, any time, anywhere, if somebody pushed him a little too far.

Ned recognized the expression well. He'd seen it often enough in his uncle's eyes.

The door to the inner room opened. A man in fluorescent, extremely expensive clothing looked out and said, "Did you say Lissea had . . . ?" He seemed to be about Ned's age, twenty-four years standard. A quick glance around the outer office, empty save for the three men, ended his question.

Tadziki answered it anyway. "Sorry, Master Doormann," he said. "I'm sure she's coming, but I'm afraid she must still be in the armaments warehouse with Herne."

The young man grimaced in embarrassment and disappeared behind the closed door again.

"Lucas Doormann," Tadziki explained in a low voice. "He's son of Doormann Trading's president—that's Karel Doormann—but he's not a bad kid. He's trying to help, anyway, when his father would sooner slit all our throats."

"Didn't have balls enough to volunteer to come along, though," Warson said, again without emotional loading.

"Via, Toll, would you want him?" Tadziki demanded. "He *maybe* knows not to stand at the small end of a gun."

Warson shrugged. "Different question," he said.

The phone rang. Tadziki winced. "Toll," he said, "how about you play adjutant for half an hour and I take Slade here over the *Swift*? Right?"

Warson's smile was as blocky as ice crumpling across a river in spring. He reached for the handset. "You bet," he said. "Does that mean I get all the rake-off from suppliers, too?"

Tadziki hooked a finger to lead Ned out of the office. "Try anything funny," he growled, "and you'll save the Pancahtans the trouble of shooting you."

Warson laughed as he picked up the phone. Ned heard him say, "Pancahte Expedition, the Lord Almighty speaking."

The adjutant paused outside the office and looked up at the vessel in the frames. She was small as starships went, but her forty meters of length made her look enormous by comparison with the fusion-powered tanks Ned had learned to operate and deploy on Friesland.

"What do you know about this operation, kid?" Tadziki asked.

"I know," Ned said carefully, "that I prefer to be called Slade, or Ned, or dickhead . . . sir."

Tadziki raised an eyebrow. "Touchy, are we?" he asked.

Ned smiled. "Nope. When I get to be somebody, maybe I'll

get touchy, too. But since it was you I was talking to, I thought I'd mention it.''

"Yeah, don't say anything to Toll Warson that he's likely to take wrong,'' Tadziki agreed. "Do you know about him?''

Ned shook his head.

"Well, this is just a story,'' Tadziki said. "A rumor. You know, stories get twisted a lot in the telling.''

''. . . could've been an officer,'' sang the joggers as they rounded the nose of the vessel. They moved at a modest pace, but one that would carry them seven or eight kilometers in an hour if they kept it up. The Racontid ran splay-legged, like a wolverine on its hind legs.

"But I was just too smart . . ."

"Seems Toll and his brother Deke had a problem with a battalion commander on Stanway a few years back,'' Tadziki said.

"They stripped away my rank tabs . . ."

"One night the CO pushed the switch to close up his command car—''

"When they saw me walk and fart!"

''—and the fusion bottle vented into the vehicle's interior,'' Tadziki said. He cleared his throat. "Toll and Deke turned out to have deserted a few hours before, hopping two separate freighters off-planet. Some people suggested there might have been a connection.''

He nodded to the boarding bridge to the hatch amidships. "Let's go aboard.''

They walked in single file, the adjutant leading. Power cables and high-pressure lines snaked up the bridge and into the ship, narrowing the track.

"He looks like the kind who'd play hardball,'' Ned said with deliberate calm, "Toll Warson does. But that's what I'd expect from people who'd—respond to Lissea Doormann's offer.''

Tadziki laughed harshly as he ducked to enter the vessel. He would have cleared the transom anyway, unlike Ned who was taller by fifteen centimeters. "You don't know the half of it, Slade,'' he said. "The battalion commander was their own brother. Half brother.''

The inner face of the airlock projected a meter into the vessel. Tadziki gestured around the vessel's main bay, crowded now by workmen in protective gear operating welders and less identifiable tools. "Welcome to the *Swift*, trooper," the adjutant said. "If you decide to go through with your application, and *if* you're picked, she'll be your home for the next long while."

Tadziki looked at Ned. "Maybe the rest of your life."

"It'll do," Ned said. "Anyway, it's roomier than a tank."

The bay was filled with bunks stacked two-high on either side of a central aisle. The pairs were set with a respectable space open between them, because they gimballed in three axes to act as acceleration couches. That meant there was no storage within the bay except for the narrow drawer beneath each mattress.

There were two navigation consoles forward, still part of the open bay. Astern were two partitioned cubicles and, against the heavy bulkhead separating the bay from the engine compartment, an alcove holding a commode. Workmen were installing a folding door to screen the commode.

"That was my idea," Tadziki explained with a glance toward the alcove. "Lissea said she didn't need special favors. I told her she might think she was just one of the guys, but things were going to be tense enough without her dropping her trousers in front of everybody on a regular basis."

Ned nodded to show he was listening while he scanned the confusion to count places. There were sixteen bunks, plus the pair of navigation couches and the private cubicles for—presumably—the captain and adjutant. It was possible but very unlikely that there were bunks in the engine compartment as well.

"Twenty places," Tadziki said in confirmation. "Six of them for ship's crew—sailors. A few of the others can double in brass. I can."

He looked sharply at Ned. "I gather from the curriculum in your ID you know something about ships yourself?"

Ned shrugged. "I've had a course in basic navigation," he

agreed. "In a pinch, I'd be better than punching in coordinates blind, I suppose. And fusion bottles are pretty much the same, tanks or starships."

The saw began to shriek again as a workman shortened the mounting stanchion of the pair of bunks which had to clear the airlock's encroachment. The sound was painful. Despite the tool's suction hood, chips of hot steel sprayed about the bay.

Ned backed out onto the boarding bridge a moment before the adjutant gestured him to do so. When the workman shut the saw down, Ned said, "I was at home in Slade House on Tethys when Captain Doormann's message came. That's all I know about the expedition—that Lissea Doormann's preparing to visit the Lost Colony of Pancahte with a picked crew."

"And," Tadziki said, nodding but smiling slightly as well, "that she invited Captain Donald Slade to accompany her."

"She could do worse than take Uncle Don," Ned said crisply. "She could do worse than take me, too."

An air-wrench began to pound within the *Swift*'s bay. Tadziki motioned Ned to follow him back down the boarding bridge, sauntering this time.

"Telaria's pretty much a family concern," the adjutant explained. "The Doormann family. There's a planetary assembly here at Landfall City, but the real decisions get made at the Doormann estate just outside the town proper."

He nodded vaguely northward.

"Okay," Ned said to show that he understood the situation—as he certainly did. Many of the less populous (and not necessarily less advanced) human worlds were run by a family or a tight-knit oligarchy. On Tethys, the Slade family had been preeminent since the planet was settled centuries before.

"Twenty-odd years ago, there was a flash meeting of the Doormann Trading board while the president, Grey Doormann, was on a junket off-system on Dell," Tadziki said. "Grey's half brother Karel replaced him as president. The genetic access codes to Doormann Trading facilities and data banks were reset to deny Grey entry."

The joggers had finished their exercise and were straggling

toward the two-story prefab beside the office building. None of the men were less than ten years older than Ned. They moved with the heavy grace of male lions.

"Okay," Ned repeated. Power was a commodity always in short supply. The events Tadziki had described were thoroughly civilized. On some worlds, a similar transfer would have been conducted by hirelings like Toll Warson and Don Slade, late of Hammer's Slammers.

The adjutant paused at the base of the boarding bridge and looked out across the dockyard. A mobile crane squealed as its boom lowered a drive motor into place. A dirigible carried a slingload of hull plates slowly across the sky to a freighter being constructed at the opposite end of the complex. The thrum of nacelle-mounted props provided a bass line to the yard's higher-pitched activities.

"Karel didn't know Grey's wife had just borne a daughter, though," Tadziki said. "They left the baby on Dell to be raised by a couple there they trusted. The parents came back and lived in a private bungalow here on the Doormann estate, as quiet as church mice."

"Lissea Doormann was the daughter?" Ned said, again to show that he followed.

"You bet," Tadziki agreed. "She had the genes, and there wasn't a specific block on her code . . . so six months ago, she waltzed into the middle of a board meeting to demand a seat and control of her branch of the family's stock. Grey had left Karel with a proxy when he went dicking off to Dell. Lissea claimed to revoke it as assignee of her father's interest."

He shook his head and smiled. "I'd have liked to been at that meeting," he added.

Ned frowned. "Weren't there human guards?" he asked.

"Close to a thousand of them," the adjutant said. "I've seen base camps in war zones that weren't near as well defended as the Doormann estate. But she *was* a Doormann, an unarmed woman. The guards didn't realize just who she was, but they curst well knew that if she was a family member, she could have them flayed if they were uppity enough to lay a hand on her."

Ned grinned and looked back at the *Swift*. "The prodigal daughter returns," he murmured. "It sure proves the expedition's leader has guts."

While the commercial liner that brought him to Telaria landed, Ned had watched the displays. The hectares of open area north of Landfall City proper (strip development surrounded it on all sides) must be the Doormann estate rather than a large public park as he'd assumed. There was a tall central spire and scores of smaller buildings scattered over the grounds.

"Oh, she's got guts, all right," Tadziki said. "Brains, too. Lissea's foster father had her trained as an electronics engineer, and she's a good one. I doubt there was ever anything Lissea really cared about besides booting her uncle out of the presidency, but she's an asset to the expedition as an engineer, believe me."

"*Why* an expedition to Pancahte?" Ned prompted.

"The short answer," Tadziki said, "is that seventy years ago one Lendell Doormann embezzled a large sum from Doormann Trading and fled, it's rumored, to Pancahte. Now, what Karel might have done if he'd had Lissea alone is one thing, but at a board meeting where everybody present was her relative as well as his, well . . . they weren't going to just call in the guards. So Karel came up with a compromise."

Ned pursed his lips. "Lissea recovers the missing assets from Pancahte, in exchange for which, Karel doesn't challenge her right to vote her father's stock."

"When she returns," Tadziki agreed. "Which Karel doesn't think she's going to do." He gave Ned a rock-hard smile. Ned was suddenly aware that Tadziki deserved to be adjutant of a force comprised of men like Toll Warson. "Me," Tadziki said, "I'm betting on the lady. I'm betting my life."

A limousine drove through the dockyard gates. Men in blue uniforms on three-wheelers escorted the car before and behind. The guards carried iridium-barreled powerguns like those of President Hammer's forces on Nieuw Friesland.

Ned thought of the veterans of Hammer's mercenary regiment whom he'd met, men and women whose scars were as often behind their eyes as on their skin. Veterans like Don Slade.

The guards looked like puppies.

The limousine drew up in front of the office. A big man jumped from one side of the vehicle and strode quickly around the back toward the other door. He wore a holstered pistol and battledress which blurred chameleonlike to match its surroundings.

"Herne Lordling," Tadziki murmured. He walked toward the office with Ned a half-step behind. "Who—whatever he likes to think—reports to the captain the same as does every other member of the crew."

The limousine's other door opened from the inside before Lordling reached it. A slim dark woman got out and started directly for the office. Lordling fell into step, but there was no suggestion that the woman would have waited if he had lagged behind.

"Time to introduce you to Captain Lissea Doormann," Tadziki said. He smiled. "Ned."

Lucas Doormann stood in the doorway to the inner office, saying, "Lissea, I'm glad to—"

Toll Warson had a broad grin on his face. He held the telephone handset out at arm's length. The gabble from whoever was at the other end of line was an insectile chirping.

"Toll, where's Tad—" Lissea Doormann said before she turned in response to the gesture of Warson's free hand. Herne Lordling bumped into her, then jumped back and was blocked by Ned Slade's forearm—outstretched instinctively to keep the big ex-colonel from crushing Tadziki against the door-jamb.

"Sorry, s—" Ned began.

Lordling cocked his fist. He was as tall as Ned and bulkier; not in the least soft, but no man of fifty was likely to be in the shape Ned was no matter how he pushed his body.

On the other hand, Lordling carried a gun.

Tadziki laid his palm across Lordling's knuckles. "Do you have business in my office, Herne?" he asked coolly. "Because I do, and brawling isn't part of it."

"Lucas, I'm terribly sorry," Lissea said with at least a pretense of sincerity. Up close, she had a sparkling hardness that belied her slight build.

She pressed Lucas' right hand in both of her own, then spun to take in the situation in the outer doorway. "Herne, *will* you stop pretending you're my shadow. Tadziki, where have you been? Herne says the arsenal's trying to fob us off with overaged powergun ammunition!"

"The invoice is for lots manufactured within the past three years, Captain," Tadziki said. "Well within usage parameters."

"That's not what's set aside for us in the arsenal," Lordling snapped.

"I don't have any control over the arsenal's procedures, Herne," the adjutant said with a politeness so icy it burned. "I *do* have control over what we receive aboard the *Swift* per invoice, and I assure you that I will continue doing my job in that respect. As no doubt you will have opportunities to do your job after we're under way."

Toll Warson chuckled. If there could have been any sound more offensive than Tadziki's tone, Warson's laughter was it. Ned noticed that Warson had dropped the telephone and was holding instead a paperweight, a kilogram lump of meteoritic iron which his callused palm nearly swallowed.

"*Stop* this," Lissea said crisply. "Toll, you're not needed here. Herne, neither are you. Tadziki, I'll expect you to double-check the ammunition before it comes aboard."

The adjutant nodded. "Yes ma'am," he said, gesturing toward Ned with a cupped hand as he spoke. "I was just showing the *Swift* to a potential recruit for the expedition here."

"*Blood*, Tadziki!" said Herne Lordling. Neither he nor Watson seemed in any hurry to leave the office. He looked at Ned and added, "The Pancahte Expedition's by invitation only, kid. Go back home till you grow up."

"My name's Slade," Ned said in a voice as thin and clear

as a glass razor. "I came in response to the courier Captain Doormann sent to Tethys."

His eyes were on Lordling, but the older man was a mass rather than a person. If the mass shifted significantly, if the hands moved or the legs, Ned would strike first for the throat and then—

"You're Don Slade?" Lordling said in amazement.

"His uncle didn't choose to accept the invitation," Tadziki interjected smoothly. "Ensign Slade here did. He's a graduate of the Frisian Military Academy and he's served with the planetary forces in pacification work."

"The Pancahte Expedition isn't for just anybody, Slade," Lucas Doormann said. The young noble wasn't actively hostile, but he *was* glad to find someone in the gathering whom he could patronize safely the way he could most of the civilians of his acquaintance.

Lissea looked at her cousin. "He isn't just anybody," she said. "He's Don Slade's nephew."

"I'm Edward Slade," Ned said, more sharply than he'd intended.

Lissea eyed Ned with the cold speculation of a shopper choosing one mango from a tray of forty. He stood at attention. Nobody spoke for a moment.

She grimaced and glanced over at her adjutant. "We've filled nineteen, haven't we, Tadziki?"

"Yessir, but—"

Lissea's focus hadn't left Ned when she asked for affirmation of what she knew already. "Sorry, Master Slade," she said. "We'll keep your name on the list if you like, but I can't hold out much—"

"As a matter of fact, Captain," Tadziki said, "I want to talk to you about the ship's internal layout. I don't think I should have a private compartment—or a single bunk."

"How many tankers do you have in the troops you've signed on, ma'am?" Ned asked. His eyes were front and level, focused on a strand that wind had lifted from Lissea's near skullcap of short black hair.

"We don't have any tanks either, Slade," Lissea said in

puzzlement at the pointless question.

"And your enemies, ma'am?" Ned said. "You're sure they don't have tanks?"

Toll Warson chuckled again, softly this time. "Nice shot, kid," he murmured.

"We don't know a great deal about conditions on Pancahte," Lissea Doormann said coolly. A smile touched her lips, slight, but the first sign of good humor Ned had seen her express. The stress on a young woman welding together men like these would be greater than that of anything Ned could imagine attempting.

"As a matter of fact," she continued, the smile flicking off and on with the suddenness of a serpent's tongue, "we know bugger-all about Pancahte, which is why it's called the Lost Colony."

She looked at her adjutant. "Tadziki, if you're so sure you want to berth in the open bay, give the orders. We'll decide what to do with the space later."

"Lissea, what do you think you're doing?" Herne Lordling demanded. "He's an *applicant*. He hasn't even passed the physical and the proficiency testing!"

Toll Warson gave Ned a speculative look, appraising him from a viewpoint quite different from the parameters against which Lissea had measured the potential recruit moments before. "I can run him through that now if you like, ma'am," he offered.

"No," Lissea said crisply. "Perhaps when we get back. Lucas?"

The nobleman, seemingly forgotten during a discussion of which he understood enough to be concerned, brightened.

"There's no problem getting Slade into the laboratory with us, is there?" Lissea said. "He has an Academy background which I think might be useful." She looked at Tadziki. "Whether or not we accept him for the expedition itself."

"Well, I—" Lucas Doormann said.

He was speaking to Lissea's back, because she'd already started out of the office. "Come along, Slade," she ordered without looking around. "You can tell us about yourself in the car."

Ned bowed to Lucas, then gestured the nobleman to precede him through the door.

"I will *not* have some kid who doesn't know his ass from a hole in the ground endangering the lives of everybody on the expedition, Lissea!" Lordling said.

Lissea, as petite as the sharp steel tip of a push dagger, turned in the hazy sunlight. "That's fine, Herne," she said. "Neither would I, so we don't have a problem."

The limousine's door was still open. She hopped in. As Lucas Doormann went around to the other side, Lissea slid over on the soft lip of the seat and motioned Ned to sit beside her.

In the office, Toll Warson was chuckling again.

The limousine had no windows, but the interior of the armored passenger compartment was covered with vision screens. The view was a little grainy, and primary colors didn't match perfectly from one panel to the next; but Ned's interest wasn't in Telarian scenery anyway.

"Why's Tadziki in your court, Slade?" Lissea asked bluntly. Her body swayed as the driver pulled a hard turn to point the limo toward the dockyard gate.

Ned locked his left hand against the panel separating the passengers from the driver's compartment; his right gripped the plush seat in determination not to slide into the diminutive woman. "Ma'am," he said, "I'm curst if I know. He read the file out of my ID, but I won't pretend I'm, well—"

Dry land on Tethys was scattered among thousands of islands and islets; aircars capable of free flight were the standard means of transport. The ride of this limousine, bonded to the ground by elastic metal tires, had a disquieting solidity.

Ned shrugged. "Look, I've been shot at, and I've shot back. But I won't pretend that I'm my uncle Don."

Lucas Doormann leaned forward to look at Ned. "Not yet, at least," Lucas said.

They were heading north on a high-speed motorway. The escort kept a clear space around the limousine, but traffic wasn't heavy.

"Whatever," Ned said. That was a polite lie. Don Slade had learned a lot of things in twenty years as a mercenary. From what Ned had seen in the brief periods the two of them were alone together, many of those were things neither Ned nor anybody else wanted to know.

Lissea sank back against the seat cushion and crossed her hands behind her neck. "My great-granduncle Lendell Doormann," she said with her eyes closed, "was one of three brothers. He wasn't interested in business—the trading side, that is."

"Or politics," Lucas said. "That's business too, if you're a Doormann."

Ned nodded, though the statement should have been broader. Politics were a part of human life. People who thought they didn't play politics, simply played politics badly.

"Lendell was a scientist," Lissea said. "He was head of research for the company—and good enough to have gotten the position even if he hadn't been family. Nobody paid much attention to what he was doing. He didn't bother his siblings, which permitted them to operate more freely in the real affairs of Doormann Trading."

"They were trying to extend family interests on Dell," Lucas said. "It ended up with the chief planetary administrator being appointed by Doormann Trading."

The limousine swung down an off-ramp framed by a pair of pillboxes. Uniformed guards presented arms as the car thundered past.

"Lendell told his brothers he was on the track of a means of instantaneous transportation," Lissea said. "Distance would no longer exist. They were interested—after all, we *are* an interstellar trading company. But they didn't understand even the first syllables of the explanation Lendell tried to give them. Afterwards, it turned out that Lendell's closest associates in his department didn't understand much more."

"Lendell's personal laboratory was in a sub-basement of

the main spire of the estate,'' Lucas said. ''The regular R&D facilities were across town in the spaceport rather than part of the estate. There's sometimes risk during testing, so that was a normal safety precaution.''

The limousine slowed, causing the passengers to bob forward. The car was on a viaduct that was about to arch over a wall. Looking down, Ned saw a six-lane highway paralleling the exterior face of the walled enclosure but set back from it by a chain-link fence and twenty meters of coarse vegetation.

The buffer wasn't a landscaping feature. Rather, it was whatever greenery sprang up in a minefield that was occasionally burned off because it couldn't be safely mowed.

The wall was about four meters high. Towers studded the circuit at half-kilometer intervals. Each tower mounted an anti-starship weapon with a bore larger than the twenty-cm main guns of President Hammer's tanks.

Two of the huge guns tracked the limousine as it approached.

''Then the bills started to come due,'' Lissea said. ''They were enormous, for the costs of Lendell's supplies and particularly for the real-time transgalactic conferencing in which he'd indulged to get the information he needed for his obsession.''

The limousine stopped. A pair of guards bent to check the identification of the driver. Because the receptors feeding the ''windows'' of the passenger compartment were on the vehicle's exterior, the driver him/herself remained invisible.

''The ultimate total,'' Lucas said, ''was nearly thirty percent of Doormann Trading's book value. The bills were years coming in. Lendell's personal holdings wouldn't have covered a fifth of the amount.''

The limousine eased down the inner slope of the viaduct, leaving the escort of three-wheelers behind. They were headed at a sedate pace toward the gleaming spire which dominated the enclave of manicured vegetation and low, classically styled buildings nestled against rolling hills.

''He'd hocused the data banks, of course,'' Lissea said. ''Even given his name and position, it was a brilliant job—

and completely secondary to his real purpose, building his . . . his . . .''

The spire was a cone with fluted exterior walls. The shallow flutes twisted slowly, describing one full revolution by the time they rose to the top of the building.

The limousine pulled up in front of the entrance. Armed guards sprang to attention. Civilian underlings, chatting as they exited the lobby, quieted and scurried respectfully aside as they noticed the vehicle. A young woman carrying an infant to show to her coworkers turned her back and cooed to hush the child.

"Matter transmitter," Lucas supplied.

"No," Lissea said, shaking her head fiercely. "That's making an assumption that *I* can't justify from the evidence."

She leaned across Ned's body—her touch was startlingly warm—and pressed a latch invisible to him until the door opened and the screen blanked. Ned got out quickly. Lissea followed, and Lucas trotted around the car from the opposite side to follow them.

The civilians who'd been walking toward the bronze-and-crystal entrance before the limo arrived held chip-implanted IDs with which to trip the electronic latches under the watchful eyes of the guards. The clear panels slid aside for Lucas and Lissea automatically. Ned and the two nobles strode inside together through a detector frame.

The lobby was floored in metamorphic stone which held tiny speckles of pure red against swirling gray shades. It reminded Ned of a starscape seen from high orbit. The joints indicated that each slab was over three meters wide and longer still.

Civilians inside had seen Lucas coming through the crystal. They crowded to the sides of the lobby. Lucas nodded to an elderly man in an expensively conservative suit; the fellow bobbed a near bow and said, "Master Lucas!"

One of the bank of elevators facing the front doors opened. The babble of its passengers stilled into silence, relieved by coughs and nervous shuffling. The people caught in the elevator cage were afraid to stay or move in any direction lest whatever they did seem disrespectful.

Tethys had never been like this. Never. But Ned's stomach turned at memory of the rank he'd taken for granted at home.

On Telaria, Edward Slade was nothing . . . and at the moment he preferred it that way.

"May we use this elevator please," Lucas Doormann said to the open cage, pleasant enough but with no more question in his words than the owner of a dog has when trying to silence the beast. The occupants scattered like roaches from a light.

Lucas got in and brushed button S3 with his fingertip. He didn't bother to check whether or not his companions were clear of the door.

Ned noticed with amusement how much the young nobleman's attitude had changed since he regained his home ground. It was a compliment to Lucas' intelligence, or at least to his instincts. His diffidence among the mercenaries meant he realized men like Warson or Lordling might shoot him out of hand, whatever his wealth or lineage.

"What *is* known," Lissea resumed, as the cage dropped swiftly, "is that when the family realized Lendell was linked to the problem—"

"They didn't know the extent of the problem," Lucas said. "They didn't dream of the real extent."

"—his brothers called on him in his personal laboratory with an escort."

The elevator slowed, then settled with a lurch. Subbasement 3 wasn't a common destination. The door opened on a lobby, brightly lighted but broken into aisles by stacks of hardboard boxes. Lucas led the way to the left.

"As they entered the lab . . ." Lissea said.

They came to a metal-finished door. A kiosk of structural plastic, clearly an add-on, stood adjacent. Someone was snoring inside. Legs, clad in a gray uniform, projected from the open door of the kiosk along a bench made of storage boxes.

"Open up there!" Lucas shouted in a blaze of real anger. "At once!"

The legs thrashed. A man bolted upright so that his head

was visible through the kiosk's front window. Then he fell off whatever he'd been lying on. "Look," he whined as he clambered to his feet, "if you were in such a bloody hurry, you could've called, couldn't you?"

He tapped the one-piece phone scabbed to the side of his kiosk, bent, and hacked to clear his throat of phlegm. He was middle-aged, wispily balding, and soft rather than fat. His face was pockmarked, and stains of some sort marked the front of his rumpled gray uniform. The name-tape read PLATT.

When Platt's eyes focused, he recognized Lucas Doormann. He gasped and bowed, furtively wiping drool from his receding chin. "Master!" He mumbled to the floor. "I've served your family all my life. I assure—"

"Just open the curst laboratory, man!" Lissea snapped disgustedly.

In any hierarchical system, there were going to be people on the bottom. The attendant at a doorway nobody used was about as low a rung as there was. It still wasn't pretty to watch.

Platt stumbled to the shining door and held his card to the center of the panel. He was more awkward than usual because of his determination to stare fixedly at the floor. "No disrespect, master," he mumbled. "Didn't imagine it was *you,* master."

The trio strode past him, controlling varying emotions. Ned's stomach turned because he was part of a social continuum that included persons like Platt.

When the door opened fully, lights came on within the laboratory. It was a big room, ten meters by thirty. The illumination by hundreds, *thousands,* of microminiature point sources was harsh, brilliant, and shadowless. For the first time, Ned got a sense of Lendell Doormann as a person—

And a very strange person he must have been.

"Is that the—" Lissea began, walking toward the dais at the far end of the room.

"Yes," said Lucas. "That's where the—the capsule was when Lendell's brothers arrived to confront him."

The laboratory was divided into specialties. Burners, sinks, and piping so clear that only the haze of decades gave it form, stood cheek by jowl with a computer console feeding a holographic display meters in diameter. An intricate test pattern ran on the display.

Ned hadn't realized that such a unit had been available anywhere seventy years before. He could only guess what resolution and computing power like that must have cost at the time.

Lissea stopped short of the empty dais. Twelve black pentagonal mirrors stood on thin wands to focus into the air above the horizontal surface. The inner surfaces were slightly concave, distorting their images of Lissea oddly. Her reflections looked as though she was drowning in tannin-rich jungle pools.

"When his brothers and the guards entered this room," she said, "Lendell was about to enter the capsule that stood here. It was described variously as egg-shaped and as a sphere compressed in the middle. There were recording devices, both as part of the laboratory equipment and in the helmets of the guards, but the shape of the device seems to vary in those images also."

"The capsule was two meters high," Lucas said. "Lendell wasn't tall, about a meter seventy. The witnesses could judge the capsule's height against his."

The air in the laboratory was dry and as dead to the nostrils as a mouthful of cotton. Ned could hear both his companions perfectly, though he still stood near the door and the two of them had advanced some distance within the room.

"They yelled at him to stop," Lissea said, running her palm a few centimeters above the surface of the dais. "No one threatened him. He was a Doormann, after all, no matter what he might have done. He looked back and called something. There was a crackling or perhaps roaring in the air, so no one could hear the words."

"One of the guards thought Lendell said, 'You'll understand in a moment,'" Lucas said. "But he wasn't sure."

"Lendell closed the capsule over himself," Lissea said. "It was split vertically in halves, and there was nothing, or at least very little inside it. But when it closed, everything on the platform vanished."

"Was there a sound?" Ned asked. "A pop, an implosion?"

Lissea turned and shrugged. "Nobody heard it," she said. "Nobody would have heard it with the noise as loud as they said it was."

"That was the transformers," Lucas said. "One of the staff from the normal R&D facility was summoned to turn them off. It turned out that Lendell had routed all the generating capacity of the *planetary* grid to his equipment for his final experiment. The spire itself was the only building on Telaria to have mains power until the transformers were disconnected."

"I thought . . ." Ned said, ". . . that Lendell fled with something. From what you say, he simply spent the money, wasted it. He didn't take it with him to wherever he went."

"My father thinks that the money wasn't wholly wasted," said Lucas, "if we find and can duplicate the capsule. Lendell's research was the bulk of the sunk costs. The incremental expense of building and operating the device might prove practical for certain purposes if in fact it did instantly transport Lendell to Pancahte."

Lissea nodded slowly, though Ned wasn't sure that it was a gesture of agreement. "Rumors came back, years after the event, that Lendell Doormann had landed on Pancahte and was living there. His siblings were still in control of the company. They'd just managed to rebuild from the financial damage Lendell had done Doormann Trading. They forbade any public mention of his name."

"They said Lendell was insane," Lucas said. "They were right, of course."

"There was never any direct trade between Telaria and Pancahte," Lissea said. "Pancahte is nearly thirty Transit hours away." Her figure, by tradition, ignored the set-up time which, depending on circumstances and the available computing power, increased elapsed time by up to three orders of magnitude.

"And it was beyond the Sole Solution," Lucas said. "A generation ago, that closed. At any rate, there's been no contact with Pancahte for at least that long."

Under normal circumstances, there was a practically infinite number of routes by which to reach any point from any other point through Transit space. There were a few anomalies. The most extreme of these was the Sole Solution, which was just that: a single point in the sidereal universe through which a vessel had to pass in order to reach certain other destinations. Pancahte was one of the worlds in that twisted gut of spacetime, the Pocket.

"Ah, Captain Doormann?" Ned asked. He didn't know how to address the person he hoped to serve under. It was very little consolation that, judging from the varieties of 'sir,' 'ma'am,' and 'Lissea,' nobody else in the expedition was sure either.

"Yes, Via, go ahead," she snapped. *"Captain Doormann" was a bad choice.*

"What is it you came to the laboratory to learn, sir?" Ned said.

"What have you learned here, Slade?" she countered. "Anything at all?"

"I learned something about Lendell Doormann," Ned said. He didn't know what she wanted to hear, so he told her the truth. "I learned that he was very sure of himself, and that he knew something. But I'm not at all sure he was right about what he thought he knew."

"He was insane!" Lucas repeated, as if the statement had any relevance to the subject under discussion.

Lissea smiled speculatively at Ned. "Do you think we should be going to Pancahte, Slade?" she asked.

"You should, sir," he replied. "Because that's how you'll get the place here that you ought to have."

He smiled back. Something in his expression surprised both his companions. "And I should," he continued, "because I volunteered to do just that."

Lissea barked a laugh. "Let's get back to the office," she said as she strode toward Ned and the doorway. "I'll tell Warson to run you through our tests."

Because of the omnidirectional lighting, she seemed a beautiful hologram rather than flesh as she approached. "If you pass them, Slade," she said, "you can call me Lissea."

* * *

Male twins in gray battledress walked toward the warehouse converted into a gym and target range as Ned and Toll Warson left it. The strangers were in their thirties, but Ned had first guessed they were considerably younger. They were slightly built, with fine blond hair and complexions of pinkish good health.

"Got a newbie there, Toll?" one of them called cheerfully. There was a scar across his temple, barely visible through the pale hair. Close up, neither of the men was quite as boyishly open as the image he obviously chose to project.

"He's passed the physical, anyway," Warson said. "Not a terrible score, either." He grinned and added, "He could give points to Cuh'nel Lordling, for one."

"I'm not long out of the Academy," Ned said, not sorry for the implied praise. "And, ah, Master Lordling has a few years on me as well."

"Captain Doormann seems to be going for experience," said one of the twins. Ned didn't know enough to guess whether or not there was a comment beneath the surface of the words.

Ned was taking deep but controlled breaths. Warson's run-through had been brutally complete. It was nothing Ned wasn't used to, though when the veteran had activated a series of pop-up targets while Ned rappelled, Ned had almost broken his neck.

He'd gotten two of the four targets with his submachine gun. "Them others would've toasted your ass, kid," Warson said with a chuckle. "Either get better, or don't get into a spot like that without backup. Right?"

"Yessir."

"Louis"—said Warson, gesturing to the twin with the hidden scar—"and Eugene Boxall. They're from Wimbledon."

"Ah," Ned said, giving the Boxalls his sharper attention.

"Yep," said Louis, "that's us."

Except that it *wasn't* Louis who finished the statement; it was his brother Eugene. The twins had traded places instantaneously and without any motion Ned could observe. Alternatively, the keloid on Louis' scalp had vanished and an identical scar had appeared across his brother's temple.

"Wimbledon teleports," Eugene said. "The future of the human race in two extraordinarily handsome packages."

"Well, on a good day, two," Louis said. *And they'd switched back again.* "Though I think *my* profile is a little more regally superior."

The twins were flushed and sweating beneath their grins, though they kept the strain out of their voices.

"They're the best," Toll Warson said with personal pride.

"So we are," Eugene agreed, his tone still light but with a dead-serious underlayer to the words. "The best teleports on Wimbledon, the best in the universe."

Wimbledon was a perfectly normal world, lighted by a K-type sun through a moderately dense atmosphere. Ambient radiation on the surface was lower than that of Earth and well beneath the norm of the planets humans had settled during the expansion.

For no reason anyone could explain, a significant proportion of children born in the Wimbledon Colony were able to teleport. The talent wouldn't make buses obsolete: thirty centimeters was a good jump, and fifteen meters was a remarkable one; but very few walls are more than thirty centimeters thick. Teleportation had its uses in military as well as civilian life.

"They tested out all right, too," Warson said. "Most ways. If one of them starts shooting, though, I suggest you stand in front of the target."

"We're lulling you into a false sense of security," Louis scoffed.

He fingered the fabric of Ned's khaki coveralls, a pair he'd left the patches on. "Hammer's Slammers, eh?" Louis said.

"I'm a reserve ensign in the Frisian Defense Forces," Ned said. "The Slammers were formally dissolved after Colonel Hammer returned home and became president. They, ah . . . There's still a social organization of that name."

"And your name?" asked Eugene.

"Sorry," Ned said. He offered his hand. He was embarrassed. He hadn't wanted to butt into a discussion among veterans. "I'm Edward Slade. Ned."

"Slade?" said Louis, shaking Ned's hand in turn. "You wouldn't have been on Crater?"

"That was my Uncle Don," Ned said.

"There was a Slade got across the Kingston Gorge," Eugene explained to Toll Warson, "to call in fire missions on the Corwinite positions. They'd wanted a cousin of ours to jump it, but it was twelve *klicks.*"

"Even the highlands of Crater are muggy," Louis said. "You can't live down in the valleys without an environmental suit, and that would have showed up like a turd on the breakfast table to Corwin's sensors."

"Uncle Don said that he'd have sweat his bones out on Crater," Ned said, "except the air was so saturated that just breathing replaced your fluid loss."

Don Slade talked frequently about the things he'd seen—climates, geography, life forms. He didn't talk about the things he'd been doing against those exotic backgrounds, though. At least not to his nephew.

"Let's get you back to the office, kid," Warson said. "I got a date in town in an hour, if I can get somebody to advance me a little money."

"Glad to have you aboard, Slade," Eugene said as the brothers entered the gym.

"I'm not aboard yet," Ned called over his shoulder.

"Tsk," said Warson. "Worried 'cause Lordling doesn't like you? Don't be. Tadziki's worth two of him."

"Well, it's the captain's decision," Ned murmured, trying to avoid getting his hopes up.

The road between the converted warehouse and the expedition office was concrete, but the expansion joints and cracks in the slabs sprouted clumps of dense vegetation. The foliage was dark green with brownish veins. It seemed lusher than that of plants growing in the unkempt grounds to either side.

"To tell the truth," Warson said, "I sometimes think Tadziki's worth two of most folks. He doesn't know the same stuff as the rest of us. But he knows his stuff.''

Ned glanced at his companion. It would be very easy to discount Toll Warson as being an extremely competent thug. Ned wondered how many people had died over the years because they made that misestimate.

They entered the office. Tadziki sat at his desk, saying to the big man bent over a document, ''You may have to wait more than an hour for the captain, Master Jones.''

''Blood and martyrs!'' Toll Warson shouted. ''What in *hell* are you doing here?''

''Signing up,'' said the stranger as he turned. ''Via, I should've known you'd be here, squirmed into some cushy wormhole, I suppose.''

He grinned at Tadziki. ''I don't guess I can be Jones anymore, huh?'' he said. Despite the nonchalant tone, there was an edge of concern in his voice.

''You can be anybody you please, Master Warson,'' the adjutant replied. ''But the authorities on Telaria aren't looking for you.''

Ned backed into a corner, staying out of the way. Toll Warson turned to him and said, ''This is my brother Deke, kid. Haven't seen him in— Via, we're both getting old, Deke.''

''Edward Slade, sir,'' Ned said. He held himself at attention. ''Ned.''

''Don't 'sir' me, Slade,'' Deke Warson grumbled. He was a centimeter shorter than Toll and perhaps a year or two younger. Kinship showed in the brothers' eyes rather than in their faces.

Deke looked at Toll and raised an eyebrow.

''His uncle,'' Toll said. ''Remember Sangre Christi?''

''I remember being glad I got out with my ass in one piece,'' Deke replied. ''I still think that was doing pretty good.''

''Tadziki?'' Toll said. ''There going to be a problem if I take Deke off for a drink and to catch up with things?''

''No problem with his application,'' Tadziki said. ''He was an invitee, though I don't think the courier ever caught up with him.''

"I been keeping a low profile," Deke muttered. "There was a little trouble after Stanway, too."

"If the two of you get drunk and tear up the center of Landfall City," the adjutant continued, "then you better hope they don't jug you for longer than three days. That's when we do the test lift—"

He nodded out the open door toward the *Swift*. Workmen were beginning to dismantle the external supports.

"—and if that goes right, it's off to Pancahte twelve hours later."

The brothers left the office arm in arm. Ned expected them to collide with both jambs of the narrow doorway, but they separated like a dance team, with Toll preceding.

Deke turned and offered Tadziki a loose salute. It could have been read as mocking, but Ned didn't think it was. There were soldiers—warriors, really—whose distaste for authority was so ingrained that it was difficult for them to offer respect even when they knew it was due.

"I, ah . . ." Ned said. "Ah, should I wait for the captain, sir?"

"Tadziki'll do fine, Ned," the adjutant said, leaning back in his chair to stretch. "And you don't have to wait unless you want to."

"I suppose she won't make a decision about a place for me until Toll gives her a formal report that I passed?" Ned said. He hadn't been able to relax more than to an at-ease posture even now that he was alone with Tadziki in the office.

Tadziki laughed. "Sit down, curse it, you make me tired to watch you!" he said. "And as for a report—if Toll Warson didn't think you were safe backing him up, he'd have told you to get your ass off-planet in the next sixty minutes. If you were smart, you'd have known he meant it."

"Oh, I'm smart enough not to think Toll's bluffing if he says something . . ." Ned said as he lowered himself into the visitors' chair. "I, ah—"

He met Tadziki's eyes. "It's down to her decision, then?" he said.

Tadziki smiled. "She made her decision when she sent you

off with Toll. Via, kid, nobody thought one of Hammer's boys couldn't handle the gym. Ned.''

Ned relaxed. His body was cold. He'd sweated like a pig as Toll put him through his paces, and the air temperature was cool enough to bite as it dried him. Only now did he notice.

"I, ah . . ." he said, "I wasn't sure."

"That's good," Tadziki said with a nod. "But everybody else was. Go clean up and—well, there's nothing on till the official banquet two nights forward. Let off some steam in town if you like. Do you need an advance on your pay?"

"Huh?" Ned said. "Oh, no thank you, I'm fine." His personal fortune would suffice to purchase a starship larger than the *Swift*, if it came to that. Tethys was a prosperous world, and generations of Slades had displayed businesslike competence in whatever they were doing.

He started to rise, but then settled back onto the edge of the chair. "I want to thank you for going to bat for me the way you did, sir," he said. "But I'd like to know why you did."

Tadziki shrugged. "Does it matter?" he asked.

"It might," Ned said.

"It hadn't anything to do with your uncle," Tadziki said. When Ned heard the words, he felt himself relax again.

"Although," Tadziki continued, "I don't suppose Don Slade would have let you come if he hadn't thought you could stand the gaff. That counts for a certain amount. But mostly it was your background."

"My background?" Ned said in amazement. He slid against the back of the chair.

"Yeah, I figured that'd surprise you," the adjutant said with a laugh. "Look, Ned. You've met some of the crew and I'll tell you, the rest are pretty much the same. What do they all have in common?"

"They're the best there are," Ned said. "They're—professionals that other professionals talk about. They're—"

He shrugged. There was nothing more to say.

"They're people who've been in just about every tight spot there is," Tadziki said, "and got out of it alive. There'll be more combat experience lifting in the *Swift* than there is in most battalions.''

''Sir,'' Ned said, ''I've got the Academy, but that's nothing compared to what any of the others has *done*. And a year of pacification.''

Tadziki nodded. ''Don't knock a formal education, Ned,'' he said. ''There are things you take for granted that Toll Warson wouldn't understand if they bit him on the ass. *Or* Colonel Lordling. But that's . . . It's not that simple.''

He opened his hands on the desk and stared at them. Ned noticed there were pads of yellowish callus at the bases of the fingers.

''I guess,'' Tadziki said, ''I thought it might be useful to have somebody along who *didn't* know the answers already, so maybe he could look at the problem instead. Somebody besides me, I mean.''

He grinned ruefully at Ned. ''And maybe it could be handy if somebody else's idea of an answer wasn't necessarily to blow the problem away.''

Ned laughed and stood up. He reached across the desk to shake the adjutant's hand. ''I'll go shower and change into civvies,'' he said. ''Hey, do you ever get some time off, Tadziki?''

''A little, I guess,'' Tadziki said.

''When I'm fit to associate with something besides a billy goat,'' Ned called from the door, ''I'll drop back by. Maybe you can show me a bit of the town tonight.''

The banquet was held in the Acme, the finest hotel in Landfall City. It was scheduled for 1700 hours the day before launch. Ned arrived fifteen minutes early.

He wasn't afraid of the expedition's dangers. Socially, though, he felt as empty as if he were leaping into a pit with no lights and no bottom.

''Yes sir?'' said a bellhop, blinking at the formal suit Ned wore for the occasion.

Nobles on Tethys went for florid effects. In this case, gold lace overlay fabric which fluoresced red or blue depending on the direction of the light. Whatever the bellhop thought about Ned's taste, the range of his net worth wasn't in question.

"The Pancahte Expedition banquet," Ned said. "Mistress Doormann's party."

"Of course, sir," the bellhop said, even more surprised than he'd been by the suit. "The penthouse, that will be. Ah—would you like me to guide you?"

"No problem," Ned said, striding toward the elevators. Tadziki had muttered that Ned could wear "any curst thing" to the banquet as he typed with both hands and the phone cradled between his ear and shoulder. From the bellhop's reaction, formal wear hadn't been the overwhelming choice among the crewmen.

In the past two days Ned had met more than half the expedition members and had at least seen most of the others. He hadn't noticed any hostility toward him—but he'd effectively been ignored.

The rest of the crew pretty much knew, or at least knew of, one another. There were cliques and in some cases mutual antipathies, but members of the *Swift*'s complement didn't disregard their companions—with the exception of Ned Slade, who might have been a plank of the barracks' flooring.

Ned had better sense than to force his company on the adjutant this close to launch. When they found a good restaurant two nights before, Ned had pumped Tadziki for details about the expedition. The exchange was a mutual pleasure, since Tadziki was glad to offer information which he had to know and most of the crew didn't care about.

Since then, however, the adjutant was swamped with work. Ned didn't know the system or personalities well enough to be more help than hindrance, so he'd kept clear.

Under other circumstances, Toll Warson might have taken Ned under his wing, but he and Deke had vanished completely when they left the expedition office the morning they'd met. No news wasn't the worst possible news: there hadn't been any calls from the Telarian police regarding the pair.

"Room for one more?" Tadziki called from the lobby as

the elevator door closed behind Ned.

Ned hit the DOOR OPEN button rather than grabbing the leading edge with his hand. Elevators at the Academy were built like firedoors and airlocks, without safety switches. It was a case where the wrong civilian reflex could get you killed in combat, so the Academy made sure the reflex was modified before cadets graduated.

Tadziki slipped into the cage and whistled. "My lord," he said, "you're beautiful! What're you doing after dinner tonight, gorgeous?"

Ned laughed. "Thought I'd cruise some navy bars and get pin money for the expedition," he said. "Via, Tadziki, you told me to wear anything, and I've always been told you can't overdress."

Tadziki wore a fawn-colored dress uniform with a white ascot. Ned didn't recognize either the uniform nor the epaulet insignia. He did note that there were four rows of medal ribbons, and that the ribbons were of slightly different heights—implying service under several flags.

The adjutant followed the flick of Ned's eyes. "I kept busy," he said, "but back where I was, it only got exciting when somebody screwed up."

"Sure," said Ned. He'd had a logistics instructor who'd used almost the same phrase; Major Kline. Besides the stories going around the Academy to make the statement a lie, there was the fact that Major Kline's legs had been burned off just above the knees.

Even before the door opened when the elevator stopped at P, the floor above 14, they could hear the sound of voices. Three attendants, a man and two young women in black-and-white uniforms, stared toward the dining room so fixedly that they jumped when Tadziki brushed one as he got out.

It wasn't a riot, not yet; but the party was well under way.

"*Very* sorry, gentlemen!" a female attendant said. "We'll take your weapons here, please."

The other woman stepped behind a counter. The man took his position at the controls of an extremely sophisticated security frame at the entrance to the dining room.

"What?" said Ned.

"Lissea thought it would be a good idea if everybody left their hardware outside the banquet," Tadziki explained nonchalantly. He handed the counter attendant a small pistol from his breast pocket. It had almost no barrel and a grip shaped like a teardrop.

"If there's a real problem tonight," he went on, reaching beneath his right coattail, "we can escort the parties to the barracks separately. That'll help some to keep the bloodshed down."

He gave the girl a thin, 10-cm rod which looked to Ned like a folding cutting-bar. She tagged both weapons and opened the lid of the counter.

"Blood and martyrs!" Ned said as he looked inside.

The tagged weapons the woman had collected ranged from a pair of spiked knuckle-dusters to—

"What's that?" Ned said. He pointed to the fat, meter-long tube fed from a box magazine large enough to hold women's shoes. Its buttstock was curved horizontally to be braced against the chest rather than a shoulder.

Tadziki leaned over his shoulder. "Oh, the rocket gun," he said. "That would be Raff's, I suppose."

"The Racontid," Ned said/asked, knowing that Tadziki would correct him if he'd guessed wrong. The recoil of a closed-tube, all-burned-on-launch rocket would be brutally punishing for even big men.

Though there were a number of other projectile weapons, most of the guns in the collection were service pistols chambered for the standard 1-cm powergun wafer. The details of the guns and their associated carrying rigs varied considerably.

The half dozen needle stunners didn't necessarily imply that some of the crewmen were more squeamish than the rest. Though the stunners were small and highly concealable, the fluctuating current from their bipolar needles could sometimes bring down a target from neural lock-up faster than blowing the heart out would manage.

As for cutting implements—both the powered and nonpowered varieties—the counter held a stock sufficient to begin clearance of a major forest.

"A lot of that's for show," Tadziki explained. "They knew they'd be disarmed at the door. I doubt most of the crew packs this kind of hardware on a normal liberty."

He stepped into the security frame. The mechanism chuckled; the attendant watching the screen nodded approvingly. Ned started through behind the adjutant.

"Sir!" called the woman behind the counter. "Please leave your weapons here."

Ned looked over his shoulder at her. "I'm not carrying any weapons," he said.

He walked through the frame. The male attendant shrugged and nodded to his companions.

"I don't need a gun to prove I'm a man," Ned muttered to Tadziki as they entered the dining room together.

The adjutant smiled. "It must have been interesting," he said, "growing up around a certified hero like your uncle."

Two elevators opened simultaneously. The Warson brothers were among the efflux, talking loudly about a woman. Presumably a woman.

Most of the *Swift*'s complement was already in the hemispherical dining room. The men seemed to have made the accurate assumption that there'd be something to drink ahead of time, and that perhaps somebody else would pay for it. A handful of them sat at tables while the rest were bellied up to the bar erected along the flat wall.

The room's outer wall and ceiling were glazed, looking northward over the city. The blur of light in the distance was the wall surrounding the Doormann estate, illuminated for security.

"Uncle Don wasn't around at all till six years ago," Ned said, looking at Telaria but remembering the roiling seascape of his home. "After he came back to Tethys, he got me a place in the Academy—"

He looked sharply at Tadziki. "*I* asked him to," he said. "It was my idea."

Tadziki nodded expressionlessly. They remained standing

just within the doorway. "Hey, Tadziki!" called a ship's crewman named Moiseyev from the bar. "Come buy me a drink!"

"So I haven't seen him much since then either," Ned continued. "Some, when I was home on leave. He's . . . I think my mother's good for him. I think he talks to her, but I don't know."

"I met your uncle once," Tadziki said. "We were on the same side, more or less." His voice, lost in the past as surely as Ned's had been, snapped the younger man back to the present.

The Warson brothers, Herne Lordling, and Lissea Doormann close behind, entered the dining room. Toll put his heavy hands on a shoulder each of Ned and the adjutant and moved the men apart. "Make way for a man who's dying of thirst!" he boomed.

A chime rang. Even the men at the bar turned toward Lissea. She lowered the finger-sized wand that combined a number of functions, including recorder and communicator, along with providing an attention signal.

"If all you gentlemen will find places," she said, "I personally haven't had a chance all day to eat."

The room was arranged with three round six-person tables in an arc that followed that of the glass wall, and a small rectangular table with three chairs on the chord. The places at the small table were marked RESERVED with gilt cards.

The crowd came away from the bar like a slow-motion avalanche: one man, three, and the remainder of them together. Ned walked around the rectangular table; Tadziki put his hand on the back of one of the reserved chairs.

Deke Warson took the reserved chair on the end opposite the adjutant.

"That's my seat, soldier," said Herne Lordling.

Deke looked Lordling up and down. "Was it, buddy?" he said. "Well, you're a clever boy. I'm sure you'll find just as nice a one over by the wall."

"Listen you!" Lordling said. Lissea said something also, but her words were drowned in the rumble of men shouting.

Toll Warson stepped in front of his brother. He put his right arm around Deke's neck in what was either an embrace or a wrestling hold, as needs required. He fished for Deke's bunched fist with his free hand.

Tadziki touched Lordling's left arm. Lordling tried to swat him off. Ned came around the other side of the table. He grabbed Lordling by the right wrist and right elbow. Lordling tensed, swore—and stopped the motion he'd almost attempted when he realized that Ned not only *could* break his arm but that the younger man was preparing to do just that.

"*Will* you stop this nonsense!" Lissea said.

Tadziki reached back with his left hand. His right continued to touch Lordling's arm and he didn't look away from Lordling's face. He picked up the card from the seat he'd taken and said, "Deke. Here's a place for you."

Deke Warson stared in the direction of the card for a moment before his eyes focused on it. He relaxed, pulled himself away from his brother, and walked around the front of the table to the seat Tadziki offered.

The adjutant let go of Herne Lordling. Ned stepped backward and only then released his own grip. There was a possibility that Lordling was going to lash out as soon as he was free. Ned couldn't prevent that, but he sure didn't intend to make it easy.

Both Lordling and Deke Warson sat down. Lissea remained standing between them until they were firmly settled. She didn't look in the direction of either man. There was a general scuffle of boots and chair-legs as the rest of the company found places.

"Blood and *martyrs,*" Ned muttered. There were patches of sweat at the throat and armpits of his dazzling suit.

Tadziki put a hand on Ned's shoulder and guided him to one side of the center table. There weren't two empty places together anywhere in the room. Tadziki gestured curtly toward a man to move him. The startled crewman obeyed.

"As cramped as we're going to be for the next however-long," the adjutant said, "I don't think we need to push togetherness right now."

It was going to be a long voyage, in more ways than one.

Lissea seated herself decorously after everyone else. She gave a regal nod toward the service alcove.

Waiters, having clustered nervously at the threatened riot, began to bring the meal in.

The Boxall brothers were at the table Tadziki had chosen, along with Raff and a ship's crewman named Westerbeke. The other five ship's personnel were together at a side table—with Toll Warson, who'd taken the seat without being in the least interested in who else might be at the table.

Toll might have traded with Westerbeke in a friendly fashion; and again, he might not, which wasn't something anybody in his right mind wanted to chance. Westerbeke looked as lonely as Ned had felt before Tadziki joined him.

Lissea seemed not lonely but alone, putting food in her mouth and chewing distractedly. Her clothes were resolutely civilian, though a great deal more subdued than Ned's: dark gray trousers, a jerkin of a slightly paler shade, and a thin tabard with diagonal black-and-bronze striping. Herne Lordling spoke to her a number of times, but Ned didn't see the woman respond.

"What's Lordling's position, then?" Ned asked Tadziki in something between a low voice and a whisper.

"Military advisor, I suppose," the adjutant explained. "Formally, he doesn't have a position—Lissea likes to have everyone reporting directly to her. But Herne had a lot to do with the list of invitees and the—the tactical planning, I suppose you'd say. He has a deserved reputation."

Tadziki took a sip of water and looked out the glass wall, ending the discussion.

As waiters removed the salad, somebody tugged the puff of fabric on Ned's sleeve. He turned in his chair. The man seated at his back on the next table said, "Hey, you're Slade, aren't you? I'm Paetz, Josie Paetz. I guess we're the up-and-comers here, huh?"

"Right, I'm Ned Slade," Ned said and shook hands. Paetz was big, red-haired, and as hard as a bodybuilder between contests. He looked much sharper-edged than other crewmen because he was so much younger: certainly younger than Ned, and possibly less than twenty standard years.

"Tell the truth," Paetz continued, "from your rep, I thought you had a few more years on you too. The time you took a platoon through the sewers on Spiegelglas, wasn't that—"

"My uncle Don," Ned said. He should have known. Waiters maneuvered awkwardly around the tables to avoid stepping between the two mercenaries. If Paetz even noticed that, it didn't embarrass him the way it did Ned.

"Oh, I got it!" Paetz said happily. "I thought, you know—for somebody like you to have that much a jump on me, I thought you must be really something. But you're just out to get a rep, same as me. Well, we'll see how it goes, won't we, buddy?"

"You bet," Ned murmured, but Paetz had already scrunched his chair back around to his own table.

"The man next to him is Yazov," Tadziki explained quietly, "his father's half brother, born on the wrong side of the bedclothes. We invited the father, who's Primate of Tristibrand. He let Josie come, and sent Yazov to keep an eye on him."

He took a forkful of pilaf. "They should be valuable additions to the company. In different ways."

"Josie isn't . . ." Ned said, ". . . one of the people you pushed as having open minds, I would judge."

"Sometimes you simply have to charge straight uphill into a gun position," Tadziki said. "Then it's nice if you've got people along who think that's a good idea."

The food was excellent in a neutral sort of way, without anything Ned perceived as Telarian national character. The hotel catered to off-planet traders and perhaps to Telarians who wanted to emphasize their cosmopolitan background.

Few of the mercenaries cared about what they were eating one way or the other. If they'd been told they were to skin rats and eat them raw, nine out of ten would have done so, if only to prove they were as tough as their fellow crewmen.

Raff shoveled through a vegetarian meal as if he were filling sandbags. The Racontid held his knife and fork in four-fingered hands. His retractile claws provided delicate manipulation when required. He showed some interest in the texture of his food, but none whatever in its flavor.

Tadziki and the Boxalls were discussing a mercenary Ned didn't know, an invitee who'd been shot by his lover as he prepared to board ship for Telaria. For a time, Ned simply ate morosely. Then out of fellow-feeling he asked Westerbeke about the *Swift*'s systems.

The crewman responded enthusiastically. The degree of detail Westerbeke offered strained the bounds of Ned's training, but he could catch enough of the meaning to nod intelligently. The capsule reading was that the *Swift* wasn't a large vessel, but she was as solidly built as any hull of her displacement. Furthermore, her major systems were redundant and better-shielded than those of many warships.

The discussion made both Ned and Westerbeke more at home at the banquet, and the details made Ned more comfortable about the voyage itself. Whatever Karel Doormann hoped would result from the expedition, Doormann Trading was sparing no reasonable expense in the outfitting.

The same was true with the complement. They were all good men, and all clearly fit despite the emphasis on experience over youth. Though tough, they weren't a gang of cutthroats either. Uncle Don would have been right at home among them.

A realization struck Ned as he viewed the assembled crew. "Tadziki," he said, "we're all males, aren't we? Except for Lissea, I mean."

"Yeah, that was a decision she made herself, though Herne and I both would have argued for it if it had come up," Tadziki said. "It's pretty tight quarters, and for a long time."

"There's Raff," Louis Boxall suggested. "You're not male, are you, buddy?"

The Racontid laughed like millstones rubbing. "It doesn't signify," he—she?—said. "You humans don't have a transfer sex."

Raff lifted his fruit cup and licked it clean with a single

swipe of his broad tongue. Waiters were removing the last of the dishes. The Racontid took a lily from the table's center-piece and began thoughtfully to munch the fleshy stem.

Lissea stood up. She looked lost and frail.

"Gentlemen," she said. The room quieted. "Fellow crew-men! We're here together for our last night in safety until we've managed to retrieve the device in which my great-granduncle fled Telaria. Perhaps our last night in safety before we disappear forever into myth and the fading memories of our loved ones."

"Don't you worry yourself, Lissea!" said Herne Lordling. There was a half-filled whiskey glass at his place, but the vol-ume and slight slurring of his words showed that this drink was the most recent of many. "You've got me along. Every-thing's going to work out just fine."

"Seems to me," snarled Deke Warson, leaning to peer past Lissea, "that being a pansy colonel doesn't make you an au-thority on much of anything except covering your ass, Lord-ling!"

Lissea thrust a hand out to either side, trying to cover both men's eyes with her fingers. "Stop this at once!" she said.

Tadziki stood up. "Captain?" he said calmly. "I wonder if you'd let me bring everyone up to speed on the plans thus far? Then they can ask questions if they have any."

Ned, who'd been poised to back the adjutant in a physical confrontation, settled in his chair again. The emotional tem-perature of the room dropped to normal as a result of Tad-ziki's tone and the volume he'd managed to project without seeming to shout.

"Yes," Lissea said. "Yes, that's a very good idea."

She reseated herself, a supple movement which her out-stretched arms turned into a dance step. Only when she was down did she lower her hands and nod at the adjutant to begin.

"The first portion of our voyage will be relatively straight-forward," Tadziki said. He moved from one side of Ned's chair to the other so that he could face all the personnel except the trio at the small table behind him. "We won't be putting in to major ports, however. We're an armed expedition. Entry checks and quarantines on highly developed worlds would add months to what's already going to be a lengthy process.''

"Hey, I'll give up my gun if you'll land on a place with decent nightlife," said a mercenary named Ingried.

"Don't worry, Ingried," Harlow called back loudly. "There'll be sheep-farmers who'll set you up with company just as pretty as what *I've* seen you with on leave."

Everybody laughed, Ingried included.

"The major question mark involves the Sole Solution," Tadziki continued when the laughter died down. "Very little has been heard from beyond it over the past generation. There've been rumors that it closed, or that it's being held by a military force that won't permit anyone through that point."

"Can we go around?" asked Yazov. Ship's crewmen chortled at the soldier's ignorance, though not to the point of openly insulting a man who'd made killing his business for thirty years.

"So far," the adjutant continued calmly, "the only person who's managed to do that is Lendell Doormann, and that's a matter of rumor rather than certainty also. But let me emphasize: I'm speaking of information available on Telaria. When we're nearer the Sole Solution, there'll be hard facts and we'll be able to refine our plans."

Tadziki cleared his throat, then sipped from the glass of hot, tart Telarian chocolate which a waiter had left at his place. "I won't claim that our information on intermediate stops is perfect either," he said. "Because we'll be touching down on minor planets, our pilotry data is likely to be out-of-date or simply wrong.

"But that doesn't matter. That doesn't matter because of *you.* You're picked men, the best there are in the human universe." His voice was growing louder, and the syllables he hit for emphasis resounded like drumbeats. "With all of us working together, there are no emergencies, no unexpected dangers that we won't be able to wriggle out of or *smash* our way through!"

"That's sure the bloody truth!" shouted Toll Warson.

Cries ranging from *"You bet!"* to *"Yee-ha!"* chimed agreement.

"And when we return," Tadziki continued, thundering over the happy assent, "we'll have more than the capsule we've been sent for. We'll have a name that nobody will ever forget. For every one of us here, there'll be a thousand others out there—"

He made a broad sweep of his extended arm, indicating the night sky beyond the glazing.

"—telling people that *they* were aboard the *Swift* too. But they weren't because they weren't good enough. *We* are good enough, and we're going to see this business through whatever it takes!"

The cheers overwhelmed even Tadziki's booming voice. Ned shouted as enthusiastically as the rest, though a part of him marveled at the expert way the adjutant had used a tense situation to weld the crew into a unity of purpose which might well last till success or disaster.

Tadziki turned, gestured to Lissea, and sat down with his arm still pointing.

Lissea rose again. She held a glass of amber wine which she extended toward her gathered subordinates. "Gentlemen," she called without any remaining indecision. "I give you ourselves and the *Swift.* May we be worthy of our triumph!"

The waiters looked on from the edges of the room, like humans watching a ritual being performed by great, bellowing cats.

The man was young, fit-looking, and above average height. His hair was light brown, almost blond at the roots, and he wore loose khaki clothing.

He stood alone in the crowd which waited for Lissea Doormann and her escort to enter the *Swift* for liftoff.

"It's so big!" said a young Telarian woman in a sundress with a cape of blue gauze over her shoulders. "I thought it was just a little boat."

Her beefy escort chuckled knowingly. "It's a *star*ship,

Elora,'' he said. He waved at the vessel a hundred meters away. ''As starships go, it's a small one. And for the distance they say they're going, it's tiny. Too small. They don't have a prayer of making it back.''

The *Swift* wore a coat of black, nonreflective paint which showed orange-peel rippling from the stresses of the shakedown run the previous day. There were striations in a reticular pattern where the plates joined, but the crewmen who magnafluxed the seams after landing had found no sign of cracks. The plates dovetailed before being welded. Repair would be difficult in anything less than a major dockyard, but the interlocked hull had enormous strength.

The *Swift* lay on its side like a huge cigar. The central airlock was closed, but the three-meter boarding-ramp hatch, forward on the port side, was lowered. It provided a good view of the vessel's bustling interior.

A man with a case of instruments and tools knelt on the ramp, adjusting the flexible metal gasket. Beyond him, two more crewmen shouted at one another, each waving a pack that bristled with weapons. The personnel were garbed in the battledress of their various former units, but all now wore a shoulder patch with the new insignia of the Pancahte Expedition: a red phoenix displayed on a golden field.

''Is that Colonel Lordling?'' Elora asked, pointing indiscriminately to the pair arguing.

''No, no,'' said an older woman the crowd pressed against Elora's other shoulder. ''Those are the Warson brothers. They've each killed *hundreds* of people.''

The pair are Bonilla and Dewey, thought the man in khaki. *They are ship's crewmen. They both know which end of the gun makes the noise, but they aren't killers by temperament.*

The rear of the crowd gave a wordless murmur. Someone called, ''They're coming!'' over the general noise.

The *Swift* set down on an open cell of the starport when she returned from testing. The crowd of thousands that gathered to watch her lift for Pancahte came from all over Telaria and even beyond. Independent news associations recorded events from the roof of the terminal building. They would sell copies to the crewmen's home worlds and to planets settled enough to have a market for vicarious adventure.

Scores of green-clad police patrolled the lines marking the safe separation from the vessel's drive motors. The police used their shock rods freely to reinforce the warning of the yellow paint, but pressure from behind still edged the crowd forward. A police lieutenant spoke angrily into her lapel mike as she scanned the sky.

Three large aircars rumbled low overhead and settled in the cleared area around the vessel. The hot breeze from their ducted fans buffeted the crowd. Elora's cape lifted from her shoulders. The man behind her caught the garment's hem and held it safe, unnoticed, until the cars had shut down.

"Oh!" cried a woman. "I've got something in my eye!"

Blue-uniformed Doormann Trading security guards hopped from the rear of the aircars. There were forty or fifty troops in each vehicle.

Instead of shock batons, the new arrivals carried power-guns: slung submachine guns in the case of enlisted men, holstered pistols for officers and noncoms. The *Swift*'s hatch filled quietly with men as the presence of armed troops drew the attention of the mercenary crew.

The police lieutenant unclipped the loud-hailer from her harness. "Stand aside!" she called, her voice turned into a raspy howl by amplification. "Make way for the honorable Lucas and Lissea Doormann!"

The company of security guards linked arms and struck the crowd as a wedge. An officer with his pistol drawn walked just behind the point of his burly men, shouting for them to put their backs into it. Civilians stumbled aside, crying out in surprise and anger.

"Go it, mob!" cheered a mercenary. *Josie Paetz,* thought the lone man. "Go it, cops!"

The guards shoved directly past the man in khaki. He concentrated on keeping his footing and moving the citizens behind him back without starting the sort of surging panic that could get people trampled to death.

Paetz wore two pistols, one high on his right hip and the

other in a cross-draw holster on his left. He also cradled a submachine gun at port arms. His burly uncle Yazov looked on from behind the young gunman with a tolerant smile.

"Move it, move it, move it!" shouted the officer commanding the guards. He was close enough that the lone man could have reached across the line of blue uniforms and touched the fellow—

—crushed his throat—

—grabbed a handful of the hair curling out beneath the helmet, jerking the head backward hard enough to—

"Hey!" said a guard in horror.

The man in khaki blinked in surprise. He looked at the guard he'd been staring *through* with an expression that he wouldn't consciously have worn.

"Sorry, buddy," he called. The guard was already gone, swept past on the current of blue uniforms which hosed a path into the spectators. Another company was carrying out a similar maneuver from the back of the crowd. The forces met midway, then squeezed outward to widen the opening.

"Look at them!" said Elora's companion. "Here they come! They're coming right past us!"

A pair of three-wheelers drove at a walking pace between the lines of guards. The vehicles were *en echelon* because the cleared way wasn't quite wide enough for them to proceed side by side. Behind them came an open-topped limousine.

The anger building in manhandled spectators evaported when the victims realized that they had the best view of the celebrities. Cursing guards flung their weight outward to counteract the nearest civilians' tendency to lean toward the oncoming limousine.

"Lissea! Lissea!"

"Oh!" said the woman on the other side of Elora. "They're too beautiful to die!"

"She sure is!" Elora's companion said, mistaking the object of—his mother's? his mother-in-law's?—enthusiasm.

The limousine was a three-axle model. The driver was covered by a polarized hemisphere in front, so that he or she wouldn't detract from the attention focused on the passengers.

Lissea Doormann rode in the backseat with her cousin Lucas beside her. He was dressed in a blue suit that might almost have been a uniform, while Lissea wore coveralls whose fabric, as lustrous and colorful as a peacock's tail, belied the utilitarian lines. She smiled tautly and waved, though her eyes didn't appear to focus on her enthusiastic surroundings.

Her right shoulder bore the same phoenix patch as did the other members' of the expedition.

Lucas was regal and perhaps a degree, self-satisfied. The fact that Lissea was getting such a send-off had to be his doing, in spite of his father.

Lissea's parents, Grey and Duenya Doormann, sat in jump seats facing the younger pair. Grey looked bewildered. Lissea's mother was crying. She dabbed alternately at her eyes and her sniffling nose. Her lace handkerchief was too delicate to be of much use for either purpose.

The Warson brothers, Herne Lordling, and Raff sat on the limo's body with their legs down inside the passenger compartment. They carried powerguns (in the Racontid's case, a rocket launcher) ready in their hands. The gun muzzles were lifted slightly and the butts were cradled rather than shouldered, but the mercenaries' readiness to use their weapons was beyond question.

"Beautiful!" repeated the older woman.

Elora nodded in agreement, though it wasn't really true. Lordling had the sort of beefy good looks that might have been "beautiful" when he was twenty years younger. The Warsons shared a craggy roughness that couldn't have passed for beauty even without the scars—the cut quirking Toll's lip, the burned speckles on Deke's right cheek. As easily claim Raff was beautiful, or that a wolverine was.

What Lissea's escort had was an aura of raw male aggression. The same was true of the rest of the *Swift*'s complement: they were men that no woman would overlook, though many would react with horror and loathing to what they read on the mercenaries' faces.

Elora's companion grimaced as Deke Warson's eyes fell across him. The mercenary wasn't threatening, just alert to possibilities for trouble. The civilian glanced away and didn't look back until the limousine had passed.

"They could cut their way through anybody, that lot," he muttered to Elora. "It's not enemies they have to worry about, just space itself. Space is too big for them, though."

Does he really imagine that twenty gunmen, no matter how skilled and brave—but courage has rarely been a short-term survival characteristic—could overwhelm all human opposition? thought the man in khaki. *Shoot it out with a column of tanks? Dance through an artillery stonk?*

Perhaps he does. He is a civilian, after all.

The limousine's driver made his vehicle pirouette, to bring it broadside to the end of the boarding ramp. Lucas Doormann got out and offered his arm to Lissea. Herne Lordling stepped from his perch in front of the young noble, then moved backward as though Lucas didn't exist.

Lissea handed her parents out of the limousine, ignoring both men. She hugged first her father, then her mother. The older woman suddenly twisted away in a fresh onset of grief.

With a final wave to the spectators, Lissea turned and walked up the ramp. The crowd cheered with the mindless abandon of a flock of birds.

The man in khaki sighed. He shook the microchip-keyed ID card he wore on a lanyard around his neck out from under his tunic.

"Excuse me," he said to the man in front of him. "Excuse me," he repeated a little louder, gripping the man's shoulder and easing him aside despite the fellow's instinctive resistance.

"Hey!" said the civilian in surprise, but he'd seen enough of the stranger's expression not to make a problem of it.

"Who is he, Chechin?" Elora asked in a voice whose emotional loading shifted from anger to interest in those few syllables.

"You can't—" a security guard began.

"I can," the lone man said, waving his ID in a short arc to call attention to it.

"Oh," said the guard. "Ah . . ."

"I'll duck under," the man said. He did so as the guards to either side, their arms still linked, squeezed as far apart as they could.

The four mercenaries of Lissea's escort formed an outward-facing line across the bottom of the ramp. When their captain entered the ship, they turned together and sauntered up behind her. Lucas Doormann stood with his feet spread and his hands clasped behind him, looking up at the *Swift*.

The man in khaki strode toward the vessel with his ID raised in his right hand. His left hand was ostentatiously spread at his side. He had to stutter-step to avoid the three-wheelers as they spun to get in front of the limousine, preparing to lead it back with Lucas.

The police lieutenant opened her mouth to shout. She turned aside when she recognized the card's phoenix blazon.

Machinery on the *Swift* gave a high-pressure moan. Lucas Doormann turned and almost collided with the man approaching from the crowd. "Slade?" he said. "What are you doing here?"

"A fair question," Ned replied. The boarding ramp was starting to rise. He hopped to the end of it and trotted into the hull of the starship. The ramp continued to grind its way closed.

"Twenty-one and all told," Tadziki said to his multifunction baton. He smiled at Ned. "I wasn't sure you were coming."

Ned shrugged. "I signed on," he said.

The vessel's interior was bedlam. Everyone *knew* how tight space would be, and the men were experienced veterans who'd often subsisted on the minimum or even less than that. Nevertheless, last-minute additions to personal belongings brought the total to half again or even double the limits Tadziki had set. It would take an hour to make the *Swift* shipshape enough to lift off safely.

Ned noted that his bunk astern was covered with gear. He laughed. None of it was his own.

"I just thought," he said to the adjutant, "that maybe I could understand what we were doing better if I looked at it like an outsider. So I was playing spectator."

"Westerbeke," Tadziki ordered, speaking into his baton. His thumb switched his booming voice through the speakers fore and aft in the bay. "Open the ramp again."

The crewman in one of the navigation consoles forward obeyed. The noise of men arguing over volume and location continued. Lissea Doormann stood in the center of the bay. Her blue-green-golden coveralls blazed like metal burning, but her face was white and silent.

Smiling coldly, Tadziki dialed a feedback loop into the speaker system. When the painful squeal died away, everyone in the bay was silent.

"Captain," Tadziki said with a nod toward Lissea, "do I have your permission to handle this?"

"Go ahead." Her voice was crisp but detached.

Tadziki smiled again. "Gentlemen," he said, "we'll all take the next fifteen minutes to separate our personal belongings into two piles. At the end of that time, the captain and I will inspect them. The pile of your choice will be tossed onto the concrete for the locals to fight over."

The adjutant's pause didn't invite comment. There were a few vague murmurs, not directed at him.

"If it turns out that both of an individual's piles are still in excess of the volume limits you were provided, then *both* piles go," Tadziki continued. "If the individual objects, his shipmates will send him out along with his gear. Any questions?"

"There will be no questions," Lissea Doormann said.

Toll Warson laughed. "Hey Cuh'nel Lordling," he said, "somebody's gonna set up a regular grocery store with what you leave behind, aren't they?"

Herne Lordling was red-faced. "No questions," he said in a clipped voice.

"Go to it, boys," Tadziki said with a nod. Mercenaries turned to their rucksacks and footlockers. Many of them began to hurl the excess directly out the three-meter hatchway.

Lissea offered her adjutant a slight smile. Tadziki leaned close so that he could speak without shouting and said, "They wouldn't be the men we want if they didn't push, ma'am. This isn't a problem."

He turned to Ned. "How about you, Slade?" he asked.

"I'm under the limit," Ned said. He grinned in a way that made the adjutant remember Slade's uncle. "I'm going to take some pleasure in clearing my bunk, though, if the dickhead who piled stuff there doesn't do it for me."

"You said you wanted to figure out what we were doing," Tadziki said. "Did you?"

Lissea drifted close enough to listen, though her unfocused eyes denied she was taking part in the conversation. The three of them were the only ones aboard the *Swift* who didn't have to comb through their personal belongings.

"I don't have a clue," Ned said. He looked at the men around him. "These guys don't have a thing in the world to prove to anybody. They've done it all, one time or another. And here they are to do it again."

He nodded out toward the spectators behind the police line. "They think we're a bunch of heroes going to certain death," he said, his tone deliberately mocking.

"And you?" said Tadziki.

"I don't think I'm going to die," Ned replied. "And I *sure* as hell don't think I'm a hero."

"Are you sure you want to be here?" Lissea said unexpectedly.

Ned looked at her. "I'm an adult," he said. "And I'm here. So this must be what I want to do."

He laughed with real humor. "But I'm curst if I could tell you why," he admitted.

Tadziki put his hand on Ned's shoulder. "Let's go clear your bunk off," he said. "Next stop is Ajax Four, and that's a long cursed way to travel standing up."

Ajax Four

---〰〰---

A YELLOW-GRAY PLUME to eastward streaked the intense blue of Ajax Four's sky. A similar trail a hundred kilometers north marked a second volcano. Droplets of spume blowing inland from the surf popped and sizzled on the barren, sun-cracked rocks.

"Fuckin' wonderful," muttered Deke Warson. "Hey, Tadziki! I'm going to fire my travel agent."

Ned opened the front of his tunic and shrugged to loosen the fabric where sweat had glued it to his skin. He felt good. Better than he'd felt since he'd last been home on Tethys.

Ajax Four wasn't a seaworld like Tethys, but the *Swift* had landed on the shore a few klicks south of Quantock, one of the planet's larger human settlements. The air was clean, and a storm had passed recently enough to give it the familiar tang of ozone.

Ajax Four wasn't home, but it reminded Ned of home; and that was a good thing just now.

The *Swift* had set down in a scallop several hundred meters across. Originally the landing site had been a miniature crater, but the sea had carved away the western third of the cone.

Lava within the volcano's channel had cooled into a basalt plug far sturdier than the cone of compacted ash. The plug provided the *Swift* with a surface as solid as Landfall City's concrete spaceport. At low tide the basalt would be a shelf well above the sea, but at the moment surf pounded its edge.

Herne Lordling had ordered six men to string a line of medium-distance sensors around the crater's lip, thirty to forty meters above the plug. Because the soft rock was weather-checked, the inner wall wasn't as difficult to climb as it appeared to be from a distance. The exterior of the cone would actually be a more difficult proposition. A climber's weight would crumble the slope into gravel with neither handholds nor footholds.

A team of ship's crewmen had unslung the pair of air-cushion mini-Jeeps from the blister on the *Swift*'s hull astern. The Jeeps would only carry two people apiece, so most of the personnel would have to hike or borrow vehicles from the colonists if they wanted to leave the vessel.

"*Sir, I still can't raise the settlement,*" Dewey reported. "*Over.*"

He was using the general push rather than a command channel, so everyone could hear him through their commo helmets. With the exception of Dewey, whose duties kept him in the navigational console, the whole complement was outside on this, the *Swift*'s first landfall since Telaria. Everyone wore his helmet visor down and polarized against the brilliant sunlight doubled by reflection from the rocks.

"*All right, Dewey,*" Lissea replied. "*Have one of the teams on the ridge relay the call. Use Yazov. He'll know what to do. Out.*"

Ned knelt and peered into a crack deep enough that spray or possibly ground water kept the interior damp. He locked his visor out of the way for a better view. There was a smudge of green against the rock. "Hey, Tadziki," he called. "Plant life!"

"It's not the plants that worry me, Slade," the adjutant said as he wandered over, faceless behind his visor. "It's the Spiders and the big nasty guns they're supposed to carry."

"Wouldn't mind having something to shoot," Deke Warson said idly. "It'd make a change."

Lissea walked over to the adjutant. "Tadziki!" she demanded. "There was no place nearer to Quantock?"

"We could have tried landing in the settlement itself," Tadziki said calmly. "The settlers here have a great deal of trouble with pirates and the interloping traders who sell weapons to the Spiders. I was concerned that if they saw an unexpected vessel coming in to land, they might shoot first and ask questions later."

Lissea raised her visor and rubbed her face with her palm. "Sorry," she said. "I feel like a fish in a barrel in this place. I—"

"Sir, I've got them on Channel Seven!" Dewey reported. *"Do you want me to patch them directly to you? Over."*

"No, hold them for a moment," Lissea replied as she strode back up the ramp. *"I'll take it at the console. Out."*

Apart from algal smudges like the one Ned had noticed, the only land-dwelling life form on Ajax Four when humans arrived was a creature whose males averaged three meters tall and a hundred and fifty kilograms. They were bipedal but four-armed. The colonists called them Spiders, though they were warm-blooded and had internal skeletons.

The Spiders ranged the interior in bands of a dozen or so individuals, living on creatures teeming in the freshwater lakes and streams. They were relentlessly hostile to the colonists, which wouldn't have made any difference—had the Spiders not also been highly intelligent.

Humans settled Ajax Four with two separate commercial purposes. The ocean provided protein, some of it of luxury quality, and algal carbohydrates which could be processed into basic foodstuffs. Oceanic aquatic fed the colonies from the beginning. It now provided most of their export earnings as well.

According to the original plan, analgesics processed from several varieties of freshwater coral would in a few years pay back the cost of settling Ajax Four. Thereafter the colonists should have become as wealthy as the citizens of *any* human planet. When Spiders with weapons made of seashells and obsidian had attacked settler foraging parties, the humans' guns cut the aliens down without loss.

Human interlopers landed on Ajax Four to scoop up coral and flee before the settlers could stop them. The Spiders traded with the interlopers instead of fighting them: traded coral for guns, and used the guns to bloodily ambush the next group of colonists who had ventured into the interior.

Since that day, the interior hadn't been safe for the colonists. They swept the vicinity of their settlements in large parties, killing the Spiders they found and accepting the inevitable sniping casualties as a cost of remaining on Ajax Four. Though the Spiders held the interior, they rarely ventured against the sensors and heavy weapons which protected the coastal settlements.

The parties' *modus vivendi* wasn't perfect, but life was rarely perfect. Since the situation hadn't changed significantly in a hundred years, it had to be considered an acceptable one.

Lissea stepped out onto the ramp. *"Captain to crew,"* she called on the general push. *"There's a party coming along the coast from Quantock. The settlement's control center has told them we aren't hostile, so they won't be shooting. Don't let's us have any problems either. Out."*

Ned looked in the direction of Quantock. Surf had battered the volcanic rock into a corniche which, except at the very highest tides, overhung a narrow shingle beach. Air-cushion and perhaps tracked vehicles could drive along the shore, though to Ned that didn't seem a safe way to approach an armed enemy. Perhaps the locals had hoped to take the presumed interlopers unaware, but that was a very risky bet.

For want of anything better to do, Ned walked toward the edge of the crater, where the settlers would be appearing. His submachine gun flopped against his right hip, so he tightened the sling. His bare forearm brushed the iridium barrel. The metal was searingly hot. Ned yelped and rubbed the red splotch which would shortly be a blister.

"What's the matter?" Lissea Doormann asked.

Ned jerked his head around. She was only a half-step from him. A commo helmet's ear-pieces cut off enough of the wearer's peripheral vision to hide nearby objects surprisingly.

"Lissea, where are you going?" Herne Lordling shouted from the hatchway.

"To make sure the first person to greet the welcoming committee isn't shooting!" Lissea called back.

"I just burned myself on my gunbarrel," Ned muttered in embarrassment. "Sorry, I didn't know you were there."

"Company coming!" Josie Paetz called in a clear, terrible voice. He stood on a ledge just below the crater rim. His submachine gun was pointed in the direction of the beach, and he was sighting along the barrel.

"Captain to crew!" Lissea said. *"Everybody take your hands off your weapons. Now!"*

She deliberately lifted her empty hands in the air with her elbows at shoulder height. Ned started to do the same, then realized he'd feel like an idiot. He crossed his hands behind his back instead.

An air-cushion truck of 5-tonne or greater payload whuffled into sight. Its skirts cast up spray on one side while the other ricocheted pebbles between the cliff and the vehicle's own flank. A civilian manned the tribarrel on the truck cab's ring mount, while other armed men—no women that Ned could see—peered over the front of the cargo box.

The tribarrel's gunner waved enthusiastically at Ned and Lissea. He was shouting something, probably a greeting, but the truck's roaring lift fans overwhelmed the words.

Though the fellow clearly wasn't hostile, it didn't occur to him to point his weapon up at a safe angle. Stupid mistakes had probably killed as many people over the years as aimed shots.

The vehicle slowed but didn't stop. Ned hopped out of the way, touching Lissea's arm to bring her with him. There was a second truck behind the first, and the vehicles had to get onto the basalt plug to be out of the surf. The first pulled far enough forward to let its companion past; then they both shut down. Though the surf instantly filled the relative silence, it was now possible to talk again.

The gunner slid down into the truck cab, opened the passenger door, and jumped to the ground. He was thirty or so, a handsome man with tawny hair and shoulders broad enough to make his waist look falsely narrow.

"Hello there, welcome to Quantock!" he called, waving his right arm like a semaphore. "I'm Jon Watford, the governor here, and I can't *tell* you how happy my wife's going to be to meet another woman from off-planet! Who's in charge?"

The truck tailgates banged down and the remainder of the locals began to get out. The insides of the cargo boxes were armored with thin concrete slabs, sandwiched three-deep to give protection against multiple hits. It struck Ned as a reasonably effective makeshift.

The men were a heavily armed militia instead of a trained military force. They carried a variety of weapons, with powerguns in the majority.

Nothing is ideal under all circumstances, but powerguns were more effective over a wide range of conditions than any alternative Ned knew of. Ajax Four had to be tied firmly into the interstellar trade network in order to be able to buy and maintain hardware so sophisticated. Of course, a gun is only as good as the gunman using it. Most of the Quantock contingent looked at least reasonably competent.

The truck bodies bore cratered splash marks from where they'd been struck by powergun bolts. As the *Swift*'s pilotry data indicated, the Spiders too were involved in interstellar trade.

"Very glad to meet you, Governor Watford," Lissea said. She extended her hand. "I'm Captain Doormann, Lissea—"

"You're in command, then?" Watford said in something between interest and amazement. He shook Lissea's hand.

Militiamen traded glances with the *Swift*'s complement. The locals were obviously taken aback by their heavily armed visitors, but they didn't seem really concerned. There were fifty-odd Quantock militiamen. They didn't have enough experience of real warfare to realize that the dozen expert killers surrounding them could have blown them to sausage before the victims could fire a shot in reply.

"Yes," Lissea said crisply. "I'm on a . . . an embassy to Pancahte. We're prepared for trouble on some of the wilder worlds, of course, but I assure you all we ask of you is the opportunity to purchase supplies at market value. We won't impose on Quantock in any way."

"Sure wouldn't mind having a decent meal, though," said Toll Warson, who'd drifted up behind Lissea.

"You'll have every facility we can provide!" said Watford. "Why, Mellie would never forgive me if I didn't bring you—and your crew, of course—to the settlement for a feast. Do come back with us. We've got room in the trucks if you don't mind squeezing a bit."

Lissea turned and looked at Tadziki. He shrugged and said, "I don't see why not. We'll leave an anchor watch, of course, but now that the sensors are in place, four men ought to be plenty."

"Might even be a woman or two looking for company," Deke Warson said to his brother in a tone of consideration.

"Warson—both of you," Lissea said as though Deke's words had thrown a switch in her tongue. "You'll provide the anchor watch with Ingried and—someone from the ship's crew . . ."

"Bonilla," Tadziki suggested.

"Right, Bonilla," Lissea said. "*If* I feel like it, you'll be relieved at around midnight. The rest of you, get aboard the trucks."

As Ned climbed into a truck box, using the latch of the tailgate as a step, he heard Toll Warson say, "You know, brother, you always did have more mouth than sense."

Jon Watford drove the leading truck and carried Lissea in the cab with him. The previous driver stood in the center of the bench seat to crew the tribarrel. There was no gun-shield. Even if there had been, the gunner's lower extremities were exposed through the windshield.

The tide was going out, exposing enough dry land for the

trucks to start back without adding to the spume. The cargo boxes were comfortably roomy for thirty-odd men on a three-klick excursion, though Ned sure wasn't going to stay aboard if shooting started.

"Do you have much trouble with the Spiders this close to the settlement?" he asked the local who was pressed against his right side. Like Ned, the man carried a submachine gun—which might even have been of Telarian manufacture.

"What?" the fellow said. "Spiders? No, no. We sweep the coast every couple months. They keep out of our way."

The deck appeared to be sheet metal. Ned toed it with his boot and grimaced when his suspicions were borne out. An air-cushion vehicle wasn't likely to set off a mine by direct pressure, but that wouldn't save this truck from a command-detonated or rod-fused mine. There ought to be floor protection—and not concrete, which would shatter into deadly shrapnel in the initial shock wave.

Tadziki, on Ned's left, noticed Ned's examination. The adjutant clung to the side of the truck with his right hand to steady himself. He raised the other hand and ostentatiously crossed his fingers while giving Ned a wry smile.

Ned looked down at the beach. Weed and occasional lumps that could be either animal or vegetable splotched the shingle, but there were relatively few signs of life. The broken tuff was too loose to anchor the shellfish and other sessile life-forms which would have populated a more resistant shore. One blob of protoplasm a meter in diameter was surrounded by hand-sized things which waved forelegs as the truck bellowed past.

When the trucks got to the fortified settlement, Ned might check the shore life more closely for old times' sake, but the Spiders weren't going to spring an ambush from the surf. Ned turned, leaning his back against the side of the truck so that he could view the corniche. He wished he'd worn body armor, to spread the jolts to his rib cage as well as for protection.

The cliffs generally ranged two to five meters above the beach's high-tide mark. One tongue of particularly refractory rock thrust so far west that the trucks had to drive around in a vast explosion of spray. Rainbows ringed the vehicles, and the salty mist cooled Ned's lungs refreshingly.

The trucks' ground pressure was too high for them to skim the wave-tops as lighter air-cushion vehicles could have done. The headland would be dangerous during the journey from Quantock at high tide.

A number of gravel-bottomed ravines drove deep into the interior. They were dry now, but they certainly held raging torrents when they carried storm water to the sea. The barren, rocky soil would do nothing to slow runoff.

The gullies were an obvious means of approach for Spiders who wished to reach the seacoast while remaining below the horizon of active sensing devices. The colonists probably planted passive sound and motion sensors in the low spots, but such gear would take a beating during every downpour.

There was nothing sexy or exciting about the business of maintaining detection apparatus. Ned doubted whether the colonists had the discipline to keep it up as religiously as safety required.

The colonist manning the cab's tribarrel raised his muzzles to a forty-five-degree angle and ripped off a burst. The cyan bolts were nearly the same hue as the sky, but their brilliance—pure energy instead of merely the diffraction of sunlight—made them stand out like pearls against linen.

All eight mercenaries in the leading truck—and probably the contingent in the second vehicle also—had their weapons raised and off safe. Lissea poked her semiautomatic 2-cm shoulder weapon out of the cab, searching for a target like the rest of them. The colonists were grinning.

The man beside Ned leaned over and shouted, "We're just letting them know in Quantock that we're back. Nothing to get concerned about."

To underscore his words, he aimed his submachine gun skyward and fired half a magazine. The pistol-caliber bolts were pale compared to the tribarrel's heavy charges. Empties spun from the ejection port, disks of half-molten plastic matrix whose burden of copper atoms had been converted to energy in the weapon's chamber. The hot plastic reeked, and ozone from the discharges bit the air.

"I prefer flares," Tadziki said with a cold disdain which probably passed right by the local.

"I told you, the Spiders don't come around here," the militiaman said.

Watford drove the truck up a concrete ramp and down into a vast polder whose floor was below water level at high tide. A seawall, anchored at either end on the cliff face, looped far into the ocean. Within the protected area were a series of square-edged ponds, some of them greenish or maroon from the crops grown there. Several hundred buildings sheltered beneath the corniche.

The polder was defended from enemies as well as the sea. Every hundred meters along the seawall and on the corniche across the chord was a fully enclosed turret. For weather protection, the weapons remained masked until use. From the size and design, Ned judged that each emplacement held a tribarrel in a fully automated or remotely controlled mounting.

People stepped outdoors as the trucks pulled up in front of the long building in the center of town. The sign over the main doors read CIVIC HALL.

The hall was a two-story structure ornamented with whimsically angled 'exposed beams' painted white against the pale blue of the rest of the facade. The whole Quantock community was decorated in pastels, and most of the residences had window boxes or planted borders.

Watford got out of the cab and started around the front of the vehicle. Herne Lordling leaped over the side and executed a perfect landing fall, but neither man was quick enough to beat Lissea to her own doorhandle.

Watford put his arm around the woman who ran up to greet him and said, "Mellie, let me introduce you to Captain Lissea Doormann, who commands the *Swift*. Lissea, this is Mellie Watford. Mellie came to Quantock as factor for a Xiphian import-export combine. She's the finest import *ever* to Ajax Four."

"We've been married a week," Mellie said. She looked down and blushed at her husband's flattery, but Ned noticed that her left hand squeezed Jon's hip firmly before she transferred her attention to Lissea.

The two women could have passed for sisters. Both were petite with dark short hair and a sort of elfin vivacity. Only in their present garments did they differ strikingly: Mellie wore a peach-colored frock, similar to those of the other women in the crowd, while Lissea was in gray utilities over which she'd slung a bandolier of reloads for her 2-cm powergun.

The sun hung low on the seawall. Its glow further softened the colors of the buildings, blending them with the ruddy tuff of the cliff face.

"I'm not really, ah, dressed for a banquet," Lissea said.

Ned exchanged bland glances with Tadziki. The captain who led a score of the most deadly men in the galaxy was embarrassed at not having a party dress.

"Come on home with me," Mellie said. "I'm sure I've got something to fit you." She caught Lissea's hand and tugged her unresisting toward a fuchsia house next door to the civic building. "I can't tell you how nice it is to meet another woman from off-planet, not that there's anything . . ."

Jon Watford glanced after the women, then returned his attention to the remaining locals and visitors. "Well, gentlemen," he said generally toward the mercenaries, "I think maybe a drink or three would be a good way to break the ice and start the celebration. Any takers?"

"Yee-*ha!*" somebody shouted. Ned wasn't sure who the enthusiast was, but a good hundred throats took up the call as the crowd surged toward the broad doors of the hall.

Six hours later, the gathering was a good-natured success. That surprised and pleased Ned, and it must have absolutely delighted Tadziki. Individual members of the *Swift*'s complement talked, in the center of large groups of locals like the grit at the core of pearls. The mercenaries were able to boast in a way they'd never have dared do among their own kind—and the listeners loved it.

The funny thing was that so far as Ned could tell, about half the stories were true and the others were fantasy. The fantasies were generally less amazing than the unvarnished accounts—which were sometimes told by the same man.

A number of the mercs had gone off with local women. That didn't seem to have caused any problems. Dewey had gone off with a local man, which *would* cause problems when Bonilla heard about it . . . but for the moment, Bonilla was safe aboard the *Swift*.

"Can I bring you anything?" asked a voice at Ned's elbow. "Another drink?"

He turned to Jon Watford. "No, I'm not that much of a drinker," he said. "I'm just looking at your chart here."

The two-by-two-meter hologram on one of the room's short walls was a 5000:1 relief map of Quantock and the terrain inland of the settlement. By manipulating the controls at the bottom of the frame, Ned found he could shift the alignment from vertical to a silhouette at any plane in the coverage area, and could decrease the scale to as low as 100:1.

"You know," said Watford thoughtfully, "I don't believe I've looked at this in the past ten years. We're pretty much focused on the sea here in Quantock. That's true everywhere on Ajax Four. But a map of wave-tops isn't much of a decoration, is it?" He chuckled.

"Has there been any attempt to, well, make peace with the indigs?" Ned asked.

"What?" said Watford.

"The indigenes," Ned said. "The Spiders."

"The Spiders aren't indigenous to Ajax Four!" Watford said with unexpected vehemence. "They're aliens, just as sure as men are, and there's curst good evidence that we were here first!"

"Oh," Ned said as his mind worked. "I didn't know that."

"There's no other land-dwelling life-forms bigger than algae," Watford said. "Do you mean to tell me that the Spiders evolved directly from algae?"

"No, I see your point," Ned said.

He pursed his lips. He wasn't looking for a fight. . . . But he *was* curious, and if he'd liked the experience of being steam-rollered in an argument, he wouldn't be the type to volunteer for the Pancahte Expedition.

"Thing is," he continued mildly, "I had the impression the Spiders didn't have any technology of their own. Not starships, anyway."

"Look," Watford said. He was getting red-faced. Ned recalled that it wasn't only mercenaries who'd been having a good deal to drink this night. "We've got *every* right to be on this planet. And I'll tell you another cursed thing: they aren't really intelligent, the Spiders aren't. They're really just animals with a talent for mimicking human beings."

"I see your point," Ned said, as though Watford hadn't made two mutually exclusive points. "You know, maybe I'll have another drink after all. What's good here?"

The funny thing was that this sort of philosophical problem concerned only decent people raised in civilized surroundings. Ned doubted that any two members of the *Swift*'s complement besides himself would even bother talking about the rights of indigenous aliens. As for the right of survival of a life-form, human or otherwise, with hostile intentions—

Pacifists didn't enter the Frisian Military Academy.

Watford cleared his throat in embarrassment. "Oh," he said. "Well, we've got a couple of good wines, but if you're willing to—"

"*Attention,*" called a voice so distorted by the hall's multiple loudspeakers that Ned didn't recognize Tadziki for a moment. The adjutant stood on the dais opposite the main doors with a microphone in his hand. "*Sorry, ladies and gentlemen, but there's some ship's business to take care of. Yazov, Paetz, Westerbeke, and Raff—you're next on the rota, and it's time to relieve the anchor watch. Our hosts are loaning us a truck, so you don't have to walk.*"

"Hey, the party's just getting started," Josie Paetz called, though he didn't look that disgruntled. The young mercenary did everything with verve, but only the prospect of combat really excited him.

Lissea stepped to the dais. She wore a tawny dress with gold polka dots. Her hand extended back toward Mellie Watford to show that she wasn't abandoning the woman who'd been her companion throughout the evening. Because the mike was live, Lissea's murmured *"Westerbeke went off with a girl . . ."* crackled through the speakers.

Ned strode toward the dais. "I'll go, Tadziki," he said.

Tadziki switched off the mike. "I want a ship's crewman, Ned," he said.

"I'm good enough for government work," Ned said. "Besides, I'm sober."

Tadziki looked at Lissea. She gave him a brief nod.

"Right," said the adjutant. "Governor, you offered us a vehicle?"

Watford had followed Ned to the dais. "Sure, no problem," he said. "Would you like one of our people to drive?"

"I'd just as soon drive it myself," Ned said before the adjutant could answer. "Got anything smaller than those behemoths you brought us here in, though?"

"Sure we do," Watford said. "Just come along with me."

The *Swift*'s complement had piled their weapons on a table near the door. The locals didn't care if their visitors were armed, but Lissea did. Watford waited while the mercenaries rummaged for their equipment, then led them outside and down a ramp to the garage beneath the building.

Ned paused a moment and studied the unfamiliar stars. He'd spent five years on Nieuw Friesland without getting used to those constellations, but recently he'd found the night sky of Tethys looked distorted also.

"You coming, Slade?" Josie Paetz called up the ramp.

"You bet," Ned said. He wondered whether or not there was a place in the universe where Edward Slade belonged.

The forty-some vehicles in the basement garage ranged from five-tonne trucks down to one-man skimmers. All were battery-powered, but two large repair vans were equipped with liquid-fueled generators as well.

The patrol radius of the heavily laden trucks would be a hundred klicks or less without a recharge. That didn't strike Ned as far enough.

Jon Watford leaned over the driver's side of the open utility vehicle he'd offered the mercs. "Here's the power switch," he said, pointing.

Ned flipped it up. The instrument panel lighted. There were a dozen individual gauges rather than a combiner screen.

"Fan switches—"

There were four of them. Ned snapped them individually, watching the dials as he did so. An unexpectedly high drain might indicate a short in one of the drive motors.

"And the collective," Watford continued, touching the control yoke. "You've handled hovercraft, I trust? With this broken lava, we don't have much use for wheels."

"I've handled hovercraft," Ned agreed. *Up to and including 170-tonne supertanks, any one of which could turn Quantock into glowing slag in three seconds flat.*

"Can we get this show on the road?" Josie Paetz demanded from the other front seat. "Curst if I don't start walking pretty quick."

The truck had seats for six people in pairs, but the two rear benches could be folded flat for cargo space. Yazov sat behind his young charge, while Raff sprawled on the rear bench with his rocket launcher pointed straight up like a flagpole. If Raff were human, Ned would guess he was three sheets to the wind, but from what he'd seen at the party, the Racontid stuck to water.

"What I figure to do," Ned said mildly, "is learn about the equipment before I take us all out in it."

He tapped a gauge. The needle didn't move. "This says we're at sixty-two percent charge," he said. "How long has it been charging?"

Watford grimaced. "It ought to have a few cells replaced," he said. "Don't worry, though, it'll get you to the ship and bring your friends back. And don't worry about the ground. We're at low tide now, so you'll have a couple hundred meters of beach to run on."

"All right," Ned said. He engaged the fans and felt the truck shiver like butter sliced onto a hot grill.

He backed into the central aisle and spun to face the entrance. The vehicle responded nimbly. Ned had forgotten how much handier an air-cushion vehicle was when the driver didn't have to contend with tonnes of armored inertia. "See you in the morning," he called over his shoulder to Watford as he accelerated out of the garage.

"Aren't you going to turn on your headlights, hotshot?" Josie Paetz asked. He reached over to the marked switch on the dashboard.

Ned raised his knee to block the younger man's hand. "No," he said, "I'm going to use moonlight. The big one's just above the horizon, but that'll do better than advertising us to anybody who wants an easy target."

Paetz sniffed and settled back in his seat. "Maybe *you're* easy," he said, but he didn't press the matter. His uncle eased slightly.

Ned took the utility vehicle up the ramp over the seawall. The salt breeze felt good and the moonlight was, as he'd expected, adequate without enhancement. Switching his visor to light-amplification mode would rob him of depth perception.

He felt himself relax. This was a nice, easy job to focus him after a social evening in which he felt uncomfortable.

Powerguns threw cyan lightning across the sky southward.

"The ship's being attacked!" Josie Paetz said. "Let's get 'em!"

"Wait for bloody support!" Yazov boomed. Several men, mercs to a near certainty, sprang out the doors of the Civic Hall with guns in their hands. The truck dipped down the outer ramp, cutting off the view of Quantock in the driving mirrors; but the *Swift*'s whole complement would be armed and on its way in a minute or less. The community militia would follow.

Raff said nothing. His rocket launcher's heavy bolt clanged to chamber a round.

"Hang on!" Ned cried. He turned the truck hard left, up a broad gully instead of due south along the shoreline. When he was sure of the surface he pushed the collective forward, feeding more power to the fans.

"What the fuck are you doing?" Paetz screamed. He

pointed. "The shooting's *there,* by the ship!"

"And that's where we're going," Ned said, "only not by the bloody front door. If you do your job as well as I do mine, sonny, then we're going to come through this just fine."

That was a crazy thing to say to the young killer, but the only sane response to combat is to avoid it. If you head toward the guns in a plastic-bodied truck, then your sanity isn't even in question.

At high speed, the truck bounced on its flexible skirts. Rocks, stream-sorted to the size of a man's fist, whopped toward the walls of the ravine. The shielded nacelles kept gravel out of the fan blades. The vehicle could move with three fans instead of four, but it would lose speed and agility. Climbing the gully wall would be a bitch even with full power.

Yazov leaned forward. "There's a lot of wasteland out here," he said in Ned's ear. His voice sounded calm.

"It's okay," Ned said, shouting as he had to do to be heard while facing front. "I'd been looking at a map. I'm going to take us back from the southeast."

The ravine kinked through ninety degrees or so for the third time since Ned had turned into it. The change was due to a dike of harder rock that pinched the gully. It made the sides steeper as well. He should have thought of that when he'd decided to climb back to the surface here.

"Hang on!" he repeated. He banked up the outside of the curve and gunned the fans. His three passengers threw their combined weight to the right without being told. Raff's snarls might have been Racontid curses. Paetz and Yazov were certainly cursing.

Centrifugal force lifted the vehicle over the lip of rock. They'd been millimeters from turning turtle and landing upside down in the ravine, but only horseshoes and hand grenades . . .

The terrain was corrugated. Tubes of lava a meter or two in diameter had hardened alongside one another in past ages. An overburden of ash had fallen across the denser lava, had been compacted and then swept away by centuries of pounding rain. The present surface was almost impossible to walk over, difficult to traverse even in an air-cushion vehicle, and provided no cover whatever for a man-sized target.

The truck rubbed and pitched. The corrugations were deep enough to spill air from the plenum chamber, so Ned couldn't proceed as fast or as smoothly as he had up the streambed. From what he remembered of the chart, they had about a klick to travel.

"Where are we headed, Slade?" Yazov said. He was using his helmet radio to avoid windrush. The high metallic content of the planet's volcanic rocks absorbed radio signals over very moderate distances, but it wasn't so bad it affected four men sitting within arm's reach of one another.

"There's another ravine," Ned explained. The vehicle bucked high. Ned twisted the bar on the dash which controlled the attitude of the fan nacelles. By angling them vertical, he managed to cushion the truck's impact.

"We'll take it back toward the coast, but south of the ship," he said, wheezing because the shock of landing had jolted him against the yoke. *"They won't expect us from that way."*

Powergun bolts streaked the sky and lit the dark mass of the crater which bowered the *Swift*. More shots reflected from the ground and glowed in the gas vaporized from gouges of rock.

Josie Paetz stood. He presented his submachine gun with both hands instead of clinging to the windshield with one or the other. His body swayed, perfectly in balance despite the truck's violent motion. His eyes scanned the horizon from that slightly higher vantage.

Ned took a hand away from the collective to key his helmet. *"Best we not call attention to ourselves too soon, Paetz,"* he said.

"Fuck off," Paetz shouted.

There was a series of bright red explosions from the battle scene. Raff stroked his rocket launcher and laughed like gears clashing.

A shadow on the ground, streaking lesser shadows. Sooner than he'd—

"Hang—" Ned cried.

They were airborne, dipping into the gully that Ned had

thought was just another corrugation until it was *real* close. He spun the yoke and leaned. The truck didn't have an aircar's power-to-weight ratio so it dropped instead of flying, marginally under control.

Paetz fell to his knees and grabbed the windshield. The clear plastic cracked across with the strength of his grip, but he didn't go out. His weapon still pointed forward in the other hand, ready to engage any Spider that showed itself.

It took ten meters before Ned thought he could get the truck stable, twice that before he did. Even then the ravine twisted unexpectedly and he tore off a chunk of front molding. Only the skirts' resilience kept them from worse trouble. Yazov cursed him for a cack-handed fool.

Paetz shot—three bolts so dazzling that Ned's visor blacked out to save his night vision. The object in the gully ahead of them was just an object to Ned, a boulder in the way. Paetz, his faceshield set to thermal imaging, recognized it as a Spider while Ned was trying to maneuver safely around.

The creature lunged upward, screaming like a glacier about to calve icebergs. It had been crouching to aim its own power-gun toward the kilometer-distant cone which protected the *Swift*. As the truck howled past the Spider, Yazov shot it with his 2-cm weapon and Raff fired his rocket launcher point-blank.

The rocket motor was of the all-burned-on-launch variety so there was no danger to the shooter from backblast, but the supersonic *crack!* behind Ned's left ear was deafening despite his helmet's protection. The Spider blew apart in a white flash. The warhead's explosion had been lost in the motor roar.

The ravine twisted. Three Spiders hunched like squat bollards across the truck's path. Instinct told Ned to brake by aiming the fan output forward. Training—*when in doubt, gas it*—slammed his throttle to the stop.

It seemed as if the whole world was shooting, but the only gunmen were the three mercs with Ned. Paetz and Yazov hit the right-hand Spider simultaneously, head-shots from the submachine gun while Yazov cratered the creature's chest with a bolt from his heavier weapon.

Recoil from the rocket launcher lifted the nose of the truck. The Racontid had to have muscles like tow cables to be able to accept the shock. The Spider in the center disintegrated. Fragments of its pelvis and torso blew into its fellows like secondary missiles.

The truck hit the left and center Spiders a fraction of a second apart. The gooey corpse Raff had shot swept away the damaged windshield and knocked Josie Paetz backward. The powergun the creature had been carrying in one of its upper hands clattered on the short hood and off the other side of the vehicle. Yazov fired again, twisting backward in his seat, and lit up the third Spider with his bolt.

The Spiders were retreating, running away when they learned that the *Swift*'s anchor watch was more of a bite than they could chew. Most of the aliens weren't going to survive to run far, though.

Ned switched on the headlights. A mass of Spiders stood like startled deer, twenty or more. Sweat and weapons gleamed on their dark gray bodies. They'd heard the shooting ahead of them, but they hadn't known how to react, and anyway, there wasn't time.

There wasn't time for the Spiders now, either.

The creatures were so tall that Ned felt he was driving into a grove with arms flailing above him like windswept branches. Paetz, flung into the well between the front and second bench, fired from a sprawling position. Yazov fired, and Raff emptied his magazine with two thunderous blasts so quick that there was barely time for the breech to cycle between the shots.

Ionized air, matrix and propellant residues, and the unforgettable reek of living creatures whose body cavities had explosively emptied, merged in an atmosphere you could cut with a knife. The truck brushed between two Spiders, one of them dying, and hit a third squarely. A headlight shattered. The heavy body skidded over the vehicle and off.

They were around a twitch in the ravine, so slight that it would appear straight to somebody looking at a map. The three-meter walls cut off view of the carnage behind the truck. There was nothing but rock in the headlight beam. Spiders were shrieking. None of them had fired during the momentary contact.

The volume of distant gunfire suddenly increased tenfold. The *Swift* wasn't the focus of the shooting. The rest of the mercenaries and the Quantock militia must have run into another party of Spiders.

The rocket launcher clanged as Raff locked home a fresh magazine. *How he stood the recoil* . . . Josie Paetz was upright, reloading also, and the shuck*clack* directly behind Ned meant that Yazov's 2-cm was ready as well.

"Go on back!" Paetz screamed. "We'll finish them! Go on!"

Ned spun the yoke with his left hand and unslung his submachine gun in his right. He pointed the weapon over where the windshield had been. "You bet your ass!" he said as the truck tore back into conflict.

The Spiders' thin bodies were exaggerated by the great length of their limbs. Their heads were nearly spherical and about the volume of a man's. The eyes were large and slightly bulged, while the mouth was a point-down triangle with teeth on all three flats.

Translucent membranes slipped sideways over the eyes as the glare of the halogen-cycle headlight flashed on them again.

Half a dozen of the Spiders were down. One had lost half its skull to a powergun bolt. Two of its fellows helped the creature stand upright, though it must have been mortally wounded.

Raff put a rocket into the injured Spider. The warhead blew the trio down like pins struck squarely by a bowling ball.

Ned hosed the aliens, keeping his muzzle low. He couldn't hope for accuracy while he drove, but he knew that being shot at didn't help *any* marksman's aim. Besides, he was bound to hit a few of them, trapped in the trough of the ravine.

Paetz fired three-shot bursts, aiming for Spiders' heads and always hitting with at least one of the bolts despite the truck's speed and the slewing turn. His uncle aimed single shots at the center of mass of each target in turn. None of the mercs knew where a Spider's vital organs were—the brain might not even be in the skull—but a 2-cm bolt packed enough energy to cook everything in the torso, and the least Josie's head-shots were going to do was blind the victim.

The Spider who'd been alert enough to aim as the truck came back was Yazov's first victim. Another of the creatures managed to swing his submachine gun to bear. The Spider disintegrated in a mix of powergun bolts and a rocket before it could fire.

Ned humped over a corpse, caromed off the legs of a Spider which stood upright but was missing two arms and the left half of its chest, and spun safely out of the killing zone again.

The iridium barrel of his submachine gun glowed white. He must have sublimed five millimeters from the bore by emptying the magazine on a single trigger-pull. There were times you had to misuse tools, waste them, to get the job done. Tools and men as well sometimes, if you were in command and the devil drove.

He tossed the submachine gun over the side of the truck. He couldn't reload one-handed with the weapon so hot, and the eroded barrel wouldn't be safe for another burst anyway.

Ned rotated the truck on its axis again, scrubbing away velocity between the skirts and the streambed. He switched off the headlight, spun the roller switch above his forehead to change his visor to thermal imaging, and held out his right hand. "Paetz!" he said. "Gimme one of your pistols!"

The butt of a 1-cm service pistol slapped Ned's palm. The weapon was already off safe. He closed his fingers about it and slammed the control yoke to the dashboard again. Stones spewed from beneath the skirts as the truck accelerated under maximum thrust.

They rounded the slight corner. The Spiders were pale wraiths against the relative darkness of rocks which had cooled during the night. Two of the creatures clung to the sides of the ravine, trying to climb, or just desperate to stay upright. A few others knelt or squatted, and limbs thrashed all over the killing ground.

Paetz, Yazov, and Raff blasted the aliens which weren't already flat on the stones. Ned emptied his borrowed pistol, but he didn't think he hit anything useful with it. There was probably nothing useful *to* hit. None of the Spiders had been able to raise a weapon against the mercenaries.

He slowed the truck to a crawl and idled back among the huge corpses. His companions were reloading.

"Wanna take pictures?" Paetz asked.

"No," Ned said. "They aren't going to walk off before daybreak."

He reached over the side of the truck and grabbed a standard-looking submachine gun from a Spider. The creature's arm fell apart under the tug of the sling. Shrapnel from a rocket warhead had shredded the Spider from skull to pelvis.

"Let's go see what happened at the ship," he said. Shooting had died down almost completely. "Besides, there may be some stragglers."

The Spiders hadn't fired a shot at them. Not one single shot.

Raff began to sing in his own language, pounding time on the flooring with the butt of his rocket launcher. His voice sounded like a saw cutting stone.

We are the best, Ned thought. His tunic was soaked with sweat and the fluids with which the Spiders had sprayed him during point-blank kills.

We are the best!

Crewmen had carried minifloods from the *Swift* to throw blue-white light over the bodies. Elongated shadows made the Spiders look even larger than they were. Most of the creatures had slid to the base of the cone in their death throes, but a few lay nearly at the rim.

"We never killed that many of them," said a marveling colonist.

"I never *saw* this many Spiders!" said Jon Watford. "In thirty-two years, I never saw this many Spiders. You're—"

He turned to Lissea Doormann. "Lissea, you're incredible,

you and your men. It'll be a generation before they get up enough strength to be a problem again.''

"I'm afraid your dress is a casualty, though, Mellie," Lissea said.

She looked down at herself ruefully. She'd dropped a bandolier over the garment as she left the Civic Hall at a run. A clasp had caught and torn the light fabric. The black smudges were iridium. The metal sublimed from powergun bores as they channeled the enormous energy downrange and redeposited on whatever was closest when the vapor cooled. Lissea's hands and the bare skin of her throat beneath the line of her visor were gray-tinged also.

Mellie, still in her own peach frock, hugged Lissea fiercely. "Don't worry about that!" she said. "What's important is that *you're* all right."

"Silly bastards thought they'd sneak up on us," Deke Warson said. The cloth facing of his hard body armor was abraded. At some point during the night, Deke must have skidded ten or twenty meters on the lava. "Because we didn't shoot the first time one of them poked his head out, they thought we didn't know they were coming."

"If that's what passes for fire discipline on Ajax Four . . ." his brother said. He spoke in Watford's direction, but he didn't raise his voice to emphasize the criticism. ". . . then I'm surprised there's any colonies left."

Virtually the whole Quantock settlement was present, *ooh*ing and *ah*ing at the windrow of huge bodies. The trucks that brought the reaction force had returned to ferry civilians. Parents carried babies to see the unique sight.

"And there's more back there along the cliffs," a colonist said. "I don't know how many there must be."

"There were half a dozen Spiders on the corniche," Tadziki said to Ned in a quiet voice. "They were going to ambush whoever came from the settlement."

The older man shook his head at the memory. "It was as though they'd never heard of thermal imaging," he said. "Or maybe they'd just never met humans who could hit anything from a moving vehicle. They scarcely got a shot off, the Spiders."

"They come up two of the gullies south of us and spread all around," said Harlow, a skeletally thin man whose skin was as pigmentless as an albino's. He had red hair. "We could see them like it was in broad daylight. We just waited till we figured we could make the bag limit."

"Amateurs," Tadziki said as he studied his hands. Like those of the other mercs, they were stained by redeposited metal. "They'll buy guns, but they won't buy support weapons like sensors and night-vision equipment to make the guns effective."

"And they act," Ned said, "as if everybody else did the same thing."

Tadziki smiled. "You all right, then?" he said.

"Sure," Ned said. "I don't know what made me do that. I'm fine."

He and the others, the *team*, reached the *Swift* less than a minute after the first 5-tonne from the settlement arrived. Ned got out of the utility truck, looked around, and vomited in the full glare of headlights.

The truth was, he still felt as though his mind was detached from the body which happened to be occupying the same space. He supposed that would pass. Blood and martyrs! He'd been shot at before, which was more than the Spiders had managed to do.

Mellie was with her husband. Jon gestured animatedly toward the fallen Spiders. Lissea walked over to Ned and the adjutant. "I hear you had some excitement of your own," she said to Ned.

Ned quirked a smile. "Seemed like that at the time," he said. "Seeing this, I don't know that we did so very much, though."

"Hey, don't sell us short!" said Josie Paetz. "We nailed every one we saw, didn't we? Musta been thirty of them, at least."

"We killed twenty-six," Raff said. "We did well, my

brothers.'' The Racontid gave his terrible equivalent of a laugh.

"When they clumped up, Bonilla stomped them with the mortar,'' Toll Warson said to a crowd of admiring colonists. "Mostly, though, it was shoot and scoot.''

He pumped his 2-cm powergun in the air. Civilians laughed and cheered. Ned noted that Toll had also been firing the submachine gun slung across his chest. Its hot barrel had seared a series of indentations in the fabric cover of his body armor.

"And shoot again,'' his brother said, "while they blew holes in the rock where the first rounds had come from. As if we wouldn't have multiple hides, with all afternoon and nothing else to do.''

"You're okay, then?'' Lissea said sharply.

"Look, I'm fine!'' Ned said. He looked away. "I did my job, all right?''

"He did better than that,'' Tadziki said. "He's the one who decided on his own hook to cut the Spiders' line of retreat—and did it too.''

Yazov turned. He was polishing the film of matrix from the ejection port of his shoulder weapon. "He can drive for me any day. Hey, Slade?''

Ned grinned at the older man. "Hey,'' he said. "We're a team, right?''

Lissea Doormann squeezed Ned's shoulder. Herne Lordling watched with eyes like gun muzzles. "That's right,'' she said. "We're a team.''

"Well, you've got to spend the night with us at Quantock,'' Mellie Watford said, linking her arm again with Lissea's. "You should all of you come. You don't need guards anymore.''

Ned winced. Some Spiders—probably a few dozen or even scores of them—would have escaped by the other ravine. Making a needless bet on how aliens would react to a disaster was naive and foolish beyond words. *He* didn't like the idea that Quantock was empty at the moment, though the settlement at least had automatic defenses.

Lissea smiled and hugged Mellie. "No,'' she said, "we'll

all stay by the ship tonight. We've got a long way to go, and I don't intend to take risks.''

"Well, you'll let us entertain you again tomorrow night, won't you?" Jon Watford said. "A victory celebration, that'll be."

Lissea shook her head crisply. "I'm sorry," she said. "We'll take on food and water from your settlement in the morning, if you'll be so kind; but we lift for Mirandola by noon."

She looked back at the ship, then faced the Quantock governor again.

"We have a mission," she said. Her voice made the night chime.

Three hours and forty-seven minutes out of Ajax Four, Ingried called from the consumables module, "Hey, why can't I get any water out of this? Hey, Bonilla—what's wrong with the water?"

Dewey, who was at the navigational console instead of Bonilla, called up the proper gauge on his screen. Then he swore and said, "Captain? Captain! The tank's open. We've voided all our fresh water!"

"All right," boomed Herne Lordling as he swung himself out of his bunk. "Who was responsible for filling the tank? That was you, wasn't it, Warson?"

He pointed a big finger at Deke Warson.

Lissea stepped out of her room. The flimsy door was opaque but didn't pretend to soundproofing.

"I'll handle this!" Tadziki said, coming off his bunk also. Ned, who'd been reading a translation of Thucydides, dropped the viewer and jumped down behind the adjutant. The whole crew was on its feet, except for Deke Warson.

"I put a load of water aboard, Cuh'nel, sah," said Warson. His bare feet were braced against the stanchions supporting Toll's bunk above him. His hands were behind his head; significantly, Deke's right hand was beneath his pillow as well. "I didn't top off the tank. There was one, maybe two bladders after the one I siphoned aboard.''

"That's a curst lie!" Lordling said. "Those were four-thousand-liter bladders, and the one you loaded was the third. The tank only holds twelve kay!"

The tank connections were badly designed. The access plate could be closed over the vent and spout even though the valves weren't screwed down to lock. For that matter, it wouldn't be the first time a seal had failed in service, particularly on a new vessel.

"I'll han—" Tadziki repeated.

"No," said Lissea. She stepped between Lordling and the Warsons. "I will. Dewey, chart a return course to Ajax Four. Westerbeke, oversee him."

Westerbeke had lurched from the commode, pulling his trousers up. He nodded and shuffled forward to the other navigation console.

Lissea looked around at her crew. "Gentlemen," she said, "this isn't a race we're in. Eight hours more or less isn't going to make a difference. But fuck-ups can kill us. Somebody didn't do his job. Somebody else didn't check that the job was done."

She looked at Herne Lordling. "And going off half-cocked isn't going to help a bad situation either. Let's take this as a cheap lesson and not do it again. Any of it."

"It was my fault, Captain," Tadziki said. "I went over the connections before liftoff, but I must have missed that one."

One of the ship's crewmen—Ned thought it was Hatton—had been officially responsible for checking the external seals.

"There's enough blame to go around," Lissea said coldly. "There aren't so many of us aboard that we can afford to trust that somebody else will make sure we all stay alive. It's over for now."

"Sir, we've got the course charted," Westerbeke called from forward.

Lissea turned on her heel. "Then engage it at once," she ordered as she strode back to her tiny compartment.

The *Swift* shuddered into Transit. Ned returned to his bunk. Like Lissea said, eight hours didn't matter a great deal.

* * *

The *Swift*'s landing motors converted the rain into visually-opaque steam. The automatic landing system used millimeter-wave radar, so optical visibility wasn't important, but the roiling gray mass on the screen above the navigation consoles didn't do anything for Ned's state of mind. He was nervous. Therefore, he kept his face abnormally calm.

"Touchdown," Westerbeke reported. Ned didn't feel the skids make contact, but the motors shut down an instant later.

"Sir, I still can't raise Quantock," Bonilla said. *"I think it's their equipment, not just the storm and, you know, the planet. Over."*

Everybody was getting up. Lissea and Tadziki walked forward. Ned stayed where he was, near the engine-room bulkhead. Lissea spoke to Bonilla without using helmet commo. Ned caught only the general drift, something about the settlement.

"All right, listen up," Tadziki said loudly. "The following personnel will put out sensors. Deke Warson, Hatton, Lordling, and myself. Get your wet suits on, boys, because it's raining like a sonuvabitch out there."

Herne Lordling turned toward the adjutant. His face was cold.

"I'll go along too," Toll Warson said. "I gave Deke a hand with the bladder."

Lissea looked at Warson and nodded.

Ned opened the drawer in his bedframe and pulled out the stretchable black overstocking of waterproof fabric. "Sir?" he said. "Tadziki? I'll take one of our Jeeps to Quantock and tell them we're back. They can bring us water in the morning."

Somebody started to lower the ramp. Water spewed in as soon as the seal broke, soaking the nearest bunks.

"Close that up!" Tadziki snapped. "We'll use the airlock instead."

"Those robot turrets'll chew you up just as fast as they would a Spider, kid," Deke Warson said. "Better wait till the storm passes and we can get a signal through.''

"I'll use laser commo when I get a line of sight," Ned said. He worked his hands through the armholes of the wet suit, then rolled the collar about his neck. He wouldn't bother with the hood. "After that I'll wait till they send somebody out to clear me through.''

"It's high tide," Tadziki said. "I don't think it'll be safe along the beach. And anyway, I don't want you going alone.''

"Hey, he's looking for a regular bed to sleep in, that's all he's doing," Louis Boxall said.

"And maybe somebody to share it?" his brother offered.

"I'll ride shotgun," Josie Paetz said.

"No, I figured to come back to the ship as soon as I'd delivered the message," Ned said, sweeping his comment across the Boxalls and Tadziki, "so that you know it's been delivered.''

Yazov put down the 2-cm barrel he'd been inspecting on his bunk. "I promised your father that I'd stick with you, Josie," he said. "If you go, I go.''

"Look, those Jeeps won't haul three!" Paetz said. From a deadly gunman he suddenly switched to being a petulant boy of nine or ten.

"Then you stay," his uncle said flatly. "Or you shoot me here.''

"Look, I don't really need—" Ned said.

"I'll go with Brother Slade," Raff volunteered. He stood up with his rocket launcher. If the Racontid even had a wet suit, he didn't bother with it.

"I'll go myself," Lissea Doormann said unexpectedly. "I'd like to see Mellie again. And anyway, I should have checked the valves myself.''

She grinned wryly at Ned. "Wait a moment while I get my suit," she added.

"I'll take longer than a moment to get the Jeep out of external storage," Tadziki grumbled. "Coyne, Harlow, both of you Boxalls—get your suits on. Setting up the Jeep's your job.''

"Lissea," said Herne Lordling, "I can't permit you to do this!"

Lissea stared at him. Lordling, with one leg into the over-stocking, looked so silly that Deke Warson had an excuse for laughing.

"That's right, Herne," she said. "You can't permit me to do anything. Because you work for me, not the other way around!"

She stamped past Ned and tried to slam the door of her room. It wasn't heavy enough to do a good job.

Ned's lips were pursed as he took a bandolier of ammunition from the arms locker. He now carried the submachine gun he'd taken from the dead Spider. It was a perfectly serviceable weapon; and it meant something, to Ned and to his companions.

"Got it!" Louis Boxall shouted as he kicked the main-pin home on the collapsible Jeep. "Your chariot awaits, milord Slade."

When the waves withdrew from the shore, the hissing roar muted to the point you could hear the sheets of rain hammering on the *Swift*'s hull. Ned's boots sloshed in a centimeter of water. The storm didn't leave it time to run off the flat, impervious surface of the basalt.

"I'm used to this," he said to Boxall as he got in on the driver's side.

"It rains like this on Tethys?" Lissea said as she scissored her legs over the Jeep's right sidewall.

The setup crew trotted back to the airlock. The last man, anonymous in helmet and wet suit, waved.

Ned threw the main switch and checked his gauges. Everything was in the green. "No ma'am," he said. "But I did a lot of diving."

Lissea chuckled. She carried a shoulder weapon slung muzzle-down to keep rain out of the bore.

Ned cleared his throat. "Ah, Lissea," he said. "There's two ways to do this: inland—where there's a couple rivers to

cross—and out to sea beyond the surf. *I* think going out over
the breakers is the better idea by far, but—well, I don't think
most of the people back aboard would like me taking you that
way."

"You're the driver," Lissea said. "I wouldn't be here if I
didn't trust you."

Ned engaged the fans and spun them up. The little Jeep
combined a high power-to-weight ratio with agile handling,
making it a delight to drive. It wasn't an aircar, but you could
glide three meters for every one you dropped if you knew
what you were doing.

"Hang on, then," he said. "The next part's the only tricky
bit."

He idled down to the shore. Because the Jeep was designed
for military use, there was a sleeve between the two seats to
clamp the butt of Ned's submachine gun. He'd covered the
muzzle with a condom, normal practice and nothing he
thought about until Lissea fingered the rubber.

"Good idea," she said.

"It's SOP in the Slammers," Ned said, keeping his voice
level.

A major wave hit the lip of basalt and cascaded almost as
far as the skids of the *Swift*. Ned eased the yoke forward,
building speed gradually to match that of the retreating seawater. Spray puffed around the vehicle as its skirts rode over
rock. When the Jeep ran into the open sea, it dipped slightly
under its own weight and that of the passengers. The plenum
chamber sealed perfectly. The Jeep, wallowing like a dory
with no rudder, began to move forward.

Ned turned the vehicle's head, fighting the sluggishness of
the fluid medium. A wave struck them. The mixture of water
and trapped air gurgled into the passenger compartment and
down across the plenum chamber. The Jeep bucked and bub-
bled higher, regaining its handling.

Ned goosed the throttles off the back of the wave. The Jeep
was dancing across the surface of the water when they met the
next big comber. They were far enough out now that they
could skid across it as a swell rather than a cataclysm.

"Next stop, Quantock!" Ned cried. Seawater streamed out the side-vents. Some rain was falling, but either the storm had slacked off or it wasn't as fierce over the ocean as it had been onshore.

"People pay good money for fun like that," Lissea said, tightening her suit's throat seal with one hand. She was being ironic, but she didn't sound angry until she added, "Just what the hell do you suppose Herne Lordling thinks he's playing at?"

Ned checked his compass direction. To gain a moment's time while he decided whether to answer, he illuminated the map display on the dashboard.

"He thinks," he said, staring far ahead of the vehicle, "that he's in love with you. And he thinks that eventually you'll, ah, fall in love with him."

He felt Lissea's eyes on him. He glanced over to prove that he wasn't avoiding her—as he was—and then focused back 'on his driving.'

"And what do you think, Ned?" the woman asked in an even tone.

Ned looked at her and away. "I think," he said, "that you're just about the most controlled person I've ever met. It'd be a disaster for the expedition if you got together with Lordling—with any of us, but especially with Lordling. So there isn't a snowball's chance in hell of that happening."

He cleared his throat. He was driving with a natural grace. For having fun in a Jeep, open water was a better medium even than a rolling meadow. There were no obstacles, and the flowing surface turned every line into a thrilling slalom.

"Why especially Herne?" Lissea asked.

"Because," Ned said, "he isn't smart enough not to get involved in things that he doesn't know anything about. Which means most things."

He didn't know how she was going to take that until she giggled. "He was a colonel, you know," she said.

"Ma'am," Ned said, "my uncle Don would say, 'There's only one Colonel, that's Alois Hammer; and I served with him.' "

"And you can say the same thing, can't you, Ned?" Lissea said.

He looked at her again. Her face in the dashlights was quiet, expectant. "Yes ma'am," he said. "In my own way. Yes, I can say that."

She faced front. "I still prefer 'Lissea,'" she said.

The first cyan ripple of powergun bolts was lost in the occasional cloud-top lightning. Three mortar shells went off, followed by three more, as quickly as the *Swift*'s crew could feed a fresh clip into the 10-cm weapon. The red flashes were unmistakable.

"The ship's being attacked!" Ned said. They were about midway on an arc between the *Swift* and Quantock, almost a kilometer out to sea. He started to swing the Jeep's bow shoreward.

Lissea prodded at switches on her commo helmet. Persistent static swamped any attempted radio communication. She snarled, "Bloody hell! They could be on Telaria for any good I'm able to do to raise them."

Ned reached down with his right hand and worked his submachine gun's charging handle. "I'll drop you at the settlement," he said.

"Like hell you will," Lissea said. "You'll bring us around the back of the Spiders and we'll light them up, just like you would if it was Paetz with you."

"Lissea . . ." Ned said. The ravines would be gushing torrents now, but the Jeep was handy enough to breast them. The very violence of the run-off would conceal the little vehicle and smother the fan's noise signature.

"And don't tell me I can't shoot like Josie Paetz!" Lissea said as she chambered a round into her 2-cm weapon. "Neither can you!"

"Yes, ma'am," Ned said. He concentrated on his driving.

All hell was breaking out around the partly crumbled cinder cone. The attackers were using at least one tribarrel. Chunks of the crater's rim dissolved.

Where the chosen ravine—now river—met the ocean, the water boiled like soup left on too high a fire . . . but there was no current since flow and counterflow balanced. Ned brought his speed up.

The Jeep's skirts dabbed at surges, causing the vehicle to pitch and yaw. He couldn't anticipate the fiercely pulsing water. The barren rocks upstream sped the runoff, but at least Ned didn't have to worry about meeting a tree-trunk rolling in the flood.

The mortar landed another triple hammerblow. Blue-and-orange flames flashed skyward in response to the shellbursts. A ripping sound indicated a powerful electrical current was shorting across the wet ground.

"That's—" Lissea said.

"Blood and martyrs!" Ned shouted, hauling on the yoke. He leaned almost across his passenger's lap to tighten the Jeep's swerve away from the sudden obstacle.

Ned was using thermal imaging rather than the vehicle's central headlight in order to achieve surprise. The river was a black mirror, sharply in contrast to the banks even though the bordering stone had been drenched by the storm.

He *knew* there would be no obstructions. Therefore he almost ran into the scissors bridge lying low across the stream, even though the stark lines of the structure were as obvious as blood on a sheet.

They bumped up over the bank of the stream. The aircushion Jeep didn't have a ground vehicle's advantage of using friction to scrub off momentum, but the lack of running gear made it very light. They skidded across the side of the approach ramp, close to the end, low, and not fast enough to rip the skirts off.

"Via," Lissea said, "the Spiders don't have gear like that. The settlers thought the *Swift* was a smuggler. They've attacked us."

"Yeah, that's what it looks like," Ned said softly.

The tribarrel had been silenced. Richly saturated bolts from the *Swift*'s defenders ripped and played across the landscape.

"Stop here," Lissea ordered. "I'll use modulated laser."

Ned skidded the Jeep to a halt. He left the fans at idle, though he was ready to shut them off if Lissea demanded that. The slight vibration wouldn't significantly affect communication, but using tight-beam laser without a clear receptor was a frustrating business. It was still raining, though maybe not enough to matter.

"Doormann to *Swift*," Lissea said. Ned, breathing hard through his open mouth, marveled at how calm Lissea kept her voice. She'd focused her faceshield's pipper on the rim of the cinder cone. The miniature laser was mounted over her right ear, with the pickup tube right above it. "Cease firing immediately. You are shooting at Quantock settlers."

The transmission was invisible and inaudible unless it painted a tuned receptor. Three quick bolts proved at least somebody hadn't gotten the word.

"Doormann to *Swift*," Lissea repeated. "Cease firing immediately. These are our friends."

A 2-cm powergun could claw a satellite from orbit through a normal-density atmosphere like that of Ajax Four. Powerguns were line-of-sight weapons, but the laser communicator was line-of-sight also.

A single bolt reflected from the cloud base. It had been aimed southward from the cone. No further shots followed.

Lissea slumped back in her seat. "I think that's got it," she said. "Whoever caught my transmission passed it on by helmet radio. Curse this planet!"

She lifted her visor and rubbed her face with her hands.

"What do you want to do now?" Ned asked. He was half-inclined to suggest that they keep out of everybody's way until daybreak. There'd been a number of hideous mistakes already this night, but there was plenty of scope for another one.

Lissea nodded forward. "Head for the *Swift*," she said. "We've got to see how much damage has been done."

"Yes, ma'am," he said.

Ned lifted the Jeep and started south, keeping his speed down to twenty-five to thirty kilometers per hour. That was plenty fast enough for the fractured terrain. The dead weren't going anywhere, and the wounded would be getting what was available in terms of help already.

Curse this planet!

He heard something ahead of them. For a moment Ned thought of another tumbling watercourse; then he recognized the intake roar of big lift fans.

"Lissea?" he said. He grounded the Jeep. "I think we're about to run into the locals."

"Via!" she said as she reached over his right knee to turn on the headlight. "Let them know we're here, then!"

A huge truck grunted over an intervening ridge of hexagonal crystals. The Jeep's headlight caught it squarely. There were a dozen or so settlers in the box. As one, they ducked beneath their concrete armor. The survivors were utterly cowed by the mauling they'd taken from the *Swift*'s professionals.

"We're surrounded!" cried the man at the cab-roof tribarrel. He'd been staring back toward the cinder cone until the light fell across him. His radio collar was compatible with the mercenaries' commo helmets.

The truck slewed to a halt as the driver threw himself on the cab floor.

"Jon, it's me, Lissea!" Lissea cried. She stood up in her seat.

"Fight, you cowards, or we've had it!" Jon Watford screamed as he swung his tribarrel toward the Jeep.

"Jon!"

Ned's burst hit the settler's leader four times in the upper chest and throat. Ned's visor blanked the core of the flashes, leaving only shimmering cyan haloes.

Watford recoiled against the back of the hatch ring. He still held the tribarrel's grips. Ned raised his point of aim. This time only two of the bolts hit, but even the pistol-caliber rounds were enough to rupture Watford's cranial vault.

"*Cease fire!*" Lissea Doormann ordered. "*All units cease fire!*"

A safety device in the truck switched off the fans after ten seconds of unattended operation. Cooling metal clicked and pinged.

Ned leaned over the side of the Jeep. He managed to raise his faceshield before he vomited.

"We saw the ship land," the settler said. His eyes were closed, and he couldn't have been really conscious with the amount of pain-blockers in him as Tadziki worked on the stump of his right leg. "We thought, 'They took care of the Spiders but we'll show we can handle smugglers the same way ourselves.' We were—we wanted to show the women what *we* could do."

"There, that's as much as I can do," Tadziki said. He stood up. "Keep him warm, don't let him go into shock, that's as much as anybody can do now."

Two colonists edged past the adjutant and put the wounded man on a stretcher. They were careful but not very adept at their task.

The surviving 5-tonne—mortar shells had left the other a burned-out wreck—was full of corpses. The wounded were moved to smaller vehicles and taken back to Quantock. The settlement's doctor was one of the fatalities, but medical personnel were flying in from other colonies.

"You know whose fault it is?" Deke Warson shouted. He pointed to a colonist. "It's you people's fault! What did you expect when you started shooting at us?"

The colonist bunched his fists and started for Warson. Toll grabbed his brother. Ned caught the settler and twisted both wrists back behind the fellow's back.

"He doesn't know what he's saying," Ned said. "He's as spooked as you are."

"Buddy," Toll Warson said, "there's no such thing as friendly fire." The big merc spoke loudly, but he wasn't looking at anyone in particular. "I'm sorry as hell, but that's the way it is."

Mellie Watford stood beside the five-tonne's open tailgate. She wore a waterproof cape over a lacy nightdress, and she had house slippers on.

Lissea tried to put an arm around her. Mellie shook herself violently, as though she'd been drenched in ice water. She began to cry, for the first time since a courier had summoned ambulance vans from Quantock and the women came with them.

"They *shot* at us," Deke Warson said. His voice was almost a whimper. "What the hell did they expect?"

"Ah, Mistress Watford?" one of the colonists said. "We're ready to start back now."

"Tadziki," Lissea Doormann said crisply. "I want the desalinization gear set up tonight. We'll lift for Mirandola as soon as we've filled our fresh-water tank."

"What the hell did they expect . . ."

Mirandola

THE FOLIAGE RANGED from azure to maroon, spreading broadly from squat tree-trunks. Ned had been raised on a planet where vegetation was sparse and thin-stemmed, so Mirandola's forests struck him as strange; but the landscape was very beautiful in its own way.

"I don't see why the settlers are so shirty about us keeping our distance," Herne Lordling grumbled. "If we were pirates, it wouldn't help them a bit to tell us to stay away, would it? Anyway, most little colonies, they're glad of some company."

"Go around the left side of this tree," Tadziki said. "It's only another fifty meters."

The adjutant was directing the five personnel who hauled a 10-cm hosepipe to a spring-fed stream to replenish the water tank. Four more men paralleled the fatigue party at some distance in the woods: pickets, in case Mirandola turned out to have dangers the pilotry data had ignored.

The hose was flexible, but it had to be stiff-walled so as not to collapse under the suction of the *Swift*'s pump. Even though the direction was basically downhill and the hose didn't bind on the surface of fallen leaves, the team doing the work mostly staggered forward with their heads down.

"I didn't even know there was a permanent settlement on Mirandola," said Louis Boxall. "It was just a stopover point from anything I'd heard, though . . ."

He looked around.

". . . it seems a pleasant enough place."

"There's nothing on file about them," Tadziki said. "Judging from orbital imaging, there's only forty-odd houses and some fields that don't look very extensive."

"Maybe they got spooked when they heard about Ajax Four," Deke Warson said.

"That's enough of that!" Lissea snapped. "Why they don't want company is their own business. We could go all the way to Pancahte on stored rations, and we can get our own water easily."

Carrying the hose required strength and weight. Lissea, though fit, couldn't compare to any of her subordinates in either aspect. She was present now because the morning the *Swift* lifted from Ajax Four the second time, she had insisted on being added to the duty roster.

She ignored Tadziki and Lordling when they told her—correctly—that her business should be with matters more important than guard-mount and fatigues. Military structures don't function as democracies, and pretending otherwise is counterproductive.

Lissea turned her head to the side and added sharply, "It's just as well that we don't have to waste time socializing, anyway."

If the captain chose to feel responsible for a tragedy that was none of her doing, Ned thought, then it was just as well that her self-punishment be limited to a few blisters. People had a right to manage their own souls, however foolish the means chosen might appear to other people.

"Here we go," said Tadziki. "Now, don't let's break our necks in the last three steps."

The loam gave way to rocks, polished and slick with moss.

Ned, at the end of the line, prepared to brace himself in case anyone ahead of him slipped.

"Captain," the commo helmets reported in Bonilla's voice, *"the colonists say they changed their mind. They want a meeting with you. The lady calling, she sounds scared to death. Just you come and one other, she says. Over."*

"Well, they can curst well wait till we get this intake set!" Lissea snarled. Her boot-heels were bedded firmly in the wet ground. *"Out!"*

Tadziki scrambled down the bank and checked the position of the filter head. He glanced back up the pipe. His expression might have been innocent, but Lissea took it as a smirk.

"Don't you patronize me, Tadziki!" she said. "I knew you were right to begin with. Okay?"

"Slade," the adjutant called. "Set a clamp to the tree beside you, will you? That ought to keep the line from lashing when we fire up the pump."

Ned flipped a coil of cargo tape around a tree bole fifty-centimeters thick. He wrapped the coil around the pipe and itself, then cut the section while Deke held the ends in place. Ned touched the piece with the electrodes in back of the tape dispenser. The calibrated current induced changes in the tape's polymer chains, bonding them to one another at the molecular level. Overall length shrank by ten percent, snugging the line firmly to the tree. Waste products driven off in the process had a faint fruity odor.

Warson stepped away, brushing together his hands in satisfaction. "Let's go home, right?" he said.

Lordling tried to help Lissea up the slope. She was closer to the top than he was. She allowed the contact, but her expression made the pointlessness of it clear.

"Tadziki," she said in a clear voice, "take me off the rota from here on out."

"Yes, sir," the adjutant said.

Lissea looked around at the men with her. "Boys," she said, "you're going to have to do the heavy stuff without me. I've got to handle deeply important discussions. With dickheads who can't make up their minds whether they want to see us or not!''

"There may be some risk involved in meeting these people, Lissea," said Herne Lordling. "I think I'd better handle it."

"I'll handle it, Herne," Lissea said in a tired voice. "I trust my diplomacy farther than I do yours."

Creatures flew and jumped about the high tree-limbs, rattling the foliage. One of them, hidden but apparently able to see, chittered down at Ned like a high-speed relay. It sounded quizzical and not unfriendly.

"They may figure to take you hostage, Lissea," Lordling said.

"Deke," Lissea said, "if I'm taken hostage by these people, I want you to get me out dead or alive. If I'm dead, I want you to kill every one of them. Think you can handle that?"

"Yes, ma'am."

Lissea looked at Lordling. Ned, watching out of the corners of his eyes, was glad the expression wasn't directed at him. "I guess that problem's taken care of, Herne," she said. "I trust you'll be able to carry out the duties that Deke assigns you."

"Lissea . . ." Lordling said. He sounded as if he were being strangled.

The *Swift* had crushed the clearing in which it landed to double the original size. The boarding ramp was clear, and off-duty crewmen were stringing hammocks from trees. If the weather held, they'd be able to sleep outside the vessel's metal walls tonight.

"Do you want a driver, Lissea?" Ned said with his eyes straight ahead of him. They hadn't spoken, she and he, since the last night on Ajax Four.

"Yes, I want you to drive me, Slade," Lissea said coolly. "I need a driver I can trust."

"I'll put on clean utilities, then," Ned said, in a similarly neutral voice. "We'll want to impress the locals."

Also, he'd clip a third magazine pouch onto his equipment belt. Just in case.

* * *

Ned's first impression of the community was its neatness. The houses arranged along the central street were built of native products, generally wood. Most had porches and many had floral plantings, sometimes within little fenced enclosures. The street had a surface of crushed stone stabilized with yellowish gum that Ned assumed was of vegetable rather than of mineral origin.

Not a soul was visible. A caged bird sang within a house whose windows were open. There were slatted blinds but no screens, though Ned had already killed a biting gnat. Mirandola had been a stopover point for starships for so long that it was inevitable some human parasites would have found a home.

"That must be the community building," Lissea said, pointing to the single-story structure forming the bar across the far end of the street. Artificial light gleamed through the open windows.

"Let's hope they all walked," Ned said as he pulled up in front of the building. He'd seen only a few parked vehicles, although there was a charging post beside every house. He didn't know where the community's generator was; the distribution lines were underground. A single fusion bottle the size of a tank's power supply would be ample for the residents' probable needs.

The wooden double doors opened as Ned shut down the Jeep. A middle-aged woman called, "Please come in, gentlemen. We're waiting for you."

"I've been called worse," Lissea muttered. She sounded detached, a sign Ned knew by now to read as nervousness. She carried her usual 2-cm weapon. She'd slung it muzzle-down, perhaps to appear less threatening.

The disquieting thing about the town was that it would have been normal on a civilized planet—and this was a frontier.

"My goodness," said the woman as Lissea walked into the building a step ahead of her escort. "You're a woman!"

"Do you have a problem with that?" Lissea snapped. "You wanted the commander and I'm the commander, Captain Lissea Doormann."

She stared around the gathering. "You're all women!"

Fluorescents in wall sconces added to the daylight in the big single room. The fixtures had paper shades which gave the effect of cressets. There were about a hundred people present, sitting on wooden benches. The furniture could be folded and added to the pile of similar benches against the back wall. The ages present ranged from early teens to quite old, but there were no young children.

And no men, as Lissea said.

"Yes," said the woman who'd greeted them at the door. "Ah, I'm Arlette Wiklander, and we've agreed that I'll conduct this meeting. That's what we'd like to discuss with you. Ah, will you come sit down?"

Arlette gestured the outsiders toward a pair of chairs set to face the benches. She touched Lissea's sleeve. Lissea twitched the cloth away.

"Let me understand this," Lissea said. There was no sign of an amplifier in the room, so she spoke in a deliberately loud, cold voice. "You're telling me that your community has no males in it?"

"No, no!" said a younger, hard-looking woman in the front row. "We just didn't think they ought to be around for this. *They* didn't think they ought to be around."

"Talia, let *me* handle the discussion," Arlette said. To Lissea she added, "Please won't you sit down. This is extremely difficult for us. Please, Captain, ah, Doormann."

Lissea sat down carefully. The iridium muzzle of her weapon clunked against the chairseat. Ned took the other chair, his face as blank as he could make it. Arlette returned to an empty space on the front bench, between Talia and a younger blonde woman.

"You see, the case is," Arlette said, "that Liberty has a problem."

"We named the colony Liberty," Talia added.

"We've been here five standard years almost," said a girl in the second row, probably the youngest person present.

"*Please!*" Wiklander said. The room hushed.

"We came here from Stadtler's Reach," Arlette continued.

"There had been political difficulties—"

"It was a coup, pure and simple!" Talia said. Her left hand gripped Arlette's right as she spoke. "The legal government was forced out by thugs on the basis of a referendum they trumped up!"

"Be that as it may," Arlette said firmly. "A number of us believed it would be better to leave Stadtler's Reach and found a new colony on Mirandola. The new government—"

"Thugs!"

"—was willing to support us in the endeavor, for their own reasons and in exchange for clear title to the property we left behind."

Ned looked slowly around the room. Some of the women refused to meet his eyes, angry or embarrassed depending on their temperament. Others were speculative or more actively interested than even that.

The latter expressions were of the sort he'd noted often enough on the faces of soldiers on leave as they prepared to hit the Strip. He'd rarely seen a woman's eyes with that particular blend of lust and intention, though.

The blonde in the front row looked anxious but determined.

"We knew we couldn't go back to the government later," Arlette said, "so we made sure we got everything we thought we might possibly need from the initial bargaining sessions. We have medical facilities every bit as advanced as those we were leaving behind. We were people of, well, influence. Power."

"Where are your men?" Lissea demanded.

"I'm getting to that!"

Arlette cleared her throat. "Please," she muttered softly, then raised her eyes to Lissea's again. "We were inoculated against diseases which might transfer to humans from the Mirandolan biosphere. That's quite possible, especially at the viral level."

"They did it deliberately," Talia snarled. "They were afraid we'd reproduce."

"No!" Arlette said. "I believe—Sean believes, and he's the medical researcher, Talia—that it was an accident. If it had been a deliberate plot, they would have attacked female fertility."

She looked from Lissea to Ned. "Instead," she continued in a voice combed to the bone by control, "the inoculations appear to have rendered every male in the community sterile. The situation might be reversible with the resources of Stadtler's Reach tackling the problem, but the government has ignored our pleas."

"Oh," Lissea said. "Oh."

Ned glanced at her. Lissea couldn't have been more stonily embarrassed if all her clothing had vanished.

"Therefore . . ." Arlette said. She faced Lissea, but her eyes weren't focused. The expressions of the two women were mirror images of one another. ". . . we were hoping that your crew might be able to help our colony. The male members of your crew."

"We're equipped to set up a sperm bank," called an older woman in the back. "There needn't be any . . . any contact."

Lissea rose to her feet. "No," she said.

Other women got up, scuffling the benches, but Arlette Wiklander remained seated. Her extended arms gestured down Talia and the softly attractive blonde on her other side. Ned didn't move either.

"Wait!" Lissea continued. She held her arm out, palm foremost. "You'll get your genes. But you'll have to pay for them."

She surveyed the room again. "I can't demand that my crew masturbate in bags for you. I wouldn't if I could. If you want sperm, you'll have to collect them in the old-fashioned way. Whatever sort of medical procedures you indulge in then is your own affair."

The blonde beside Arlette gave a smile, half real and half sad. "Live cover or nothing," she said. "Well, we expected that."

"Yes," said Arlette to her hands as she folded them again in her lap. "Well, Captain Doormann, I've drawn up a series of—guidelines. Which I hope will be acceptable."

She removed her hologram projector from its belt sheath

and switched it on. Some of the women who'd risen were seating themselves again, trying to be unobtrusive about it.

"Wait," said Ned. He hadn't spoken since he entered the building, and his voice was much louder than he'd intended. Everyone stared at him, Lissea included. "Where *are* your men?"

Arlette nodded heavily three times. "We had a town meeting last night, as soon as we knew a ship had landed. We—all of us—decided it would be best if the men camped ten kilometers outside Liberty for as long as you stay. When your ship leaves, it'll be—as if it never was. We're a small community. We can't afford to have . . ."

"Memories," said the blonde beside her.

Arlette cleared her throat. "Now, about the guidelines . . ." she said.

"They're coming!" Westerbeke called from a navigation chair. Liberty was three klicks away, but the *Swift*'s sensor suite registered the vehicles as soon as they switched on. Half the men rushed toward the boarding ramp.

"Wait!" said Lissea Doormann. "Everybody back inside. I have things to say to you."

She pushed through her crew and turned, facing them from the bottom of the ramp. Ned was at the back of the crowd. He put his boot on a bunk's footboard and raised himself so that he could see as well as hear Lissea.

"You may have heard," she said, "that the citizens have agreed among themselves that everyone is available to any crew member who wants to date her."

"You bet your ass!" somebody said.

"Hey, that's a thought!" another replied.

"Shut up, curse you!" Lissea's face had gone from white to flushed. Men's heads jerked back.

"What I'm telling you is this," Lissea resumed in mechanically calm tones. " 'No means no.' Maybe she thinks you're ugly, maybe she thinks you've got the brains of a sea urchin—maybe she's really got a headache. No means no!"

She glared across the men generally, then focused for a moment on Ned. He met her eyes, but he swallowed as soon as she'd looked away.

"There's plenty of pussy out there for every one of you," Lissea continued coldly. "Nobody's going to have to date the five-fingered widow tonight. But if anybody pushes in where he isn't wanted—*for any curst reason!*—I'll leave him behind to explain himself to the colony's menfolk when they return. Is that clearly understood?"

"I'm bloody well a believer!" Deke Warson said, and he sounded as if he meant it.

It was dusk. The lights of wheeled vehicles from the community glittered among the trees.

Lissea shuddered. She suddenly looked very small. "All right, boys," she said, "have a good time. If anything breaks, Raff or me'll give a buzz through the external speakers of your commo helmets, but you can pretty well expect to be clear till ten hundred hours tomorrow."

"Bless them all," Harlow sang. *"Bless the fat and the short and the tall . . ."*

The first vehicle pulled up at the base of the ramp. It was a tractor pulling a twin-axle flatbed trailer. A cab-over pickup truck followed, and there were two or three similarly utilitarian vehicles behind those.

Men piled onto the trailer. Toll Warson got up on the tow bar and began chatting with the driver.

Dewey and Bonilla headed for the pickup. "Hey, Dewey!" Westerbeke called. "Why're *you* going along?"

"Hey, I've got nothing against women!" Dewey replied.

"I haven't had anything against a woman in seventeen years," Bonilla said. "But that doesn't mean I'm going to turn down a chance at booze and a cooked dinner."

The tractor pulled around to circle back. The motor had a heavy flywheel/armature to prevent it from stalling in a muddy field. It thrummed with a deep bass note.

"Lissea," said Herne Lordling. "I want you to understand that I'm doing this only—"

"Get aboard, Herne," Lissea said tiredly. She turned her back on the scene.

The pickup drove away with a full load. A Jeep and another pickup took its place. Herne got into the Jeep beside the driver. The Boxall brothers took the back pair of seats.

Arlette Wiklander drove the second pickup. She looked at Ned and said, "Are you the last, then?"

He nodded. "I guess," he said. "I wasn't sure, but I guess I am."

He put a boot on the side-step and lifted himself into the back instead of riding in the cab with the driver. "Ready when you are," he said.

Arlette turned sharply. The headlights flashed and flickered from the tree-trunks. Ned looked over his shoulder. Lissea was watching him. Her face was without expression.

The clear sky above Liberty was bright in comparison to the forest canopy, but at ground level the truck's headlights slashed visible objects from a mass of blurred shadow.

Many of the houses had their porch lights on. In a few cases, mostly at the end of the street near the community building where the tractor-trailer was parked, the exterior bulbs were switched off but light glowed through heavy curtains.

Several houses were dark and shuttered; but as Lissea had said, there were still plenty of willing takers for the *Swift*'s small crew.

Toll Warson stood on the porch of a house with blue trim. He was turning to leave. When he saw Ned in the back of the pickup, he called, "Hey Slade! This one says she's waiting for you. Shag her twice for me, okay, handsome?"

Warson waved cheerfully as he walked toward the house next door. The brothers had bragged that they were going to fuck their way up one side of the street and down the other, but that was just the friendly exaggeration of men old enough to wonder secretly about their performance.

Arlette slowed the truck to a crawl. "Ah—sir?" she called

out the side window. "Shall I stop?"

"Yes ma'am," Ned said. *May as well.* "Please."

He hopped down from the bed and dusted his palms against his utility trousers. There was a pistol in the right cargo pocket, not obvious to an outsider but a massive iridium pendulum every time his thigh swung.

He didn't imagine the weapon would serve any practical purpose. It was a security blanket in a situation that confused Ned more than it seemed to affect the other mercs.

"Her name's Sarah," Arlette said quietly. "She sat beside me when we met with you and Captain Doormann."

The blonde, then.

"I'm the community's doctor," Arlette said. "Well, Sean and I, though the hands-on side never appealed to him." She looked down the street. Most of the mercenaries had disappeared within houses by now. "I'm going to be busy tonight."

Ned walked up the three steps to the porch. The door was already open halfway. Behind him, Arlette drove off in the truck. As Ned raised his hand to knock on the jamb, Sarah appeared in the opening and swung the door wide.

"Will you come in please, Master Slade?" she offered. "I was hoping you might . . ."

Sarah's dress was a lustrous beige synthetic, probably one of the cellulose-based polyesters. The cutwork collar was handmade but not particularly expert. She moved with a doe-like grace and beauty.

How did she learn my name? Maybe from Toll Warson?

He stepped into a parlor furnished with a sofa and three chairs, all very solidly made from wood with stuffed cushions. Though they were all of similar design, the sofa's cabinetry was of a much higher order than that of the smaller pieces. The differences probably indicated the learning curve of a white-collar professional finding a new niche in the colony.

The shaft of the floor lamp was a column of three coaxial helices. It was an amazing piece of lathework which would have commanded a high price on any planet with a leisure class.

Sarah closed and barred the door; there was no key lock. The windows were already curtained.

"I'm Ned," he said. "And Dr. Wiklander said that your name is Sarah?"

Sarah looked up in startlement. "She told you that? Ah—but yes, I'm Sarah. I, ah . . ."

She looked away. The parlor filled the front of the house. Behind it was a kitchen/dining room with separate doorways from the parlor into either half, and a staircase to the second floor.

"I've made supper, it's a game stew and vegetables or there's cold ham if you'd like it," she said in a quick voice like a typist keying. "And I have drinks, it's all local but I've bought some whiskey from Juergen that's supposed to be very—"

"Sarah."

"—good!"

Ned put his hands on the woman's biceps, just touching her, until she raised her eyes to meet his. She giggled.

"Look," he said, "dinner later would be very nice. But you're nervous and I'm nervous. Either I ought to leave, which wouldn't be my first choice. Or we ought to make love."

"You're direct," she said. "That makes it easier."

She stepped away from Ned and turned off the lamp. The kitchen was still lighted. When Sarah came back, she pressed her body close and kissed him. He turned slightly to prevent her from noticing the pistol. He undid one of the front buttons of the dress. She wore no undergarments above the waist.

Sarah's breasts were fuller than he'd expected beneath the slick, stiff fabric. Ned took off his commo helmet with his free hand and tossed it onto the shadowed sofa.

"Upstairs," she said. She giggled again. "Maybe on the sofa later, if you like."

She drew him after her up the narrow staircase. The open jalousies let in moonlight, though the sun was fully down. The upper story was a single room, narrowed by the roof's pitch.

The bed stood in the center, with storage chests lining the long sides.

Sarah turned at the head of the stairs. She kissed Ned again as he stood on the step below her. He slipped her puffed sleeves further down her arms to bare her breasts, then kissed them.

"Most of the colony came as couples," she said, playing with his hair. "I was . . . Sean and Arlette are my parents. I married Charles here in Liberty."

She twisted back into the room proper and began undoing the rest of her buttons. Ned took off his tunic. He slit open the pressure seal of his utility trousers with an index finger, then realized that he needed to take off his boots first. He undid them, glad of the semidarkness because he felt as clumsy as a mule in ballet class. After you knew somebody a while, you didn't think about that sort of thing anymore; but he never would know Sarah better than he would this night.

He lowered the trousers carefully to keep the pistol from banging against the wooden floor.

"Come," Sarah said, sitting on the edge of the bed and drawing him over on her as he knelt to kiss her, "later we can . . ."

Somebody began hammering on the front door.

"What?" said Sarah as she sat bolt upright.

"It's one of the guys who forgot the ground rules," Ned said grimly, feeling for his trousers. He took the pistol from the cargo pocket and held the garment as a shield in front of him and the weapon. "I'll go talk to him."

His penis had shrunk to the size of his thumb. He wished he had time to put the trousers on. They wouldn't stop a determined mosquito, much less a powergun bolt, but they'd make him *feel* less vulnerable.

He didn't recall ever having been this murderously angry before in his life.

"Sarah, you whore!" the man on the porch shouted. "Open the door! I know you're in there!"

"Good lord!" she said. "It's Charles. It's my husband."
Oh boy.

"Look, I've got to go down to him," Sarah said pleadingly.

"Lord, yes!" he agreed as he stuffed the pistol back in his pocket. He began pulling the trousers on. He'd stopped using underpants when he noticed that none of the *Swift*'s veterans wore them.

Sarah took a robe from the rack beside the mirror-topped dresser and wrapped it around her. She padded quickly down the steps, still barefoot. "Charles!" she called. "I'm coming."

Ned grabbed his socks and boots. The tunic could wait, but he wanted his boots on no matter which way the next few moments went.

The door bar slid back on its staples. The man's voice boomed again, though it quickly sank to noise rather than words Ned could understand. Charles was either drunk or so angry that he slurred his syllables. Sarah's voice lilted like a descant above the deeper sound. The parlor light went on.

Ned donned his tunic, but he didn't bother to squeeze the seam shut. He stepped to the big window at the end of the room opposite the dresser. The glazed sashes were already latched open. The jalousies were mounted on dowels, not cords, but he could swing the whole set out of the way.

The stairs creaked behind him. He turned, stepped away from the window that would have backlit him, and reached into his pocket.

"Ned?" Sarah whispered from the doorway. She was tugging the robe close about her with both hands.

"Right," he said, also pitching his voice too low to be heard on the ground floor. "Look, I was just about to leave."

"Oh, Lord, I'm so sorry," she said. She stepped toward him, then stopped and convulsively smoothed the patterned bedspread where their bodies had disturbed it. "You can come down the stairs. Charles is in the kitchen. I'm so sorry, but I think you'd better leave."

"No problem," Ned said. He pulled the jalousies back from the window ledge and looked down. Less than three meters, and smooth sod to land on. He'd had to jump farther in training while wearing a full infantry kit.

"I hope it works out for you all," he said as he swung himself from the window. Sarah started toward him again, perhaps to kiss him good-bye, but he deliberately let himself drop before she reached him. The wooden slats clattered against the sash.

An easy fall. The physical one, at any rate.

Though the ground-floor windows were curtained, Ned ducked low as he rounded the house. A high-wheeled utility vehicle pulled into the yard, but Charles hadn't stopped to connect it to the charging post.

The parlor was dark again, perhaps to provide privacy for Ned leaving. It was a useful reminder that when reason fought with emotion, the smart money was on emotion to win.

A pickup accelerated down the street from the community building. Ned stepped off the pavement—the small community didn't have sidewalks—but the vehicle pulled up beside him.

"Is there a problem?" Arlette Wiklander asked. "I heard shouting."

Ned squatted to put his face on a level with hers, so that he didn't have to speak loudly. "No problem," he said. "Ah—the lady's husband seems to have had second thoughts, but it's no problem."

Arlette winced. "I see," she said. "Ah . . . There are other, ah, houses."

Ned looked down the street. Several mercenaries were walking from house to house already. Like the arsenal disgorged at the banquet on Telaria, it was a form of boasting; but the weapons the crew carried to the banquet had been real also.

"No, ma'am," Ned said. "That's all right. I'd appreciate it if you gave me a lift back to the ship, though. Or—"

"Master Slade, I'm very sorry," Arlette said. Her intonation was almost precisely that of her daughter. "Of course I'll take you back, if that's what you want."

"Bloody hell!" Ned said. "I've left my helmet in there, on the sofa!"

Arlette shut down the truck and got out. "I'll take care of it," she said.

Ned stayed by the vehicle. He didn't hide, but he was ten meters from the door and as much out of the way as he could be. Arlette marched up on the porch, knocked hard, and called, "Sarah, it's your mother. Would you come to the door, please?"

The panel jerked open. The man who stood in the doorway said, "Couldn't wait to come laugh, could you, bitch?"

"Charles, I need to talk to Sarah for a moment," Arlette said. "Then I'll get back to my other business."

"Sure you will, *Mother* dear," he snarled. "You didn't want her to marry me from the beginning, did you?"

Charles was tall but stooped. He looked down as he fumbled with his belt. His bald scalp gleamed in the light from the houses across the street.

"Charles, let me see what mother needs," Sarah said softly from within the parlor.

Charles turned his head. He hadn't hooked his belt properly. When he took his hands away, his trousers dropped around his ankles with a loud *thunk!* against the board flooring.

He bent down and came up, not with the garment but with a pistol.

"You think it's fucking hilarious that I'm not any kind of man, don't you, *Mother?*" he shouted.

Sarah grabbed her husband's arm from behind. He shrugged violently and threw her away from him. His right forearm was vertical. The gun muzzle pointed skyward.

"That has nothing to do with being a man, Charles," Arlette said in a calm voice. "And we've always wanted the best for you and Sarah."

Part of Ned's mind wondered at her control. He'd drawn his own powergun, but he kept it out of sight at his side. He wasn't a good snap-shot, not good enough to trust himself in this light and the two women in the line of fire. He didn't dare aim now, though, for fear of precipitating the violence.

"Charles . . ." from within the room.

"Sure you did," Charles sneered. "You and dear Sean, such *sensitive* people. I'm sure it really pains you that your son-in-law can't get it up!"

He put the muzzle of the gun against his temple. Arlette reached for him. He fired. The red flash ignited wisps of Charles' remaining hair as the bullet kicked his head sideways.

He fell onto the porch. Sarah screamed. Charles' heels drummed against the boards and his throat gurgled, "K-k-k . . ." The sounds weren't an attempt at words, just the result of chest convulsions forcing air through the dying man's windpipe.

Both women knelt over Charles. Mercenaries and some locals poked their heads out of windows, wondering whether they might have heard a door slam closed.

Ned thrust his pistol back into his pocket. He got into the truck and switched the motors on. "I'm going back to the ship," he called generally to the night. "The truck will be there."

He still didn't have his commo helmet. He wasn't about to go back for it now, though.

Lissea was sitting on the ramp when Ned parked the truck. She drank from a tumbler. Only the cockpit lights were on, so the illumination spilling from the broad hatch was soft and diffuse.

Ned got out of the vehicle. "There was a problem in town," he said carefully.

Lissea nodded. "All taken care of," she said. "Arlette Wiklander radioed us."

She tapped the ramp with her fingertips, indicating a place for Ned at arm's length from her. "Want something to drink?"

"I'm fine," he said. He sat down. He supposed he was fine. His blood and brains weren't sprayed across a doorjamb, at any rate.

Lissea drank from her tumbler, looking out into the night.

"Arlette says nobody blames you," she said.

Ned laughed. "I don't blame myself," he said. "I'll take responsibility for what I've done, but that whole business was somebody else's problem."

He stopped talking, because he could hear his voice start to rise.

"Arlette said the husband had had more than his share of problems in the past," Lissea said to the night. "He was a good deal older than the girl. The . . . It was the sort of thing Arlette had worried about happening years ago. The sort of thing."

The communications suite crackled. Lissea turned her head alertly, but Raff handled the query himself. Night creatures trilled.

"Do you ever think about what makes somebody a man, Lissea?" Ned said.

She frowned. "As in 'human being,' " she said, "or as in 'male human being'?"

"Not exactly." Lissea's tumbler was three-quarters full. "Can I have a sip of that?"

She handed it over. She was drinking water laced with something tart.

"You know," Ned said, "man—as opposed to wimp or pussy or whathaveyou."

Lissea laughed harshly. "Having doubts, Slade?" she asked.

"Not really."

"Well, don't," she said. "You became a fully certificated Man the moment I signed you on for this expedition. Is that why you volunteered?"

He shrugged. "I don't know," he said honestly. "I'd like to think there was more to being a man than that. I'd like to think there was more to it than being able to get my dick hard, too, though that isn't something I worry about either."

Lissea held a mouthful of water for a moment, then swallowed it. "My parents think I want to be a man myself," she said. Neither of them looked at the other. "My mother, especially. She's wrong."

She turned fiercely toward Ned. "I only want what's mine!" she said. "Do you have to be a man to get what's due you?"

"You shouldn't have to be," he said. He sniffed or laughed. "A lot of things shouldn't be the way they are, though."

"Don't I know it," Lissea muttered. She drank the tumbler down to the last two fingers of its contents, then offered it again to Ned. He finished it.

"Arlette says," Lissea said in the direction of the trees, "that her daughter Sarah is in a pretty bad way. She could use some company just now. I said I'd see what I could do when you got back to the ship."

Ned looked at her. "I . . ." he said. "I didn't want to make a bad situation worse."

"That's always a possibility," Lissea said. She stood up. "You're the man on the ground. I won't second-guess your decision."

Ned stood up also. He felt colder than the night. The radio inside the *Swift* was live again.

"Captain?" Raff called.

"In a moment, Raff," Lissea said. She looked at Ned. He stood below her on the ramp, so their faces were level. Very much as . . .

"Well?" she demanded.

"I left my commo helmet back in Liberty," he said. "I'll go get it now. I'll probably return with the other personnel in the morning."

Lissea nodded crisply. "As you wish," she said.

He looked away but didn't move. "It's Paixhans' Node for our next landfall, Tadziki was saying?"

"That's right. It's a long run, but nothing that should present real problems. We should be able to update our data on the Sole Solution there."

"Right," Ned said. He reached into his pocket and brought out the pistol. "Will you stick this back in the arms locker for me?" he said. "I don't know why I brought it in the first place."

Lissea took the weapon and nodded again.

Ned glanced in the rearview mirror as he drove away. Lissea still stood in the middle of the hatchway, silhouetted stiffly against the soft light.

Paixhans' Node

—◆—

PILOTRY DATA INDICATED the airlock/decontamination chamber of the Paixhans' Node Station could accommodate two suited humans at a time. There was nothing about the landscape to attract strollers, so the *Swift*'s complement left the vessel in pairs at the three-minute intervals the entry process required. Ned accompanied Louis Boxall near the end of the slow parade.

"I think," Boxall said, "that my ancestors must have had Paixhans' Node in mind when they wrote about Hell. Sang about Hell."

Ned looked around him. The atmosphere was breathable, as close to Earth Normal as, for example, that of Tethys. The communications station which the Bonding Authority maintained here filtered and heated the air to one hundred fifty degrees Celsius to kill possible spores, but there was no need to supplement the atmosphere to keep the station personnel alive.

The station person, actually.

Apart from that, however, Paixhans' Node was dank,

wretched, and purulent with life—all of which was fungoid. Water condensed from the air, dripping over every surface. Sheets and shelves and hummocks of fungus grew, rotted to slime, and were then devoured by their kin.

The highest life-forms, the Nodals, were human-sized and ambulatory. They had a certain curving grace, like that of a fuselage area-ruled for supersonic operation. The Nodals crawled a millimeter at a time as though they were osmosing across the surface of the rocks. The contact patch served also for ingestion, absorbing all the stationary fungus in the Nodals' path.

The Nodals were the closest thing to beauty on a world with a saturated atmosphere and a sky that glowed white at all times from the light of billions of stars. They were also the only real danger here, not for themselves but because of the spores which ejected from the core of a ripe Nodal.

"Hell's supposed to be hot and fiery," Ned said. He picked his way carefully across the slippery rocks. The *Swift* had put down half a klick from the station because the ground closer to it was too broken to be a safe landing site. It didn't make a great footpath, either.

"Not on the Karelian Peninsula," Louis said. He gestured. "This would do fine."

They used their external helmet speakers to talk. Normally when personnel wore protective suits, they spoke through radio intercoms. On Paixhans' Node, electro-optical radiation from everywhere in the Milky Way galaxy converged at the apparent distance of forty-one light-minutes. Ordinary communications gear was swamped to uselessness; though for properly filtered apparatus, the unique conditions were of enormous value.

The Bonding Authority was the lubricant that made the interstellar trade in mercenary companies work. The Authority guaranteed the table of organization and equipment of mercenary units to the parties who wished to hire them, and guaranteed to the mercenaries that they would be paid per contract.

For the Bonding Authority to function efficiently, it needed something as close as possible to real-time communications across the galaxy. The communications station on Paixhans' Node acted as a transceiver serving the Authority and, at considerable fees, the needs of other users.

"Well," said Ned, "I won't tell you your ancestors were wrong."

Their path would take them within arm's length of a Nodal. It swayed gently to a rhythm beyond human comprehension. The creature's upper portions swelled slightly from a pinched waist. Bubble-like vacuoles as well as chips of solid color were visible beneath the translucent skin. The axial core had a pale yellow tinge.

"Via!" Boxall swore. "Don't touch it or you might set it off."

"They've got to be as bright as tractor enamel before they're really ready to burst," Ned said. He angled well away from the Nodal nonetheless. "That's what the pilotry data says."

"The pilotry data isn't going to be dissolved from inside if a spore lands on it," Boxall said. He laughed sharply. "Come to think, I guess it might. But it wouldn't care the way I do."

They were nearing the station. It was a hemisphere over a hundred meters in diameter. Antennas of complex shape festooned the dome and were planted in farms some distance away.

"I hear," Boxall said after a moment, "that you might know something about the guy who mans the station. Gresham?"

Ned nodded, though he wasn't sure how visible the action was beneath his suit. "I made something of a study of it," he said. "Of him."

There was a lot of information on Friesland, in the Slammers' archives. Uncle Don had never said anything about it, except that he'd seen the prettiest sunset of his life once on Taprobane.

"Gresham worked for the Bonding Authority," Ned said. "He was a field agent, new to the job. He talked too much. At least that was what prisoners said later."

"He was bribed?" Boxall asked.

"No, he just talked. While he was inventorying mercs hired by the Congressional side on Taprobane, he let out that while there was supposed to have been a battalion of Slammers' tanks landed in the capital to support the Presidential party and secure the spaceport, it was really only two infantry companies."

The external speaker distorted Boxall's whistle. "So the Congressional party took the spaceport," he said.

"Nope," Ned Slade said coldly. He'd watched images of the battle, mostly recovered from the helmet recorders of dead troopers. "But they sure-hell tried. And it wasn't cheap to stop them, even for the survivors."

They'd reached the dome. Close up, the structure loomed over them. Water condensing on the curved sides dripped down in sheets of gelatinous fungus—orange and saffron and a hundred shades of brown.

The light above the airlock blinked from red to green. Boxall pressed the latch button.

"Afterwards," Ned said, "there were discussions between the regiment—"

"Colonel Hammer?"

Ned nodded. "Colonel Hammer. And the Bonding Authority. Everybody knew what Gresham had done, but all the evidence was secondhand. Handing Gresham over to the Slammers for execution would compromise the Authority's prestige and neutrality. That was what the higher echelons felt, at any rate."

The airlock door slid abruptly into the side of the dome. The chamber within was a meter square. The walls were glassy and faceted internally.

"What they did," Ned said, "the Authority did, was to offer Gresham a contract. So long as he worked for the Authority, his life was safe. Not even Hammer's Slammers were willing to murder an Authority employee."

The door slammed home with the enthusiasm of a guillotine's blade. Ned's visor went opaque for protection. Infrared light bathed the men from all six surfaces of the chamber. Ned bumped his companion as they both turned slowly, making sure that the light cleansed every crevice of their suits.

"And then they transferred Gresham here, to Paixhans' Node," Ned said. "For as long as he lived. Seventeen years so far."

His visor cleared. An instant later, the lock's inner door shot open. Ned and his companion stepped into the foyer where empty suits stood or lay on the concrete floor. The air was muggy.

They stripped off their own suits and followed the sound of voices down a hall to a large room with equipment built to waist level around all the walls. Surfaces above the electronic consoles were of a gleaming white material that cleaned itself.

Most of the *Swift*'s complement stood and looked with neither comprehension nor particular interest at the equipment surrounding them. The Warson brothers squatted before a console. They weren't touching the access plate in the front, but they were *pointedly* not touching the access plate. The fragments Ned heard of their low-voiced discussion were surprisingly technical.

"Look, Master Gresham," Lissea said in the tone of someone forced to argue with a senile relative, "that's between you and your employers. We're perfectly willing to pay you— we'll pay you in rations, if that's what you'd like. But—"

"It wouldn't do any good," said the man to whom she spoke. He hunched in the room's sole chair, a black structure which appeared to have been scooped from an egg. Its flat base quivered nervously at the floor, like a drop of water on a sea of mercury.

Gresham was sallow. His bones stuck out, and there were sores on his elbows and wrists.

"Master Gresham," Tadziki said calmly. "We can't afford to offend the Bonding Authority. All we're asking from you is information on the Sole Solution."

"On Alliance and Affray, you mean," Gresham said. As he spoke, Ned noticed that the man's teeth were black stumps. "On the Twin Planets."

Gresham grinned with something approaching animation. "But you don't know that. Yet. I'll tell you everything you want to know. But you have to stop whoever's stealing my food."

"We'll give you food!" Lissea repeated.

"It won't help!" Gresham cried. He tried to get up from the chair, but he couldn't summon the strength. He began to cry. Through the blubbering, he mumbled, "I have to eat the fungus. The rations dispenser drops a meal for me. And they steal it! They steal it! I have to eat what I gather outside or I'd die."

In a tiny voice he added, "I want to die. I can tell you anything about anything in the galaxy. But I want to die."

"Well, that could be arranged," said Josie Paetz.

Yazov gripped his nephew's jaw between his thumb and forefinger. "Don't speak like that!" he said. "He's a Bonding Authority employee. If he wants to die, then he can kill himself!"

Yazov released Paetz as though he was flinging away a bloody bandage. The younger man was white-faced. He swallowed before he holstered the pistol which he'd thrust into his uncle's belly.

"Who steals the food?" Lissea asked. She seemed to have swept frustration out of her mind. "Not the Nodals, surely."

"Who else is there?" Herne Lordling asked.

"I don't know," Gresham said. "I'll show you, though. It's almost time."

Gresham snuffled loudly to clear his nose. He seemed almost oblivious of the presence of other human beings. Resupply ships would arrive on an annual, or at most, a semiannual schedule. The number of other vessels which touched down on Paixhans' Node must be very small.

"Time for what?" Coyne asked. Everybody ignored him.

Gresham got up from his chair and stepped to the hallway door. He walked like an old man, his head down and his legs shuffling forward mechanically. Though he couldn't have been much over fifty years old, deficiencies caused by a diet of local produce had aged and weakened him. He was lucky to be alive.

Or perhaps not.

Across the foyer from the control room was a chamber one

meter by ten, with a high ceiling. The long wall facing the foyer was of a gleaming, glassy material like that which lined the airlock. There was a niche at waist height in the center of it.

"A Type Seven-Six Hundred Rations Dispenser," Tadziki said approvingly. "Or maybe a Seven-Eight Hundred—it's a matter of storage capacity, and I can't be sure how deep the room is. It's a bulletproof design. Trust the Authority to buy the best."

"What *is* it?" Ingried said peevishly.

"When somebody's alone in a station like this," the adjutant explained, "you don't want to leave all the rations under his control. People get funny. A dispenser like this provides his meals one at a time, so that he doesn't decide to make a bonfire of a six-months' supply when he's having a bad time one night."

"This poor bastard's had a bad time longer 'n that," somebody muttered.

A chime sounded softly in the bowels of the mechanism. A sealed carton about thirty by thirty by ten centimeters in size dropped into the niche. Gresham reached out as if to take it.

"As if," because after seventeen years he certainly knew it was going to vanish again, as it did.

"Via! Bloody hell! Blood and martyrs!" across the semicircle of mercenaries standing behind Gresham. He turned, looking almost pleased.

"Stop that happening," he said, "and I'll help you. I'll *save* you; I know how. You can't give me my freedom, but let me eat food again."

Lissea looked at Tadziki. He pursed his lips and said, "There's the question of your employer's intention in this matter—"

"No," Gresham said. He fumbled carefully in a breast pocket of his coveralls and brought out a folded sheet of hard copy between two fingers. He handed it to Tadziki.

Tadziki opened the document. " 'Inspection of the Type Seven-Six Hundred dispenser by manufacturer's representatives indicates the unit is in proper working order,' " he said/

read aloud. " 'This office will not authorize further off-site repair expenditures. If station personnel desire, they may procure local support and charge back costs within Guidelines Bee Three three-nine-four to Bee Four ought-ought-seven inclusive.' "

Gresham began to cry again. "Sixteen years ago they sent that," he said. "They don't care if I starve so long as they can *say* they stood up to Colonel Hammer!"

"Seventeen years seems a pretty long time," Lissea said doubtfully.

"It's that much longer than some eighty poor bastards got on Taprobane," Deke Warson said in a voice that could mill corn. Ned wasn't the only member of the company who knew why Gresham had been exiled to this planet-sized dungeon.

"Which brings up the other question," the adjutant went on. "I think we can presume the problem with the food— whatever—isn't the Authority's doing, though it doesn't appear to bother them a great deal. I suspect that—President now, isn't it?—Hammer might still be displeased by meddling with what he considers his business."

Lissea looked puzzled. "Surely that's no concern of ours, is it?" she asked.

The Boxall brothers had been talking in low tones ever since the meal container vanished. Now Louis looked up and said, "If it's a choice of the Bonding Authority or Colonel Hammer wanting my hide, I guess I'd choose Hammer. But believe me, Gene and me aren't going to fix this if Hammer *is* involved."

"You can fix it?" Tadziki said sharply.

"We might be able to do some good," Eugene said in the tone of someone making a promise with everything but the form of the words.

"But not if it pisses off Hammer," Louis repeated. "Sure, it's a big universe, but I don't want to spend the rest of my life looking over my shoulder."

"I think I can clear things," Ned said. His hands were trembling, but he kept his voice steady.

"You, Slade?" Herne Lordling sneered. "You're going to

use your vast influence as a reserve ensign to bring President Hammer around?''

"Herne!" Lissea said.

"Slade?" said Gresham. "You're *Slade?*"

"You're thinking of Uncle Don," Ned said to Gresham. He looked at Lordling. "I don't have any influence with President Hammer," he said. "I saw him once on a reviewing stand, that's all. But my uncle commanded the regiment's initial force on Taprobane."

"You're Slade," Gresham whispered. He reached toward Ned but his hand paused a centimeter away, shaking violently.

Ned gripped Gresham's hand. "I'll need to send a real-time message to Nieuw Friesland."

His eyes focused on Lissea. "I'll pay for it personally," he added.

She shook her head. "It's an expedition expense," she said.

Gresham began to giggle hysterically. Ned had to hold the older man to keep him from falling.

At last Gresham got control of himself again. "I've been here for seventeen years," he said. "They pay me well—there's a hardship allowance. And there's nothing for me to buy. *I'll* pay for the cursed message!"

They walked back into the control room. Ned and Tadziki supported Gresham; Ned thought of offering to carry the man but decided it might be an insult.

Gresham unlocked a keyboard. A holographic screen sprang to life above the console. He typed in his access code, summoned a directory for Nieuw Friesland, and added an address to the transmission. He seemed both expert and much stronger while he worked.

He lurched out of the chair. "There," he said to Ned. "Go ahead. When you're done, hit SEND."

Ned sat down, paused, and began by typing his serial number. He heard his fellows whispering behind him. The two men who'd come from the ship most recently hushed as others filled them in on events in the dome.

Letters of gray light formed in the hologram field:

RESERVE ENSIGN SLADE, E., WISHES TO INFORM PRESIDENT HAMMER THAT HE PROPOSES ON HIS SOLE RESPONSIBILITY TO CORRECT AN ANOMALY IN THE FOOD DISTRIBUTION SYSTEM OF THE BONDING AUTHORITY STATION ON PAIXHANS' NODE. THIS ACTION WILL TAKE PLACE IN THREE STANDARD HOURS FROM SLUG TIME. OUT.

"How do you walk with balls that big, kid?" Toll Warson asked in a friendly tone.

Ned tried to get up from the chair. The first time, his legs failed to support him and he fell back.

"So now we wait three hours," Tadziki said in a neutral voice.

"Captain," Louis Boxall said, "we'll need some apparatus to make this work. Can you give us a hand with the shopwork? You're the best hand with the hardware on the *Swift.*"

"I'm not sure I'm willing to go through with this, Tadziki," Lissea said. Her eyes were on Ned.

"It's my responsibility!" Ned shouted. "You will *not* interfere with matters that are my responsibility!"

Men looked away. "Touchy little feller, ain't he?" Deke Warson murmured to the ceiling.

"All right, Boxall," Lissea said. "Come back to the ship with me and we'll build your apparatus."

"We can only clear one suit at a time with the hand sterilizer, ma'am," Eugene said doubtfully. "Should we wait a couple minutes, Lou and I?"

"No, you can curst well stand outside the ship while I clear through the airlock!" Lissea replied as she stamped into the foyer. "This is your idea!"

To Ned's surprise but perhaps not to Tadziki's, there was a reply. Gresham's console logged it in eighty-eight minutes after Ned had sent the query on its forty-one-minute route to Nieuw Friesland. Hard copy scrolled from the printer, but the assembled men read the message from the screen:

INFORMATION NOTED. IF YOU'RE WILLING TO ANSWER TO YOUR UNCLE, THERE'S NOTHING USEFUL I COULD SAY. HAMMER.

Herne Lordling swore under his breath.

Ned said, "My uncle Don understands what it's like."

He spoke loudly but without a specific listener in mind. His mind was a collage of memories, views of a big man with a smiling mouth and eyes that could drill an anvil.

"He won't second-guess the man on the ground."

Gresham was crying.

Save for the anchor watch, the *Swift*'s complement was assembled in the station foyer. It was a change of scenery from the interior of the vessel, though a sterile one. Paixhans' Node wasn't a world which encouraged spacers to sightsee during their stopovers.

"Ten minutes till the next feeding, then?" Tadziki said after glancing at the clock above the door to the supply alcove.

Gresham nodded sluggishly. He'd eaten a ration bar from the *Swift*. It was the closest thing he'd had to a balanced diet since a similar offering from the most recent supply ship months before.

The station ran on Zulu Time: a twenty-four hour clock based on that of Earth at the Greenwich Meridian. It was as good a choice as any, since planetary rotation didn't affect the bright skies and the personnel weren't expected to go outside often anyway.

The inner lock cycled to admit the Boxall brothers and Lissea. The three of them had squeezed into the decontamination chamber together.

"That's not safe," Gresham complained. "You might miss a spore—"

Lissea opened her helmet. "Shut up, Gresham," she said.

Ned looked away from her.

"Well, I suppose if you're careful . . ." Gresham mumbled.

"We got it done," Eugene Boxall said. "Are we in time?"

Tadziki shrugged. "Eight minutes," he said. "Then twelve

hours to the next, ah, load."

"Plenty of time," said Louis. *"Plenty* of time."

He opened the front of his pressure suit and held out the egg-shaped case he'd carried inside the garment. "We're going to need one of you to go along with us," he continued. "Slade, that's you if you're up to it."

Ned reached for the egg. "You bet," he said.

Herne Lordling snatched the object from Boxall's hand. "Negative," he said. *"I'll* go."

Eugene dropped his suit on the floor of the foyer. "Look, Lordling," he said. "This isn't about shooting. This *particularly* isn't about shooting."

"Give him the scrambler, Herne," Lissea said. "Ned was my recommendation for the job."

Lordling glared at the Boxalls, then Lissea. He refused to look at Ned, and he continued to hold the object. Without speaking to one another, the Warsons shifted in concert to put themselves at two corners of an isosceles triangle with Lordling the third point. If shooting started, the brothers wouldn't be in one another's line of fire.

"We're not," Tadziki said, "in that much of a hurry." He stepped forward so that he was between Lordling and the Warsons, looking from Deke to Toll and back with a glum expression.

"Take the curst thing!" Lordling said. He thrust the object out to the side, not so much handing it to Ned as dissociating himself from what happened to it.

The egg was heavy. Within the clear plastic case, Ned could see a power supply and what he thought was an oscillator.

"Whoever's taking the food," Eugene resumed, "he's got to be a Wimbledon teleport like ourselves. Now I know, five meters is usually good distance and here we're maybe talking thousands of parsecs."

"But this is the Node," his twin said, taking up the theme. "We figure he could be coming from anywhere, anywhere in the galaxy. In and out like a pop-up target."

"Fine, but why?" Toll Warson asked.

Lissea looked at Gresham coldly. "I assume because some-body paid him to make this gentleman's life a little more mis-erable," she said. "But not to kill him."

"You see what we meant about Colonel Hammer," Louis said. "Seventeen years means a long memory."

"We don't want the guy killed," Eugene said. "Not if there's any other way. He's just doing his job."

Harlow laughed. "I've killed lots of people who was just doing their job," he said. "Via, I killed plenty who just hap-pened to be standing on the wrong piece of real estate. We all of us have."

He looked around the band of mercenaries, inviting argu-ment.

"Wimbledon isn't a very big place," Louis said. When his face flushed, the scar on his temple stood out more sharply. "We're doing this our way or not at all."

"I said that Ned," Lissea said, "could be trusted not to shoot unless there was no other choice.

Ned dabbed his lips with his tongue. "Thank you, Lissea," he said.

"We're going to carry you with us," Eugene said to Ned.

"You can do that?" Westerbeke demanded. "Carry stuff with you when you teleport?"

"It's a lot harder to jump out of your clothes than it is to wear them with you," Louis said. "Likewise the bubble of air around you."

"Him, he's heavy enough to be a problem," Eugene said with a nod toward Ned. "But we're good."

"Via, we're the best!"

The twins looked scarcely teenaged in their glow of antici-pation. They knew as surely as everyone else in the company did that there were stronger men and better shots on every side of them now—but this was *their* skill, and there was nobody like them in the galaxy.

"When he comes, we follow him," Eugene continued. "We don't know where that'll be. Anywhere in the galaxy, like I say. When we get there, you trigger this."

His index finger indicated the thumb switch on top of the egg in Ned's hand.

"It's an RF scrambler," Louis explained. "It'll disorient any teleport within maybe five meters of it. Us included, that's the problem."

"Optical would work as well as radio frequency," Eugene said, "but we don't know where we're going. It has to function if he's turned away or there's a wall between us or something."

"Via! I forgot the tape," Louis said. "Did you bring the tape?"

"*I* brought the tape," said Lissea. She handed Ned a roll of black, 75-mm tape. The adhesive was alcohol-soluble, but you could lift the bow of a tank on a properly rigged cable of the stuff.

"When we get there," Eugene repeated, "you trigger the scrambler. The guy'll probably fall down."

"We'll sure fall down," Louis said. "It's like having the worst headache ever in your life."

His twin shrugged. "It stops when the oscillator stops," he said. "But *don't* turn it off till you've got his eyes bandaged with the tape. Otherwise he'll likely jump again, and maybe we won't be ready to follow."

"One minute," said Tadziki.

Ned had come to the station unarmed. Lissea held out to him the submachine gun she'd brought on this trip from the *Swift.*

"I don't think I'll need this," Ned said.

"The teleport should be helpless," Lissea said, "but he may not be alone wherever he comes out. Take it."

Eugene Boxall shrugged. "Hey look," he said. "We don't want anybody croaking us while the scrambler's on, either. Do what you've got to do."

"Nearing time!" Tadziki said sharply.

Ned slung the submachine gun over his shoulder and stuck his right arm through the spool of tape. The twins gripped his wrists firmly, as if they were preparing for a trapeze act.

A chime sounded in the dispenser. The meal packet landed

in the niche with a *choonk*—

Ned's mind everted in a blaze of dazzling light.

The room was sunlit through a netlike screen across one whole wall. The Boxalls gripped Ned's wrists crushingly. The figure directly in front of the mercenaries was turning as Ned's thumb mashed down the scrambler switch.

The stranger, a woman with long, curling hair, flung up her hands with a cry of pain. Louis Boxall collapsed like a steer in the abattoir, but Eugene thrashed wildly and continued to hold Ned.

The switch had a detent to lock it until a second thrust released the spring. Ned dropped the unit. It bounced on a floor covered with long, meter-wide rugs laid edgewise and overlapping by half their width. He used both hands to break Eugene's grip, then turned his attention to the woman.

She was short, young, and strikingly beautiful in a smooth-skinned, plumpish style. The scrambler's invisible impact had driven her to her knees. Her eyes were closed, and she squeezed her temples with clenched fists while she made cackling sounds.

Ned yanked the roll of tape off his arm. He stretched a length, slapped it over the woman's eyes, and knocked her hands aside so that he could complete the loop around her head.

The submachine gun swung like a heavy pendulum, getting in his way. He set it on the floor with hasty care—there was one up the spout, and *no* safety could be trusted absolutely—before he finished the job of blindfolding the woman.

Breathing hard, more from stress than actual exertion, Ned looked for the scrambler. It had rolled beneath the legs of an intricate brass floorlamp. Ned poked the switch again to release it.

This was a *very* nice room, tasteful as well as expensively decorated. The window overlooked a parklike city from thirty stories up. The glazed surface curved to include half the ceiling as well, showing that this was the penthouse. The long wall opposite displayed two large abstracts, coolly precise, which flanked a curtained doorway. There was relatively little furniture, but pillows heaped against the short walls would serve as chairs or couches.

Louis Boxall raised himself to a squat. "Lord, Lord," he muttered. "Did anybody get the number of the truck that hit me?"

"Hey, it's a girl," Eugene said with considerably more animation. He still lay on the rugs, but his eyes were open and turned toward the captive. She was beginning to stir also.

"Rise and shine, troopers," Ned said. "I've done my part. The rest is up to you."

A man walked through the curtained doorway. "Tanya?" he said. His face blurred in surprise at the scene. He reached into the pocket of his flaring jacket.

Instead of snatching the submachine gun, Ned grabbed a double handful of a rug. He yanked at it, thrusting off with his legs as well as using his upper body to pull.

The newcomer's feet flew up. His arms flailed and the back of his head clunked into the wall. A needle stunner flew from his hand into a corner of the room.

"Father?" the girl called. She jumped to her feet, her face terrified beneath the band of tape. *"Father!"*

"He's all right!" Ned said as he grabbed the man. He pulled the man's jacket down to bind his arms while he was still logy, then checked the pockets for further weapons. There were none. The fellow's hair was coarse and black, but by the looks of his facial wrinkles he was probably in his sixties.

"Father?"

"Who are you?" the man asked.

"Hold him," Ned said, swinging the stranger toward Louis. He scooped up the submachine gun and quickly checked the remainder of the suite. There were two large bedrooms, two baths, and a fully equipped kitchen/dining room. No one else was present, and the exterior door was secured with a 5-cm steel bar as well as a pair of electronic locks.

Ned walked back into the living room. "All clear," he said. He tossed Eugene a bottle of clear liquor.

"Meet the Glieres, Slade," Louis said. "Oleg, and his daughter Tanya. We're just explaining to them that their contract with Colonel Hammer is now at an end."

Eugene wetted the tip of the neckerchief he wore over his tunic with the liquor. It had a minty odor. He dabbed alcohol onto the tape, starting at the woman's hairline. Oleg watched nervously. There obviously wasn't any fight in him.

"Where are we, anyway?" Ned asked, looking out the window. It was a lovely city, wherever it was.

"Wonderland," Tanya said. She had a throaty, attractive voice that fit her physical person. "In the Trigeminid Cluster."

Ned shrugged. He'd never heard of the place—which implied that Wonderland had never been a market for mercenary soldiers, an even better recommendation than the broad swathes of landscaping among the buildings below.

"I . . ." Oleg said. He looked as though he wanted to sit down but didn't dare to. Louis gestured him toward a pile of pillows. "We'll of course do what you say. But I hope Colonel Hammer won't be offended."

"Oh," Ned said, rummaging in his breast pocket. He came out with two flimsies: the hard copies of his message to Friesland and Hammer's reply. He handed them to Gliere, who read, then reread the documents to be sure of their meaning.

Eugene lifted the cargo tape from Tanya's eyes. She had remained perfectly still during the process, but now she shuddered and said, "Oh thank God, thank God. I was *blind*."

"We needed to talk with you," Eugene said, "so that, you know, it could stop with talking."

Louis took the liquor bottle from his brother and swigged it. "I don't know about you," he said, "but my head feels like somebody's been using it for a rabbit hutch."

"You're from Wimbledon too?" Tanya asked.

"Where else?" Eugene said. He loosened the last tag of adhesive and dropped the blindfold onto the floor. "You've both been doing this, then?"

"I don't jump very well anymore," Oleg said. "My age, you know."

A muscle in Louis' cheek quivered. Nobody likes to be reminded that he will inevitably grow too old to perform his specialty.

"Tanya has taken over the duties this past five years," Oleg went on, "so that we didn't lose the retainer."

"We don't need the money!" his daughter said sharply. "My paintings already earn more than this *theft* does." She looked from Louis to Eugene and patted her disarranged hair. "I'm glad it's over."

"It's got to be," Eugene said. He offered the bottle to Tanya, then drank after her. The twins' eyes were approving.

"Do you suppose we could get back to Paixhans' Node?" Ned said. "They're going to be wondering about things until we report."

"Slave driver," Louis said. He bent and scooped up the meal container Tanya had dropped when the pursuit arrived. "Look, though," he said, glancing between the Glieres, "I'll be back to visit, if you don't have objections."

"*We'll* be back," Eugene added. He put his boot on the scrambler and crushed it, despite the layers of carpet beneath the object. "We don't meet many of our sort off Wimbledon."

"*We,*" Tanya Gliere said, "would like that."

Half a dozen of the mercenaries in the foyer were singing "Sam Hall," entranced with the acoustics of the room and the long corridors curving off it. Deke Warson reached into the guts of the ration dispenser and shouted over the racket, "Who wants a . . ." He paused to rip open the meal packet. "Roast duckling!"

"Warson, both of you!" Tadziki ordered. "Go easy on the food. Remember it'll be two months before the next supply ship."

Deke and Toll had opened the loading gate of the dispenser so quickly and easily that Ned didn't imagine the resupply crew could have beaten their time. Whether or not the two *had* rigged their brother's vehicle to blow up, they certainly had the expertise to do so.

"My Nellie's down below all dressed in blue."

"I assure you, Master Gresham," Lissea said, "that we'll leave ration packets to make up for those we're consuming tonight. I can't pretend the quality will be up to those the Authority supplies, though."

"Says my Nellie dressed in blue—"

Gresham laughed so hard that he began to hiccup. "Oh, Mistress Doormann," he said. "Oh, Mistress Doormann, there's always the fungus outside."

"—now I know that you'll be true—"

He'd eaten half a packet of spiced meatloaf, then had promptly vomited the whole contents of his stomach back up. Now he wore a fresh uniform and picked carefully at the remainder of the meal.

"Yes I know that you'll be true, goddam your eyes!"

Tadziki looked from the cheerful mercenaries to Gresham. "You agree that we've carried out our part of the bargain, I trust? Then it's time for you to do your part."

Gresham and the *Swift*'s complement ate at tables and benches built from maintenance stores: plating, tubes, and boxes that could be used to repair the antennas outside and the electronic modules within the dome. Minor tasks were a part of Gresham's duties, while larger ones—a tower which collapsed in a storm, for example—had to wait for the supply ship to arrive.

Gresham blinked as the adjutant spoke. He started to rise immediately, mumbling, "Of course, of course—"

He was trying to lever himself up from the table, but his wrist buckled. Ned grabbed the frail civilian before he fell facedown in the meatloaf.

Lissea looked fiercely at Tadziki. "I don't think we need be in *that* much of a hurry," she said.

The Boxall brothers stepped into the makeshift banquet hall, carrying a case of bottles between them. They set the load down on the concrete.

"Hey, come and have dinner!" Deke Warson called from the dispenser. He reached down for another pair of meals.

"Have a good trip!" Louis replied. The twins vanished in the same eyeblink.

Everyone looking in the teleports' direction fell silent. Ned and Tadziki both jumped to their feet, but Lissea beat them to the case of bottles.

There was a note on it, folded into a fan. She opened it. "Shut up, you lot!" Tadziki ordered.

" *'Dear Captain,'* " Lissea read aloud. " *'We're going to leave you here. Hope you think we were worth our rations, and you can keep the pay.'* "

She looked up. "They both signed it," she added.

"Deserters!" Herne Lordling said.

The adjutant lifted a bottle from its foam cocoon. "Iron Star Liquors," he said, reading the label. He shook the clear liquor.

"It's mint-flavored," Ned said. *And it cleaned the adhesive off cargo tape about as quickly as industrial alcohol could.*

Lissea looked at Ned and raised an eyebrow.

"They made a friend on Wonderland," he said. He didn't have any idea of what domestic arrangements on Wimbledon were like. "I guess they figured they . . . Well, I don't know how long it'd take to get to the Trigeminid Cluster in normal fashion."

Lissea shrugged. "They earned their keep," she said. She tossed a bottle to Toll Warson, another to Westerbeke in the center of the singers, and a third to Coyne at the far table.

Noisy enthusiasm echoed around the foyer.

Lissea looked at Ned. "And so did you," she added in a barely audible tone.

"There's been no astrophysical change in the Sole Solution," Gresham said from the console attached to a projection screen. "The change—the problem preventing normal navigation—was wholly political."

The station administrator was a different man since the thefts of his food were ended. He hadn't regained his physical health from a few normal meals; in some ways, long-term deficiencies had damaged him beyond complete recovery. Mentally, however, Gresham was free of the strain that had hagridden him over his years of exile. He spoke distinctly and with obvious command of his material.

"The Twin Worlds," he continued, "Alliance and Affray, are close enough to the Sole Solution through Transit space that they are virtually a part of the anomaly. A generation ago, the Twin Worlds completed the cooperative project that had absorbed a significant portion of their planetary output for nearly twenty standard years."

A torus bloomed in the center of the holographic projection. The object had no scale, no apparent size. Gresham worked a detached control wand with a cold smile on his face, focusing the image on half the screen down to increasingly small portions of the doughnut displayed in full beside it.

"Blood and martyrs!" said Westerbeke. "How big *is* the fucker?"

"There are occupied satellites of considerably smaller diameter," Gresham said with cold amusement. "It doesn't have a name. Technically, it's Twin Worlds Naval Unit One. They call it the Dreadnought."

The small-scale image focused on a weapons blister from which three tubes projected. *A tribarrel,* Ned thought; until the scale shrank still further and he saw that the specks on the outside of the turret were men. *The guns must have bores of nearly a meter.*

"But what do they do with it?" Lissea asked. "You could never invade a planet with that."

All of the ship's crewmen—save Dewey, on anchor watch—were in the station's control room. Some of the other off-duty mercenaries hadn't bothered to come. They didn't regard navigation as anything to concern them. Even on a planet as boring as Paixhans' Node, they preferred to play cards and drink the remainder of the Boxalls' parting gift.

"The Dreadnought was built to control trade through the Sole Solution," Gresham said. "To end all trade except for what was carried on Twin Worlds hulls. They require merchants to land on either Alliance or Affray and to transfer their cargo to local vessels."

"Will they sell ships to outsiders?" Tadziki asked.

"No," Gresham said. "Nor, if you were considering it, would they permit you to reflag the *Swift* as a Twin Worlds vessel."

"I suppose they charge monopoly rates for their services?" Ned said. The point didn't matter since Lissea wasn't about to leave the *Swift* behind, but it showed that he was awake.

"Of course," Gresham agreed. "Since the Dreadnought has been operating, the value of trade through the Sole Solution has dropped to five percent of the previous annual total. This has hurt many planets, particularly those of the Pocket. The situation is satisfactory to the Twin Worlds themselves because *their* combined planetary income has increased markedly."

"Why doesn't somebody do something about it?" Toll Warson asked.

His voice wasn't quite as relaxed as he had wanted it to sound. The Warsons were as close to being functioning anarchists as anyone Ned had met. The notion of imposed authority was genuinely offensive to them. That they'd spent all their lives in the rigid hierarchies of military systems implied an insane dichotomy.

It also implied they'd been very good to have survived this long, but that was true of almost everybody aboard the *Swift*.

By now, everybody. Even Ned Slade.

"Economics," Lissea said before Gresham could answer. "There are planets and planetary combines which could take this *thing* out of play."

She gestured at the hologram. The scale had shrunk to show that the Dreadnought did mount tribarrels. The installations on the main battery turrets looked as though they had been planted on flat steel plains.

"But a fleet that could accomplish that would take years to build, decades. Nobody with the resources had a good enough reason to employ them for the purpose."

"Precisely," Gresham said, a teacher approving his student's answer. It was hard to equate this man with the whimpering wreck who'd greeted the *Swift* on its arrival.

"We'll come back to the problem," Gresham continued. He blanked the display. "Now, as to a rest-and-resupply point on this side of the Sole Solution, you'll land at Burr-Detlingen."

"Will we, now?" Deke Warson murmured.

The screen panned across a gullied plain with little vegetation. There were occasional human-built structures, all of them in ruins.

"There's no settled agriculture," Gresham said. "No human society since the wars, really. The atmosphere is ideal, and you'll be able to replenish your water supply from wells. Do you have equipment for processing raw biomass into edibles?"

"No," Tadziki said. "That'd be too bulky for a ship of the *Swift*'s size."

"Well, you should be able to shoot animals for fresh meat," Gresham said. The image slid across a family of rangy herbivores, perhaps originally sheep or goats of Earth stock.

"On the other side of the Sole Solution," Gresham said as he blanked the display again, "is Buin. I can't really recommend it as a stopover, however. I think you'd be better off to continue to one of the developed worlds further into the Pocket."

"We'll need copies of all your navigational data for the Pocket," Lissea said.

"We've already downloaded it into the *Swift,*" Westerbeke assured her.

"All right," Lissea said. "I want to avoid developed worlds wherever possible."

"And there's the time factor," Tadziki said. "The nearest alternative landing point is another five days beyond Buin."

"Bugger *that* for a lark," a mercenary muttered. Under weigh, the *Swift* differed from a prison by having far less available space for those enclosed.

"Yes," Gresham said tartly. "The problem with Buin is the autochthonal race."

The display flopped from a pale white glow to the image of

a gray-skinned creature beside a scale in decimeters. The Buinite was about two meters tall, within the human range, but its legs were only half the length of its arms and torso. The jaw was square, with powerful teeth bared in a snarl. One big hand carried a stone. Ned couldn't tell from the image whether the stone had been shaped or not.

"They don't look like much of a problem," Harlow said. "Nothing a shot or two won't cure."

"Individually, you're correct," Gresham said with no hint of agreement. "The autochthones' technology doesn't go beyond stakes and rocks—"

The hologram shifted to a panorama. Buin was rocky, and the vegetation tended toward blues and grays rather than green. A band of twenty or so autochthones was scattered across the field of view, turning over stones and sometimes probing holes with simple tools. They wore no clothing, though some of the medium-sized adults slung food objects on cords across their shoulders.

"Nor have they traded with travelers to gain modern weapons," Gresham continued.

"Do they have anything to trade?" Ned asked.

"Not really," Gresham said, "but the question doesn't arise. The autochthones invariably kill everyone who lands on their planet, unless he escapes immediately."

"I'd like to see them try *that*," Herne Lordling said. For once, the muttered chorus of other mercenaries was fully in support of his comment.

"You will, sir," Gresham said. "You assuredly will, if you land on Buin."

He switched the image to an overhead view of a mound. Vegetation hadn't started to claim the raw earth mixed with boulders the size of cottages.

"Artificial?" Lissea said.

"Yes," said Gresham. "And at the bottom of it, there's a starship, the *Beverly*. Autochthones damaged her engines with thrown rocks—"

The hologram switched to a Buinite stretching his left arm out behind him, then snapping forward like a sprung bear trap.

The stone that shot from his hand sailed a hundred, perhaps a hundred and fifty meters in a flat arc before it hit the ground. Ned judged that the projectile weighed about as much as a man's head.

"And then they buried her, as you see," Gresham said. "Don't confuse intelligence with technology, mistress and gentlemen."

"Twenty of them did that?" Toll Warson wondered aloud.

"Probably two thousand," Gresham said. "Perhaps twenty thousand. Male Buinites concentrate on any ship that lands, like white cells on a source of infection. They appear to be telepathic. They are careless of their individual lives, and they are utterly committed to destroying the intruders."

He cleared his throat. "There have been cases where a vessel was undermined rather than being overwhelmed by advancing siege ramps," he added.

"But they *are* intelligent," Lissea said musingly.

"Clearly," Gresham agreed.

"That will help," Lissea said. "I'll want full data on the Buinites, physical and psychological. I assume that's available?"

Gresham looked surprised. "Why, yes," he said. "Everything is available here, in a manner of speaking. But I strongly recommend—"

"Before we worry about Buin," Tadziki interrupted, "we've got to get through the Sole Solution. Now, either it *isn't* the only way into the Pocket through Transit space—"

"It is," Gresham said, nodding vigorously.

"—or we've got a real problem," the adjutant continued. "I don't see any way in hell that we can get past that Dreadnought in the time it'll take to recalibrate for the next Transit."

"We bloody well aren't going to fight it," Deke Warson agreed.

"There is, I believe, a way," Gresham said. He was smiling. "I've had a great deal of time to consider the matter."

His expression didn't look sane. Ned supposed that nobody exiled to Paixhans' Node could remain sane.

"Your *Swift* has a lifeboat with stardrive, I presume," Gresham continued.

"Yes," Lissea said.

"Then this is how you will proceed . . ."

Burr-Detlingen

—⫘—

NED CARRIED THE submachine gun in his hands, not slung. The sky of Burr-Detlingen was white with occasional hints of blue, darkening now toward the east. The sun was just above the horizon, though in these latitudes full darkness would be some while to come.

It was still no time, and certainly no place, for Tadziki to be off wandering alone.

"Tadziki!" Ned called toward the masses of iridium armor, polished to a soft patina by windblown grit. "Hey, Tadziki! Anybody home?"

The *Swift* was a kilometer to the south. Ned had been on the crew that had reopened the well from which the vessel was now replenishing its water supplies. The thousand-meter shaft, a relic of human civilization on Burr-Detlingen, had been partly choked with sand.

Four of the men had gone off in the Jeeps, to hunt for meat, and for the fun of it. Bonilla, deck watch at the navigation console, told Ned that the adjutant had taken a walk toward the vast boneyard of military equipment near the landing site.

There was enough wind to scour away sound as well as all the paint and insignia from the shot-out vehicles. A yellow haze on the northern horizon indicated a storm sweeping across the badlands. If it changed direction—and who knew what the weather patterns of this place were?—getting back to the *Swift* would be a bigger problem than a dry walk.

"Tad—" Ned called. A figure stepped away from the bulk of a vehicle. Ned presented his weapon, then lifted it when he recognized Tadziki.

"Hey, I was looking for you," he said. "You, ah . . . Your helmet radio?"

"Sorry, I didn't mean to bother anybody," the adjutant said. He touched a switch on the side of his helmet. "I set it to ignore nonemergency calls. Even I ought to have a few hours off, eh?"

"Via, I'm sorry," Ned said. "I was—well, not worried, but there's supposed to be bands of locals running around. I just thought I'd, you know, make sure everything was okay."

The tank directly before him had been hit three times by kinetic energy shot. Two of the rounds had failed to penetrate but the projectiles had blasted deep pits in the tank's frontal slope. The sides of the craters were plated a purple that the sunset darkened.

The third shot had punched through the side of the turret. The interior of the tank burned out with such violence that the thirty-plus–tonne turret had lifted from its ring and resettled at a skew angle before being welded to the hull.

"The locals aren't any threat," Tadziki said. "They've sunk so far that it's hard to imagine them as being human. Sometimes passing ships capture them as slaves. Sometimes they're shot. Just for the fun of it, you see."

He spoke without emphasis, and his eyes held a blank fatigue that Ned didn't like to see—see in anybody, and Tadziki was by now a friend.

"That wasn't in the pilotry data," Ned said carefully. Tadziki carried a ration pack and a condensing canteen, but he appeared to be unarmed.

Either there was more in Ned's expression than he thought

there was, or the two men were linked to a degree beyond that of physical communication. Tadziki reached into a breast pocket and pulled out a needle stunner.

"I suppose I'm making a statement, Slade," he said, "but I'm not trying to commit suicide."

Ned smiled. "Well, you can never tell," he said lightly.

"Come on and take a look at this," Tadziki said. He waved at the vast junkyard, armored bulwarks squatting in mounds of fine sand. "It's an interesting experience."

They walked past a command car whose fusion bottle had failed. The gush of plasma had not only eviscerated the vehicle, it had sucked the relatively thin armor inward so that the wreck looked like crumpled foil.

"This is my second trip to Burr-Detlingen," the adjutant said.

Ned looked at him sharply.

"No, no," Tadziki explained. "Not during the fighting—that was nearly a century ago. A cartel on Thunderhead got the notion of salvaging the equipment here. I was part of the team they sent to assay the possibilities."

Three armored personnel carriers were lined up nose to tail. Each had taken a powergun bolt through the center of its broadside. All the vehicles' plane surfaces were bulged convex by internal explosions.

"Salvage this?" Ned said.

"Yeah, well, they hadn't seen it," Tadziki explained. "They'd just heard about all the high-quality equipment abandoned here with nobody to claim it. We spent a week on the survey without finding a single piece that was worth more than metal value."

"Metal value" meant "worth dirt." Every planetary system had an asteroid belt which sorted metals in pure form and rich alloys, ready for the taking. Only colonies which had lost the ability to travel in space placed a premium on metal.

Tadziki climbed the bow slope of a tank and onto the turret. Ned followed him onto the artificial hillock. The barrel of the main gun had been shot out so badly that there was no way to tell from the cone-shaped remnant what the bore's original diameter had been.

"This is where the final battle of the war was fought, did you know?" Tadziki said. He gestured again at the field of gigantic litter.

"Really?" said Ned. "I would have thought it was just a salvage yard."

"They fought with spears and clubs," Tadziki explained. "One side built rock walls between the carcases of the vehicles and used them for fortifications."

He pointed.

Ned could see signs of artifice, now that they were pointed out to him. "The other side attacked them. Nobody won, of course."

"I think it was a religious war," Ned said. He looked down. Sand had eroded the join between the hatch cover and the coaming into a deep, thumb-thick gully. He couldn't see any sign of battle damage to the tank, however. "We studied one of the battles at the Academy. In Intermediate Tactics class, I think."

"It was excellent equipment!" Tadziki said angrily. He stamped his foot on the turret roof. It was like hitting a boulder: the armor was too thick to bell at the impact. "There isn't one planet in a thousand today who could build or afford to buy hardware like this."

"Yeah," Ned agreed as he surveyed the hectares of sophisticated equipment. "I was wondering about that myself. This isn't exactly a land flowing with milk and honey."

The sun was down, though the sky still looked bright. "You know," he said. "It wouldn't be a bad idea for us to be getting back to the *Swift*, whether or not the locals are a problem."

"They grew citrus fruit," Tadziki said. He showed no signs of planning to leave the graveyard. "Lemons in particular—Terran lemons naturalized here. They had a unique flavor. Burr-Detlingen exported fruit all over the galaxy."

Ned looked around. Except for the vicinity of the *Swift*, nothing in the landscape moved but what the wind blew.

"Any of the groves left in driving distance?" he asked. "If we have to wait here three days before trying the Sole Solution, maybe we could get a Jeep."

"There's nothing left," the adjutant said. "They weren't groves; they were individual trees in walls to keep the wind from stripping them. The walls became pillboxes, and of course the irrigation system was destroyed early on. There's nothing left that anyone would want to have."

It was becoming appreciably darker. Well, the charge-coupled devices in their helmet visors could increase ambient light by three orders of magnitude. Lack of depth perception wasn't a problem in terrain this barren.

"I'd never have come back here if there'd been a choice," Tadziki said. "There wasn't a choice: no planet close enough for us to launch the lifeboat into the Sole Solution in a single Transit."

Everybody had moods. Tadziki was under greater stress than anybody on the expedition except Lissea herself. Maybe more than Lissea, even, because the adjutant had enough experience to know how bad it could get.

Ned reached down and twisted the hatch's undogging lever. To his surprise, it rotated smoothly. "You couldn't have checked all these vehicles in a week," he said as he lifted the hatch open.

The stench hit them like a battering ram. The tank hadn't been opened in the century since it had been destroyed. The crewman who died lifting his hands toward the inner hatch release had mummified. His teeth were a polished yellow against the coarser saffron skin. The eyes had sunken in, but they were still open.

And the stench . . .

The two men tumbled down the sides of the tank as if a grenade had burst between them. Ned wheezed and gagged. He closed his eyes for a moment, then found that it was better if something other than memory provided his mind with images.

"Why do men go for soldiers?" Tadziki shouted. They were walking back toward the *Swift,* wallowing in sand which had drifted around the skirts of the vehicles. "Do they believe in *that?* Is that what they want?"

It was too dark to see clearly unaided, but Ned didn't want to shut his visor. Concussion from a large mine could have killed the tank crew, crushing their internal organs without penetrating the hull of their vehicle.

"It's not that simple," he said.

"On the contrary, boy," Tadziki said. "It's *exactly* that simple."

After a moment, he reached out and gripped Ned's shoulder. "I'm sorry," he said.

Ned reached up and squeezed the adjutant's hand against him. "No sweat," he said. He looked back at the armored wasteland, tombstones for a whole planet. "I'm sorry too," he added.

The Sole Solution

—◆—

"S TAND BY FOR Transit," Westerbeke announced.

Lissea was at the backup console, though Ned doubted she'd had much more navigational experience than he'd had. She was nervous, just like the rest of them. If she wanted to be in position to see disaster instantly, then nobody aboard could deny her the right.

"Via," said Ingried plaintively. "The worst it can be is they tell us we're bad boys to try to run the Solution, and they make us land on Alliance. Right? Maybe we get fined."

"The *worst* it can be," Yazov said in a harsh, no-nonsense voice, "is that they figure out we're the ones that tried to kill them all, and then they torture us to death. Maybe the same way that we tried to do them."

"*Shut up, both of you,*" Tadziki said, using the vessel's PA system.

"Transit."

Ned felt the flip-flop passage from one bubble universe to another with wholly different physical laws, then back again to the first. He deliberately prevented himself from gripping his bunk rails fiercely. Part of his mind *felt* that could help him against a bolt of plasma devouring the entire vessel.

"No sign of the Dreadnought," Westerbeke said. *"No sign of the Dreadnought, but there's our lifeboat."*

"Boys, I think we did it!" Lissea cried.

She adjusted the holographic display at her console, projecting the view at maximum enlargement. The lifeboat the *Swift* had launched from orbit above Burr-Detlingen hung in vacuum; there was nothing material within a light-month of the Sole Solution.

Men cheered and swung out of their bunks—Ned as quickly as any of the others. The *Swift* had the traditional 1-g way on, so there was considerable risk if the vessel made another Transit while the complement was out of its couches. Fifteen minutes was as fast as the AI could recalibrate, though; and anyway, it was worth a bruise or even broken bones to release the tension of the last few hours.

"Here, I've got the data dump," Lissea said. She touched her controls. The starscape shifted to a recording made inside the lifeboat during its unpiloted Transit into the Sole Solution. Initially, that meant the holographic display was a pulsing purple, the closest the equipment could come to reproducing the absolute lightlessness within the little vessel.

"Unidentified ship," snapped a transmission-modulated laser rather than a radio, judging from the static-free reception. *"Heave to immediately. This is Twin Worlds Naval Unit One. You will not get another warning. Over."*

The lifeboat's interior lights went on at full intensity. The six Nodals within were of an unhealthy translucence from days of lightlessness. Their flesh, yellow and pustulant, began to firm up visibly under the illumination.

"This is trading vessel Southshields *out of Nowotny,"* the lifeboat's AI replied on cue. *"We are heaving to. We have a load of cacao and worked bronze only. What's the trouble? Over."*

The voice from the Dreadnought laughed harshly. *"No problem at all,* Southshields," it said. *"We'll just confiscate your ship and cargo for entering closed territory of the Twin*

Worlds. Unless you try to get away, in which case we'll blast you to vacuum, and that won't be a problem either.''

"Southshields, *stand by to be boarded,''* another voice interjected.

The lifeboat's navigation display was crude, and the images were further degraded by copying and retransmission from the internal camera. The Dreadnought was visible as a vast doughnut, but the catcher boat launched from it was no more than an approaching quiver of light.

The Nodals were becoming active now that the lights were on. At this final stage of their breeding process, their bases remained fixed. Ripples like slow tides worked up their swaying bodies. The yellow tinge of the creatures' flesh became brighter and more saturated.

The lifeboat's hull thumped, then rang metallically as the lip of a boarding tube clamped around the hatch. The boat didn't have an airlock—most low-end cargo vessels didn't. The catcher vessel was equipped to board without putting the Twin Worlds crew to the discomfort of suiting up.

A Nodal's skin ripped from top to bottom as if a seam had given out under pressure. Yellow spores exploded in a haze that hid the interior for a moment. The spores began to settle on all the surfaces of the vessel.

The hatch opened. Spores swirled in the air currents.

A burly man with a fat-muzzled pistol stood framed by the coaming. He wore an airpack but not a pressure suit. Behind him stretched the boarding tube to his own vessel. The tube's reinforcing helix acted as a light guide, illuminating the pathway.

A second Nodal ruptured.

The Twin Worlder's scream was loud despite being muffled by the airpack. He opened fire with his pistol, the worst thing he could have done—

Though at this point, there wasn't anything he could have done that wouldn't have been disastrous.

The weapon fired charges of airfoils shaped to spread from the muzzle into a broad, short-range killing pattern. They sliced the remaining Nodals into geysers of spores, seconds or minutes before the creatures would have opened naturally.

The atmosphere of the cabin was yellow mud. As the air cleared, the camera showed that tendrils of spores had followed the panicked Twin Worlder back down the boarding tube. Thousands—*millions*—of them clung to the man's flesh and clothing.

"Good enough!" Deke Warson cried. The *Swift*'s bay was alive with glee. "That'll teach the bastards!" several men shouted at once.

"What they should do," Tadziki said, "is to blow themselves up right now. It's the only way."

"Nobody wants to die," Ned said from beside him.

"They're going to die, quickly and certainly," the adjutant said. He sounded detached, as though he were assessing the state of play in a bridge rubber. "Not quickly enough, though. There's no cure for the spores once they've infected a human. Cauterizing heat, that's all, heat beyond what flesh can stand. UV and hard radiation simply stimulate growth."

"I think," Toll Warson said, "that this calls for a party!"

Lissea got up from the console. Men clapped her on the back as she walked down the aisle. "Yes," she said. "We can break out a double liquor ration. Herne, you're in charge of dispensing it."

The boarding tube ripped as the catcher vessel powered up without going through the time-consuming procedures to release it. Automatic systems within the device immediately clamped it shut at the break. Vacuum wouldn't have affected the spores one way or another, but the lifeboat's navigational equipment depended on an atmosphere to reveal its holographic images.

Most of the men ignored the display as soon as Lissea ordered a liquor distribution. Westerbeke, on duty while the AI calculated the next Transit, glanced toward the hologram occasionally. Mostly he watched his fellows queued before Lordling at the liquor cabinet.

The fleck of the catcher vessel merged again with the shape of Twin Worlds Naval Unit One. "They wanted medical help," Tadziki mused aloud. He still stood at Ned's elbow.

"People don't like to believe how serious a crisis is at first."

"If they'd reported the situation," Ned said, "they'd never have been allowed to dock. But they should have had the balls to report anyway!"

The adjutant shrugged. "They aren't fighting men," he said. "They just happened to have a job on a warship so powerful that it could never be used. They didn't *believe*, none of them, that they'd ever be in a life or death situation."

"Oh, dear, what can the matter be?" Coyne sang, waving a tumbler of ruddy brandy in the air.

"Shut the fuck up!" Harlow said. "You got a voice to scare crows."

"And the Dreadnought left station," Ned said. "They went back to the Twin Worlds, I suppose? One or the other of them."

"Seven old maids, locked in the lavat'ry," Coyne and Yazov continued.

"Who's got the dice? Shmuel, you've got dice, right?"

Tadziki nodded. "Presumably," he said. "There's really nowhere else they might have gone. They may not be planning to land."

"They were there from Sunday to Saturday," crewmen sang. Several of them had surprisingly good voices. *"Nobody knew they were there!"*

"They can't land the Dreadnought," Ned said. "But no matter what, some of them'll get down in gigs and catcher boats. And some of those will already be infected."

"Yes," Tadziki said. "That's what I think too. Now I'm going to have a drink."

Ned walked to his bunk. The bow and center of the bay were a party room, but the back was empty.

He didn't want his liquor ration. He could trade it to somebody, but there wasn't anything else Ned wanted, either. Nothing that a human being could give him, anyway.

Ned picked up the microchip reader. He still had Thucydides loaded. The author's introduction claimed he was writing a paradigm for human behavior. The work itself was an account of two powerful nations lurching toward mutual destruction; not inevitably, but with absolute certainty nonetheless.

Lissea retched behind her thin door panel.

Ned got up. He dampened a towel at the water dispenser, then gently tried Lissea's door.

It was locked. He glanced toward the bow. The party went on merrily. Lordling and the Warson brothers were singing with linked arms.

Ned took a finger-sized probe from his equipment belt and tried the lock. The telltale on the probe's back flicked from red to green in less than a second. The latch wasn't much of a challenge to equipment and training by which Ned could bypass the security devices on a tank.

He checked the party again, then slipped into Lissea's compartment with the wet towel. The door closed behind him as part of the same motion.

She'd been sick into a bag. She looked up, her eyes red and furious.

"Brought you a towel," he said, turning his back as he thrust it toward her.

"Yeah, I see that you did," Lissea said. She didn't shout or curse, as he'd expected and as he knew he deserved. Her voice was husky, burned raw by stomach acid. She took the towel from his hand.

"Go on, sit down," she said. "Want a drink?"

Ned sat down on the end of the bunk. The bulkheads provided privacy but actually reduced Lissea's apparent space, because they cut her off from the volume of the bay.

"No thanks," Ned said.

"I do," Lissea said. The locker beneath her bunk was of double depth. She leaned over, opened it, and took out a bottle with conifers on the label.

"Wood alcohol," she said. "That's a joke, boy. It's what we brew on Dell." She drank directly from the bottle. The towel lay crumpled at her feet.

A craps game competed with the singers in the bay. From what Ned could tell, there might have been two songs going on at the same time.

"They don't know what they've done, do they?" Lissea said brightly. "—what we've all done, I should say, shouldn't I?"

"They know," Ned said. "They've killed the crew of the Dreadnought, however many thousands of people that was."

"And how many people on the Twin Worlds?" Lissea said. She flung the bottle down. The container bounced, spilling liquor from the mouth, but didn't break. "And to the next planet and the one after that, and the one after *that*."

Ned set the bottle upright. The stopper was still in Lissea's hand. He didn't ask for it.

"No," he said. "On the Twin Worlds, maybe. One or the other of them. But there's no place except Paixhans' Node where Nodals can get the permanent illumination they need to thrive. Maybe a few of them will get to the fruiting stage. But not many, and none beyond one or two generations.

"I'm supposed to feel good that I've only killed thousands, not millions?" she said. "Is that it?"

"You knew," Ned said coldly, "what was going to happen when you made the decision to proceed. The only way this wouldn't have been the result is if the plan had failed—and we all died instead, most likely."

"All right, Slade, you've—"

"No!" Ned said. "Nothing's changed. *Don't* second-guess yourself. We all knew what we were doing and we did it. Now we're going to go on. And there'll be some hard choices to make later, too. We *know* that."

Lissea laughed. "You haven't told me that they were evil bastards and no better than pirates," she said. "Do you want to tell me that, too?"

"What's done is done," Ned said softly. "If you don't like the way things look from this side, then pick another route the next time."

He thumbed toward the bulkhead and the noise beyond it. "Most of the people here, they've got a lot less trouble with what happened than they would've with getting greased themselves." He grinned. "Which is why you hired us, I suspect."

Lissea chuckled again, this time with more humor. She

picked up the bottle. "Want a drink?" she offered again.

"No, thanks though."

She stoppered the bottle. "Thanks, Ned," she said. "Let's us go join the party now. I wouldn't want anybody to get the wrong impression."

There might have been a speculative tone behind her words; but Ned was a man, and he knew that men thought that way.

Buin

—⟋⟋⟍—

"WE'RE STILL GETTING *signals from the crashed vessel's crew,*" Bonilla reported from the backup console. Westerbeke always had the con in tight situations, and powered flight through Buin's atmosphere was certainly that. *"The survivors have abandoned their ship and headed for high ground. They say they can't hold out much longer. Over."*

Buffeting made all objects within the *Swift* rattle, adding considerable noise to the wind-roar through the thick hull. All personnel were in their bunks, wearing body armor and festooned with weapons and equipment.

Ned was dry-mouthed. He'd never before had this long to expect certain combat.

"Lissea, the indigs'll be concentrated on the downed ship," Herne Lordling said. His helmet gave him the ability to enter the command net rather than simply listen to Channel 1 traffic, the way other personnel did. *"We shouldn't land within fifty klicks of them. Let the fools get themselves out of their jam. Over."*

Ned suspected Lordling spoke for most of the complement. The *Swift* wasn't crewed by Good Samaritans, and this looked like a dicey business at best. The crewmen of the vessel that had either crashed or foolishly landed on Buin—it wasn't clear which—were in desperate straits, but that wasn't a problem the Warsons, for example, felt they were being paid to solve.

Ned was green enough, he supposed—soft enough—to be willing to help. He just didn't see there was a thing in hell he could do.

"Westerbeke," snapped Lissea's voice, *"land us as planned if the site is clear. Lordling, you have your orders."*

"All personnel prepare for landing," Westerbeke ordered. The pilot sounded cool, almost bored.

The boom of the jets segued into a ringing *blammm!* as Westerbeke or the ships' AI doubled the number of lit nozzles and shifted the direction of thrust. Flat clamps held Ned to his bunk when inertia tried to shift him first forward, then up.

Reflected exhaust hammered the *Swift*, a warning that the vessel was within meters of the ground. The touchdown itself was accompanied by a series of raps on the lower hull.

Ned's first thought was that the Buinites were already attacking. Tadziki, who was importing visuals from the navigational console to his visor, said, *"Loose gravel, boys. It's all right."*

The main hatch began to open an instant before the jets shut off and the couch clamps released. Mercenaries swung from their bunks with a long crash of boots against the decking. The ramp was only halfway down when Herne Lordling's four-man team pounded across it and leaped to the ground. The second team was a stride behind them; Ned and Lissea were half of the third.

It must have rained recently. The brush was alive with yellow, white, and orange flowers which almost hid the cooler-colored foliage that Gresham's holograms had led Ned to expect. Between bushes scattered at several-meter intervals, the stony soil had a white crust that could be either salt or lichen.

The *Swift*'s external cargo blisters were already open. The Warson brothers had lifted out one of the Jeeps and were reaching for the other. Ned didn't recall having ever before seen such a casual expression of strength.

He unlocked the fan nacelles of the first Jeep and levered them up into operating position. Somebody fired from the other side of the vessel. The plasma discharges sizzled through the commo helmet an instant before the sonic hiss-*crack!*

Crewmen with bundles of poles, wire, and directional mines staggered through the brush under guard of their fellows with weapons ready. Three men remained aboard the *Swift:* Westerbeke and Petit, at the navigational and engine-room consoles respectively, and Tadziki—against his will—to take charge from the vessel if things went badly wrong. The adjutant stood in the center of the main hatchway with a 2-cm powergun ready.

The *Swift*'s upper hull was the best vantage point for a kilometer in any direction. The two-man crew who'd set up the tribarrel there cried out. They pointed over the Jeeps toward vegetation lining an underground watercourse; then cut a long burst loose. Cyan bolts blew stems upward in a haze of soapy black flames.

Lissea lurched into the Jeep with the device she'd built in the *Swift*'s maintenance shop. The electronics chassis mounted three separate lenses on the front, with a shoulder stock and a clumsy-looking handgrip underneath. From the way Lissea struggled, the apparatus must weigh twenty kilos.

"Are you ready?" Lissea shouted as Ned dropped into the seat beside her. She glanced around at the other Jeep. "Is everybody ready?"

"Let's get 'em," Deke Warson said with his hands on the driver's yoke. His brother lifted the muzzle of his 2-cm powergun slightly. He'd slung an identical weapon across his chest. This wouldn't be a good time to have to clear a jam.

Three Buinites ran from the shelter of a flat-topped tree half a kilometer away. A merc guarding the wiring party fired and spun the middle indig. The remaining pair dropped flat, then rose again together. A storm of cyan bolts devoured them before they could release the stones their arms were cocked to throw.

"Get a move on, Slade!" Lissea shouted, though the only delay had been that of the fans accelerating the loaded Jeep after Ned shoved his controls forward.

By plan, Ned's Jeep—Lissea's Jeep—was to lead. Ned was pretty sure that the actual reason he was a nose ahead of the Warsons as they raced toward the knoll just within the gap in the new-strung wire was that the brothers and their equipment were that much heavier than the load Ned's vehicle had to carry.

The crews had laid a conductive net as fine as spider silk between posts at hundred-meter intervals. The wires weren't so much material presence as scatterings of sunlight. They sagged at some points and were twisted around brush.

With luck, the net would provide a stable base for the minutes Lissea needed to carry out her plans.

The rocky knoll was the only high ground—three meters above its surroundings, putting it above the treetops—in the vicinity. The tribarrel on the ship fired a long planned burst, blasting the site clear of vegetation. Ned steered by memory, because he wouldn't be able to see the rise until it was right on top of him.

Somewhere a Buinite hit the net. Electricity from the nuclear batteries in the nearest post coursed through the creature in a long, drawn-out thunderclap. Cross-wires were insulated from one another, guaranteeing a current path whether or not the victim was grounded.

A dozen more Buinites reprised their dead fellow's actions within the next ten seconds. None of the victims screamed.

The roots of bushes held soil together, forming squat plateaus like the drums carnivores perch on in a circus act. Ned skidded between a pair of the short columns. He wasn't driving a tank, though with a load like this the little Jeep handled as sluggishly as a tank did. He had to go around things, not over them, and there wasn't any protection for when—

A submachine gun and three or four 2-cm weapons opened

up. They were a good distance away and hidden by the brush. Somebody shouted.

"Up here!" Lissea called, but Ned was already steering to hit the rise bow-on. If he tried to climb the knoll at a slant, the loaded Jeep might turn turtle. Ash and bits of charred brush-wood sprayed from beneath the skirts, but the plasma-lit fires were barely smoldering.

Ned halted, spinning the Jeep to put its bow inward again. The braking force threw them against the seatbacks rather than forward toward the windscreen. He unslung his subma-chine gun and glanced to the right, toward where the commo-tion was occurring.

The Buinites had rolled a mass of brush into a fascine four meters in diameter and twenty meters across. The crude con-struction rocked across the landscape like a bad clockwork toy. Powergun bolts lit the face of it, shattering stems without penetrating.

When green, the local vegetation didn't burn hot enough to sustain combustion. Veils of dirty smoke swathed the fascine, but the autochthones protected behind it continued to advance the cylinder unhindered.

Ten Buinites trotted toward the knoll. Deke and Toll War-son opened fire from beside Ned and Lissea. Their single aimed shots cracked as quickly as those of an automatic weapon.

"Don't shoot, you bastards!" Lissea screamed.

Autochthones spun in cyan flashes. The survivors dropped to cover.

A Buinite jumped upright. He was a hundred meters away. Lissea's device hummed, bathing the autochthone and a one-hundred-twenty-degree swathe of the landscape in pulsing light.

The creature's whole body snapped forward like the arm of a ballista. The Warsons fired together. The autochthone's head and upper thorax gouted blood and fierce blue light, disintegrating under twin megajoule impacts.

"Don't—" Lissea said as she thumbed a dial to a higher setting. Three more Buinites stood, arched, and blew apart as the device in the captain's arms hummed uselessly. The last of the creatures died with four bolts from Ned's submachine gun flashing across the gray chest.

All the Buinites were down, but more rushed from concealment. They'd reacted instantly to the *Swift*'s arrival. Their speed and organization was remarkable, even granting the previous shipwreck had concentrated them only a klick away.

Lissea adjusted the frequency of her device again. The Warsons waited, and Ned waited. Heat waves trembled above the iridium barrels of their powerguns.

The Buinite fascine staggered under the impact of four rocket shells from the Racontid's launcher. The cylinder, brush bound with branches, ruptured and spread like a jellyfish cast onto hot sand.

Powergun bolts released their energy on the first solid object they intersected. They could only claw the outside of the fascine. Raff had adjusted the fusing to burst the warheads of his projectile weapon a tenth of a second after impact. The charges went off deep inside the tight-wrapped brushwood, ripping it apart from within.

There were at least forty autochthones behind the fascine, protected by the cylinder's bulk as they pushed it toward the vessel. Crumpled, the loosened pile still provided cover from ground level, but the men atop the *Swift* had a better angle.

The tribarrel ripped a bloody swath through the Buinites. As survivors rose to scamper away, individual marksmen knocked them down with stark flashes.

An autochthone threw a rock more than one hundred fifty meters to the knoll. The missile thumped down in a cloud of ash between the two Jeeps.

Then a group of a dozen or so approached by short rushes, two or three moving at a time. As each team lurched forward, occasionally dabbing their hands down as they moved, the rest crouched and waited. The Buinites were obviously preparing to loose a shower of stones together while the gunmen focused on the party making the rush.

A Buinite cocked his arm back.

"Next one's *mine,* ma'am!" Deke Warson cried.

Lissea triggered her device on the new setting. The Buinite preparing to throw and his crouching fellows all collapsed limply as if shot through the brain stem. The three running autochthones weren't affected. They hunched as they scampered, so they hadn't been looking in the direction of the device.

Lissea held her finger down. The runners flopped to cover, peered upward, and sprawled mindlessly in turn.

"Go!" Lissea ordered as Ned shifted power to his fans.

"Yee-*ha!*" Deke Warson cried as he did the same, guiding the yoke with his knees while he kept the powergun's shimmering muzzle aimed toward the fallen Buinites. He'd have to take the controls normally in a moment . . . or maybe he wouldn't—the Warsons were good, *everybody* aboard the *Swift* was good, incredibly good at what they did.

By itself, that would just have increased the cost the autochthones incurred when they—crushed, buried, destroyed—the *Swift*. Lissea's nerve scrambler emitted a pattern of light on the critical frequency on which the Buinites' central nervous system operated.

The scrambler's broad-angle effect would not be enough to stop such dedicated creatures either. In a short time, they would find a way to overcome it.

The Jeeps bumped awkwardly across the remainder of the knoll, spitting out bits of charred brush. The downslope gave the little vehicles a gravity boost. Ned's controls felt lively for the first time since they'd gotten the Jeep operating this morning.

The wiring crew had left a gap two meters wide in front of the knoll. Harlow stood behind the self-setting post at one side of it, looking outward.

A Buinite who wasn't part of the previous squads rose from cover with a rock in his hand. Lissea swung her heavy scrambler toward him.

Toll Warson's bolt blew the autochthone's arm off. The limb, still gripping its fistful of basalt, spun in one direction while the torso contra-rotated more slowly in the other. A splash of greenish, copper-based blood dissipated in the air between them.

"We've got enough down now," Lissea muttered to Ned. "If they'll stay down."

"So far, so good," Ned said as he lunged back. He used his weight as well as the nacelle angle to help the Jeep clear a jut of harder rock running unexpectedly above the scree to either side.

"It took me three *tries* to get the frequency!" Lissea said. "*A* frequency. It may not give us ten minutes; they may be hopping up right when we get to them!"

"Then we'll put them down again, won't we?" Ned said, guiding the Jeep around the stump of a tree, blown apart in smoldering needles where a plasma bolt had struck it. The first of the catatonic autochthones lay just beyond. The others of the creature's—squad? family?—sprawled back over a distance of fifty meters.

"Jump!" Ned ordered as he slowed. "I'll take the other end!"

They hadn't discussed procedures at this stage, because they hadn't known how the comatose victims would be arrayed. Lissea didn't argue: Ned was right, Ned was driving, and anyway, there was no time to argue.

She rolled out of the vehicle, dropping the scrambler onto the seat as she left it. She managed to keep her feet despite the Jeep's forward motion.

Ned accelerated again toward the middle of the straggling line.

Two more fascines rolled toward the *Swift* from opposite sides of the perimeter. The rocket gun hammered again. Raff was beside the tribarrel on top of the vessel now, so that he could swing his rocket gun in any direction.

The mortar, set up near the *Swift*'s ramp, fired a ranging shot. Using the high-angle weapon hadn't been part of the plan, but the crew hadn't expected the autochthones to concentrate and to deploy siege equipment so quickly. Pretechnological, *hell!* If the Buinites were hunter-gatherers, it was because they wanted to be hunter-gatherers.

And the *Swift* would leave them to run their planet the way they wanted to; but first the crew needed water and a break, and that meant discussions with the Buinites on the terms that the Buinites understood.

Two mortar shells burst with pops rather than bangs, ejecting submunitions to cover a wider area than individual blasts could do.

A moment later, the bomblets detonated with a sound like the snarl of a huge cat. If Tadziki had placed his rounds correctly, the autochthones behind one or both the fascines were now flayed corpses.

Killing them wasn't enough unless every male autochthone on the planet could be killed. Killing and the nerve scrambler were only the preliminary parts of Captain Doormann's plan. Lissea was just as good at *her* job as the men she commanded were at theirs.

Ned stopped the Jeep by venting the plenum chamber while the fans continued to run. He jumped out, leaving the vehicle howling. Shutting down would save power, but battery life wasn't likely to be a problem. Ned might not have a lot of time to spin the fans up to operating speed when he wanted to leave.

He wanted to leave now, but he had a job to do.

The submachine gun banged against his breastplate. He ignored it: the Warsons were providing cover. Ned drew the knife from the sheath outside his right boot and knelt beside a Buinite.

The creature lay on its back. Its mouth gaped. Oils blasted from the vegetation by powergun bolts had a strong, spicy odor. Perhaps that was why Ned's eyes started to water.

The Buinite's muscles were lax. Ned spread the short legs apart and went in with the knife, following his instructions precisely. A bone held the penis semierect at all times. The gonads were internal, but they bulged the flesh of the buttocks obviously. The scales there were white and finer than the mottled gray which covered other parts of the autochthone's body.

The knife was a weapon, not a tool. Its straight, twenty-centimeter blade was double-edged and narrow; not ideal for gelding, but it served well enough.

Ned stabbed, twisted as if he were coring an apple, and pulled the knife away. The ugly gouge filled with blood smearing over the lips of the cut. The excised organs hung by tags of skin. The Buinite remained flaccid, breathing in shallow gusts through its open mouth.

Ned ran to the next victim. If this were a commercial operation rather than punishment and a warning, he would have some means of cauterizing the terrible wounds. The fighting knife was razor-sharp, with an edge of collapsed matter which would stay sharp despite brutal use. It severed the arteries so cleanly that the cut ends shrank closed, leaking relatively little blood.

Not perfect, but good enough. Ned stabbed, twisted, and moved on. The third Buinite slicked nictitating membranes sideways across its eyes as the knife slipped in. The scrambler's effects were beginning to wear off.

Another victim, this one humped on his face. The limbs splayed as Ned tried to operate from behind, so the knife cut an accidental collop from the autochthone's thigh. Ned botched the job, leaving the parts still attached but so hideously mutilated that they would never heal normally. He wondered if microorganisms on Buin carried the equivalent of gangrene.

The autochthones were beginning to move. One of those Lissea had gelded moaned loudly.

Ned's right boot slipped on a stone because the sole was bloody. His arms were sticky green to the elbows. His knife stabbed and turned, this time completing the operation perfectly even though the Buinite tried to rise to its hands and knees while he cut.

Ned wished he were dead rather than doing this.

The next autochthone turned its head as he approached. The creature's eyes were still mindless.

Guns fired. The tribarrel swept very close and the Warsons let off aimed shots as steady as metronome strokes. A bolt struck an active Buinite so close by that its body fluids sprayed Ned.

Ned wished he were dead, but he had a job to do. He knocked the autochthone unconscious with the butt of his knife, then used the point and edge with practiced skill before he got up; there were no more victims to be mutilated and he hurled the knife into the brush with as much strength as his arm retained.

"Ned, come on for the *Lord's* sake!" someone was shouting—Lissea, as she struggled to lift the nerve scrambler with hands as bloody as Ned's own. He ran for the Jeep thirty meters away.

Toll Warson stood on the seat of the other vehicle. He aimed at Ned and bellowed, "Ge' *down!*"

Ned dropped, twisting his face back. He saw an autochthone standing by the body of his mutilated fellow. The stone the creature had already thrown exploded in a cyan dazzle because Toll had shot the missile first. The second bolt, quick as a finger twitch, hit the base of the Buinite's neck and blew the head off in a high arc that looked like a planned effect.

Maybe it was. Toll was very good, and Ned Slade was good enough to have done his job without the slightest hesitation because he had his orders and it had to be done.

Ned got into the Jeep and slammed the vents closed. The Buinites' blood was tacky, so his hands wouldn't slip on the controls. He spun the vehicle. Lissea was saying something, mumbling. He couldn't understand her and he didn't much care whether the words were directed to him.

Harlow had already withdrawn. Two Buinites lay outside the wire, shot dead, and three others hung on the gossamer. The limbs in contact were burned to husks of carbon by the amperage which coursed through the net's seeming delicacy. Ned drove past. He was controlling his speed carefully. If he let instinct slam the yoke to the dash, the Jeep would pogo on the rough terrain and lower the actual speed over distance.

He skirted the knoll. They didn't need to look for anything; they'd seen and done all that was required. The Warsons followed, Toll facing the rear and his brother driving with one hand while the other held his 2-cm weapon ready.

Deke fired once, shattering a stump that could have been an

indig but wasn't. He hit it squarely though the bolt snapped close past the lead Jeep in order to find the target.

Huge hollow explosions hammered the air from the other side of the vessel. The crew had set a thin belt of directional mines midway between the *Swift* and the wire to gain additional time for the withdrawal. The mines were going off now, blasting cones of shot outward toward the Buinites.

Ned had hoped—they'd all hoped—that the shock of mangled bodies would cause later waves of autochthones to pause. Nobody who'd seen the Buinites in action still believed that was a realistic likelihood. It was going to be close, one way or the other.

The *Swift* quivered on its lift engines. Two men carried a third into the vessel while six or eight mercenaries fired from the hatchway. More directional mines detonated, a multiple stroke like thunder glancing from all the sides of heaven.

"Drive straight aboard!" Lissea cried, twisting backward in her seat with her powergun gripped in her bloody hands. She didn't fire—the other Jeep was right behind them.

Ned didn't back off the throttle until his skirts brushed the ramp; *judging* the slope would brake them enough to keep control. He popped the vents and let inertia fling them into the bay as the skirts sagged with a great sigh.

Ned hadn't thought there was enough room for the Jeep, but there was—barely. Hands gripped him and yanked him out of the vehicle, out of the way. His boots tangled with the Jeep's sidepanel and he flopped clumsily in the aisle, on top of the reeking mortar tube.

The interior was a chaos of men and weapons. The tribarrel lay across somebody's bunk. The shimmering barrels had cooled themselves by melting the synthetic bedding into a cocoon about the iridium. It would take hours to chip and polish the gunk out of the workings so that the weapon could function again.

"Leave it!" Lissea screamed from the hatchway as Deke Warson drove the other Jeep up the ramp. "Leave it!"

Men were firing past the brothers. Ned could see Buinites running from the shelter of trees, rocks in their hands. He tried to clear his submachine gun but the sling caught in the mortar's elevating screw.

The Warsons jumped from either side of their vehicle as though they were making a combat drop. *"Leave—"* Lissea cried, but they grabbed handholds meant for two men per side and lifted the Jeep with the fans still howling in the nacelles.

Josie Paetz fired his pistol. A stone slammed Toll in the back, ricocheting upward from his body armor and taking his helmet off. He grunted, then regained his balance. The Warsons threw their Jeep on top of Lissea's, trusting everybody else to get out of the way in time or take the consequences.

Rocks clanged on the *Swift*'s hull. She was already lifting with a tremendous roar: cargo blisters open, ramp down, and Moiseyev—his right cheek bruised and bloody—gripping Deke Warson's arm, the only thing keeping the big mercenary from tumbling out as a final missile dropped onto the surface of Buin.

Despite the windrush and buffeting, the hatch closed in ninety seconds. That was nearly up to the best speed the hydraulic jacks could have managed ahead of a normal liftoff. The bay was thunderous hell as Westerbeke carried out his instructions: one low orbit and back to the point of departure.

Ned stood still-faced beside somebody's bunk. He'd washed the blood from his skin though not his memory. Lissea was near the ramp. They'd cleared the hatchway by hauling the Jeeps down the aisles on their sides. The heavy weaponry that should have been stowed in the external blisters with the vehicles lay on bunks. Nobody was pretending to bother with normal landing procedures on this one.

Ned gripped the bedframe as though his hands were cast around it. Hatton chortled something to him, looked at the younger man's face, and began talking to Yazov instead.

They couldn't go any distance from Buin like this. Even if the water held out, the weeks of Transit and recalibration before the *Swift* reached Pancahte would drive everybody aboard mad. At worst they'd have to touch down to hurl out the Jeeps and heavy equipment if there wasn't time to stow the gear properly.

"Captain, there's movement at the site," Westerbeke warned. *"There's indigs all over the ground where we landed the first time! Over."*

"Set down on the knoll," Lissea ordered. *"Be ready to make a touch-and-go if we need to. Out."*

"The locals'll ring us if they've got a problem," one of the mercenaries shouted. Other men laughed. Either they were genuinely unconcerned that the rocks clanging against the hull would smash an engine nozzle, or they were determined to give a carefree impression.

Ned latched his faceshield down and thumbed the rotary switch on the lower edge till it gave him visuals from the navigational console. He normally didn't like to do that because when the visor was opaque to the outside world, it made him feel as if he were trapped in somebody's fantasy.

Right now, he could use fantasy.

The directional mines had blown great wedges out of the landscape so that the *Swift*'s former landing site seemed ringed by pointers. Smoke drifted downwind from one of the abandoned fascines. Tadziki had fired a charger of incendiary shells from the mortar. He hoped that the flames would prevent fresh autochthones from replacing the team pushing the fascine, as would happen if he'd used normal antipersonnel bomblets.

Buinites were all over the site, like bees preparing to swarm. In pairs and quartets they carried away the bodies of fellows who'd been killed while attacking the *Swift*. The fenceline, still deadly despite the scores of victims it had claimed, was buried under a mound of brush—further proof that the autochthones could respond effectively to the starfarers' technology.

The vessel roared with braking effort as it settled toward the knoll. Buinites turned their long-jawed faces upward to watch.

"Adjutant to crew," Tadziki said. *"I won't—repeat, will*

not—open the ramp until I'm sure we're staying, so don't be in a hurry. Out.''

Scattering rocks, ash, and brushwood, the *Swift* landed where Ned and Lissea had waited for their victims to come to them. The knoll wasn't big enough for the vessel's length: bow, stern, and even the tips of the landing skids overhung the outcrop.

Tadziki, at the backup console, set the visuals to magnify two autochthones carrying a headless corpse, and behind them, a third living Buinite with a smashed arm. The injury was the result of a mine blast, not a powergun's concentrated hellfire. The creatures stared at the *Swift*. Their eyes quivered as the vessel shuddered to stasis with the ground.

Moving with the unified precision of a flock of birds, the three living Buinites turned and loped off through the brush. The corpse lay where it fell. The wounded autochthone spurned the body with his clawed foot as he ran.

Tadziki pulled back on the image area. Buinites fled the *Swift*'s return on all sides. They ran *away* rather than toward anything: every figure in the sensors' quick panorama was vectored directly outward from the vessel, like chaff driven by a bomb's shockwave. The autochthones threw down whatever they'd been holding in the moments before they recognized the *Swift* as the same vessel that had landed an hour and a half before.

Those who were missing a leg hopped. Those who had lost both legs dragged themselves by hands and elbows. *Away.*

Westerbeke shut the engines off. Hissing gases and the ping of metal parts filled the *Swift* with their relative silence.

''Master Tadziki,'' Lissea said, *''you may open the hatch. I believe the locals have decided to leave us alone from here on out.''*

Tadziki didn't hit the hatch switch instantly. *''Adjutant to crew,''* he ordered, using the PA system rather than radio. *''Starboard watch stays with the ship to clear and stow cargo. Toll, you're in charge. Out.''*

The ramp began to whine open. Lissea turned in the hatchway and called, ''Don't stow the Jeeps. We'll need them to check out the people from that other ship. Are we still getting calls from them?''

Westerbeke peered past the back of his couch. ''Negative,'' he said. ''Nothing since they reported they were leaving the wreck.''

''Well, maybe they abandoned the commo gear for its weight,'' Lissea said. She hopped gracefully through the hatch ahead of the mercenaries.

They might well have pushed her if she'd delayed much longer. Nobody wanted to be trapped within the vessel's bay in its present condition.

Ned was the last of the port watch to disembark. The duty crew had already begun to clear the bay of damaged and temporarily stored equipment. One bunk was ruined. The sooner the stink of its melted bedding was removed from the closed atmosphere, the better for the *Swift*'s complement.

Lissea walked downslope to where the autochthones were gelded. Herne Lordling was beside her, ordering her to be more careful. Several other mercs accompanied them with fingers on their triggers. Ned fell in behind them.

Tadziki was still aboard, keeping watch on the surrounding terrain. It was difficult to see any distance in this flat, brush-speckled landscape, but the *Swift*'s sensor suite could identify individual Buinites up to a kilometer away. The party would meet no hidden threats.

Ned's eyes felt hot and gritty, and his skin prickled. He didn't remember these trees with yellow seedpods among their thorns, but the whorls of lighter soil indicated the Jeeps' air cushions had swept the rocks here.

The leaders came to the nearest of the mutilated victims. He—*it*—was alive and sitting up. The stone he'd been carrying when the scrambler anesthetized him lay at the creature's side, but there was no sign of intelligence in the dull eyes.

''Bloody hell, Lissea!'' Lordling said with what was, for him, restraint. ''Not a very neat piece of work, was it?''

''It did the job, Herne,'' Lissea replied in a brittle voice. ''I said I would do what was necessary to make the autochthones leave us alone while we restocked and rested.''

''It wouldn't have done any good to neuter them with a jolt of radiation, Lordling,'' Ned said. He'd heard other men speak in the tone he was using now, but he'd never imagined he would join their number. ''We didn't dare be neat. They had to know instantly that they'd been emasculated, that any of them who fought *us* would either die or be emasculated.''

''They don't mind dying,'' Lissea said. ''That we knew. But they couldn't be sure.''

She walked on. The mercs following her skirted the first victim gingerly, staring with sick fascination at the creature's bloody groin. The Buinite had no expression at all; nor did Ned as he brushed past.

The second Buinite was dead—not from the knife wound or from shock, but because the creature had begun to chew off its limbs when it awakened. Its powerful teeth had crushed through both arms at the elbow joint and were working on the right knee when blood loss accomplished the desired purpose.

''I think we've seen enough,'' Lissea said. She turned and started back toward the *Swift* without seeming to look at her companions. ''Slade, take the Jeeps and three men. See what you can learn about the castaways. Tadziki will download navigational data to your helmet.''

''Yes ma'am.'' He'd take Raff, and the Warsons would drive. *Good men to have at your back in a tight place . . .*

Herne Lordling's lips pursed. He glanced at Ned, then side-long back toward Lissea. ''The locals may not have run far,'' he said. ''There could be an ambush.''

''I figured to carry the scrambler myself,'' Ned said before Lissea could speak. ''And I'll replace the knife I lost. We'll be all right.''

The look on Lordling's face as he stared at Ned was one of pure loathing. That was fair enough, because it only mirrored the way Ned felt about himself.

But he would do what had to be done.

* * *

"Think your little toy's going to scare all the locals away from us, then?" Deke Warson asked as he guided the lead Jeep expertly with his left hand alone. He held the butt of his 2-cm weapon against the crook of his right elbow instead of trusting it to the sling or the clamp beside his seat.

"No," Ned said. "It was for use in case the *Swift* herself didn't scare them out of our way. As she fortunately seems to have done."

Each Jeep left behind it a plume of dust high enough to call autochthones from klicks distant if they wanted to come. Behind Ned, Toll kept the second vehicle slightly to port, the upwind side, instead of tracking his brother precisely.

"Via, boy," Deke said. "I swapped barrels on the old girl here"—the muzzle of his weapon nodded—"and I'm ready for a little action."

Some of the trees rose from ten or a dozen separate trunks, individually no more than wrist-thick, on a common root system. Often the lower branches appeared to have been browsed off so that the surviving foliage formed a bell like the cap of a mushroom. Ned knew nothing about local life-forms except for the Buinites themselves.

"Deke," he said, "you're welcome to all the kind of action Lissea and I had on the first touchdown. If the locals come round again, we'll be reinforcing that lesson the same way."

Ned's submachine gun was slung. The nerve scrambler filled his arms, and he was using the lower half of his visor as a remote display for the *Swift*'s sensors. He wanted all the warning he could get if there were autochthones in their neighborhood.

Warson chuckled. "It's not like they're human, boy," he said. "Even if they was, what happens to the other guy don't matter."

They passed a fresh cairn at the base of a thorn-spiked tree. The stones in this region of Buin oxidized to a purplish color when exposed to air for a time, but the undersides remained yellow-gray. The cairn melded the colors into a soft pattern like that of a rag rug.

"We're on the right track," Deke said, pointing.

"A local marker?" Ned asked. The drivers were navigating by means of a map projected onto their visors, a twenty-percent mask through which they could view the actual terrain. Under other circumstances, Ned would have checked the heading, but he had to concentrate on the autochthones—

And the chance of Deke Warson getting lost because he misread a chart wasn't worth worrying about.

"Naw, I figure there's some poor turd from the wreck smashed to jelly down there," Deke said. "The locals, they don't do a job halfway."

There was approval in his voice.

"*Rescue party?*" said a voice on Channel 12. That wasn't a push the expedition normally used, but the commo helmet scanned all available frequencies and cued the transmission. "*We see your dust. Are you a rescue party? We are the survivors of yacht* Blaze. *Ah, over?*"

Half a klick away, basalt in the form of hexagonal pillars cropped out ten to twenty meters high above the scrub. Broken columns lay jumbled below. Sunlight reflected from the pinnacle, a space of no more than a hundred square meters.

"*Telarian vessel* Swift *to survivors,*" Ned replied. "*Yes, we're a rescue party, but we're not going up there to meet you. Come on down. The locals have cleared out. Over.*"

"How'd they get up there to begin with?" Deke said.

Ned cranked his visor to plus-six magnification. The angle wasn't very good. Three human figures waved furiously toward the Jeeps.

"Looks like an aircar," he said. "Pull up here. If we get any closer to the rocks, we won't be able to see the people."

"*Rescue party, are you sure the nonhumans are gone?*" the voice asked. "*Our car has been damaged and we won't be able to get back to safety again.*" A pause. "*Over.*"

"We're here, aren't we?" Deke Warson interjected. "*Come on, buddy. If you don't want to spend the rest of your lives on a rock spike, you better come down and let us escort you to the ship. Fucking out.*"

He looked at Ned and grinned through the faint haze of topo map on his visor. "Somebody scared like that, don't screw around with them. Slap 'em up alongside the head if you're close enough, or anyway don't give them a choice.''

The grin became broader. "Or we could just leave them," he added. "It's not like we've got a lot of extra room about the *Swift*.''

"Blaze *to rescue party*,'' the voice said. *"We're coming down. Out.''*

Ned cleared his visor to watch without magnification or a clutter of overlays. The figures got into the aircar. The vehicle lurched over the edge with only marginal control. The lower surfaces had been hammered by thrown rocks. One of the four nacelles—providing enough power for the car to fly rather than merely skim in ground effect—had been smashed out of its housing.

"Five to three they don't make it!" Toll called from the second Jeep.

"You're on in Telarian tellers!" Deke called back.

The car did make it, though it rotated twice on its vertical axis before the driver brought it to a skidding halt in front of the Jeeps. The occupants were male. One of them had his left arm bound to his chest by bandages torn from what had been the tunic of his white uniform. The survivors carried carbines, but they didn't look as though they were practiced gunmen.

The aircar's driver got out. Ned swung from the Jeep to meet him. The stranger was young, with dark hair and a large, gangling frame. Instead of a uniform, he wore a robe that billowed freely when he moved but tailored itself to his body when he was at rest.

"I'm Carron Del Vore," he said, extending his hand to Ned. "I—we—we're very glad to see you. More glad than I can say.''

He looked worn to the bone. Nobody had bothered to inform the castaways of Lissea's plan before the *Swift* lifted off again. They must have felt as though their guts were being dragged up to orbit on the same vapor trail.

"Edward Slade," Ned said. "Ned. I believe you sailed out of Pancahte?''

Carron smiled wryly. "Yes, we're from Pancahte,'' he

said. "As a matter of fact, my father is Treasurer Lon Del Vore."

When he saw that the term and name meant nothing to Ned, he added, "That is, he's the ruler of the planet."

Buin's atmosphere was clear, so the stars gleamed from it like the lights of plankton feeding at night in one of Tethys' crystal atolls. In the background, the *Swift*'s drill sighed softly as it cut its way to a deep aquifer.

"Yes, certainly Lendell Doormann came to Pancahte," said Carron Del Vore. "I've seen him myself, when I was very young. Walking into Astragal, up the old road from Hammerhead Lake to talk to my grandfather."

The crew had spread a tarpaulin of monomolecular film from the *Swift* as shelter, though there seemed no threat of rain. The thin sheet hazed but did not hide the stars when Ned looked up through it.

They'd replaced the wire perimeter and directional mines as well. Buin wasn't a place to take chances.

"Maybe he's still alive," Carron said. "Though . . . it isn't clear that he was ever present *physically.*"

The Pancahtan noble sat on the ramp. Lissea and Herne Lordling knelt before him, and the remainder of the *Swift*'s complement lounged on the ground further back to listen. The mercenaries were interested not only because this was a break from the boredom of Transit, but also because Carron was speaking about Pancahte, the expedition's goal.

One of the yacht's other survivors was present for the company. The third lay anesthetized on a bunk while the vessel's medical computer repaired injuries from the rock that had broken his arm and several ribs.

A stone had dished in the skull of the last of the common sailors who'd escaped with Carron in the aircar. As Deke surmised, his body was beneath the fresh cairn.

Ned squatted at the rear of the gathering, beyond the edge of the tarp. He felt alone, dissociated even from himself. Part of his soul refused to believe that he was the person who had

gelded Buinite warriors and who was coldly prepared to repeat the process if the needs of the expedition required.

"Present on Pancahte?" Lissea asked.

Tadziki knelt down beside Ned in the clear darkness. Insects or the equivalent burred around the light, but none of the
local forms seemed disposed to regard humans as a food
source. "Good work today, Ned," the adjutant murmured.

"No, in the Treasurer's Palace, I mean," Carron explained.
"Lendell Doormann seemed to walk normally, but his feet
weren't always quite on the ground. A little above or below,
especially when the footing was irregular. Nobody mentioned
it, at least in my hearing. Perhaps my grandfather knew more;
he and Lendell often talked privately. But my grandfather
died twenty years ago, and Lendell appeared for the last time
months before that."

"But the ship that Lendell arrived in," Lordling said, "is
that still around? That's what we've come for."

"Thanks," Ned whispered to Tadziki. "I wish I felt better
about it, though."

"When you start feeling good about that sort of duty,"
Tadziki said, "I won't want to know you. But it had to be
done."

"Is it a ship?" Carron said. "We always called it 'the capsule.' It's a tiny little thing, scarcely more than a coffin. Yes,
it's still there. Not that anyone really sees it, except through
long lenses. You see, the area five kilometers around Hammerhead Lake in all directions is patrolled by tanks. Two of
them. They don't let anyone any closer than that."

Several men spoke at once. Lissea touched the key on the
side of her commo helmet and murmured something to
Dewey, on duty at the console. An air-projection hologram
bloomed above the Pancahtan's head. Details were less sharp
than those of an image on a proper screen, but the display was
big enough that everyone present could see it.

Carron looked up. "Yes, that's one of the tanks," he said.
"They were on Pancahte before the settlers landed there five
hundred years ago—that's standard years. There are other artifacts from that time, too. I was on my way to Affray to see

whether there are any leavings from the . . . the earlier race there, or whether Pancahte is unique."

Tadziki leaned close to Ned and said, "He had quite a library with him. Lissea converted one of our readers to project the chips."

"He might better have grabbed another box of ammo when he ditched from the yacht," Ned whispered back.

As he spoke, however, he knew he was wrong. The Pancahtan castaways couldn't have survived more than a few hours had the *Swift* not rescued them. A few hundred rounds more or less wouldn't have made any difference. Carron was a scholar, and he had chosen to save his research materials rather than leaving them to be flattened beneath the hammering stone weapons of the autochthones.

"Looks man-made to me," Lordling said. "*How* old do you claim it is?"

"Older than the colony," Carron repeated. "More than five hundred standard years."

"Balls," said Lordling. "Pancahte was a first-dispersion colony, right after human learned to use Transit space. Nobody sneaked in there first and left a couple tanks."

"Parallel evolution works with machines as well as with life-forms, Herne," Lissea said. "Until the laws of physics change, equipment that does the same job is likely to look pretty much the same."

"It's not just the tanks," Carron said without apparent anger. "There are structures on the near peninsula of Hammerhead Lake that are equally old."

Lissea handed him a control wand. Carron twitched it, displayed an index, and summoned an image that seemed to be from an orbital camera. Though the Telarian equipment was unfamiliar at least in detail, Carron used it with the skill of an expert.

The map first established scale by including a community of ten thousand or so residents at the bottom of the image. At the top of the frame was a sparkle of water more than a kilometer through the long axis. It was clearly artificial, consisting of two perfectly circular lobes joined by a narrow band of water.

"Below is Astragal," Carron said. "That's the capital of Pancahte. And this—"

The image focused on the body of water. Scores of other pools and lakes dotted the landscape, but none were so large or so regular in outline.

"—is Hammerhead Lake."

A pair of pentagonal structures stood on the lower peninsula. Fat spits of land almost joined to separate the lake into two round ponds. As the scale shrank, Ned used shadows to give the buildings a third dimension. They were low and had inner courtyards of the same five-sided shape. One building was slightly larger than the other, but even so it was only twenty meters or so across.

"What are those pentagons?" Lissea asked.

"Nobody knows," Carron replied. "Nobody can inspect them because of the tanks. They shoot at aircraft as well as ground vehicles. These images were made from orbit."

"I don't see why," Deke Warson said, "if these tanks are so much in your way, that nobody's done something about them. I might volunteer for the job myself, if we're going to be there on Pancahte a while."

"They aren't particularly in the way, sir," Carron said. He continued to lower the scale of the display. One of the pentagonal buildings swelled and would soon fill the image area.

Deke's voice was thick with the sneering superiority of an expert speaking to someone who hadn't dealt with a problem the expert viewed as simple. Carron Del Vore responded with an aristocrat's clipped disdain for a member of the lower classes who was getting uppity. That was an aspect of the Pancahtan's character which Ned hadn't seen before.

Toll Warson grinned at his brother. It was hard to tell just what his expression meant.

"There," Carron said, pleasantly informative again. "In the center of the courtyard."

He played with the control wand for a moment. A red caret sprang into the center of the holographic image and blipped toward a round object. "This is the capsule which brought Lendell Doormann to Pancahte. It isn't really big enough for a ship, is it? And it certainly couldn't hold enough food and water for the fifty years he visited Astragal, but he never took anything while he was with us."

Men looked at one another. Nobody spoke for a time.

"I want to see that tank again," Deke said in a colorless voice.

"Yes, all right," Lissea said. "If you would, Master Del Vore?"

"Of course," he replied. "But I would prefer to be called Carron by one of your rank, mistress."

The display flipped back in three quick stages to a close-up of the tank. The vehicle was low-slung. It had a turret and a single slim weapon almost as long as the chassis. No antennas, sensors, or other excrescences beyond the weapon marred the smoothly curving lines.

There was no evident drive mechanism. The hull seemed to glide a few centimeters above the ground. Where the terrain was sandy, the vehicle left whorls on the surface as it passed, but the weight wasn't supported by an air cushion as were the supertanks on which Ned had trained.

"What kind of armor does that have?" somebody demanded. Ned's mouth was already open to ask the same question.

"We don't know," Carron said. "Neither projectile nor directed energy weapons have any effect on the tanks. I should rather say, no effect save to stir the tanks up. When they're attacked, they respond by destroying all artificial devices within their line of sight—rather than limiting themselves to their normal radius. That means among other things that they knock down all communications satellites serving the capital."

"What's its power source?" somebody asked. "Five hundred years is a lot of power."

Simultaneously, Lissea said, "Do you know how the gun operates? It's an energy weapon, I presume?"

"This was recorded a century ago, when a member of the

Treasurer's Guard decided to prove he was a better man than his rival for the same woman," Carron said. "We don't have satellite views, for obvious reasons."

The image had been recorded at night, from ground level. Buildings in the foreground suggested it had been taken from Astragal itself. There was a great deal of ground fog.

A ribbon of light wavered across the sky. It seemed smoky and insubstantial. "The discharge," Carron explained, "if that's what it was, didn't give off energy. What you're seeing is a reflection of external sources, stars and the lights of Astragal itself."

"Reflection in the *air?*" said Herne Lordling.

"No," Carron said. "The effect occurred in hard vacuum as well. At the far end of the beam, a communications satellite vanished into itself. That's as accurate as anyone was able to describe the result."

He surveyed the mercenaries, a sea of faces lit gray by scatter from the hologram display. "And no," he added, "we don't have any idea what the vehicles use as a power source. Only that it seems inexhaustible."

"We . . ." Lissea said. "Ah, as Herne said a moment ago"—

And had no business saying, but what was done, was done—

"We've come to retrieve the device by which my great-granduncle traveled to Pancahte. It wasn't his to take away the way he did. I've been sent to your planet by the proper owners in order to retrieve it."

"I don't see that that's possible," Carron said. "Because of the tanks, of course. But I don't really see my father approving a . . . ah, strangers coming to Pancahte and taking something."

"It's no bloody use to him, is it?" Deke Warson said.

"I'm afraid that Lon's attitude is if something is valuable to anyone, it's valuable to him," Carron said. "He's not a charitable man. Nor a kindly one."

Lissea cleared her throat. The streak of frozen destruction in the screen above her was a stark prop. "Perhaps," she said, "he'll be moved to a friendlier state of mind by the fact we've rescued his son and heir."

"What?" Carron said. "Oh, I'm not his heir. That's my brother Ayven. Frankly, I doubt that even Ayven's life would affect my father's actions very much, and I don't know that Ayven would want it any other way. They're very much alike—hard-handed men both of them."

He touched the display control and projected instead a landscape of fog and bright, glowing streaks of lava. The view was twilit, though Ned realized after a moment that the point of light at zenith was the system's sun.

Much of the sky was filled with the great ruddy arc of a planet. Pancahte was the moon of a gas giant rather than a planet in solar orbit. The regular shapes in the middle distance were buildings, or at least man-made objects.

"Madame Captain, gentlemen . . ." Carron said. "Meeting you was a great day for a person of my interests. On Pancahte, there's very little interest in artifacts of the Old Race. Not among the general populace, and certainly not within my family."

"You'll help us with your father?" Lissea asked.

"Well," Carron said. "I'm sure I can show you the collection of Old Race artifacts in the Treasurer's Palace. The only collection on Pancahte, really. I doubt if anyone but me has viewed it in my lifetime. And a few kilometers from Astragal, there's a dwelling of some sort, a bunker, that I believe was built by the Old Race. I'll take you there. It isn't dangerous, the way the tanks are dangerous."

"What do you expect in exchange for helping us?" Herne Lordling demanded harshly.

"Herne," Lissea said.

"Besides expecting you to save my life again at some future date, you mean?" Carron said ironically. "All right, then."

He stood up. He gestured with the wand, flicking off the display so that it didn't detract attention from him.

"Note that all my life I've worked to understand the artifacts of the Old Race," Carron said, arms akimbo. He was a handsome man in his way, though in the company of these killers he looked like a plaster cherub. "Note, *sir,* that my present journey was to Affray, to see whether the Twin Worlds have Old Race vestiges also."

"Look, buddy," Herne Lordling said. "Don't use that tone with *me.*" He started to rise. Lissea gripped his biceps firmly and held him down.

"You asked the question, Lordling," said Deke Warson. "Hear him out."

"Note," Carron continued in a ringing voice, "that if you are able to avoid or deactivate the Old Race tanks I will gain information about them that no one in five centuries has had. So it's purely out of self-interest that I'm willing to help you, sir. You can rest easy on that score."

The Warson brothers started the laughter, but much of the company immediately joined in.

"On the other hand," Carron said, lapsing into what seemed to be his normal manner, that of a subordinate briefing superiors, "I can't offer you much hope of being allowed to remove the capsule or even being allowed to try. My father simply wouldn't permit that. He's quite capable of killing me out of hand if he feels I'm pressing him excessivly."

Lissea stood up. "I'll want to discuss the situation on Pancahte with you in detail," she said. "We'll use the navigational consoles and their displays."

"Of course, Lissea," Carron said.

"I'll come too," said Herne Lordling. "This is military planning."

"I trust not," Lissea said, though there was little enough trust in her voice.

She stepped into the vessel's bay, between Carron and Lordling. Mercenaries stood up, brushing their elbows and trousers and stretching.

"I'd best get in there also," Tadziki said without enthusiasm. He looked at Ned and added, "It doesn't appear that we're much closer to Lissea achieving her goal than we were on Telaria."

Ned shrugged. "If I'd known what we were really getting

into,'' he said, ''I wouldn't have bet there was a snowball's chance in hell that we'd get as far as we have already.''

''If you'd known,'' Tadziki said. ''Understood, that is. Would you have still come on the expedition?''

Ned laughed. ''I suppose so,'' he said. He looked at himself in the mirror of his mind.

''The person I am *now* would have come anyway,'' he said.

Tadziki walked up the ramp to join Lissea in the nose of the vessel. Ned watched him, thinking about changes that had occurred since he'd signed aboard on Telaria. He wondered what his kin would think of him at home on Tethys.

And he wondered if he'd live long enough to get there.

Pancahte

—〰—

PANCAHTE WAS AS grim a world as Ned had ever seen. The primary's bloody light filled the sky, and the atmosphere was thick with mist and the reeking effluvia of volcanos. For all that, the temperature was in the middle of the range Ned found comfortable, and the *Swift*'s sensors said that it wasn't actively dangerous to breathe the air.

The sailor with the broken arm waited until the boarding ramp clunked solidly into the crushed stone surface of the spaceport. He took two steps forward, then ran the rest of the way and threw himself on the ground mumbling prayers.

The other Pancahtan sailor moved with the same initial hesitation. A squad of guards wearing powered body armor began to approach the *Swift*. A woman holding an infant pressed past them. She and the sailor embraced fiercely. Other civilians, mostly women, scuttled around the guards also. They stopped in frozen dismay when they realized that no more of the yacht's crewmen were disembarking from the rescue vessel.

"We radioed from orbit," Ned muttered. "Why did they have to come? They knew there wasn't going to be anything for them."

"It's no skin off our backs," Deke Warson answered, curious at the younger man's concern.

"I'd rather lose some skin," Ned said, "than be reminded about Buin."

Deke laughed.

The spaceport was designed like a pie. Blast walls divided a circle into sixty wedges, only half of which were in immediate use. The administrative buildings were in the center. Rows of rectangular structures to the south of the circular landing area contained the shops and warehouses.

The guards walked toward the *Swift* from the terminal. Their suits were bright with plating and inlays, though Ned presumed the equipment was functional also. The men's only weaponry was that which was integral with their armor.

The powered suits struck Ned as a clumsy sort of arrangement—overly complicated and hard to adapt to unexpected conditions. The armor might stop a single 2-cm bolt, but it was unlikely to protect against two—or against a well-aimed burst from Ned's submachine gun. Still, like anything else in life, proper equipment was mostly a matter of what you'd gotten used to.

Lissea stood beside Carron Del Vore in the center of the hatchway. Tadziki and Herne Lordling flanked them. The rest of the *Swift*'s complement waited behind the leaders, wearing their best uniforms and carrying only minimal armament.

The gold-helmeted leader of the guards stopped before Carron, raised his faceshield, and said, "Prince Carron, your father welcomes you on your return to Pancahte. We have transportation to the palace for you."

Carron nodded. "Very good," he said. "I'll be taking Captain Doormann, my rescuer, with me to the palace. She has business with the Treasurer."

The guard's body was hidden beneath the powered armor, but his face gave its equivalent of a shrug. "Sorry sir," the man said. "We don't have any orders about that."

Carron's jaw set fiercely. "You've got orders now," he said. "You've got my orders."

"The car won't handle the weight," another guard volunteered to his chief. Ned couldn't be sure if Pancahtan etiquette was always so loose, or whether Carron's father and brother were so public in treating him as the family idiot that the guards too had picked up the habit. "We'll have to leave Herget behind to get off the ground, like enough."

"Then two of you will stay behind!" Carron snapped. "Do you think I'm in danger of attack on my way to the palace? You—" he pointed to the man who had just spoken "—and *you*—" to the guard beside him with green-anodized diamonds decorating his suit "—stay behind! Walk back!"

The guards were obviously startled by Carron's anger—or his willingness to express it. How much did Lissea's presence have to do with what was apparently a change? "Well, I suppose . . ." the leader said.

"Captain," Carron said, offering Lissea his arm.

Lissea laid her hand in the crook of Carron's arm, but she turned to her men instead of stepping off with the Pancahtan.

"Their armor empty weighs as much as a grown man," she said. "If two of them stay behind, four of us can ride. Tadziki, Slade—come along with me. Herne, you're in charge of the ship till I get back. Break out the Jeeps, and I'll see about arranging to replenish our stores."

"Yes, of course," Carron agreed. "You should be accompanied by your chiefs. Your rank requires it."

"Hey Slade-chiefy," Deke said in a loud whisper as Ned stepped through the front rank of men, "see if your chiefness can score us something better than water to drink, hey?"

"This isn't my idea!" Ned snapped back. Except for the stares of his fellows—Herne Lordling's eyes could have drilled holes in rock—he was both pleased and proud to be chosen.

The guards fell in to either side of the contingent from the *Swift*. The powered armor moved with heavy deliberation as though the men were golems. The suits' right wrists were thickened by what Ned surmised was the magazine for the coil gun firing along the back of the palm. A laser tube on the left hand was connected to the power supply which bulged the buttocks of the suit.

"It's through there, in the admin parking area," the leader muttered, pointing. He frowned as he studied Carron, both irritated and concerned by the young prince's assertiveness. "The car, I mean."

Twenty-odd civilians watched Carron go past. Some of them were crying. A young boy tugged on a woman's waistband and repeated, "Where's daddy? Where's *daddy?*"

Ned avoided eye contact with them, the widows, orphans, and bereaved parents. He'd never seen the *Blaze,* so he had no idea how many crewman the yacht had carried. More than would ever come home, certainly.

The knife grated on bone as he cut too deeply into the Buinite's crotch. He twisted the blade—

Tadziki gripped Ned's hand. "What's wrong?" the adjutant demanded. "Why are you smiling like that?"

"Sorry," Ned muttered.

He didn't want to think that way. There were things you had to do—but if you started to justify them, you were lost to anything Ned wanted to recognize as humanity.

The port buildings were of stone construction rather than the concrete or synthetics Ned would have expected. The blocks were ashlars, square-cornered, but the outer faces had been left rough and the courses were of varied heights.

The finish and functioning of Pancahtan powered armor, and the ships docked at neighboring landings, looked to be of excellent quality, so the rusticated architecture was a matter of taste rather than ability. Ned found the juxtaposition of high technology and studied clumsiness to be unpleasant; but again, style was what you were accustomed to.

A few spectators watched from behind the rails of upper-level walkways or through the gap at the inner end of the blast walls while they took breaks. Maintenance and service trucks howled across the spaceport on normal errands. All the vehicles were hovercraft, even a heavy crane that Ned would have expected to be mounted on treads.

Ned tapped the armored shoulder of the nearest guard. The man looked at him in surprise and almost missed a step. Servo lag in the suit's driving "muscles" meant that you had to take care when changing speed or direction. The armor's massive inertia could spill you along the ground like an unguided projectile in the original direction of movement.

"Do you have wheeled vehicles?" Ned asked. "All I see are air cushions."

"Huh?" said the guard.

Carron looked back at Ned. "There's too much vulcanism and earthquakes for roads," he said. "Induced by the primary, of course."

He nodded upward toward the ruddy hugeness of the gas giant which Pancahte orbited.

"The buildings are on skids," Carron added, "with integral fusion bottles for power. Other structures—"

He gestured toward the blast walls. Ned now noticed that the repaired stretches, differing slightly in the color and surface treatment of the concrete, were more extensive than the normal frequency of landing accidents would account for.

"It's simpler to rebuild when they're knocked down."

It was easy to spot the vehicle they were headed for in the parking area. All but a handful of the forty-odd cars and light vans were hovercraft. The exceptions were a few aircars, whose lift-to-weight ratio permitted them to fly rather than merely to float on a cushion of air trapped beneath them by their skirts. Most of the latter were delicate vehicles like the one Carron had carried on his yacht.

The only exception was truck-sized and armored. The roof and sides were folded back, displaying spartan accommodations and surprisingly little carrying capacity. Most of the bulk was given over to the drive fans and the fusion powerplant that fed them.

Lissea stopped and looked at the sky, arms akimbo. "Does it ever get brighter than this?" she asked. "I mean, is this daylight?"

"Well, yes," Carron said. "It's daylight, I mean."

He looked upward also. Somewhere in the port a starship was testing its engines. A plume of steam rising from geysers at the edge of the port drifted across the parking lot, almost hiding the members of the party from one another.

Carron's voice continued, "It's really—well, it's bright enough to see by easily. The primary provides quite a lot of energy, particularly in the infrared range, so we're always comfortable on Pancahte."

"I'd think people would go mad in these conditions," Lissea said. "Even after, what, twenty, twenty-five generations?"

Carron cleared his throat. The band of steam drifted on, dispersing slowly in the red-lit air. "Well, there are social problems, I'll admit, at full primary," he said. "Suicide, domestic violence . . . Sometimes more serious outbreaks. We tend to live in communities on Pancahte rather than in isolated houses, even though most dwellings are self-sufficient."

His face was set firmly again. He crooked his finger in a peremptory fashion to Lissea and resumed walking toward the vehicle to catch up with the guards who waited two paces ahead. "Sometimes we visit, well, brighter worlds. But very few Pancahtans leave permanently. It—the world—it's our home."

Ned looked up at the primary also. The planet's mottled red appearance was no more than a mixture of methane and scores of other gases, not a promise of blood and flame. . . .

But all the male civilians he'd seen on Pancahte, workmen and lounging spectators alike, went armed. Even Carron wore a pistol, a jeweled projectile weapon scarcely larger than a needle stunner.

The knives and guns were simply parts of their dress, like the vivid neckerchiefs they affected. The choice of weapons as fashion accessories said even more about Pancahtan society than Carron's halting defense of it had done.

The guards had a quick argument among themselves at the aircar. Two of the men stepped aside.

Carron pointed to a different pair. "I said that *you* two would walk!" he said. "If you forget my orders once more, you needn't bother returning to the palace at all because you won't have a post there."

The guards glanced at one another in rekindled surprise. "Yessir," mumbled the two Carron had indicated, who weren't the ones culled on the basis of seniority. The man wearing the diamond-pattern decorations even bowed before he backed out of the way.

Lissea looked at Carron. With only an eye-blink's delay to suggest that she'd hesitated, she said, "Will you hand me in, then, Carron?"

"Milady," Carron said with nervous smile. He bowed low and offered Lissea the support she claimed as right rather than need. The primary's light accentuated his flush.

Lissea stepped lithely into the big aircar, her fingertips barely resting on Carron's. The open cabin contained six oversized bucket seats arranged in pairs. The backs of the forward four were fitted with jump seats. Lissea sat on the edge of a bucket seat and patted the expanse of padding beside her. "Room enough for two, Carron," she said archly.

Tadziki took the other bucket seat of the center pair. His lips were pursed. Ned avoided meeting the adjutant's eyes as he got into the vehicle, and he particularly avoided looking at Lissea and Carron. Squatting in the gap between the two forward seats, he looked out over the raised windscreen.

It wasn't that he didn't know what was going on. It was just that he didn't much like it.

Guards got in. The weight of their armor rocked the aircar on its stubby oleo suspension struts. The remaining pair trudged toward a terminal building, to cadge a ride or call for another vehicle.

The Treasurer's Palace was ten klicks away, on the north side of Astragal. Walking that far in powered suits would bruise the wearers as badly as a kick-boxing tournament. Ned wasn't sure the suits' powerpacks would handle the drain, though that depended on how good Pancahtan technology was. From what he'd seen, it was pretty respectable.

"Now, the bunker—I call it a bunker, but you'll be able to judge for yourself—is only two kilometers from the port, due east," Carron said, answering a question of Lissea's about Old Race sites. It wasn't what most people would call a romantic discussion, but it was the subject nearest to the Pancahtan prince's heart.

Carron didn't have much power in his own family. That would have been obvious even if he hadn't said as much himself. If Carron was the only help the expedition had on the planet, the *moon,* then they might as well have stayed home.

The car lifted, wobbled queasily as the automatic control system found balance, and flew out of the lot. The vehicle accelerated slowly because of its load.

The guards locked their faceshields down. They were probably talking by radio. Ned's commo helmet could access the conversation—signals intelligence was a skill the Academy taught with almost as much emphasis as marksmanship. He didn't care, though. Right now he didn't care about anything that he had any business thinking about.

Tadziki tapped Ned's elbow and pointed down at the port. The car had risen to fifty meters, giving the occupants a good view of the other vessels present. There were a dozen or more large freighters and double that number of smaller vessels, lighters and yachts presumably similar to the one in which Carron had been wrecked on Buin.

Tadziki indicated the three obvious warships, each of five to seven hundred tonnes. They were streamlined for operations within atmospheres; one, slightly the largest, had bulges which held retractable wings for better control. Shuttered turrets for the energy weapons and missile launchers were faired into the hull.

The ships would be formidable opponents for vessels of their own class. The *Swift* was designed for exploration, not war. Any one of the Pancahtan ships could eat it for breakfast.

The car flew over the city of Astragal. Buildings were low and relatively small, though grouped structures formed some sizable factory complexes.

Lines of trees bordered and frequently divided broad roadways. The grounds in which structures stood were generally landscaped as well. Pancahtan foliage was dark, ranging from deep magenta to black.

The buildings were skewed in respect to one another and to the streets. The straight lines of one house were never quite parallel to those of its neighbors. It was that slight wrongness, rather than the occasional major break where a road axis leaped three meters along a diagonal, which most impressed the lower levels of Ned's consciousness. He found Astragal profoundly depressing, even without the fog drifting across the landscape and the yellow-red glow of lava in the near distance.

Lissea and Carron talked loudly on the seat behind him. That didn't help his mood. He couldn't make out words over the windrush.

They were nearing the largest single building Ned had seen on Pancahte, though the suggestion of unity was deceptive on closer look. The structure was really four separate buildings arranged as the corners of a rectangle. The curtain walls connecting the blocks showed signs of frequent repair. The inner courtyard was a formal garden in which numerous people paced or waited near doorways.

The aircar's driver adjusted his fans to nearly vertical and let air resistance brake the vehicle. He angled toward a landing area of crushed rock beside one of the corner buildings, rather than toward the larger lot serving the gated entrance in a wall.

Ned noticed a double-row missile launcher tracking the vehicle from the top of the structure. When the aircar dipped below the cornice and out of the missiles' swept area, it was still in the sights of two guards at the entrance.

The guards' weapons were unfamiliar to Ned. They seemed to be single-shot powerguns with an enormous bore, 10-cm or so. Perhaps the mass of the powered armor permitted the guards to handle weapons whose recoil would ordinarily have required vehicular mounting.

Carron claimed Pancahte had a unitary government which dated back to the colony's foundation, but this certainly wasn't a peaceful world. Well, that needn't matter to Ned. He wasn't going to stay here any length of time, at least if he survived.

The driver shut off the fans, stood up, and shouted, ''Prince Carron Del Vore and companions!'' toward the entrance guards, using a loudspeaker built into his powered suit.

The guards didn't respond. More particularly, they didn't lower the fat energy weapons, one of which was pointed squarely at Ned's chest. The mirror-surfaced door opened in response to an unseen controller.

"Captain Doormann," Carron said formally as he extended his hand to Lissea. "Permit me to lead you into the presence of my father, the Treasurer."

Ned and Tadziki pressed back so that the two leaders could step between them and out of the aircar. The adjutant looked up at the walls: concrete cast with engaged columns between pairs of round-topped windows. "Looks sturdy enough," he said.

"It's old," Ned said. "When they built the spaceport buildings, they used stone. This place dates from before they had much time for frills."

They hopped down to follow Lissea and Carron inside. The aircar took off again behind them. The entrance guards had put up their weapons. They now looked like grotesque statues, men modeled from clay by a child.

The interior of the building was a single large room with a seven-meter ceiling and walls covered with vast murals. There were hundreds of people present: guards, clerks, officials, and petitioners. Everyone but the guards in powered armor seemed to be talking simultaneously, creating bedlam.

The twelve floor-to-ceiling pillars weren't structural—the coffered concrete vault was self-supporting. Rather, the columns were giant light fixtures, and their white radiance lifted Ned's spirits the instant he entered the room.

The throne room, near enough. The burly man sitting on a dais opposite the door must be Lon Del Vore. He was framed by the double line of columns. Guards stood before the dais with the integral weapons in their forearms pointing outward.

The guards weren't really protection. Every civilian present, including the visitors, wore a holstered pistol. A good gunman could draw and fire before the armored men could react. Ned knew that as a pistolero he was at the low end of the *Swift*'s complement, but he was confident he could assassinate the Treasurer if it came down to cases. Lon's willingness to expose himself in this fashion was a comment on his physical courage.

Three men were on the dais with Lon, standing rather than seated. Two of them were old. They dressed in bunchy dark fabrics and used small electronic desks that looked like pedestals.

The third man was small, blond-haired, and about thirty standard years of age. By looking carefully Ned could see that the blond man, Lon, and Carron all had similar features, though their body types could not have been more varied. *Ayven Del Vore, the Treasurer's heir—and from the look of him, a very hard man despite his slight build.*

Lon's chair was ornate and decorated with hunting scenes in blue enamel, but there was a keypad built into one arm and a hologram projector in the other. As one of the older men spoke earnestly, the air in front of the Treasurer quivered with images which couldn't be viewed from the rear of the coincidence pattern. The holograms distorted his face with shifting colored veils.

At Lon's feet lay a carnivore of a type depicted frequently in the room's murals. It was four-legged and rangy, so that it would weigh less than a man of similar torso length. The claws on the forepaws were fifty to eighty centimeters long. Too big to retract, the claws pivoted up so that they curved against the ankle joint with their needle points forward.

The beast had a hooked beak, though its body was covered with brown fur worn down to calloused skin over the joints. When Ned first noticed the creature, it was lying on its back to scratch itself under the chin with a dewclaw that could have disemboweled an ox. Though one of the guards stood with his laser focused on the beast at all times, the Treasurer's choice of a pet also indicated his contempt for personal danger.

An usher whose blue robe fluoresced in vertical lines stepped close to Carron. They exchanged details in tones lost in the surrounding babble.

The official turned and strode down the aisle with his arms akimbo, shouting "Make way!" as he advanced. His chest and elbows thrust people aside to create a zone in which Carron with Lissea, then Ned and Tadziki behind them, could walk without themselves bulling through the crowd.

Ayven glanced at his brother without interest, but his eyes lingered on the *Swift*'s three personnel. Ayven wore a big-bore powergun in a shoulder holster. The rig was out of the way during normal activities but was almost as accessible as a hip carry should need arise.

Carron's brother was the first Pancahtan Ned had seen who looked as though he might have earned a place on the *Swift*. From the way Ayven watched Ned and Tadziki, Ned suspected Ayven was making a similar assessment of the visitors.

"Prince Carron Del Vore and companions!" the usher bawled, his face centimeters short of the guards at the foot of the dais.

Lon shut off the holographic screen which had blurred his face till that moment. He was balding and heavier than he probably wished to be, but he remained a powerful man with features that could have been chipped from stone.

"You're back soon, aren't you?" he said. He spoke over the ambient noise without giving the impression he was shouting the way the usher had done. "Thought better of that nonsense, have you?"

"We landed on Buin, Father, because the auxiliary power unit was overheating," Carron said. His voice sounded brittle in contrast to that of the Treasurer. "By great good fortune, Captain Doormann of Telaria and her vessel arrived on Buin at the same time. She and her crew were able to rescue me and the survivors of my yacht from the natives, who would otherwise have infallibly slain us all."

"Lost the ship, did you, brother?" Ayven said. He didn't sneer, exactly. Rather, he displayed the sort of amused contempt a man might for the mess a puppy had made in someone else's house. "Well, I suppose you could have gotten into worse trouble if you'd been fooling around here. I've always been afraid you were going to manage to destroy the satellite ring with your nonsense."

"Go on, boy, introduce your friends," Lon said. "I'm going to be up half the night with this curst redevelopment scheme for the Foundation District as it is, so I don't have a lot of time to waste.''

"Sir," Carron said with spots of color on his cheekbones, "permit me to introduce Mistress Lissea Doormann, captain of the vessel *Swift* out of Telaria. These are two of her officers, Masters Tadziki and Slade.''

"Where's Telaria?" Ayven asked sharply.

Lissea stepped forward. She didn't shove Carron aside, but her hand on his shoulder urged him to leave her in charge. "Telaria is a world well outside the Pocket, sir," she said.

"Impossible!" Lon said. "The Twin Worlders don't let any ships through the Sole Solution. Unless— *Telaria,* you said?"

"The Twin Worlders don't command the Sole Solution anymore, sir," Lissea said. "But if you think you recognize the name, you probably do. Lendell Doormann was my great-granduncle, and it's to retrieve the capsule that he stole from Telaria that I've come here.''

"You *fought* your way through the Sole Solution?" Ayven said in wonder.

Other conversations hushed throughout the hall, though the shuffle and rustling of bodies continued to create background noise like that of distant surf. The carnivore on the dais stared at Lissea. Its eyes had horizontally slitted pupils and golden irises.

"The Twin Worlds will not be interdicting the Sole Solution in the future," Lissea said. "There was no fighting involved. We've come to Pancahte in peace, and with the intention of bringing your world and mine into closer relations.''

Ayven knelt beside the chair and used the keypad. A miniature image trembled before him, unreadable to the visitors.

"Don't talk nonsense," Lon said with a quick wave of his hand. "Telaria's half a galaxy away. What *I* want to know is how you got past the Dreadnought.''

Telling him wouldn't do Lissea's cause any good. If the Treasurer learned the expedition had been willing to use biological warfare against whole planets, he was very likely to forestall a similar attack with a quick massacre.

"The Twin Worlds ended the blockade by their own decision," Lissea lied. "The Dreadnought wasn't on station when the *Swift* reached the Sole Solution."

We wouldn't land Nodals on a world as dark as Pancahte. They wouldn't ripen here. . . .

"So you're diplomats, are you?" Ayven said as he stood again. The image he'd summoned from Pancahte's data net sprang to large size and rotated toward the audience. It was a view, possibly real-time, of the *Swift* with members of her complement amusing themselves around her in the landing area:

Yazov threw gravel up in the air, several bits at a time. Josie Paetz blasted the pebbles with his pistols, trading weapons between his right and left hand after every shot like a juggler. Other men watched, cheered, and occasionally fired shoulder weapons.

The Warsons squatted in the shelter of the hull with a box between them for a table. They were playing cards and occasionally swigging directly from a carafe. The ship's liquor supply was supposedly locked up in the absence of the captain and adjutant, but Ned had already seen what the brothers could do to electronic security.

Even so, it would have been a placid enough tableau, except that Deke and Toll between them carried enough hardware to arm a squad. Ned knew the Warsons well enough by now to read the seemingly aimless glances they gave their surroundings. They were hoping somebody would view their feigned nonchalance as an opportunity to attack.

Herne Lordling stepped to the middle of the hatchway. He yelled at the shooters. The projected display didn't include an audio track. Josie fired one more round and turned insolently. The breeches of his pistols were locked back, empty. A gray mist of matrix residue streamed from them as air cooled the bores.

Herne turned toward the recording instrument and shouted again. He outstretched his left arm, pointing with the index and middle fingers together. His right hand hovered over the grip of his holstered pistol—

The image quickly jumped away, then ended.

"Diplomats?" Ayven repeated. He laughed.

Ned made a decision because he'd noticed that besides Lissea, there were only two women in the big room. He didn't have time to discuss the matter with his captain.

"Sir, if we were only diplomats," he said as he stepped forward, "we wouldn't have survived to rescue your son."

The analytical part of his mind noted approvingly that his voice rang across the hall like the note of a bar of good steel.

"I'm Slade, nephew of the Slade of Tethys." The nouns wouldn't mean anything here, but the statement's form would. "The other members of Mistress Doormann's company are of similar rank on their own worlds. We come to you in peace, aiding a worthy lady to redress the wrong done by a kinsman of hers."

Ned was glad that he couldn't see Lissea's face as he spoke, but they both knew by now that the way forward needn't be a pleasant one. Twenty gunmen couldn't gain Lissea's ends by main force, so they had to adapt themselves to circumstances.

Lon Del Vore straightened in his chair; Ayven's stance became a challenge. For all that, the two men relaxed somewhat, because *this* was a situation they understood.

"I'd say that after seventy years," Lon said, "that this capsule you claim is forfeit to the state of Pancahte for nonpayment of personal property taxes."

His face broke into a smile like a landslip. "But if you choose to contest ownership, you can apply for appointment of three assessors under our laws. With right of appeal to the Treasurer."

"We're of course willing to pay for your help," Tadziki offered quickly. "In currency, if you will, or in our labor. The matter is a moral obligation for our mistress, you see."

Ned risked a glance back at Lissea. She stood with her lips composed, her hands folded demurely before her, and hellfire glaring from her dark eyes.

"There's no more possibility of bank transfers between our planets than there is of trade," Lon said irritably. "And as for labor—the men of Pancahte can arrange their own disputes without need of diplomats of your sort.''

''It's moot anyway,'' said Ayven. Behind the mocking smile, his mind had given the question serious consideration. ''The capsule is on Hammerhead Lake. Nobody can get close to it without being fried.''

''Father!'' Carron said. Ned started. He'd forgotten that Carron still stood just behind him. ''Seventy years ago a Doormann reached Hammerhead Lake despite the tanks. Perhaps now another member of the family can do the same and teach us how to do so. That would be of enormous value.''

''Value to boys who don't have anything better to do than play with old junk, maybe,'' Ayven snapped. ''No value to Pancahte, that we should turn over property on the say-so of a woman who claims a relative of hers stole it.''

The carnivore became restive. It got to its feet, turned toward Lon, and made a mewling sound. Lon rubbed the beast's throat with the toe of his boot, calming it again.

''You offer labor,'' he said, speaking toward Tadziki. ''Well and good. I'll make you a proposition. The tanks—I suppose my son has told you about them?''

''Yes I have,'' Carron said crisply.

''The tanks kill a certain amount of livestock and a few careless people every year,'' Lon continued. ''They're an irritation. If you can destroy them, then I'll let you have the capsule you claim.''

''Or you can leave Pancahte immediately,'' Ayven said, ''with as much help from me and the Treasurer's Guard as it takes to shift you.''

''Yes, I accept,'' Lissea said. ''I'll need a few days to prepare for the operation, however.''

''Three days, then,'' Lon said. Ned stepped sideways to remove himself from the discussion. ''But if you think you're going to look the tanks over from close up—well, their weapons don't leave enough to require burial, so it's no concern of mine.''

''I'll order supplies to be sent to the *Swift* to replenish her stores,'' Carron said.

"*Will* you, brother?" said Ayven.

"They rescued me and my men at considerable personal risk," Carron said with a cold power that his voice hadn't held before in this audience hall. "They fed us during the journey. I don't believe the state of Pancahte is so poor that we can't show such persons hospitality."

Lon grimaced. He pointed to one of the old men on the dais. "Make it so," he said.

Returning his gaze to Lissea, he went on. "Three days. Or you leave Pancahte and return at your peril."

Lissea nodded with cold contempt and turned on her heel.

Carron started to go out with her. "Not you, son," Lon said. "You've trespassed long enough on our visitors' hospitality. From now on you'll leave them strictly alone."

Carron blinked like a burglar caught in the act.

Tadziki tapped Ned's wrist, then nodded toward the official on the dais. "I'll stay back a time," he whispered. "Take care of Lissea."

Everyone in the room watched Ned trotting to catch Lissea before she left the room. He supposed it was his imagination that he could actually feel the carnivore's eyes on him.

The view of the audience with Lon Del Vore and Ayven was an amalgam of the recordings Lissea's helmet and Ned's had made. As a result, the hologram played back by the *Swift*'s equipment differed subtly from Ned's memory. That disturbed him, as did watching himself on a tightrope between the Pancahtans and Lissea—without the adrenaline rush that had carried him through the event itself.

"Those *bastards*," Herne Lordling said, facing the projection from the bottom of the ramp. The *Swift*'s entire complement, save Tadziki—who was still in town—and the man on instrument watch, sat or squatted before the hatchway to watch.

The image of the door swelled on the display until the hologram dissolved. The crew had rigged translucent tarpaulins between the ship and the blast walls as protection against both the elements and Pancahtan eyes. The filmy sheets were sullen with the primary's shadowless light.

"It's their planet," Lissea said. "They've agreed to let us proceed, which is as much as we could ask for."

Her voice was emotionless. She was so angry that she'd shut down to keep from exploding, but Ned wasn't sure Lordling realized that.

Herne stared at Lissea. "But their *attitude,* woman!" he said. "They're sneering at us! These hicks are sneering at *us.*"

"I'm not unfamiliar with the experience of being patronized by my inferiors, Herne," Lissea said coolly. "Let's get on to the problem at hand."

A ship lifted from across the circular port. There was a quick shock as the engines came up to full power, then a sustained roar which faded slowly as the vessel rose into the thinner layers of the atmosphere. The ship was a big freighter. Pancahte had an extensive trade network among the worlds of the Pocket.

"They don't believe we can really evade—overcome, whatever—the tanks," Ned said while the rumbling continued. "If we accomplish that, we may still have difficulty getting the Treasurer to honor his agreement. He wasn't just joking when he let us know that he personally is the highest law on the . . . the world."

"What somebody ought to do is to give that Treasurer a third eye-socket," Lordling said. "And that somebody just might be me."

"And what would that gain us, Herne?" Lissea snapped.

"It'd gain us the bastard being dead!" Lordling said. "Look, Lissea, you can't let pissants think they can push you around. It's—well, you'll have to take my word for it."

"No, I won't have to do that, *Master* Lordling," Lissea said. "Because *I'm* in charge." She pointed toward the hatchway. "Go relieve Harlow on the console. Now!"

Lordling looked amazed. He didn't move. Ned leaned forward, his eyes on Lissea. He reached across her and put fingertips on Lordling's knee.

She grimaced. "No, cancel that order," she said. "But

Herne, stop acting like an idiot.''

"The capsule's not so big that we'll have trouble handling it,'' Toll Warson said. "I can borrow a van easy enough to hold it. What we ought to do is make a quick snatch and run before Del Vore has second thoughts.''

"Steal one of the trucks right out there?'' Petit asked, nodding in the direction of the terminal parking area.

"No, no,'' Toll said. "Via, off a street. We just went through the lot to check out door and power locks. It won't be a problem.''

"What about the tanks?'' Ned asked.

"Some people like to think tanks can stand up to anything an infantryman can dish out,'' Deke Warson said, loud enough to focus attention on him. He was at the back of the audience, where Ned couldn't have seen him without standing up. "The tanks *I've* run into, that's not the way it is. I'm willing to bet these are no different.''

"Worst case,'' Toll said, "we take out the running gear and then keep clear of the guns. Our Carron may be a very bright lad, but he's sure no soldier.''

Toll met Ned's eyes with a degree of amusement, though without malice. By this point he respected Ned, but he still felt there was a lot the boy had to learn.

Which was true. But the Old Race tanks, which glided above the ground without any visible running gear, were as new to the Warsons as they were to Ned. And the Warsons couldn't accept that. . . .

"Captain, there's a truck seems to be heading for us,'' Harlow warned. *"They come from town and turned through the terminal. Over.''*

Everybody moved, fast but smoothly. Deke Warson twitched aside an edge of the tarp to look around it. His 2-cm weapon was muzzle-up in his hand, though hidden to the oncoming vehicle.

Josie Paetz climbed the three-meter blast wall with a short run and a boot-sole partway up to boost his head over the lip, pushing the top sheet out of the way. He clung there one-handed. Unlike Deke, he didn't have the least hesitation about presenting the pistol in his right hand.

"It's Tadziki," Deke reported in a tone of disappointment.

"*Adjutant to* Swift!" Tadziki rasped over the general push. "*Blood and martyrs, you curst fools! Don't be pointing guns at me unless you want to eat them! Out!*"

Paetz dropped down from his perch. "Talks big for an old guy," he muttered.

Yazov cuffed him. Paetz grunted and turned his back on his uncle.

The vehicle was a hovercraft with an open box rated for a tonne of cargo. The fans would lift all the men you could cram onto the vehicle, but if there were more than a dozen they would have to be good friends. A similar truck had carried Lissea and Ned back from the palace. Tadziki had relayed their request for transport to the Pancahtan official with whom he was discussing the expedition's supply requirements.

The adjutant was driving this one. No one else was in the vehicle. Mercenaries held the side tarps out of the way, but the overhead sheets bellied down dangerously in the suction before Tadziki pulled up beside the *Swift* and shut the fans down. He got out, looking worn and angry.

"I held a meeting to discuss what our next move ought to be," Lissea said by way of greeting.

"Did you come up with any good ideas?" Tadziki asked. It disturbed Ned to hear the adjutant's tone, though sneering irony was common enough among other members of the expedition.

"Take out the tanks and take off with the goods before the authorities know what's happened," Toll Warson said, agreeably enough. You had to look carefully in the odd light to note the slight frown indicating that he, too, was concerned by Tadziki's uncharacteristic display of irritation.

Lissea touched Tadziki's hand. "No, we didn't," she said. "Should you and I go inside and discuss privately what you've learned at the palace?"

Tadziki looked at her. "Bloody hell," he said. "I'm sorry. Yeah, maybe we ought to talk, just you and me."

He rapped the side of the truck. "We've got this on loan for while we're on the ground here. Yazov, take three men at any time past oh-five-thirty standard and pick up our supplies. I've got the coordinates downloaded, it's a warehouse on the west of the city. You can drive a hovercraft?"

"Yeah, I can drive one," Yazov said. "But you know, I think if you've got something to say that concerns all our asses, it'd be nice if all of us heard about it."

"Anybody tell you this was a democracy?" Herne Lordling snapped.

"Nobody tole me I was cannon fodder, either," Yazov said.

He put his arm out to his side, so that it lay across the chest of his nephew. Josie Paetz wore the kind of smile Ned had seen on his face once before, when they prepared for the second pass through the Spiders on Ajax Four. If Yazov held a grenade with the pin pulled, his gesture couldn't have been more threatening.

"Guys," Lissea said, stepping between the men. She sounded like the boy the whale flopped on. "Guys? Let's all sit down, all right?"

She shook her head. "You know, if I had it to do over, I'd take a female crew." She smiled, still tired but no longer looking frustrated. "Except if I'd done that, none of these Pancahtan bastards'd do anything but pat me on the head and tell me go off and be a good girl. Eh, Ned?"

He grinned back. "Hey, the universe wasn't created on *my* watch," he said.

Tension eased. Ned lowered himself onto the gravel by crossing his ankles and sitting straight down. Other men followed his lead with more or less effort, depending on the technique they chose and how flexible their joints were.

A nearby ship ran up its engines, but that was apparently only a test rather than preparation for immediate takeoff. The port quieted enough for normal speech again.

"All right, Tadziki," Lissea said calmly. "Tell us what you've learned."

The adjutant began. "Though the Treasurer ordered Carron to keep away from us . . ." He was seated beside Lissea on the ramp, so he would have had to turn his head to meet her eyes. He did not do so. ". . . he, the boy, wants to meet with you secretly at the Old Race site he mentioned. The bunker. He's given me the coordinates."

"That makes sense," Lissea said. "What's your opinion?"

Tadziki nodded twice, as though he had to jog the data loose within his mind. "I think," he said toward the men seated before him, "that Carron is interested in more than the technology, Captain. But I don't see any choice other than you meeting him. Going up against those tanks unaided is like stepping out a window in the dark. It might be survivable, but the chances are against it."

"You want her to be a whore, is that it?" Herne Lordling said. He didn't jump to his feet, but that might have been because Toll Warson sat beside him with a hand poised to grab Lordling's belt. "Go on, Tadziki, say it: you want her to fuck this boy on the off chance that he knows something useful!"

"No," the adjutant said tersely, "I do not want that."

"Not that it matters a curse what anybody else wants on that subject," Lissea said, cool as winter dawn. "How soon is he willing to meet?"

Ned expected silent anger from Lissea like that which she displayed when he interrupted to save the audience with Lon Del Vore. Instead, Lissea seemed to have stated a simple truth, that the subject was one on which she would make the decisions without consultation.

Tadziki unclipped a control wand from his breast pocket and brought the hologram display live. A topo map formed in the air. "He wants the meeting at Hour Nineteen local. That's in three hours twenty-two minutes standard. Here."

A red spot glowed on the map. "And here we are."

Lissea looked at Lordling. "The Jeeps are ready to roll?" she said.

"Yes, ma'am," Herne replied in a husky voice. "But look, *Lissea*. There needs to be ten of us with you in case it's a trap."

Lissea made a moue with her lips and shook her head. "Herne—" she said.

"I'm not claiming the boy's deliberately setting you up,"
Lordling continued. The harsh timbre of his voice indicated
he was conceding Carron's goodwill from policy rather than
belief. "But his brother and father, *they* may be using the boy
for bait. The rest of the unit stays aboard the *Swift* with engines hot, so—"

"*Stop*, Herne," Lissea said. A Warson chuckled.

She looked at Tadziki. "What're our chances if the locals
launch an attack on us here in port?" she asked.

"None," Tadziki said. He looked around the gathering, not
so much inviting comment as projecting his flat certainty.
"They'd have casualties. Worse casualties than they'd probably expect. But there's no question of the outcome."

None of the mercenaries spoke. A few of them avoided the
adjutant's eyes, but they couldn't argue with the assessment.
As Yazov had said earlier, they hadn't joined the expedition to
become cannon fodder.

"Right,," Lissea said. "If I go with a mob behind me,
it'll destroy any chance of empathy with Carron. So I'll go
alone."

"Empathy?" Deke Warson called from the back of the
group. "Gee, I never heard it called that before. I should've
stayed in school longer, huh?"

Everybody laughed. Almost everybody. Herne Lordling
got to his feet and walked stiffly up the ramp. "I'll relieve
Harlow on watch," he said hoarsely.

"It might," Ned said, looking toward the triple-headed
hologram projector within the vessel's bay, "be desirable for
you to have a, you know, driver, a radio watch along, though.
If you're going to be down in a bunker that may be shielded."

He felt Lissea's head turn. He lowered his eyes and met
hers. "Yes," she said crisply. "That's a good idea. Slade,
you'll drive me."

She got to her feet. Others followed. "I'm going to change
my uniform. Tadziki, do we have enough water for a shower
before the locals come through with resupply?"

Tadziki nodded. "I'll rig shelter and a hose on the other
side of the ship," he said. "Warson, both of you. Westerbeke,

Paetz. Get out another tarp, some high-pressure tubing for a frame, and the welder. I'll be along in a moment to supervise you.''

Lissea entered the *Swift*. The meeting broke into half a dozen separate conversations. Some of the men were speculating on their chances of leave in Astragal and the possible opportunities there.

Tadziki gestured Ned toward him. The men stood shoulder to shoulder. Their heads were turned toward but not *to* one another. They stared at the gravel.

''That was a good idea about you going along,'' the adjutant said. ''But you'll make sure that the principals have privacy for their discussions, won't you?''

''I'm not a kid, Tadziki,'' Ned said. He sounded angrier than he'd intended to let out. ''And I won't be a third wheel, no.''

He stamped back aboard the vessel. Before he drove off tonight, he wanted to check his submachine gun and ammo bandolier again.

''Half a klick to the bunker now,'' Lissea said, the first words that had passed between her and Ned since they drove away from the *Swift*.

Most of the trees had spongy, pillarlike trunks only six to ten meters high. The black-red fronds grew out in a full circle from each peak like a vertical fountain spraying. There were exceptions that spiked up twenty meters and more didn't have branches at all. Their trunks were slender cones covered with a fur of russet needles.

Bits of plant matter danced from beneath the Jeep's skirts, though Ned kept his speed down. ''Keep an eye out,'' he said. ''I'm busy not running into a tree.''

The primary had set beneath the curve of Pancahte, but the sun was up in the east. The star was a Type K4 whose light was balanced toward the red also, but it seemed white by contrast to the glow of the near-stellar primary. Pale sunlight flickered through the forest's veiling fronds.

"I'm going to go back with Lendell's capsule, Ned," Lissea said quietly. "And I'm going to take my place on the board of Doormann Trading."

"You bet," Ned said. "And we're here to help you do that."

"There," Lissea said, pointing to a delicate four-place air-car like the one which the Pancahtan yacht had carried. She'd held her 2-cm weapon on her lap during the ride. Now she thrust its butt into the socket beside her seat.

Carron Del Vore stood up in the waiting vehicle. He was alone. Ned swung the Jeep in so that Lissea was on the Pancahtan's side.

"Did we mistake the time, Carron?" she asked. Her helmet sensors would have noted the heat and sonic signatures of the aircar's passage if it had arrived any time in the past five minutes.

"Oh, no, Lissea," he said. "I was—well, I thought I'd get here early to mark the spot. It's hard to find if you're not familiar."

He stumbled getting out of the aircar. Lissea waited a beat, then raised her hand so that he could help her from the hovercraft.

They were in a forested valley. To either side, the ground had cracked open millennia before and oozed lava into parallel basalt ridges a kilometer apart.

The *Swift*'s navigational system plotted a route from the spaceport using satellite charts which Carron provided. The necessary data was then dumped into Ned's and Lissea's helmets. There was no more chance of them missing the bunker than there was of them missing the floor if they rolled out of bed.

But then, Carron's nervous anticipation didn't have a lot to do with Old Race artifacts. Despite his rank—and he wasn't a bad-looking guy—he must not have known many women.

There weren't many women like Lissea Doormann.

Ned stepped around his side of the Jeep. His right arm cocked back so that his hand could rest lightly on the butt of the submachine gun, slung with the muzzle forward.

The vehicles were parked in a perfectly circular clearing, obviously artificial. Ned lifted his visor with his left hand. He no longer needed the line projected onto the inner surface to give him a vector to their goal.

Ned laughed without humor. Lissea and Carron looked at him. "Um?" Lissea said.

"We got here," Ned said. The bunker was the physical location at which the two principals hoped to reach their separate goals.

"Yes, I haven't been here in years myself," Carron said. The center of the clearing was sunken. He reached down for the hasp which barely projected from the leaf mold. When Carron straightened, a flat, rectangular plate, about a meter by two, pivoted upward with him. It spilled soil and debris to the sides.

Carron moved without effort. The plate was over a hundred centimeters thick and burdened with a considerable accumulation of dirt and decaying fronds, so the hasp must merely trigger a powered opening mechanism.

Ned touched Carron's wrist with his left hand. "Let me take a look, if you will," Ned said with no hint of question. He grinned. "I'm expendable. Then I'll come back up here and keep out of the way."

"I'll determine where you'll go and when, Slade," Lissea said in a thin voice.

He looked at her. She nodded toward the opening. Now that she'd greeted Carron peacefully, she'd taken her heavy powergun back from the Jeep's clamp. She held the weapon ready.

"Really, there's never anyone here," Carron said plaintively.

Steps led from the above-ground shadows to darkness. The staircase had no handrails.

Ned twisted a lightball clipped to his belt, breaking the partition between the chemicals so that they bloomed into white effulgence. He pulled the ball free and lobbed it one-handed into the bunker. It clattered around the interior. The bioluminescent compound would gleam with cold radiance for an hour or so, depending on the ambient temperature.

Ned walked deliberately down the first five steps. They were of some cast material with a nonslip surface on the treads. The material sounded brittle beneath his boots, like thermoplastic, but it showed no signs of wear.

The interior, which unfolded as Ned stepped downward, was light gray. There was nothing visible except dirt that had fallen in when the hatch opened.

Ned suddenly jumped to the floor and spun behind the submachine gun's muzzle.

"There's really no one here," Carron repeated.

He was right, and Ned felt slightly more of an idiot than he had before.

"Looks good to me," he said with false nonchalance. He started up the steps. Lissea, descending, waved him back down again. She'd slung her powergun and carried in her left hand the heavy testing kit she'd brought from the *Swift*.

"There were no artifacts at all in the bunker?" she asked Carron over her shoulder.

"The bunker itself is an artifact," he corrected her. "When I first located it—from records in the palace library—the hatch was open and the cavity was half filled. Mostly leaves and branches, of course. At some point the settlers must have used it for storage and perhaps living quarters, though."

He waved a hand around the circular interior. "I had the contents cleaned out and sifted. There were some interesting items from the early settlement period—some objects that must have traveled from Earth herself, five hundred years ago. But the settlers *found* the bunker here, they didn't build it. And there's no sign of whoever did build it."

The bunker was about ten meters in diameter. Floor, walls, and ceiling appeared to have been cast in one piece with the staircase. Ned picked up the lightball and set it on a tread at the height of his chin, so that it illuminated an arc of wall evenly.

"What are these?" Lissea asked, touching the wall beside a spot of regular shadow, four-millimeter holes in the material. "Ventilation?" There was a sparse horizontal row of similar markings, midway between floor and ceiling.

"No," Carron said. "There's a gas exchange system within the wall's microstructure. If we could determine how that worked, it would be"—

He lifted his hands in frustration—"of incalculable value. I think the holes may be data-transmission points and I even manufactured square wave guides to fit them. It would make a . . . a *burp* at me. But I haven't been able to get a response."

He looked around and added peevishly, "I should have brought ch-chairs. There's nothing to sit on."

Lissea brushed the comment away. "I've sat on worse than a clean floor," she muttered. She bent close to the hole, then knelt and opened her case.

Carron noticed Ned's eyes counting holes. "There's ten of them," Carron said. "Every ninety-seven centimeters around the circumference. Almost ninety-seven centimeters."

"If the ventilation system works and the door mechanism works," Lissea said as she chose a cylindrical device from her case, "then the powerplant's still in operation. The place should be capable of doing whatever it was built to do."

She looked at Carron. "Square wave guides. You brought some, didn't you? Where are they?"

He blinked in surprise at her tone. Carron might have been used to being ignored, but he didn't expect to be spoken to as if he were a servant.

"Yes, why I did," he said. He opened the lid of his large belt pack, flopped the front down into a tray, and took two square tubes from pockets within. The pack was a small tool-kit rather than a normal wallet of personal belongings.

"I'll go up to the surface," Ned said quietly.

"Yes, do," Lissea said. She didn't look up as she spoke. She'd taken another tool from her case and was cutting at the end of a wave guide with a tiny keening noise. "Both of you go up, will you? I don't know how long this is going to take."

Ned turned without speaking and climbed the stairs, two steps at a time. He heard Carron's feet behind him. The staircase, though apparently flimsy, didn't spring or sway under foot.

By the time he stepped over the lightball, his head was above ground again. It felt good.

Carron snicked closed the catch of his belt pack, rotating so that a spear of sunlight illuminated the task. He avoided eye contact with Ned.

The immediate forest held nothing of interest on any of the spectra Ned's helmet could receive and analyze. He squatted to watch through the hatchway as Lissea worked. Carron moved a little farther back in the clearing so that he too could see without rubbing shoulders with Ned.

Lissea had broken her case into three separate trays which she'd laid out to her right side. She used the floor in front of her as a worktable, picking up and putting down items with precise movements. A lamp extending from one tray threw an oval of intense light across the floor. Occasionally a welding head sparkled viciously.

Ned had seen Lissea perform as the female captain of a band of hard-bitten, intensely *masculine* men. She'd done a good job, a remarkable job; but that was all on-the-job training. This was the first time Ned had seen Lissea doing the sort of engineering task for which she'd been formally educated.

Repeatedly, Lissea held a device against the wall, touched a switch, and went back to work. She was proceeding by trial and error, but there was no waste motion whatever. Each action was calculated to determine a particular question, yes or no, and thus take another step toward the goal.

"She must be incredibly brave, isn't she?" Carron said quietly.

Another step toward *Lissea's* goal.

Ned gave Carron a friendly but neutral smile. "You bet," he said. "In some ways, I don't think I've ever met anybody braver."

Because she had something to lose. There were no cowards aboard the *Swift,* but most of the men knew they'd be doing this or some equivalent of this until the law of averages caught up with them.

"Aside from being brilliant, that is," Carron added hastily. "I've been . . . consumed with the Old Race since—well, since I can remember thinking. And she dives in with a plan only minutes after she gets here!"

"A lot of times it's having a fresh perspective," Ned said dryly. Pancahte wasn't the sticks, exactly, but the whole Pocket would have been a backwater even without the Twin Worlds strangling access. "But I agree: Lissea is brilliant."

He waited a beat to add, "Besides being beautiful, of course."

Carron grimaced as though by forcing his face into a tight rictus he could keep from blushing. He couldn't. "Ah, yes," he said, staring toward a tree ten meters away, "I think she's very attractive too."

Ned looked down at Lissea again. He couldn't really see much of her at this angle. She'd lowered her faceshield to protect her against flying chips and actinic radiation from the welding.

What he saw when he looked at her was the image his mind painted. That was more than a trim body and precise features, though it included those aspects. He wouldn't define Lissea Doormann as being the ideal of physical beauty . . . but beauty wasn't solely or even primarily physical.

And yes, she was beautiful.

"I suppose that she . . ." Carron said. "Does she have a protector?"

Ned looked at the tree on which Carron's eyes were focused. It was one of the tall cones. Tiny blue flowers grew among the shaggy needles. "She's got twenty of us," Ned said with unintended harshness. "Well, eighteen, now. But if you mean—"

He fixed Carron with his gaze and waited for the Pancahtan to meet his eyes before he continued. "—is she involved with anybody, no, I don't think she is. Certainly not anybody aboard the *Swift.*"

Carron nodded and let out a breath that he might not have been aware he was holding. He opened his mouth to say something noncommittal.

The bunker roared.

The interior was a hazy ambience rather than clear air and

pale walls. Glare quivered through the mass like lightning across cloudtops. The bioluminescent globe had faded to a shadow of itself.

Carron started to jump down the hatch. Ned grabbed him across the waist left-handed and flung him back. Lissea might be trying to run up the stairs.

"It's all right!" she shouted as thunder coalesced around her. "I've gotten it to work!"

Ned dropped into the bunker in three strides, judging where the treads were by memory. He held his submachine gun like a heavy pistol so that his left hand was free to take the shock if he slipped.

His soles hit the floor. He reached out for Lissea. She was there, her shoulder warm through the tunic and her hand reaching up to clasp Ned's.

The wall before them erupted in a massive bombardment taking place on a horizon kilometers away. White, red, and yellow light gouted, and the air shook with repeated concussions.

The image vanished rather than faded. On the opposite side of the room, blue light limned a gigantic structure composed of pentagonal facets. Either the object was hanging in space or it was so huge that the supporting surface was beyond the image focus. Bits of the ship/building hived off as bands of non-light struck and scattered and collapsed in searing bolts which flashed from corners of the pentagons.

As suddenly as the conflicting images had appeared, the circular wall cleared again. The air still had a shimmering materiality: the lightball glowed as if it stood behind a dozen insect screens.

Ned couldn't be sure where the air stopped and the wall began. He didn't reach out, because he wasn't sure what his hand would touch—

Or whether it would touch anything.

Carron Del Vore stood with them. His eyes brushed Ned's with a cold lack of expression. Ned took his hand away from Lissea and stepped to the side.

"I loaded a vocabulary cartridge and told the system to

switch on," Lissea said to the men. The room hissed with sound that was barely noticeable until someone tried to speak over it. "There weren't any input devices, so it's likely the system was voice-actuated. But it had to recognize my words as data, so I made a core load through a guide hole."

"Ready for instructions," a voice said from the whole circumference of the bunker at once.

"Well, I'll be hanged," Ned said. "You mean it's a data bank with no security gate controlling access?"

"You loaded a vocabulary?" Carron said. "But how did that help? How did it translate the words into information it could process?"

Lissea squeezed Carron's hand. Ned looked at his feet. He'd flipped over one of the trays when he leaped into the bunker. Now that the light was steady, Ned bent and concentrated on picking up tools he'd scattered.

"A seven-hundred-thousand-word vocabulary of Trade and Standard English," Lissea said, "is enough self-consistent information to provide its own code—for a sufficiently powerful processor. This one was."

Presumably the bunker didn't care where the controller was facing, but human beings like to act as if there were a point of focus. She turned to the wall again. "There are two tanks defending a perimeter around Hammerhead Lake, fifteen kilometers north of Astragal," she said. "How can the tanks be shut down or destroyed?"

"Define Hammerhead Lake or Astragal," the environment said.

"I'll handle it," Carron said with matter-of-fact firmness. He took the control wand from Lissea's breast pocket without bothering to ask. "Project a relief map of the ten thousand hectares of surface centered on this bunker."

Carron was taking charge rather than begging a favor. Ned had noted the dichotomy in the young noble's personality before.

The interior of the bunker changed. Ned felt an instant of vertigo. A vast map curved into view some meters beyond where the wall should have been. Either the illusion of flying tricked the balance canals in his ears, or for a moment gravity had shifted and he was looking straight down at Pancahte itself.

A flat, palm-sized disk from Lissea's toolcase hung in the air, attached to nothingness by one of the wave guides Carron had provided. She hadn't removed the device after she dumped data into the vast bank encircling them. Ned wondered what storage method the builders had used, and how long ago they had lived.

Carron adjusted the wand's lens into a needle of light. "This location," he said, flicking the beam around the easily recognizable dumbbell silhouette. There was no sign of Astragal or any human construction on the projected map.

"Do the tanks you're concerned with look like this?" the bunker asked.

The image of an object with twenty pentagonal sides appeared. The topographic map was still there. The projections neither masked nor intersected one another even though they should have been occupying the same points of space.

The tank, if it was a tank, had no weapons or other bulges to mark its flat sides. The vehicle rotated like an ill-made wheel across waste terrain, leaving cracked indentations on the surface. Broken rock spewed out whenever a corner bit. The vehicle looked like nothing Ned had ever seen in his life.

"No," Carron said. "It's a . . . there's a hull and on top a—"

Another vehicle replaced the first against the same setting. The change was so complete and sudden that Ned wasn't aware of any point of transition. This tank was identical to those whose images Carron had showed them on Buin, except that the details were precise, down to splotches of tarnish on the flanks. There was either a persistent highlight or an emitter on the gun mantle.

"Yes," said Carron. "Like that. How can we get past them safely?"

"Describe the behavior of the tanks," the bunker directed.

Ned was beginning to get used to the omnipresence of the voice. What he still found disquieting was the background vibration. The longer he listened to it, the more it sounded like a battle of enormous scale going on in the far distance.

"They circle the lake," Carron said. "They shoot at anyone or thing that comes within six kilometers of it."

"They've been operating for at least five hundred years," Ned added.

Perhaps the hum was merely the operating frequency of the vastly complex computer in which they stood. Or again, Ned might be reading his own fears into random images which the system displayed as it booted. . . .

But he didn't believe that.

"The tanks are on autopatrol," the bunker said. The system's designers had made no effort to humanize the voice. The words were dead and *wrong* without a tone of satisfaction to accompany them. "They can be disarmed by anyone they've been programmed to recognize as friendly."

Ned and Lissea exchanged glances—she frowning, he with lips pursed in consideration.

"It is unlikely after five hundred years," the bunker continued, "whether standard or local, that anyone from the contemporary population would remain alive. Did you have another type of year in mind?"

"No," said Carron tightly.

"Then the only way the tanks can be disarmed is through the use of a standard key," the bunker said. "This is a standard key."

A flat, square object some sixty millimeters per side appeared in front of Lissea and the two men. It had a wristband, though Ned thought the object was too large to be comfortable when worn that way. There were no distinguishing marks on the smooth gray surface.

The third image appeared with/over the topo map and the vision of the tank maneuvering across rocky terrain. The combined views were simultaneously clearer than any one of them should have been, no matter what distance from which they were seen. The bunker's display certainly wasn't holographic, and Ned now wondered whether it had any presence in the physical universe whatever.

"All right," Lissea said. "That's how the tanks can be disarmed. Now, how can they be destroyed?"

"The tanks can be destroyed by the application of sufficient energy," the bunker said. "The flux required is of stellar magnitude. Nothing within the information you have provided me suggests that you have knowledge of the principles necessary to apply such volumes of energy."

Ned didn't look at his companions. He was also only marginally aware of the map, tank, and key before him. The rumble of warfare, cataclysmic and unimaginably distant in time, filled him like flame in the nozzle of a rocket.

"I've seen a . . . a key like that," Carron said. "My father has one in the collection of Old Race artifacts in the palace."

"You've *got* one?" Lissea said. "Wonderful! When can you bring it to me?"

"The top lifts up," Carron said, gesturing toward the display. "There's points marked on the inner surface. When you touch them, light flashes from the back of the lid."

The bunker changed the image as Carron spoke. The lid raised ninety degrees; the view rotated to show ten unfamiliar symbols arranged in pyramid fashion with a solid bar across the bottom. The image turned again. The raised back emitted pulses modulated in both time and hue—spectrum—across the entire surface.

"Carron," Lissea said. "You have the key. Our lives depend on it, *my* life. When can you bring it to me?"

"Lissea," the Pancahtan said, *"I* don't have the key, my father does. I can ask him to loan it to you; I'll do that—"

"A little thing like that?" Ned interrupted harshly. "You say nobody ever looks at the artifacts and your *father* certainly doesn't care. He'll never miss it!"

"He'll see you use it, though!" Carron said. "You can't hide *that.* He'll see and he'll understand, and then he'll have me killed. Probably kill me himself. You don't *know* Lon!"

Ned turned his back to the Pancahtan.

"If you ask your father to let me use the key," Lissea said, ticking off probabilities without particular emphasis, "then he'll know its significance—guess, at any rate. After that, you won't be able to remove the key yourself.''

Carron nodded miserably.

"I don't think there's any likelihood of his agreeing to your request," Lissea continued. "Especially since he's ordered you to keep away from me and the expedition members in general. Is that correct?"

"I don't know," Carron said, knotting his fingers together before him. "Yes, I suppose so. Yes."

Lissea nodded, her eyes empty. "Yes," she said, "that's what I thought."

She shrugged. Her visage and stance shifted with the movement, becoming as hard and brilliant as an oxy-hydrogen flame. "Slade," she said, "go back to the Jeep and monitor radio traffic. Don't disturb me unless there's an attack on the *Swift.*"

"Yessir," Ned said. He turned to the steps, putting his left hand on an upper tread to guide him in the surreal half-light.

"I'm going to get additional information on these keys," Lissea said in a brittle voice. "Perhaps we can build one from equipment aboard the *Swift.*"

Perhaps pigs can fly. Perhaps the lion will lie down with the lamb.

"And Slade?" Lissea called. "Close the hatch behind you, will you?"

"Yessir."

Echoes of fire and bloodshed reverberated, in the bunker and in Ned's mind.

The sun had set while the three of them were in the bunker. The primary had not yet risen.

Given the size of Lon Del Vore's pet, the variety of life in the forests of Pancahte shouldn't have surprised Ned as much as it did. He sat with his back to a tree-trunk at the edge of the clearing, as still as a sniper: watching, listening, trying not to think.

The largest creature of this night was a snuffling omnivore the size of a raccoon. Its long snout delicately skimmed the

leaf mold. When scent located a target, one or both of the
creature's thumb-claws swept sideways and down. Each
stroke was as quick and startling as the snap of a spring trap.

In the air, other hunters patrolled. Small, scale-winged
creatures drove ceaseless spirals and figure-eights across the
clearing, sucking gulletfuls of the chitinous insect-equivalents
that chose the open space in which to dance and mate.

Twice while Ned waited, a hook-beaked flyer stooped from
its vantage point on the peak of a cone tree. Both times the
killer smashed an insectivore to the ground, pivoted on one
wing, and snatched its prey back up to its eyrie. The flight was
a single complex curve, executed as smoothly as a sailor ties a
familiar knot.

With magnification at ten-power and his helmet's micro-
processor sharpening the infrared images, Ned watched the
killer shred its prey. The victim's skin and wings, stripped
away by tiny cuts of the beak, fell to the floor of the clearing
in tatters before the creature bolted the remainder whole.

Ned watched; and, despite himself, thought.

The hatch opened partway. The bunker was silent. The system's own illumination had shut down, and the lightball was
by now only a flicker of gray.

Lissea held the hatch vertical. It shielded her from the vehicles, though Ned had a perfect view of his companions from
the edge of the clearing. She bent down, kissed Carron as he
stood two steps below her, and then shook free of his would-
be embrace.

She flung the hatch fully open and called exultantly, "All
right, Slade. We're ready to go. Fire 'em up!"

"You've got interesting bird life here, Del Vore," Ned said
easily as he rose to his feet. "Do you call them birds,
though?"

He rolled the switch over his visor to restore an unmagni-
fied field of view, though he left the receptors on thermal
imaging.

Carron tripped on the last step and almost dropped Lissea's
toolbox. Lissea continued to walk to the Jeep. She neither
paused nor looked back.

"I can take that," Ned said, reaching for the toolbox and removing it from Carron's grip.

"Ah, yes, we say birds," Carron said, but Ned was already striding for the hovercraft behind Lissea. "I, ah—Lissea, I'll be there."

She was in the driver's seat. "I'll take us back," she explained as Ned settled the case carefully into the small luggage trough behind them. "I like to drive, sometimes."

Carron had jumped into his vehicle. The aircar spun its fans up loudly, howling before Carron suddenly coarsened the blade angle. The car jumped vertically and bobbled as the AI kept it balanced with difficulty. Carron waved over the side as he flew out of the clearing, fifty meters high and rising.

"Not a natural driver," Lissea said mildly as she engaged the Jeep's fans. "But he's going to steal the key we need from the collection in the palace."

"I thought he might," Ned said. He removed his commo helmet and massaged his temples with his eyes closed.

"The bunker provided full instructions as to how to use the key," Lissea said. "There's a virtually infinite number of settings, but only three standard ones. The bunker thinks that in these circumstances the people who set the tanks on auto-patrol would have used a standard setting."

What circumstances are these? Ned thought, but he didn't say that aloud. Instead he said, "Carron seems a nice fellow. Certainly bright enough. Seems a bit, you know . . . young for his age."

"Slade," Lissea said without looking away from her driving, "drop it. Now."

A lot of us guys are young for our age.

There was a party going on around the *Swift* when Lissea pulled up.

The wedge-shaped landing site was big enough to hold a freighter forty times larger than the expedition's craft. Shelters of canvas, wood, and plastic sheeting had sprung up in the vacant area between the blast walls. Ned wasn't sure the light structures would survive a large vessel landing in one of the immediately neighboring berths, but the spaceport authorities were routing traffic to the opposite side of the field for now.

The Pancahtan official with whom Tadziki negotiated had been willing to find accommodations for the crew within Astragal. Tadziki refused the offer because he wanted to keep the men close by the vessel, but he'd parlayed it into supplies with which the crew could build their own quarters.

With the supplies and privacy had come local companionship. Privacy wasn't, as Ned remembered from field service, an absolute requirement.

"I figured on the merchants," Lissea said to Ned. "But I didn't expect so many women."

"The men did," Ned said. "Wonder what they're using for money, though?"

"Let's hope nobody's managed to trade the main engines for a piece," Lissea muttered as she shut the Jeep down.

The *Swift*'s boarding ramp was raised. Deke Warson sat cross-legged in the open airlock with a 2-cm weapon across his lap.

A redhead with blonde highlights and more drink in her than she had clothes on tried to climb over Deke. He turned her around with a gentleness that belied the strength he applied as he set her back on the gravel. "I come off watch in forty-three minutes, sister," he said affectionately. "I'll look you up then, okay?"

Deke noticed the Jeep and waved. "Hey, Cap'n!" he said. "Don't you got your suit on inside out?"

"Aw, I never get classy women," Toll Warson called from a bench at the table set up along one blast wall. "The ones I meet never bother to take their clothes off."

Men cheered and catcalled. Herne Lordling wasn't visible. Tadziki appeared at the hatchway behind Deke, wearing a reserved smile.

"Hey, what do you mean?" cried the woman seated beside Toll. Ned wasn't sure how serious she was. "I'm classy, honey. *I'll* take my clothes off!"

She started to roll her tube-top down over a bosom that

looked outsized even on a torso which no one would have described as slim. Toll laughed and stopped the woman by gripping her hands and burying his face between her breasts.

Lissea stood up. She stepped from the driver's seat to the Jeep's slight hood, a framework joining the two forward fan wells.

"Ned," she ordered, "blip the siren."

Still-faced, Ned leaned over and obeyed. He kept his finger on the button for three seconds, letting the signal wind to the point at which everyone in the encampment could hear it.

The locals—whores, gamblers, and the tradesmen who provided food and drink—blatted in surprise. The *Swift*'s mercenaries didn't speak. Breechblocks clashed as men made sure their weapons were charged before they lunged from their shelters. Some of the mercs appeared undressed, but none of them were unarmed.

"Crew meeting in the *Swift* in one—that's figures one—minute," Lissea shouted. "All personnel need to be present; nobody else will be."

Lissea looked around at her crewmen. "I'll keep it short, gentlemen," she added. "Then you can get back to what you were doing. Sorry."

She hopped down from her perch and strode to the airlock so swiftly that Deke had to hop to clear her path. Ned followed, wearing a cold grin. "Game point to the lady, Toll," he called over his shoulder as he entered the *Swift*.

Tadziki, careful as always, had kept a four-man watch. The vessel could take off at a moment's notice. Ned was the next man aboard. He squatted in front of the navigational consoles. They'd been rotated rearward for the moment. Dewey reclined in one, the adjutant in the other.

Lissea stood between the consoles with the control wand in her hand, watching her crewmen come through the airlock in various states of dress and drunkenness. Her face was unreadable.

Deke Warson cycled the hatch closed behind his brother, who lurched aboard carrying Coyne over his shoulder. "Forty-seven seconds!" Deke announced.

"Gentlemen," Lissea said. She didn't use the internal PA system. Men held their breath or shielded their open mouths with their hands.

"The operation will proceed tomorrow morning," she continued. "I'll have a device that will freeze the operations of one tank at a time. Cause the tank to pause, that is. Somebody has to enter each tank to shut it down."

"Who's in charge of the attack?" Herne Lordling asked from the back of the gathering. He'd been drinking, maybe more than most of the crew, but he held himself straight as a gunbarrel. He spoke in a truculent tone.

"I'm in charge, Herne," Lissea said. "I'll be operating the key, the device. I've had training regarding the device—"

A few minutes with a nonphysical simulacrum in the bunker.

"—and anyway, it's my line of work. For the first phase, all I need from most of you gentlemen is the absolute certainty that you won't try to get involved in the operation. In particular, that you not shoot at the tanks. If anybody shoots, the tanks switch from standby to attack mode. The key won't affect them in attack mode, and they'll quite certainly kill me. Does everybody understand that? *Clearly?*"

"What the hell did we come for, then?" Harlow muttered. Tadziki looked at him hard, but the mercenary sounded puzzled rather than angry.

Lissea raised a data disk fitted with a wave guide like the one with which she'd entered the bunker's memory. "The key works on one tank at a time. Then somebody has to enter the unit and load its internal computer with a language chip so that it can understand commands. The bunker, the Old Race system that provided the information, tailored a pair of language chips so that the less powerful computers aboard the tanks will be able to convert the data."

"Sounds like a job for me, Cap'n," Deke Warson said. Because he'd been on watch, his information-processing faculties were a hair sharper than those of his brother who'd been drinking.

"What?" said Herne Lordling. "No, that's my job!"

"I'm not ready for comment, yet," Lissea said harshly. "While my subordinate shuts down the first tank, I'll pause the second and shut it down myself. *Then* and *only* then, the rest of you will be responsible for proceeding to the lakeside complex, removing the capsule, and bringing it aboard the *Swift*."

"We'll have to move quickly, before the Treasurer decides to go back on his word and stop us," Tadziki said from the console. "But if we enter the patrolled area while the tanks are still operating, we blow the operation sky-high. Timing is critically important."

Lissea looked across the crowd to the Warsons. "Deke," she said, "Toll—there may be electronic locks on the buildings. I expect the two of you to get our people inside. Do you think you'll be able to open up an unknown system?"

Toll Warson raised his closed right hand. "Like a fish, Captain," he said. As he spoke, a shimmering blade snicked from between his fingers and snicked back.

"Worst case," Westerbeke volunteered, "we go over the roof into the courtyard and hump the curst thing out on our backs. Shouldn't be a big problem."

Other men nodded.

"Captain," Tadziki said, "I recommend that Slade act as your subordinate for the disarming process. He won't be necessary for moving the capsule. And he's got experience with tanks besides."

Tadziki's gaze was bland. Ned knew that Lissea and her adjutant hadn't had time to set this up since she'd returned from the bunker.

Lissea looked down at Ned as though the suggestion was a surprise to her. "Yes, all right," she said. "That's the way we'll do it. Herne, you'll command the anchor watch, and Tadziki will be in charge of retrieving the capsule. Any questions?"

"Wait a minute," Lordling said. *"Wait* a minute!"

"If there are no further questions," Lissea said, switching to the vessel's PA system to overwhelm the babble, "you can go back to your recreation."

"Curfew is in four hours standard," the adjutant added, rising to his feet. "We've got work to do in the morning."

"Wait a minute!" Lordling repeated.

"Shut up, you dickhead!" Josie Paetz snarled. "Uncle and me got a girl *good* and ready about the time we got called away!"

"Dismissed," Lissea said. Deke hit the ramp switch to empty the vessel fast. There'd be no problem with locals boarding while the herd of mercenaries thundered in the opposite direction.

"Slade," Lissea said, speaking unamplified again, "you and I will need to go over familiarization procedures for the tanks. I've brought data from the bunker in holographic form."

"Yessir," Ned said as he stood up. He kneaded the long muscles of his thighs. It felt like it'd been a long day, but he hadn't done anything yet. "Yes, Lissea. I'm looking forward to that."

The sun and the primary were near opposite horizons. Ned, at the controls of one Jeep, watched the faint double shadow they cast around the *Swift*.

A Pancahtan driver pulled up in an empty 1-tonne truck and got out. He waved gaily toward the mercenaries as he joined the spectators clogging the terminal area.

This was the most exciting event on Pancahte in decades. People from all across the world had turned out to watch it.

Yazov's five-man team leaped aboard the second of the trucks Pancahte was loaning the expedition for transport. Deke Warson and his team were on the vehicle Tadziki had borrowed the day before, while the adjutant himself manned a powerful sensor suite on a Jeep with Toll Warson driving.

"*Ready when you are, Cap'n,*" Deke reported.

"*Let's do it,*" Lissea said.

Ned twisted the throttle to three-quarters power and tilted his yoke forward to follow at a comfortable ten-meter separation behind the Jeep Toll drove. The borrowed hovercraft slid in behind the Jeeps with their fans bellowing. A single truck could have carried all ten men, but not ten men and the capsule they meant to return with.

The crowd cheered. Hovercraft and a few aircars paralleled the expedition as Toll swung east to skirt Astragal. Streamers flew from the vehicles, and many of the brightly caparisoned passengers waved enthusiastically.

Ned hadn't expected the locals to be supporting Lissea. In all likelihood they were just cheering for the excitement. A public execution would have done as well.

That might be next.

Crops grew in vast fields illuminated by tethered balloons which emitted light at the high-energy end of the spectrum that the Earth-derived vegetation required. Local plants couldn't supply human nutritional needs, though Pancahte's animal life was fully edible.

"How do you like being star turn at the circus?" Lissea asked.

Their commo helmets clicked—leakage from the microwave links transmitting power from each field's fusion plant to the balloons. Ordinary pole-mounted lights would be toppled within days by Pancahte's seismic activity.

"Let's see how the performance goes," Ned said. "Just now, I'm thinking farming—*that's* a worthy occupation."

She laughed, squeezed his biceps without looking at him, and went back to studying the minute projection of a tank's interior on her visor.

Ned hadn't carried his submachine gun. There wouldn't be room for the weapon within the fighting compartment of the Old Race tank which the bunker had displayed. There shouldn't be need of the weapon—any weapon—if it came to that; but Ned had stuck a pistol in the right breast pocket of his tunic. It only weighed a kilo, and it didn't cramp his movements.

A quartet of big aircars loaded with members of the Treasurer's Guard in powered armor fell in behind the expedition. A few of the civilian vehicles sheered off, and the enthusiasm of the remaining spectators was noticeably muted.

"Adjutant to captain," Tadziki reported from the lead Jeep. *"There's quite a reception committee waiting for us three klicks ahead, just short of the start point. Over."*

"Noted," Lissea replied. *"As we expected. Captain out."*

She glanced over at Ned. "Usually about half the men carry submachine guns," she said. "Today everybody's got a two-centimeter instead. What do you think?"

Ned smiled. The big shoulder weapons were medicine for powered armor.

"I think you hired the best there is, Lissea," he said. There was a trill in his voice that surprised him. Adrenaline was already making his muscles shiver, bucking against the limited movements that driving a Jeep permitted. "My money's on the visitors if something pops."

"I'll have the balls of any of my people who starts it," Lissea muttered; which was a way of saying the same thing: that both of them expected to survive, and *that* was an irrational attitude if Ned had ever heard one.

The lead Jeep carried a portable sensor suite nearly comparable to the unit built into the *Swift*. Toll would halt on high ground outside the tanks' patrol area. Tadziki would monitor the sensors, providing remote data to Ned's and Lissea's commo helmets on call—and, in an emergency, without being asked. The need to judge when to interrupt somebody in a life-threatening situation was the reason Tadziki and not another crew member was in charge of the equipment.

The country south and east of Astragal was flat between volcanic dikes and had good soil. Where the ground hadn't been cleared for agriculture, it was covered by native forests.

North of the city, the land became broken and sandy. Trees dwindled to stunted individuals spaced ten or twenty meters apart, then were replaced by a species of ground cover that was so pervasive as to constitute a virtual monoculture.

Purple-black leaves spread from spiky centers like lengths of carpet. They completely hid the soil. Where the skirts of the lead Jeep bruised a track across them, the leaves curled up and exuded a spicy fragrance. Droplets of condensed dew glittered among the undersurface hairs.

Ned worked cautiously over a jumble of rocks that were almost big enough to force him to take the Jeep around. "There's the welcoming committee," Lissea said. She was able to watch the horizon while the driver's attention was focused just ahead of the flexible skirts.

Thousands of Pancahtans waited near a ridge of rock or hard-packed sand. The civilians wore the bright garments that most on this dismal world affected, but there were over a hundred guards in powered armor as well.

Toll Warson curved his Jeep off to the left, heading for a single gigantic boulder which had collected a ramp of sand up its lee side. Topo maps showed the boulder was the best nearby vantage point. It provided a view across to the other side of Hammerhead Lake.

Lissea and Ned might have used the Pancahtans' own satellite imagery. Neither of them wanted to trust the goodwill of the Treasurer, who was at best a very doubtful neutral.

The ridgeline and the reverse slope were in the area which the tanks defended. Ned would enter while terrain blocked both tanks' line-of-sight weapons, but there'd be no chance of withdrawing over the crest once he'd committed. The ridge was quite literally a deadline.

He drove toward the array of Pancahtan troops. Lon Del Vore and Ayven wore gold and silver armor respectively. Their faceshields were raised. The powered suits were so brightly polished that reflections turned their surfaces into a harlequin montage.

"Pretty little peacocks, aren't they?" Lissea murmured, but that was probably bravado. She knew as well as Ned did that mirrored metal would scatter much of the effect of a powergun bolt.

Lon, Ayven, and the six guards closest to them sat on two-place aircars with spindly fuselages. The fan nacelles were mounted on outriggers. There was a small cab to protect each fabric-uniformed driver, but the soldier behind him had only a saddle and footboards.

The six cars lifted in unison and flew toward the Jeep in two parallel lines. Ned slowed without orders. He heard the note of the trucks behind him change as the mercs driving flared to either side, ready to spread their troops in a line abreast if shooting started.

The aircars roared down. Each pivoted on its vertical axis like members of a drill team. The Treasurer was showing off the proficiency of his troops; but no argument, they *were* proficient.

Lon flew at ground level to the right of the Jeep; Ayven, to the left. They'd closed their faceshields. *"I want you to know,* Captain *Doormann,"* Lon's amplified voice boomed, *"that I'm aware you came to Pancahte to scout us for pirates. Well, your plan won't work. Off-world thugs will get no more from us than enough ground to scatter their ashes!"*

Lissea touched a switch on her commo helmet. *"Sir,"* she said on a push the locals had used in the past, *"we came in peace and we hope to go in peace. All we want from Pancahte is the loot my kinsman stole—and that on the terms you set, after we first disarm the tanks which have heretofore inter-dicted this portion of your planet. Over."*

The lines of aircars accelerated away in a pair of fishhook curves without further comment. They stayed low. The pow-erful downdraft of their fans flung long leaves about like sheets flapping from the line on a windy day.

Carron pulled out of the mass of armored men in an even smaller vehicle, a one-man hovercraft. It swayed and hopped across irregularities hidden beneath the vegetation. Lon bel-lowed something from his aircar, but he didn't attempt to in-tercept his son.

Ned slowed the Jeep as Carron brought his vehicle in close on the passenger side. "Stop us here," Lissea ordered, adding a hand signal in case her soft words were lost in the intake rush. Ned eased them down gradually, so as not to surprise either Carron or the vehicles following.

Carron reached over and gripped the side of the Jeep. He'd taken off his jacket and held it crumpled in his hand. "Lis-sea," he said, "I've thought it over. Lon will kill me—*kill* me when he learns that I've taken the key."

"Carron, my life depends of you keeping your word," Lis-

sea said. There was a hint of desperation in her voice. Ned
didn't know how much of it was assumed—for the purpose of
convincing a needed supporter who'd gotten cold feet at
something beyond the last minute.

"I'm going to keep my word," Carron said, "but you've
got to help me. Lissea, *do* you love me like you said?"

Ned's eyes studied the ridgeline ahead of them. His skin
prickled as if it was being rubbed with a wet sponge.

"Yes I do, darling," Lissea said with soft certainty. "I
never dreamed I'd meet a man who shared my own soul so
completely."

"Then take me away with you!" Carron said. "That's the
only way I'll be safe. We can stay on the Twin Worlds and
study how the capsule functions!"

"All right, Carron," Lissea said. "If that's what you want,
I'll take you away with me. I love you, darling."

"Oh, Lissea . . ." Carron said. He straightened, balancing
again on his vehicle, and sped back toward his armored kins-
men.

His jacket was still draped over side of the Jeep. Lissea felt
the fabric, then reached into a side pocket. "It's here," she
said.

She looked at Ned.

He shrugged. "Whenever you want to, Lissea," he heard
his voice say.

"Then let's do it," she replied, rocking forward and back
as Ned shunted power again to the fans.

Ned keyed his helmet's Channel 3, a link to Tadziki that not
even Lissea could enter. Channel 2 was reserved for her and
the adjutant. "Give me three-position topo"—his Jeep and
both tanks—"on the left half of my visor, fifty-percent
mask," he ordered.

The vehicles—red, orange, and the white Jeep—appeared
against a sepia-toned terrain map through which Ned's immediate surroundings were still visible. He had full binocular vision, though the map was a hazy intrusion on the landscape.

Lissea sat in a state of apparent repose. She'd strapped the
key onto her left wrist; its lid was closed. She showed no signs

of impatience, though the Jeep idled when she had given the order to execute. The operation wouldn't begin until Ned was good and ready to commit.

"Mask the beaten zones in blue and yellow," Ned said.

Tadziki's response was only a heartbeat behind the last syllable of Ned's command. The beaten zones, portions of the terrain on which the tanks' weapons could bear, appeared as irregular, ever-changing blotches across the map display. Where both weapons bore, the colors merged into bright green.

Because the tanks were moving, the beaten zones varied from one moment to the next depending on where the vehicles were in regard to the broken terrain. Tongues of rock, boulders higher than the gunmount, and the slopes when a tank cruised along a swale—all reduced the area the weapons covered. By the same token, a tank that crested a ridge could suddenly sweep twice the ground it had a moment before.

The tanks were moving slowly, about—

"Eighteen kay-pee-aitch," Lissea said, as though she'd been reading Ned's mind.

"Any data on what their maximum speed is?" Ned asked as he watched the soft lights and waited to move—another thirty seconds unless the tanks reacted before then. . . .

"No," said Lissea. "A lot faster than this, though."

"That we can count on," Ned murmured as he slid his throttle and yoke forward.

He leaned slightly as he steered for one of the ten-meter gaps between civilian vehicles and the central mass of armored soldiers. He wanted an angle on the slope ahead, anyway.

"Go get 'em, Cap'n!" a mercenary shouted. Curst if a few of the Pancahtans didn't cheer as well.

It didn't matter. Nothing mattered but washes of blue-and-yellow light, and the white point accelerating toward them.

At the base of the ridge, air bleeding from the Jeep's plenum chamber made leaves hump and flail. Some of the foliage slapped the skirts angrily.

Ned brought his speed up. The sand higher on the slope

wasn't as well compacted. A few of the spike-cored plants had taken root, but they were small and their leaves were mere tendrils. The Jeep spat them away in clouds of sand drifting downslope. It wasn't a good surface even for an air-cushion vehicle, but the Jeep was light enough to maintain the momentum it had gained in its running start.

"They're reacting," Lissea said, a trifle louder than the howling fans required.

"Roger."

Ned and Lissea had considered timing their intrusion so that the tanks would be at the east and west limits of the patrol area when the Jeep entered the zone from the south. They'd thought the better of it when they realized that would leave them facing the both tanks simultaneously, with only a single key to disarm the pair of them.

Instead, one tank was on the far side of Hammerhead Lake. The other, though within a klick of where the Jeep would appear on the ridgeline, was in a channel. The surface rock had cracked and been wedged farther apart by lava that hardened into basalt at the base of the trough. For the ten or fifteen seconds the tank was in the narrow passage, its long gun could only bear frontwards.

The ridge was a spit of red sandstone too dense for the roots of normal plants to find purchase. Lichens marked the surface in concentric rings of varied hue, often brightly metallic.

"Hang on!" Ned cried, though he scarcely had to. The Jeep whooped onto the crest, bounced, and skidded down the reverse slope with gravity speeding its progress.

The more distant tank was marked orange on the display and its beaten zone was blue. It was accelerating but continuing to follow its previous patrol track. That was good. Ned had been afraid—and he'd seen the thought in Lissea's eyes, though neither of them had mentioned it—that the tanks might be able to cross the lake in an emergency rather than going around it.

The nearer tank stopped on a dime and backed, instead of proceeding to the far end of the channel it had entered. The turret rotated as soon as the sandstone walls permitted it to do so.

On Ned's visor, the yellow mask of the killing zone washed down from the ridge crest, pursuing the white dot but not quite catching it before the howling Jeep hurtled into a meter-deep gully as planned. Ned and Lissea shrieked triumphantly though the shock slammed them bruisingly forward.

Ned dumped the plenum chamber. He and Lissea dived from the Jeep to opposite sides. They and the vehicle were now safe until the tanks approached from one end of the gully or the other.

As they would surely do.

Lissea raised the lid of her key and touched markings on the formerly covered surface. Ned crouched against the wall of the gully, watching a schematic of his life or death played out on his visor against a background of grainy stone. The plot of the gully was a brown streak across the yellow of the beaten zone.

The red dot wobbled toward the gully. Topography prevented the tank from describing a perfectly straight line. Lissea took a deep breath, touched a point on the key, and raised the device over the rim of the gully. The Old Race vehicle didn't fire at her, but neither did it slow its advance.

Ned took the pistol out of his shirt pocket. It was something to do with his hands, as useful as whittling though no more so. Lissea lowered her device and punched another set of points, numbers, onto the markings.

The tank was two hundred meters away. In a moment, the vehicle's path would intersect the ravine and its weapon would rip across the intruders. A roar like the crackling of water poured into boiling grease accompanied the tank.

Lissea raised the key again. Light from the lid flickered over Ned's face for an instant.

The crackling stopped. The red dot on Ned's visor halted, and the ground shook as the vehicle dropped.

Ned jumped up. The second tank was moving fast, but it'd be out of sight for another minute, perhaps a minute and a half. "Come on!" he shouted as he climbed behind the yoke of the Jeep.

Lissea swung herself doubtfully into the vehicle. She held her left arm toward the tank and braced the wrist with the other hand. "Careful!" she said. "If you jar me out of line with this thing, they won't find enough of us to bury."

"Via, they won't come looking!" Ned said. He slammed closed the shutters and used the bounce of the plenum chamber filling abruptly to lift them over the lip of the ravine. Lissea's upright torso dipped and bobbed, but her arm remained pointed like a tank's stabilized main gun.

The gun of the Old Race tank was at a safe forty-five-degree angle; the turret was aligned fore and aft. The vehicle rested on the ground rather than drifting above it.

The smoothly curved tank was only six meters long and three meters in maximum breadth and height, but it must have weighed at least a hundred tonnes. Its weight had shattered the rock beneath in a pattern of radial cracks.

Ned pulled around to the rear of the vehicle where the hatch was supposed to be. Lissea pivoted on the seat beside him, pointing the key over his head. He vented the plenum chamber and leaped out as the Jeep skidded to a halt.

The surface of the tank had an opalescent shimmer like that of black pearl, irrespective of light from the sun or the primary. There was a sharp tang to the air, not ozone. Ned sneezed, then sneezed again.

According to the images the Old Race bunker supplied, a hasp on the rear of the tank would raise the hatch. There was no hasp on the glowing surface before him.

Ned opened his mouth to call for help. Nobody knew any more about the situation than he did. He patted the curved smoothness in hopes of finding a hidden mark or indentation.

There wasn't any mark, but an oval portion of the armor slid within itself when Ned touched it.

"Get on with it!" Lissea cried. "The other one's going to be on top of us!"

Ned flipped up his visor, then tossed the whole commo helmet to the ground. He slid feet-first into the tank. It fitted him more like a garment than a hundred-tonne machine.

A dull red lightbar glowed across the upper front of the cockpit. Except for that, the interior was as featureless as the inside of an eggshell. None of the controls or displays the bunker had briefed him to expect were present. This tank was similar to the bunker's examples, but it was a later model.

"Ned, for the *Lord's* sake!" Lissea screamed.

The bunker said the controls were smoothly rounded knobs on the dashboard. Ned visualized their location, then set his hands where they should have been.

The Jeep exploded in actinic brilliance that flooded through the open hatch. The gun of the oncoming tank seemed to fold matter inward along the path of its discharge.

"*Ned—*"

So she was all right, keeping the first tank between her and the weapon of the second, and the knobs *were* there; the controls sprang up beneath his palms, molding themselves to the shape of Ned's hands. Gunnery on the right, movement on the left.

The hatch behind him closed with such silent precision that Ned was aware only of the silence that now wrapped him. A panoramic display that gave the impression of sunlit solidity surrounded him. The other tank rippled forward, proceeding like a well-found ship over rough seas.

Ned was supposed to insert the language chip as soon as he got aboard, then shut the tank's systems down by verbal command. Instead, he pressed up and left on the gunnery control. The knob remained fixed. A white targeting circle slid down across the panorama. The displays didn't move, but the walls of the turret slid behind them as silent as quicksilver. He twisted the unmoving knob counterclockwise, tightening the circle to a white dot at the base of the other tank's gun mantlet.

The oncoming tank halted and crunched into the ground. The long-barreled weapon that had been questing for Lissea rose to its safe setting. She jogged around the bow of Ned's tank, holding the other vehicle in the key's calming transmission.

Ned let his breath out. He must have dropped his pistol in

the ravine or the Jeep. He didn't have it now.

He took his left hand from the unseen control and fished the language chip from his right breast pocket. The square, four-millimeter input point in the center of the dash had appeared when the systems came live. Ned inserted the wave guide and switched the chip to dump to the vehicle's computer. He didn't suppose it was necessary, but it was what they'd planned to do.

"Go to standby," Ned ordered.

The panoramic display vanished, leaving only the lightbar and cool gray surfaces. The turret aligned itself. Probably the gun rose to a nonthreatening slant as well, but Ned couldn't tell from where he was. The dash ejected the data disk and the input hole blanked over.

The hatch behind Ned opened again, to his sudden relief. He'd had a momentary vision of his body entombed in an armored coffin no one could breach. Perhaps Lissea would drape a banner reading MISSION ACCOMPLISHED on the tank . . . except that she'd be trapped forever in the other vehicle, wouldn't she?

Ned levered himself backward through the hatch. His arm muscles wobbled in reaction to the hormones that he'd finally burned away. He wondered if the Old Race crewmen had helpers or special equipment to ease the job of boarding and evacuating their vehicles.

Lissea crawled from the other tank. She looked as wrung-out as Ned felt, but he noticed that she'd brought her data disk out. He hadn't bothered to pick his up.

The tanks were dull. They looked like clay mock-ups rather than the glowing, vibrant terrors they'd been moments before. Ned ran his hand curiously over the flank of his unit. The surface felt vaguely warm.

A wave of vehicles swept toward the tanks across the previously forbidden area. The three hovercraft holding the *Swift*'s personnel were in the lead. Lissea spoke into her commo helmet's internal microphone.

Ned walked over to pick up his own helmet. His legs were unsteady for the first few steps.

The Jeep Ned and Lissea had ridden smoldered in a tiny knot that couldn't have contained more than a tenth of the mass the vehicle had had in the instant before the tank weapon had hit it. But all's well that ends well. . . .

Yazov's truck and the Jeep carrying Tadziki and Toll Warson pulled up beside the tanks. Scores of vehicles filled with Pancahtan civilians rocked along behind them.

Deke Warson waved from the cab of the other one-tonne without taking his eyes off the terrain in front of him. He kept going toward the lakeside buildings. The hovercraft was moving fast for the conditions, but Ned noted Deke made constant minute corrections to his vehicle's course and speed. He was driving with ten-tenths' concentration, not simply barreling straight ahead.

Lon Del Vore and most of his troops advanced only to the ridge marking the area which the tanks had interdicted. Ayven, however, in company with another two-place aircar and a pair of the larger vehicles loaded with six of the Treasurer's Guards apiece, sailed along fifty meters up and that far behind Deke's truck.

Though the aircars could easily have passed the air-cushion vehicle, Ayven and his troops instead matched speed. They followed like a pack of hunting dogs running down an antelope.

The four mercenaries in the back of Deke's truck eyed their escort with a deceptive nonchalance. Each man rode with a hand on the grip of his weapon and the muzzle cradled in the crook of the opposite arm. If trouble started, the sky would rain powered armor and bits of blasted aircars in a fraction of a second.

Lon's silver-armored son certainly knew that, so he wasn't planning to start trouble.

Toll skidded to a halt. Tadziki lifted himself from the Jeep one-handed before the skirts had braked to a complete halt. With his boot-soles as fulcrum, the adjutant used momentum to swing his body upright from the carefully chosen angle at which he'd left the vehicle. Whatever Tadziki's claims to have been strictly a noncombatant, the guy who performed that maneuver without falling on his ass had made more than his share of hot insertions.

"Slade, are you all right?" he demanded. "What happened to your helmet?"

The ground shook, though not as fiercely as some of the shocks Ned had already felt on Pancahte. The tanks jiggled, grinding the rock beneath them into gravel of a smaller size. The trembling impacts sounded like heavy machinery working—as, in a manner of speaking, it was.

"I took it off," Ned said. "It's like wearing a glove inside those things."

He stepped toward the back of Yazov's truck. Josie Paetz reached down to help him board.

"Tadziki, Warson," Lissea said brusquely, "go on with Yazov. Slade, we'll take the Jeep."

Toll rose from the driver's seat as though he'd expected the order. Maybe he had; Ned certainly hadn't.

Half the civilian spectators followed Ayven at a respectful distance. The others were circling or had parked near the tanks.

Carron broke through the pack and drove straight to where Lissea stood. His one-man hovercraft had a narrow footprint and a proportionately high center of gravity with a man aboard. It wasn't a good choice for terrain so rough. Plant juices staining Carron's cheek and right sleeve suggested that he'd managed to low-side when the little vehicle went over.

"Lissea!" he said. "Remember your promise. You're going to take me along?"

Toll Warson withdrew his head from the hatch of the nearer tank. "Sure doesn't look like much," he said. Ned looked at him sharply.

"If you're going to come," Lissea said, "then get moving! We're heading for the lake."

She took the Old Race artifact from her wrist and tossed it to Carron as she got into the Jeep. He squawked and caught it.

The sensor suite bulged from the luggage trough and added

nearly fifty kilos to the Jeep's burden. If the loaded vehicle could carry the two big mercenaries, it ought to manage one man and a small woman, though.

"Bloody hell, Slade, drive!" she said. "Do you need an engraved invitation?"

Ned fumbled clumsily with the controls for a further instant before he got them sorted out. Toll had feathered the fans as he cut power, while Ned always left the blade angle coarse. The fans sang as Ned pushed the throttle forward, but it wasn't until he changed the unexpected setting that the Jeep lurched ahead.

The ground trembled again, without violence but continuing over a thirty-second interval. Ned wondered whether the crust of Pancahte was setting up for a major displacement. Worse come to worst, open country like this was as good a place as any in which to ride out an earthquake.

"But Lissea?" Carron called.

Pancahtan aircars marked the position of the leading truck like vultures following a dying horse. Yazov put his boot to the firewall as soon as Lissea implied he was clear to follow Deke's truck. Tadziki and Toll Warson boarded the 1-tonne on the fly, drawn onto the bed by the men already there.

Ned slid the Jeep's throttle to the stop also. He could adjust his speed by tweaking blade pitch and the angle of his fan nacelles, lifting high enough that the skirts spilled air when he needed to slow. The battery temperature gauge began to rise with the constant high-rate discharge, but that was nothing to worry about.

Some of the hurry was justified. Lissea was in command, so she ought to be present when her personnel reached the capsule. Less creditably, a part of Ned had no intention of losing a race to Yazov in a locally built truck.

Least creditable of all, Ned wanted to leave Carron Del Vore as far behind as possible. That was petty, but Ned didn't claim to be perfect.

On smooth stretches, the 1-tonne might have had a speed advantage, but on this terrain the Jeep's agility put it ahead early and kept it there. A bulge in a spreading leaf might be no more than a kink of growth, but it might as easily conceal a boulder big enough to rip the skirts off a hovercraft. The two mercenary-driven vehicles skidded and wove about the potential hazards.

Pancahtans took chances in an attempt to keep up with the *Swift*'s experts. Some of the locals flew up, flailing as their vehicles cartwheeled and scattered bits of bodywork across the landscape.

The peninsula was nearly three hundred meters long. Some of the civilian craft had stopped or were idling at the near end. Because all the Pancahtans were looking in the other direction, dicing between the vehicles brought shouts of anger and surprise. When the Jeep's skirts brushed an enclosed sedan, the civilian driver reached out to shake his fist—

And almost lost it when the 1-tonne blasted by, thirty meters behind. Several men in the box of Yazov's truck kept their weapons pointed while Josie Paetz jeered and pumped his right index finger through his left fist.

On both sides of the peninsula, Hammerhead Lake danced in vertical spikes. The Jeep's air cushion and the howl of its fans masked the vibrations agitating the water. Ned wished he'd learned more about the amplitude of the quakes to be expected on Pancahte.

The buildings and vehicles at the end of the peninsula were fifty meters ahead. "Hang on!" he ordered.

The nacelles were in the full-aft position to provide maximum forward thrust. Rather than reverse their angle with the wand on the left side of the control column, Ned spun his yoke to pivot the Jeep at the same time he dumped the plenum chamber.

The combination of active and passive braking slowed the vehicle from seventy kilometers per hour to a dead stop in less than twenty meters—excellent performance for a hovercraft. Besides, deceleration stresses pushed Ned and his passenger comfortably into their seatbacks instead of trying to bounce them off the dashboard.

Ned added a bit of tricky reverse steering to fishtail the Jeep between the big Pancahtan aircars. Guards with their faceshields raised gaped at the exhibition.

Ned hadn't thought about Lissea since he had got the Jeep under weigh. His attention had been limited to the potential threats and potential obstacles in all directions of his vehicle. Now he looked at his commander in sudden trepidation—*the sedan their skirts had brushed, that was on Lissea's side.*

She was smiling and relaxed. "Not bad," she said as she scissored her legs over the sidepanel. "Not bad at all."

Via, they'd both been tight as cocked pistols when they got into the Jeep. The fast ride had let out tensions. The business with the tanks was more like waiting for the guillotine to drop.

Deke Warson knelt beside the circular door of the nearest building. "Knelt" was the operative word: the opening was only a meter-fifty in diameter, and the wall from soil to roof was less than two meters high. A sunken floor could explain the outside height, but the door was presumably sized to its builders.

Who were unlikely to have been human—though the Old Race tanks had to be crewed by beings the size and shape of men. As Ned had said, the tank fit him like a glove.

Three Pancahtan soldiers stood in line abreast on either side of Ayven in his silver armor. They watched the mercenaries involved with the building five meters in front of them.

A severe shock—the first Ned had noticed during this spasm—rocked the site. One of the armored men fell down. He jumped upright again and backed into his proper space. Hammerhead Lake was beginning to boil.

"Got it!" Deke shouted, oblivious to external events while he concentrated on the lock. A kit of delicate electronic tools lay open beside his right boot. The circular doorpanel rotated outward and up from a hinge concealed at the two-o'clock position.

Harlow and Raff jumped onto the roof from the inner courtyard. "No problem!" Harlow called. "We can just lift it over."

Lissea slipped between Pancahtan guards. Ned followed a pace behind her. As a reflex, he put his hand on one man's shoulder.

That was a waste of effort. The fellow didn't feel the contact. When he lurched, startled by Lissea's sudden appearance before him, he knocked Ned into his fellow. It was like jumping between moving buses: nothing an unaided human did was going to affect his mechanical neighbors.

"Like hell we're going to lift the sucker!" Deke called as he squatted in the low entrance with his 2-cm weapon pointing forward. "We're going to take it right through this door I got open!"

"Shut up, Deke," Tadziki ordered. "We're going to do exactly what the lady behind you says we're going to do. Now, get out of her way!"

Deke glanced over his shoulder in surprise. "Sorry, Cap'n," he muttered.

He hunched quickly through the opening instead of hopping aside. Lissea followed. Ned gestured Tadziki to go through behind her, then gripped the roof's coping with both hands. Harlow reached down to help. Ned got his boot over the edge unaided and straightened again on top.

Ned wasn't claustrophobic. After his moment of fear in the Old Race tank though, he didn't feel an immediate need to enter another strait enclosure.

Like the Old Race bunker, this building appeared to have been cast in one piece. The roof was unmarked by antennas, ventilators, or support devices of any sort.

The walls of the inner court were pentagonal and parallel to those of the exterior. The enclosed area was about five meters wide. Flanked by Harlow and Raff, Ned reached the inner edge just as Deke Warson led Lissea into the courtyard on her hands and knees.

Raff spun twice, aiming his rocket gun at what turned out to be nothing—smoke or the brightwork of a civilian vehicle catching the late sun. His disquiet bothered Ned. The Racontid generally seemed as imperturbably as a rock.

"See, it's just a little thing," Deke said. "We'll get it through the doors easy." He gestured to the capsule as though it was his sole gift to Lissea.

The ground shook again, violently. The building moved as

a piece, but Ned noticed the ancient structure fifty meters away was dancing to a slightly different rhythm. He bent to rest the tips of his left fingers on the roof to keep from falling.

A crevice opened beneath a Pancahtan hovercraft, then slammed shut again to pinch the flexible skirt. The occupants bailed out, bawling in surprise. This couldn't be a common occurrence, even for Pancahte.

Hammerhead Lake shuddered. Great bubbles of steam burst in a warm haze that drifted over the buildings.

Carron Del Vore was in the courtyard with Lissea and six of the mercenaries. Toll Warson waited at the outside entrance, his weapon held across his chest as if idly.

Several of Ayven's companions had fallen because of the most recent shock. The Treasurer's son remained upright. The primary washed the left side of his powered armor blood red.

"Lissea?" Ned called. "Better move it out. I don't like the look of the lake."

He gestured. She couldn't see the lake's surface, but the plume of steam must by now be visible from the courtyard.

"What do you figure's going on, Master Slade?" Harlow muttered. He was as nervous as Raff, or he wouldn't have asked the question in a fashion that tacitly granted Ned officer status.

Lissea gave a curt order and pointed at the capsule.

"Lava must've entered the water channel feeding the lake," Ned said. "We're going to have a geyser or worse any minute now."

The capsule rested on an integral ring base. Four of the mercenaries gripped the ovoid and tilted it end-on so that they could manhandle it through the doors. It was heavy but not too heavy to carry.

Carron reached between two of the men. He touched what must have been a latch because the whole upper surface of the capsule pivoted upward. Deke Warson cursed and bobbed his head as the top opened toward him.

Inside the capsule was the wizened yellow mummy of a man. They'd found not only Lendell Doormann's capsule, but the desiccated remains of Lendell Doormann as well.

"All right, let's get it moving," Lissea ordered. She slammed the capsule closed again. "We can look at all that later."

Her voice sounded thin against the background rumble of Hammerhead Lake. Ned wished he had a gun, even if it was no more than the pistol he'd lost while deactivating the tanks.

Feeding the capsule through the doorway was a two-man job. Deke took the front of the load; Coyne, who was bigger than he was strong but was strong nonetheless, took the back.

Lissea was talking to Tadziki and Carron. The men bent with their heads cocked to hear her over the voice of Pancahte.

"Come on," Ned muttered to Harlow and Raff. "We can help out front when they get it clear."

The other men in the courtyard couldn't get through the doorway while the capsule blocked it. Dewey looked up and called to the trio on the roof, "There's nothing but dust inside. What do you suppose this place is? It's *old.*"

Ned nodded. All they could prove was that the bunker, the tanks, and these very different buildings predated the settlement of Pancahte five hundred years before. His instinct told him that they were at least an order of magnitude more ancient yet; which of course was impossible, if the Old Race was really human.

If humans had evolved on Earth.

"Let's go," he repeated to his companions. He crossed the roof in quick strides. The land shuddered in an undertone. The vibration wasn't immediately dangerous, but it seemed even more menacing that the fierce jolts of moments before.

"Toll, we're coming," he called and dropped down beside Warson.

Toll grinned sidelong at him. "Our friends there are getting nervous," he said with a nod toward the guards in powered armor. Ground shocks had kinked the parade-ground line. Even Ayven stood skewed a little from his original stance.

"They're not the only ones," Ned said.

Deke backed through the doorway, cursing the load and the building's architect. He kept his end of the capsule centered perfectly in the circular opening. Ned stepped in beside him.

There were no handholds on the top end of the ovoid, so it was a matter of balancing the weight on spread hands. A patina roughened the capsule's metal surface enough for a decent grip.

Raff and Harlow took opposite sides in the middle. More men spilled through the doorway behind Coyne, but there was no need for them now.

Toll Warson walked to the bearers' right front like a guide dog. He waved with his left hand to Ayven Del Vore. "Give us a hand, then," he warned. "Or get out of the way."

"What is it?" Ayven said. His voice was harsh and metallic through the suit's amplifier, but even so it sounded weak beside the crust's groans.

"Show him what it is!" Carron said, stepping between the capsule and the line of guards. "Set it down for a moment so that my brother can see exactly what he's trying to steal."

"Yes, do that," Lissea said.

"I represent the government of Pancahte!" Ayven rasped. *"I have a right to know what strangers are trying to take from our world!"*

The mercenaries lowered carefully. The ovoid wasn't intended to rest on its side. Ned stuck the reinforced toe of one of his boots out to cushion the capsule from ground shocks. The adjutant muttered an order to Coyne, who did the same on the reciprocal point.

"Blood and martyrs!" Josie Paetz said. Hot water slopped over the shoreline and swept across the rock.

When the wave withdrew, it left a slime of mineral salts. The water lapped one of the Pancahtan guards to the ankles of his armored boots. He backed farther away, staring at the lake's roiling surface.

Carron worked the capsule's latch again and drew the lid open. Ayven started back, throwing a hand up reflexively to shield his armored face.

"It's a coffin, brother dear!" Carron cried. "Do you begrudge Captain Doormann the corpse of her great-granduncle? Do you?"

The two-place aircar which Ayven had ridden jiggled on

the ground. The driver looked nervously out of his cab. The similar vehicle whose soldier passenger was still astride the saddle now hovered twenty centimeters above the rock.

Ayven spun on his heel. His armored foot struck sparks from the rock. *"Go on back to Astragal,"* his amplified voice commanded. *"The body you can have, but the capsule my father will decide on."*

The men lifted. Lissea stepped close to Ned to swing the lid down with her extended arm. The Pancahtan guards stepped clashingly out of the way. Had they never seen a dead man before?

Though the remains of Lendell Doormann had an eerie look to them. It wasn't that the wizened corpse seemed alive: the rings of blue-gray fungus on the sallow skin belied that notion. Rather, it seemed that the body had been dead and mummifying in the sealed capsule for the entire time since Doormann vanished from Telaria—despite the fact that he had carried on intercourse with the Pancahtans for another fifty years yet.

A double wave broke over the margins of Hammerhead Lake. The pulses washed across the peninsula from three directions. "Bloody *fucking* hell," Deke muttered, stepping through water as high as his boot tops with the same mechanical precision that he had maintained when the surface was dry.

Yazov was already in the open cab of the nearer 1-tonne, though it wasn't the vehicle he'd driven to the site. The hovercraft's flexible skirts dampened the quick choppy motions of the ground into longer-period motions. The truck surged and fell slowly. By contrast, the two big aircars of the guards hopped and chattered despite the shock absorbers in their landing struts.

The mercenaries handed the capsule to their fellows waiting on the bed of the 1-tonne. "Tilt it back on its base," Lissea ordered.

"And two of you hold it there," Tadziki added as he helped lift the ovoid straight himself. "Paetz and Ingried."

Ned's helmet hissed, static leaking from a nearby transmission. Ayven had given an order to his men, who stamped toward the six-place aircar. One of the guards slipped on yellow-white froth that had been left when the waves receded. He hit the rock like a load of old iron.

A shock knocked down almost all of the people standing on the peninsula, Ned among them. The open door of the pentagonal building flapped with the violence of the quake. Hinges which had survived centuries and perhaps millennia snapped off. The panel clanged down on edge and hopped around an inward-leaning circle until it fell flat.

Hammerhead Lake belched again. Because of the steam, Ned thought another wave was oozing over the shore.

Yazov ran up his fans. Air spewed from beneath the truck's skirts. Ned stepped back, peering toward the lake.

"Get going!" Lissea ordered. Her shout was barely audible. Carron was at her side, looking concerned but not frightened.

Yazov pulled the 1-tonne in a tight turn. Mercenaries on the truck bed braced themselves against the capsule to steady it.

It wasn't a wave. It wasn't a geyser either, though steam and water roaring a hundred meters high made it look as though it might be.

Ned ran toward the parked Jeep. He keyed the general push on his helmet radio and shouted, "Don't anybody shoot! This is Slade! Don't anybody shoot or we're all dead!"

The thing rising from the lake was faceted and huge, towering a hundred meters above the shoreline before anyone could be sure it was a solid presence. Its bulk walled the three sides of the peninsula into what had been Hammerhead Lake. The lake was the pit which had held the thing, and the thing filled that kilometers-long cavity as a foot does its sock.

The thing was a starship, a pair of dodecahedral masses joined at the center by a pentagonal bar. Though three hundred meters long and nearly as thick from base to peak, the bar looked tiny compared to the twelve-faceted balls it joined together. Lightning flashed from one lobe to the other. The enveloping steam flickered like a fluorescent tube warming up.

"Don't anybody shoot! Don't shoot!"

Beside Ned, the guard riding the two-place aircar twitched

forward the fat-bored powergun slung across his back. He aimed upward at a forty-five-degree angle and fired. The concussion knocked Ned down again.

Recoil from the big weapon made the struts of the hovering aircar tap down. It slid back toward the larger unit with six guards aboard.

A spark snapped from one of the starship's triple angles. The shooter's head and helmet vanished in liquid fire. The guard toppled backwards out of his saddle. The large aircar behind him exploded, punched through by a five-sided beam that expanded during its passage.

The vehicle doubled in on itself. Men in powered armor tumbled to either side. Four of them were uninjured, but the two on the center seats had lost everything between waist and knees. Rock beyond the collapsing aircar gouted up as lava, twenty meters high, spraying as far as the civilians at the base of the peninsula.

The driver grounded his vehicle, jumped from his cab, and collided with Ned. The Pancahtan ran blindly toward Hammerhead Lake, and the starship still rising from it.

Ned grabbed the handhold on his side of the small aircar's cab. There was a folding step, but he couldn't flip it down with his boot toe and he didn't dare risk taking his hands off the grip while the driverless vehicle slid sideways.

Something whanged off the opposite side of the cab, a fan-flung pebble or a bullet loosed wildly by a man trying to fight the terrors in his head. The aircar pivoted in a half circle as Ned pushed it in his desperate attempts to board. He finally got his leg over the frame connecting the cab to the rear saddle, then dragged himself through the cab's side door.

The starship continued to rise. The upper angles of the lobes were lost in haze and lightning half a kilometer high, but the lower surfaces were still within the margin of the pit. Twice sparks licked away swatches of rocky landscape. The discharges might have been retribution on human gunmen, though there was no evidence left in the bubbling lava.

Ned had never driven a Pancahtan aircar before, but there were only so many ways to arrange the controls of a vehicle meant for general use. He checked for the throttle and found it as an up-and-down motion of the control column. He lifted, spun, and hauled back on the wheel. The car rose to ten meters in a climbing turn, accelerating above the ground traffic as Ned drove toward the deactivated tanks.

The Old Race hadn't left the tanks to keep later humans away from Hammerhead Lake. The tanks had held something else down in that pit. It was up to Ned to undo his mistake of an hour before.

If it was possible to undo the mistake now.

Pancahtan hovercraft tore across the ground like wind-blown scud. They dragged humps and tangles through the vegetation to mark their passage.

Ned had lost his commo helmet when he'd struggled aboard the aircar. He didn't know what was happening to the rest of the *Swift*'s complement, didn't know if any of the others were alive, and that couldn't matter now.

He didn't know if Lissea was alive.

The tanks were where he and Lissea had deactivated them a hundred meters apart, skewed and lonely on the purple-smeared landscape. Ned brought the aircar down hard and too fast. He was ham-fisted in reaction to the second adrenaline rush in an hour. The skids banged to the stops of their oleo suspension, then bounced him up and sideways.

Ned didn't have the right reflexes for this particular vehicle. He tilted the column against the direction of bounce, but he must have managed to lift the throttle also. Increased power to the fans flipped the vehicle to the ground on its back. Momentum then rolled it upright again.

The cab was dished in, wedging the driver's door. Ned put his boot-heel to the latch, smashing the panel outward as violently as if a shell had hit it. He was all right. He'd clamped his legs beneath the seat frame to keep from rattling around the cab like the pea in a whistle. He'd feel it in his calf muscles in twelve hours or so, but he was fine for now.

And now might be all there would ever be for Edward Slade.

He ran toward the tank. The hatch was open as he'd left it.

The massive vehicle quivered in response to high-frequency shocks pulsing through Pancahte's crust.

The alien starship had risen completely above ground. The lower surfaces appeared to rest in a pillow of steam bloodied by the light of the primary. Beams sprang from a high point on either bell. Their tracks looked as if matter had been pressed flat in their path and twisted.

Ned grabbed the edges of the tank's hatch to support himself. Previous blows by the starship had been quick, snapping sparks. These beams differed in type and intensity. They augered south, beyond the visible horizon. The beams had no identifiable color, but they throbbed dazzlingly bright on a world where ruddy light muted all other brightness.

The horizon swelled into a bubble glowing with the colors of a fire opal, as furious as the heart of a star. The Old Race bunker. The starship was attacking the Old Race bunker.

Ned squirmed feet-first into the Old Race tank. The bubble at the point of the intersecting beams burst skyward like a lanced boil, spewing plasma and vaporized rock into Pancahte's stratosphere. The whole sky shimmered, white at the core of the jet and a rainbow of diffracted hues shimmering outward from that center.

Ned gripped the dashboard. The controls shaped themselves to his palms; the visual panorama sprang into razor-sharp life. The hatch thudded closed behind his head an instant before the shock of the bunker's destruction reached him through the rocks of the crust.

The landscape hunched upward in spreading compression waves, then collapsed in the rarefactions that followed. The Old Race tank had lifted on its propulsion system when the controls came live. Even so it pitched like a great turtle coming ashore. The atmospheric shock seconds later was mild by comparison, though it must have been equivalent to that of a nuclear explosion at a comparable distance.

Despite Pancahtan construction methods, there couldn't have been a building undamaged in Astragal. As for the *Swift*—

The *Swift* would have to wait. Ned focused his targeting circle on the center of one of the alien starship's huge lobes.

He pressed his right thumb down. The springiness of the tank's controls shifted to something dead and dry, like old concrete. The panoramic screen didn't blank, but the real-time visuals switched to icons: the starship was a red crosshatch, while the Pancahtan landscape became a sweep of tan polygons over which skittered blue blobs in place of the hovercraft fleeing from the peninsula.

The white targeting circle had vanished from the new display. The dull lightbar across the front of the fighting compartment shifted through bright red to orange.

The display returned to normal visuals. The tank gave a great lurch upward. The controls were live again, but the beam of the tank's weapon ripped a hole almost vertically into the sky, above the starship even though the vast construct continued to rise.

The rear hull of the tank had sunk turret-deep in lava so hot the rock curled in a rolling boil. When the propulsion system came on again, the tank sprayed upward to hover above the dense liquid as if it were still solid rock.

The starship lashed out again with the paired beams that had destroyed the Old Race bunker. The other tank was at the beams' coruscant point of intersection. The vehicle tilted, sinking into the molten rock as Ned's own tank had done a moment before.

The other tank's gun had sheared a collop out of one of the starship's lobes. Ned lowered his targeting circle to the upper edge of the pentagonal tube joining the bells. He cut downward.

The bar across the front of the tank bathed him in lambent yellow light verging toward green. The starship rotated around the vertical center of the tube. Ned's beam pared metal away from the alien construct like whiskers rising from the workpiece on a lathe.

The controls went dead; the display returned to icons. The second Old Race tank became a white star that dominated the dull landscape around it.

The color of Ned's lightbar rose from bright green to blue.

His hands had a leprous cast. He thought of the fungus on Lendell Doormann's face. He licked his lips, but his tongue was dry as well.

The visuals returned, flaring. The pool of lava encircling Ned's tank was white and meters deep, but his massive vehicle broached like a huge sea beast. The magma was unable to harm the tank so long as the vehicle's defensive systems had power, but if the rock hardened it would entomb Ned until the stars grew cold.

The other tank fired also, its beam a chain of hammered light. The starship's lobes had separated and were drifting downward in reciprocal arcs.

Ned focused his targeting circle on the lower edge of a bell. He held his gun steady as gravity dragged the ship fragment through his beam. Fiery streamers sparkled from the point of contact, twisting like octopus arms. They gouged away more of the ship's structure wherever they curled back against it.

The lightbar was vivid indigo, except where patches were beginning to sink into violet and blackness.

The other tank shot at the same lobe as Ned. An irregular wedge peeled away from the great dodecahedron and smashed into the ground an instant before the mass from which it had separated did. Sparks gouted skyward like kilotons of thermite burning. The sparks enveloped the larger portion as 't fell into them, warping the hull plates inward.

The tank's hatch shot open behind Ned. *"Eject at once!"* cried a voice that rasped directly on the human's lizard brain. *"This vehicle will terminate in ten seconds!"*

Ned had concentrated on gunnery, ignoring the movement controls because his tank could neither pursue nor flee from the starship lowering in the heavens. Now, the lava that glowed beyond the hatch was a ram battering the back of Ned's neck. He spun the live but unmoving knob within his left hand. The tank rotated on its axis, swinging the rear opening away from the pool of bubbling rock. Ned heaved himself clear.

The remaining lobe of the starship hit the ground kilometers away a few seconds after its sectioned fellow had struck.

The glare was a sparkling echo to the southern aurora where plasma from the bunker's destruction cooled and dissipated in a broad cloud.

Ned lay on sand and broken rock. The vegetation that had covered the ground was dead. Leaves were seared to a brown tracery of veins which themselves crumbled at the touch of Ned's hand.

Heat hammered Ned every time his heart beat. He stayed low, but sulphurous gases from the melted rock made his throat burn and his eyes water. He began to crawl toward where the other Old Race tank had been.

The vehicles rotted like sodium in an acid atmosphere. Bits scaled away from armor that had withstood forces that devoured living rock.

The groundshocks had ceased when the alien starship rose fully clear of its pit. The pop and crackle of huge explosions scattered the remaining wreckage, but that was a mild substitute. Occasionally a fireball sailed thousands of meters in the air, burning itself out to fall as ashes.

A breeze blew from the south to feed the flames of the starship's immolation. The air was fierce and dry, but cooling. Ned rose to his hands and feet, then stood upright.

Lissea was staggering toward him. She'd somehow lost the trousers of her utility uniform, and her right arm bled where the tunic sleeve was torn—

But she was alive, they were both alive, and the distant flames laughed as they cleansed Pancahte of the gigantic starship which had laired so long in its crust.

Light flickered from a dozen places on the horizon, as bright in total as the half-risen primary. A vehicle was coming toward Ned and Lissea from the east. Ned couldn't make out what it was.

"I saw you go off," Lissea croaked. "I . . . First I thought you were running away."

"I wasn't running away," Ned said. His voice sounded as though he'd had his throat polished with a wire brush.

Lissea nodded. "I know that. How long do you suppose it's been there, waiting?"

Ned looked toward the broad expanse of the starship's crash and shrugged. The white sparkle was dimmer than it had been initially, but parts of the mass would burn for days. "I don't want to think about it," he said. "If there was one, there could be others—here, maybe anywhere. *We* couldn't have done anything to stop it."

"No, I don't guess we could," Lissea agreed. She still wore her commo helmet. She adjusted the magnification control on her visor and said, "Carron's returning to pick us up. He brought me to the tanks when I realized what you were doing, but he had to get clear of the area at once. The car was no protection."

"*Carron* brought you here?" Ned said in amazement.

The aircar was a big, six-place unit like the ones that had carried sections of the Treasurer's Guard. It was the surviving member of the pair that had accompanied Ayven. Carron brought it down twenty meters from Ned and Lissea. The stubby landing legs skidded on the rock, striking sparks.

"Yes—Carron," Lissea repeated. She and Ned jogged drunkenly toward the aircar. Carron might have landed closer—but he might have put it down on top of them if he'd tried. The Treasurer's younger son hadn't become a better driver in the past hour. After Ned's own "landing" in the smaller car, he was willing to be charitable.

The sky toward Astragal glowed. Parts of the city were afire.

"Do you want to drive?" Carron shouted as Lissea climbed into the car. He didn't take his hands off the controls to help her. The fans buzzed angrily because of his unintended inputs. "If you want, you can drive, either of you!"

"Not in the shape we're in!" Lissea said. "Get us to the *Swift* as fast as you can."

She threw herself onto the other forward seat. Ned squatted behind and between the pair. Lissea seemed oblivious of the fact that the tail of her utility jacket barely covered her—lacy, black—underwear. An explosion had partly stripped her without taking either her boots or her commo helmet.

Carron lifted the big aircar to fifty meters and pointed it south. As soon as it was airborne, the vehicle's automatic controls took over, leveling and smoothing the flight. Ned hadn't realized how much the car's nervous hopping on the ground had irritated him until the motion stopped.

"How did you get this car?" Ned asked. "The guards didn't just let you have it, did they?"

"I EMPed them," Carron said. The smooth ride of the vehicle's own systems had calmed him also. He gestured toward the large attaché case lying in the midsection of the car beside Ned. "A cold electromagnetic pulse to freeze their armor. The powered suits have some shielding, but I scaled my generator to overcome it at short range."

At the end of the gesture, Carron put his hand on Lissea's bare thigh. She laid her own hand on top of his.

They passed an overturned civilian hovercraft. The survivors waved furiously. Carron ignored them. They'd probably be as safe where they were as they would in ravaged Astragal.

"I thought Ayven might have his men arrest me," Carron continued. "For the, you know, the key. I couldn't shoot my way through them, but a pulse that burned out the circuits of their suits all at once . . . So I carried a generator with me today. And I used it on the guards because I knew we couldn't get clear of that *thing* in a ground vehicle."

Carron was talking to Lissea. Ned avoided looking directly at the other man and calling attention to himself.

That Carron was technically capable of preparing such a plan shouldn't have been a surprise. He clearly wasn't stupid, and he was well enough versed in electronics to discuss the subject with Lissea, who was expert by galactic standards.

That Carron was ruthless enough to carry out the plan in the fashion described, leaving six men to die because he'd fried their circuitry and turned their powered armor into steel straitjackets—

Maybe that shouldn't have been a surprise either. He *was* Lon Del Vore's son and Ayven's brother.

The car reached the northern outskirts of Astragal. They'd

risen to a hundred meters, high enough to get a broad view of the chaos occurring in the city.

A series of parallel cracks arced through the developed area, about a kilometer apart. Extended, they would form circles centered on the site of the Old Race bunker.

When the bunker's defenses failed, the shock was sudden and from virtually a point source. At its highest amplitude, the wave front created stresses beyond the elastic limits of the rock on which Astragal was built. Everything along those points on the radius of expansion had been shattered to rubble.

People huddled in the streets, looking up at the aircar. Fires burned in many places, ignited by internal damage to the structures or by blazing matter slung from the bunker site. There was neither water nor the coordination necessary to extinguish the fires, so the situation was rapidly getting out of control.

"Lissea," Ned said, "the spaceport was closer to ground zero than the city was."

"Do you think I don't know that?" she snapped.

Carron, struck by the tone though the words weren't directed at him, snatched his hand away from Lissea's thigh.

He gestured again toward his case. "I brought an alternate routing out of the Pocket," he said. "The navigational logs of the original settlers are in the palace library. I've gone through them, looking for information on the Old Race. If we try to go back through the Sole Solution, I'm afraid my father will hunt us down."

"There isn't any other way into the Pocket," Lissea said querulously. "That's *why* it's the Sole Solution."

Ned raised himself, gripping the seat backs for support against the one-hundred-fifty-kilometer-per-hour windrush. He squinted toward their destination. The spaceport seemed in relatively good condition, though ships lay like jackstraws rather than in neat, gleaming radii pointing toward the terminal buildings at the hub.

A large freighter lay on its side. The gray smoke leaking from ruptures in the hull plating was the only sign of movement about the vessel.

"There's only one way *in*," Carron corrected. "But there's another way out. And I've brought the navigational data."

"Blood and martyrs, man!" Ned snarled. "That's the ship! Don't fly us off into the desert!"

"Oh!" Carron blurted. He'd set the course when they lifted from the battle site, but he'd forgotten to take the car off automatic pilot. Now he shoved the column forward and banked around the vessel he'd overflown.

Both 1-tonne hovercraft were parked in what had been the *Swift*'s landing segment. The blast walls had collapsed into twisted ribbons; one of the borrowed trucks lay beneath concrete and strands of wire reinforcement—the remains of the nearer wall.

The vessel herself was undamaged, though she now rested on the ruins of the other wall.

"They lifted off!" Lissea said. "Thank the Lord, somebody had sense enough to get them airborne before the worst of the shockwaves hit."

"Score one for Herne," Ned said, though he was by no means sure Lordling was responsible for the decision. Westerbeke and Petit were on anchor watch as well. Ned disliked the ex-colonel so much that he forced himself to give the man his due and more whenever he had to speak of him.

Pancahtans had waved at the aircar or merely stared apathetically as it flew overhead. The men crouching in the rubble about the *Swift* watched the vehicle through the sights of their powerguns. At least some of them had their fingers on the triggers.

Carron was too focused on his landing to notice the overt threat, but Lissea keyed her commo helmet. *"Captain to* Swift *personnel,"* she said. *"Don't shoot; I'm in the approaching aircar. Over."*

Ned noticed that she didn't sound angry, just fatigued. He was suddenly tired also. He could melt onto his bunk now, no matter what was happening around him.

Carron landed in two bounces, the second of which put the car's legs into the jumble of the blast wall and almost overset the vehicle. The *Swift*'s ramp was raised but not quite closed.

It began to lower again as Tadziki and Herne Lordling sprang out of the narrow airlock.

"Are we prepared to lift?" Lissea demanded as those men and other mercenaries ran toward the aircar. She started to get out but stumbled because her legs didn't want to support her.

"Lissea, what happened to your clothes?" Lordling demanded. He kept her from falling, then picked her up bodily despite her struggles.

"We're ready, but we don't have clearance to lift," Tadziki said. "We were hovering, but the tower threatened to turn the port's defensive batteries on us if we didn't set down."

"Herne, curse you for a fool!" Lissea snarled. "Put me down!"

"I can take care of that," Carron said as he hefted his case out of the vehicle. "We've got to leave at once, before Lon is able to take control again. He won't let us go."

"Tadziki, help him," Lissea said, nodding toward Carron. "He'll need access to the navigational system. Make sure he gets it."

The adjutant put his hand on Carron's shoulder to guide rather than force his attention toward the *Swift*'s landing ramp. "Yes, we've got to hurry!" Carron agreed.

"I'm going to take a party to the terminal building and clear it out," Lordling announced. "Yazov, Paetz, Warson—yes, you—Harlow . . ."

"No, no, I can take care of the tower," Carron called as he shambled up the ramp. Tadziki's hand was out to help with the case of heavy equipment, but Carron didn't appear to notice the offer. "Don't worry about that."

"*Captain to* Swift *personnel,*" Lissea ordered. "*Everybody board ASAP. I want to be able to lift the instant we get clearance. Over.*"

"A mother-huge rock hit us aft, Captain," Dewey reported. "It smashed hell out of the lifeboat bay. We were going to put the capsule there, but it's all bunged in."

They'd gotten back with the cursed thing, then. Ned had almost forgotten that the expedition's purpose was to retrieve the capsule.

"Lissea, you can't trust that pissant!" Lordling said. "Come on, boys, let's take care of this. It's not far enough to drive."

"Sounds to me like mutiny, Herne," Toll Warson called from the left side of the airlock hatch. He was right-handed, and only his right arm and eye were visible beyond the hull metal. His brother squatted behind the lowered ramp with his submachine gun in his hands.

"*I* think it's a pretty bloody good idea!" Josie Paetz said loudly. He put his hands on his hips and turned to face around the whole assemblage.

"It is not a good idea, nephew," Yazov said. He stepped chest to chest with Paetz and grabbed the younger man's wrists when he tried to pull away. "It is *not* a good idea to side with a fool against your commanding officer."

A warehouse of flammables blew up on the outskirts of Astragal. There was a bubble of liquid orange, followed by another on a slightly different center. The third blast hurled entire drums hundreds of meters in the air. Some of them fell into the city proper.

"Let's get aboard, Herne," Lissea said. She put her hand on Lordling's shoulder. He shook her off.

"Carron's got a pretty good track record thus far, Herne," Ned said. The *whoomp* of the third explosion hit the port area hard enough to shake the crumbled blast walls into lower piles. "He—"

Lordling punched him in the face.

Ned fell onto his back and elbows. He wasn't sure what had happened. He was dizzy, and hot prickles spreading from his mouth and nose made his vision pulse between color and black-and-white.

Herne Lordling turned on his heel and stamped up the boarding ramp, his back as straight as the rope holding a hanged man.

Lissea holstered her pistol before she bent to help Ned rise. "Are you all right?" she asked. "Your lip's cut."

It wasn't the punch, it was everything else that had happened. Ned felt sick to his stomach, but that passed a moment after he stood upright again.

"Let's get aboard the ship," he said, leaning on Lissea's arm. Men stood close, ready to help but unwilling to interfere until asked to. Their gun muzzles were vertical. "We've got to get out of this place."

A plume of smoke curled up like an auger from the site of the warehouse explosions. The light of the primary tinged it dirty gray. Filth and blood, that was all that remained on Pancahte since the expedition had arrived.

Tadziki met them at the top of the ramp. "He's loading a new navigational program into the data base," he announced without preamble. "Del Vore, I mean. Do you want us to use it when we lift? Westerbeke sounds doubtful."

"Yes," Lissea said. "Yes, I suppose he's right. He ought to know what his father's like. It's best we avoid the risks when we can."

Ned grabbed the frame of the nearest bunk and transferred his weight to it. The troops who'd been outside the *Swift* clomped up the ramp, trying not to jostle their captain and adjutant.

Westerbeke came aft to join the officers. Lissea glared angrily past him, but the pilot had left Bonilla in the console beside Carron. Bonilla was competent and anyway, they couldn't lift until things were sorted out further.

"Captain," Westerbeke said, "that course the kid's loaded, the system rejects it as outside parameters. We'll have to override the system to use it."

"You *can* override the system?" Lissea said.

"Ned," Tadziki said in an undertone, "get aft to the medicomp and tell Deke to take care of the swelling and abrasion. If you let it go and it gets infected, you'll be out for the next week."

"Yeah, I can, but it may Transit us off to West Bumfuck with no way to get back," the pilot explained. "It's a big universe. If we don't have reference points, our chances of getting any bloody where are less than zip."

"I'll do that," Ned murmured. He made no attempt to let go of the bunk.

The ramp rose with the last man, Josie Paetz, still on it. Paetz backed aboard, watching for an excuse to shoot until the rising slope forced him down to the deck proper.

The capsule was secured in the center aisle, where they'd heaved the Jeeps during the first hurried getaway from Buin. Lendell Doormann's creation wasn't quite as much in the way, but neither did the capsule improve traffic flow within the small vessel.

"Two, maybe all three of those Pancahtan warships are operable despite the commotion," Tadziki reported unasked. "They'll take a while—a day or so unless they're kept on hot standby—to load supplies and get the crews aboard."

"We'll chance the new course," Lissea decided aloud. In deliberate echo she added, "Carron's got a pretty good track record so far." She gave Ned a lopsided grin. "Get forward to the controls, Westerbeke. You'll take us up when I tell you to."

The tannoys rasped, *"—not lift off! I repeat, Telarian vessel* Swift, *you do not have permission to lift off. If you lift, you will be destroyed! Over."*

Bonilla peered around the enveloping back of his seat, waiting for orders. He'd patched the transmission into the PA system in order to get his superiors' attention. The tower must have noticed that the *Swift*'s crew had come aboard and the ship was buttoning up.

Westerbeke hastened forward, shoving past men trying to sort their gear and to understand the situation. Carron stood. "It's ready!" he called. "I'm ready to shut down the tower."

Lissea keyed her helmet to access the ship's external commo system. "Swift *to Astragal Tower,"* she said. *"We hear and understand. We're just checking airtightness following hull damage.* Swift *out."*

She glanced at Tadziki. "We *are* airtight, aren't we? How much damage do we have?"

The adjutant shrugged. "Nothing we can't fix at the first layover," he said. "Some leakage, yes, but nothing that would keep me on Pancahte."

"All personnel in place for liftoff!" Lissea ordered. The

tannoys thundered her words an instant out of synch with her lips. "Carron, when Westerbeke tells you, shut down the tower."

Ned stepped down the aisle to where the capsule was stored. He paused for a moment. Raff picked him up bodily and handed him over the obstruction to Yazov on the other side.

"How's he going to fix the tower?" Josie Paetz demanded from his uncle's side. "Is he going to blow it up?"

"My guess is he's going to send a shutdown signal to the terminal's powerplant," Ned replied. "But I didn't ask. Maybe he *will* blow them up. He's capable of it."

The part of his mind that answered the question floated some distance above the body it putatively occupied. Though Lissea's voice was strong and controlled, her face looked as though she'd been dragged from the same coffin as her great-granduncle.

Ned pulled himself onto his berth and closed his eyes. He felt the paired bunks sway as the adjutant got into the lower unit.

Ned lifted himself onto an elbow and looked around. "Hey Tadziki," he said. "Where *are* we going then? I didn't ask."

"Wasatch 1029," Tadziki said. He sounded tired as well. The past several hours hadn't been a rest cure for anybody. "It's a listed planet, not that there's anything there according to the pilotry data. We'll have to hope our—Master Del Vore is correct about the routing."

The *Swift* shook herself. Westerbeke was clearing the fuel feeds before he applied full power.

"*Tower to Telarian vessel* Swift!" the PA system snarled. An image of the terminal complex filled the main screen forward. Smoke from the overturned freighter drifted past the buildings, and there seemed to be a fire in the parking area as well. "*You have been warned for the last time! A detachment of the Treasurer's G—*"

The Pancahtan voice crackled silent. All the terminal's lighted windows went dark.

"Lift off!" warned Westerbeke, and the *Swift* began to rise on full power.

Wasatch 1029

—◦—

WASATCH 1029 WAS brilliant in the blue sky of its human-habitable planet. The air was like summer in the mid-latitudes of Tethys, though the vagrant breezes didn't leave a taste of salt on Ned's lips to make him feel completely at home.

"Blood and *martyrs*," Deke Warson snarled. "This place gives me the creeps."

A saw screamed on the other side of the vessel. Three men under Tadziki were cutting and welding plastic sheet-stock into a casket for Lendell Doormann.

Lissea and Carron Del Vore had spent the uneventful Transit from Pancahte studying the circuitry beneath the capsule's outer plating. They wanted to remove interior plates as well, but not even the *Swift*'s hard-bitten complement was willing to share their limited interior accommodations with a grinning mummy.

Deke struck viciously with his gun butt at what Ned called a plant for the lack of a better word. A gnarled bloom the size of a man's fist grew on a meter-long stalk. Its form was as insubstantial as patterns of dust motes dancing in sunlight, but the shape retained itself until the plastic butt smashed through it. Bits of bloom, vaguely russet, drifted away in the air and settled slowly.

"Look at that!" Deke said. "How does that happen? What if we're *breathing* them?"

Ned looked down. His boots and those of the rest of the *Swift*'s personnel had crushed other, infinitely varied "plants" into the soil around the vessel. It was inevitable and no different than what would have happened on a planet whose vegetation was more similar to that of Earth. The fragility of the trampled forms made the destruction seem worse, though.

He ought to be used to destruction by now.

"It's no problem, Deke," Ned said aloud. "You breathe microbes and bits of plant life on every planet you've ever been on. This place isn't dangerous."

He looked at the sunlit hills. He didn't suppose he'd ever see the planet again after the *Swift* lifted for Kazan. "It's clean here. I like it. Especially since Pancahte."

"If you like this place . . ." Warson said as he turned away. He swatted at another bloom, scattering it like a bomb blast. ". . . then you're fucking nuts!"

The *Swift* would leave Wasatch in a day or two, carrying Lendell Doormann's casket in the external lifeboat bay. Toll Warson and another team were repairing damage caused by a hundred-kilo chunk of lava. The impact had sprung plates and probably would have smashed the lifeboat if the *Swift* still carried one.

The hilltops were forested with larger versions of the plants here in the valley. The planet had animal life as well, though none of the reported larger forms had appeared since the *Swift* landed.

Some of the men compared the local life-forms to jellyfish, but the creatures were really more similar to ripples in a running stream. A ripple is a disruption to a fluid's smooth flow. It remains essentially unchanged so long as the flow maintains, even though the molecules forming its pattern shift rapidly and constantly. Life here imposed its patterns on the environment as surely as hidden rocks did on the water of a stream.

Half the men aboard the *Swift* hated Wasatch as much as Deke did. The other half relaxed for the first time since they'd lifted from Telaria, and neither party could imagine why the others felt the way they did. Funny to think that people similar in many ways would react so differently to a planet: rock and air and water. It was a mistake to believe every ruthless killer was the same. . . .

Lissea loved Wasatch. She and Carron had wandered off together, taking a break from their concentrated examination of the capsule. The ground would be pleasantly warm on the south slopes.

Herne Lordling came out of the hatchway and stood on the ramp, looking around. He didn't carry a tumbler, but he'd been drinking. Like Ned, he was off duty at the moment, and he had a right to his liquor ration.

"You," he called. "Slade."

The men nearby grew quiet. Moiseyev, on top of the vessel, slid down the opposite side to where Tadziki was.

"Got a problem with me, Herne?" Ned asked. His upper lip began to itch, though during Transit the medicomp had repaired the damage the punch had done. The physical damage.

"No problem," Lordling said. His face was flushed. Ned couldn't read his expression, but anger and embarrassment were both part of it. "I just want you and me to talk. We can take the Jeep."

"Take the Jeep where, Herne?" Tadziki asked as he walked around the stern of the vessel. His casket-builders, Raff among them, sauntered along behind him. Unlike Ned, they were all armed.

Lordling turned. "Just out a ways," he said. He wiped his mouth with the back of his hand as if to scrub away a bad taste. "Look, I want to talk to Slade, that's all. Do you have a problem with that?"

"*I* don't have a problem with it," Ned said. "But I'll drive. And we're not heading east."

"I don't give a fuck where we go!" Lordling said. "I just want to get away from this place, all right?"

The adjutant nodded slowly. "Sure, Herne," he said. "That's all right. But don't get out of helmet range—"

About two klicks with the *Swift* in a valley and no repeaters set up—

"—and be back in an hour. We might need a Jeep for something, and we've only got the one now."

Lordling jumped from the ramp without responding and strode to the little hovercraft waiting by the bow blister.

"Hey, kid?" Deke Warson called.

Ned looked up. Deke held his 2-cm weapon by the balance. He pitched it muzzle-up to Ned, who caught the heavy weapon.

"He won't need that!" Herne Lordling said from the passenger seat of the Jeep.

"That's good, Herne," Warson replied. "Because it'd be really too bad if he did."

Lordling faced front. Ned got in, stuck the borrowed weapon in the butt sock, and switched on.

"Where do you want to go, then?" he asked quietly. The inner muscles of his forearms were quivering in hormonal expectation. Herne was the bigger man by twenty kilos and not much of it was fat, but the day Ned couldn't handle somebody twice his age— Well, he wasn't worried.

"Just get the fuck out of here!" Lordling snapped. He shook himself. "Look, Slade, I don't want to fight. Okay?"

Ned engaged the fans and pulled away from the vessel. "That's your choice, Lordling," he said, making an effort to prevent his tone from turning the statement into a challenge.

He headed west, because the sun was already in the tops of the tall trees there, and because Lissea and Carron had gone east. He hoped he'd be able to drive between the insubstantial trunks rather than tearing a swath through them.

"Look, Slade, I wanted to talk to you because I think you respect Lissea," Lordling blurted. "Those other bastards, all they care about in a woman is her cunt and if she gives good head."

"We're not on a church outing, Herne," Ned said carefully. "If Lissea doesn't mind people treating her like one of the guys, then I don't see where the problem is. It's not as though anybody's made trouble about taking orders from a woman." *Except maybe you.*

"It's not that!" Lordling said. "It's what she's doing with this pissant she's brought along. That's got to stop, and if she doesn't see it, somebody's got to stop it for her."

Ned drove through a band of brush several meters tall. The branches spread into bell-shaped tips, like morning-glory flowers, from which dangled veils of fronds. The shapes were immeasurably more delicate than could have been achieved by denser matter which had to support its structure physically.

The Jeep tore the bushes like violet fog. Ned thought the air was suddenly cool, but his mind could have been playing tricks on him.

"Herne," he said as if each word were a cartridge he was loading in preparation for a duel. "I don't think Lissea's private life is any business of ours."

"Look, Slade," Lordling said hoarsely. His big hands knotted on the Jeep's dashboard and his eyes were straight ahead. "I'm not saying a woman ought to be alone, it's not like that. But this *puppy.* She's wasting herself just to look at him!"

The Jeep was among the tall trees. They grew more like coral branching in a fluid medium than internally supported plants. The bases were a meter or two across, but vast pastel arrays lifted to spread and ramify over hundreds of square meters at their tops.

Driving through the forest was like entering a cathedral with groined vaults. The sound of the Jeep's fans was an intrusion.

"Herne . . ." Ned said. He stopped, because he didn't know how to continue.

"Well say it, then!" Lordling snapped. "Are you just like the rest? I tell you, Lissea's *different.*"

Ned saw a patch of direct sunlight and steered for it. He couldn't talk while he was driving, not about this. His hands were sweaty, and his muscles jumped as they had before the firefight on Ajax Four.

"She's different, we're all different, Herne," he said. He'd been all right because he hadn't let himself think about it, he was good at not thinking about things, but Lordling wouldn't leave it at that. "It's our job to leave her alone!"

Full sun struck them on a tongue of rock which stabbed into the next valley. Ned reversed his nacelles quickly and dumped the plenum chamber. The Jeep stopped a few meters from the edge of a seventy-degree escarpment.

The immediate slopes were covered by the big trees, but the valley floor was open. On it were hundreds of golden puff-balls the size of Terran hippopotami. Some of them drifted against the wind. Ned had found the animal life of Wasatch.

Ned stepped from the Jeep, staring across the valley. He thrust his hands into his side pockets. "Look, I don't much like the guy," he said, "but I don't have to. He got us out of a couple tight places. I could say, 'Lissea pays her debts,' and that'd be enough."

"That's how a *whore* pays her debts!" Lordling said. "She's not a whore!"

The golden creatures were nearly globular. They began to move as a group up the valley's western slope. As the herbivores moved, three streaks of silvery translucence shifted from among the golden creatures to space themselves along the eastern edge of the herd.

"She's a person," Ned said. The silvery figures were more than three meters tall, slim and as supple as willow wands. "She's got a lot in common with Del Vore—"

"She's got nothing in common with him!"

Ned turned. "They're of the same *class,*" he said harshly. "They've both been stepped on by their families. They're both engineers. Grow bloody up, Herne! He didn't hypnotize her, he didn't hold a gun to her head. She's doing what she wants to do!"

Lordling looked around for something to hit. He took a step toward a tree, thought the better of it, and kicked the Jeep's skirts as hard as he could. His boot rebounded and spun him halfway around.

Ned faced the valley again. The distant crest was unforested. Sunset turned the herbivores into disks of molten gold as they eased out of sight. The silver figures moved slowly up the hillside after their charges, staying always between the herd and the watching humans.

"I thought," Lordling muttered, "that if we arranged it together . . . I thought you'd understand."

"I understand," Ned said. *I understand that I'd like to stick a pistol in Carron Del Vore's mouth. I'd like to make him bite on it before I pulled the trigger.* "If I thought he had to be killed, I'd kill him myself and not worry about what happened next. But it's her choice. It's Lissea's choice."

Lordling muttered something, probably a curse. "Let's go back, then. I was wrong about you."

"In a moment," Ned said.

The herbivores had vanished. The silvery figures stood on the far crest with the low sun behind them. Ned bowed toward them, as though he were greeting Councillors of Tethys at a formal gathering.

One after another, the shimmering silver creatures bowed also. Then they drifted out of sight.

"Now we'll go," Ned said.

He felt calm. It had been a long time since he last felt calm.

Kazan

—⅏—

WESTERBEKE WAS AT one of the aft-rotated navigational consoles; Lissea was in the other. Facing the seats and the projected display was the rest of what had become the *Swift*'s command group: Tadziki, Herne Lordling, Carron, and Edward Slade.

Kazan, their planned layover, was the blue-green ball forming a backdrop to the defensive satellite on which the *Swift*'s sensor inputs were focused. Ned wasn't good at keeping his face blank, but the others didn't look happy at what they saw on the display either.

"*Intercourse with this world has been proscribed by the Sextile Alliance,*" the tannoys said, broadcasting the warning from the satellite by modulated laser. "*Vessels which approach within one light-minute will be destroyed if they attempt to leave the proscribed region again. Vessels which attack a satellite of the defensive cluster will be destroyed. There are no exceptions. Intercourse—*"

Lissea touched a switch and shut off the sound. The remainder of the crew, watching over the shoulders of the command group, muttered and argued among themselves. Their lives were at risk also. Though none of them expected their opinions to affect the captain's decision, they *had* opinions.

The satellite was one of a quartet forming a tetrahedron to enclose Kazan. Each satellite contained enough directed energy and missile weapons to ravage a continent.

"After two hundred years," Herne Lordling said without enthusiasm, "the systems may have broken down."

"The sensors and commo haven't," Westerbeke said. "Look, I don't like this. We can hold out till Celandine."

Several of the men behind Ned growled.

"If we don't land here," Tadziki said, "then I advise sequestering all the weapons. It won't do a great deal of good, of course, as there's no one aboard who isn't capable of killing with his bare hands."

The *Swift*'s complement had accumulated gear at every layover, and the initial tight stowage of Telaria had long since gone by the boards. Boxes, bags, and bottles covered bunks and the spaces between them. The interior fittings themselves had never recovered from damage inflicted during the panicked rush from Buin.

Partially dismantled for examination, Lendell Doormann's capsule blocked the aisle even more thoroughly than it had when the crew brought it aboard. The ship stank like a pigshed despite constant filtering by the environmental system.

Tempers were short. As Tadziki had implied, lethally short.

"We'll proceed," said Lissea, "on the assumption that we're going to land." She smiled coldly. "Landing's easy, after all. The trick will be lifting off again."

Kazan was a jungle planet with a considerable resource base. The colony's population was split between a ruling oligarchy and—the ninety-eight percent remaining—workers whose very lives were forfeit at the oligarchs' whim.

None of that would have been a matter of concern off Kazan, were it not that the oligarchs visualized themselves as rulers of a multi-planet empire as well. Manpower was no problem for them. Just as European colonizers had conquered Africa with native African troops, and millennia earlier Spartan nobles had gone to war accompanied by ten times their number in armed slaves, so the underclass of Kazan fought with a mere leavening of oligarch officers.

Three times Kazan attacked its neighbors—and was driven back, but at the cost of enormous disruption to the victimized planets. After the third time, the six worlds under potential threat had banded together to end the problem once and for all.

Cities could be bombed, but the oligarchs had dispersed their industry widely. Invading the planet was out of the question. The population of Kazan would inevitably outnumber whatever ground forces could be transported across interstellar space, and none of the Alliance's planners had had the stomach for guerrilla warfare in a jungle against a fanatical foe.

So the Alliance had opted for quarantine instead. It cut Kazan off from the rest of the universe with a constellation of unmanned satellites, programmed to destroy any vessel that attempted to leave the planet.

That had been two hundred years before. No one knew what Kazan was like now, but the planet was still the only charted layover point between Wasatch 1029 and Celandine. Given the conditions aboard the *Swift*, the risk was one the complement was willing to accept—*if* they could avoid the defensive satellites.

"We can enter the satellite's control system through the communications channels," Carron said. He stood with his heels twenty centimeters apart, toes splayed outward, and his hands crossed behind his back. "When we have gotten access, we need only to exempt ourselves from the parameters of ships to be attacked."

"If it were that easy, somebody would have tried it before now," Herne Lordling said, glaring at the Pancahtan.

"The satellites were built two centuries ago," Lissea said. "The *Swift*'s systems are Telarian state of the art *today*. We have more processing power than the Alliance's engineers dreamed of—or Kazan's."

"They don't *have* a commo system," Westerbeke said.

"What they've got is a warning beacon, but you can't talk *back* to the satellites. There's no way in like that."

"They have sensors, though," Ned said. "They have to, for targeting. There's a channel to their control system that way. It ought to be possible."

Lissea looked sideways at Westerbeke, then across the display to the four men standing in front of her. "All right," she said. "That should be possible. Are we agreed?"

Westerbeke grimaced. The others nodded, even Lordling.

Lissea nodded also. "Agreed, then. Carron, Ned—the next step is up to us, I believe. We need to find both an access channel and the codes with which to insert our requirements in the satellite's data base."

She frowned. "Will one satellite be enough, or will we have to deal with the entire constellation?"

"If we remove one satellite from the array," Tadziki said, "it leaves a gap through which we can exit the planet if we're careful."

He looked at Westerbeke.

"Oh, we'll be careful," the pilot said. "Don't worry about my end of this. But you'd better be right about making friends with their AI. The first we'll know if you screw up is the fifty-centimeter bolt ripping us inside out."

After seven hours thirty-two minutes, Ned made the last keystroke and rocked back from his cross-legged sitting position to lie on the deck. The other two team members were slumped in the navigational couches.

" 'She has wrapped it in her kerchief, she has cast it in the sea,' " Ned quoted in a loud voice to the ceiling. " 'Says sink ye, swim ye, bonnie wee babe, you'll get no more of me!' "

"What the hell's that?" Herne Lordling growled. He and Tadziki sat on the lower forward bunks, by their presence closing access to the team working at the computer stations in the bow.

"It's an old song about a woman who found a way out of her problem," Ned said. "Her name was Mary Hamilton, and they hanged her. Hung her?''

He closed his eyes, then quickly opened them again. When Ned's eyes were shut, his brain pulsed with the sine curves that they'd been using as code analogues. Yellow and blue—green for a match, but always with tiny spikes of yellow and blue to mar the chain. Not much of a difference, but a man with a bullet hole through the forehead isn't much different from a living man—to look at.

''Have you gotten us clearance to land, then, Lissea?'' Tadziki said. ''To lift off again, that is.''

''Yes,'' said Carron.

''No,'' said Lissea a half-beat later.

Ned lifted himself onto his elbow. Lissea and Carron raised themselves on the couches and looked at one another.

''Well, it's the same thing,'' Carron said to her. ''Just as good.''

'' 'Just as good' *isn't* the same thing,'' Lissea said tartly. They were all frazzled by the project. The rest of the crew, left twiddling their thumbs while the experts worked to enter the satellite's control system, probably wasn't in a much better humor.

''Instead of fucking around,'' Deke Warson asked in a voice as soft as a snake crossing a bedsheet, ''would somebody like to explain what's going on?''

''The folks who built the satellite, may they rot in Hell,'' Ned said without turning his head, ''designed two separate systems. One collects and analyzes sensor data.''

''Tracking and targeting,'' Lissea said. ''That's the system we can access.''

''And when it's done,'' Ned resumed, ''it hands the data over to a wholly separate chain which makes the decision to fire. The second system is a closed loop and we can't touch it.''

''Can you adjust the sensors to feed improper range and course information to the gunnery control?'' Westerbeke suggested.

Carron waved his hand to brush the suggestion away. ''That wouldn't do any good,'' he said. ''It's self-correcting.

The second salvo will be on top of us if the first one isn't. I came up with a solution: change the firing order of the batteries that engage us.''

"What the hell does that mean?'' Josie Paetz growled.

"Hey, Slade?'' said Toll Warson.

Ned lurched upright again and swung to look at the gathered crew. The men were drawn and angry. Several of them were playing with weapons.

"Yeah, Toll?''

"This going to work?''

"You bet your ass,'' Ned said. He smiled coldly.

Warson smiled back. Between them, it must have looked like feeding time in the lion house. "Cap'n,'' Toll said to Lissea, "if we're going to go, let's go. Sitting around like this just makes it worse, it always does.''

There was a rumble of assent from the crew. Herne Lordling turned and glared a challenge to Lissea.

"Yes,'' she said, "all right. Westerbeke, take the helm again. Carron, go to your bunk. The same with the rest of you. We'll transit within the proscribed area, between the satellite and the planetary surface. Is that understood?''

Carron rose, but the arc of men watching and listening didn't break up for him to pass them to what had been Louis Boxall's bunk.

"What happens then?'' Herne Lordling asked.

"Then there's a choice,'' Lissea replied in a cool tone that ignored the fact her orders were being disregarded for the moment. "Either we land on Kazan, or we make an immediate attempt to lift out of the gravity well. The choice, which is *mine,* is that we lift. That we know immediately whether or not we've gimmicked the satellite sufficiently to keep us alive.''

Westerbeke laughed grimly as he pushed past Carron. "No, ma'am,'' he said as he seated himself and began setting up the Transit parameters. "We only know if it *did* work. Otherwise, we don't know any bloody thing at all.''

Deke Warson stretched and sauntered back toward his

bunk. "You know," he said, "nobody'd ever believe it if I was to die in bed. . . ."

They came out of Transit within the orbits of the constellation of satellites, nearly into the upper reaches of Kazan's atmosphere. The planet more than filled the frame of the main display forward. Ned switched his visor to accept a close-up view of Satellite III, the nearest of the array, instead.

At standby, the satellites were spheres overlaid with smooth bulges. That shape changed in the view Ned watched.

The *Swift*'s systems chuckled and groaned. The navigational computer was updating the vessel's real position against the one it had calculated before Transit. Even after so short a hop, less than three light-minutes, the calculations required for another Transit would take the better part of an hour.

The preliminaries to Transit would require minor attitude adjustments to align the vessel perfectly with the gravitational field. At the point the *Swift* began making those adjustments, Satellite III would convert the vessel to an expanding fireball.

Because the *Swift* had entered the proscribed region, Satellite III unmasked the batteries that would be required if the interloper attempted to leave. Covering plates opened so that missile carousels could extend. Turrets rotated and their shutters withdrew to expose the huge powerguns within—50-cm, Westerbeke had guessed. The weapons were at least that big.

Westerbeke wasn't going to Transit away from Kazan. All he had to do to trigger the satellite's response was to trip the main engines for a second or two to raise the *Swift* into a higher orbit.

"*Stand by for acceleration,*" Westerbeke warned. Then, muttered but still on intercom, "*If we had a lifeboat, we could use it for the guinea pig.*"

"*We have used the lifeboat for other necessary purposes, Master Westerbeke,*" Tadziki said in a voice colder than Satellite III's unfired cannon. "*Get on with your duties. Now!*"

The engines snarled, thrusting Ned against the contoured

cushions of his bunk.

The image of Satellite III rotated and began to expand. There was a blue flash, copper ions from ten or more big-bore powerguns firing simultaneously—

Into the shutters that protected the weapons from cosmic dust and radiation. A moment later, missiles launched from within closed batteries ruptured the structure still further. Though the warheads didn't have time to arm, rocket exhaust had the effect of explosives when vented within the satellite.

"*Good* fucking job, Slade!" Deke Warson shouted down the bay.

"Wasn't my idea," Ned called back. "Thank Prince Carron."

They—Lissea and Carron, but particularly Ned, because he was the one who was familiar with weapons systems—had switched Satellite III's firing order. Instead of the guns and missiles prepared for use, the firing signal had gone to batteries that didn't bear on the *Swift* and therefore hadn't been deployed.

The control system would have corrected the error with its second salvo—if there had been anything left of system or satellite after the first.

The explosions that vaporized half the structure provided a violent thrust to spin the remainder around the center of mass. Satellite III ripped into three large chunks, a spray of fragments, and a cloud of gas and plasma. Centrifugal force flung the portions apart in a glowing, glittering starburst.

"*Take us in closer for reconnaissance, Master Westerbeke,*" Lissea ordered from the backup console. "*I don't think we need to worry about the defensive cordon when we're ready to leave.*"

Men cheered from their bunks. There was still the situation on Kazan to worry about, but when Coyne shouted, "I'm going to find me a girl with tits so big I'd smother if she got on top of me!" he was voicing the optimism of most of the complement.

"*Prepare for—*" Westerbeke began.

The *Swift* shuddered.

"What the hell was that?" Bonilla said, his voice high in the sudden silence.

"That was the satellite," Lissea said in cool assurance. *"We were close enough to feel the gas ball from the explosion. Gentlemen, prepare for acceleration as we drop into a lower orbit to choose a landing site. Captain out."*

As the engines fired, Ned switched on the remote image on his visor. Kazan rushed up at him, a green surface that took on form and texture with the passing seconds.

From a reconnaissance orbit, the trees looked like the tops of green thunderclouds, surging with death and rage.

On the second orbital pass, Lissea switched the imaging system to ground-penetrating radar. It quickly limned the geometric outlines of a city hidden from optical scanners by the vegetation. There was a circular crater in the center of the thirty-hectare sprawl.

"Did the Alliance bomb Kazan?" Ned wondered aloud. "There isn't any record of that in the pilotry data. Just that they'd built the satellite array."

While the *Swift* was in unpowered orbit, he didn't need to use his commo helmet to speak. Tadziki could answer or not, as he saw fit.

"There wouldn't necessarily be a record," Tadziki replied. He sounded vaguely doubtful also. "Our data base was assembled on Telaria, after all; and in a war, not everything gets reported."

He paused. "It may be that the damage occurred after the quarantine, though. It's unlikely that a society like the one described became peaceful when it was forced in on itself."

The damage—the bomb damage, nothing else could have caused it—hadn't been repaired.

"All right, pilot," Lissea ordered. She used the general channel so that everyone aboard would be clear about the intended course of events. *"Set us down on the outskirts of that settled area on the next pass. Adjutant, prepare a security detail for following the landing. Over."*

"Roger," Tadziki rasped. *"Yazov and Paetz, you Warsons, Harlow and Coyne, and I'll take Slade for the fourth team. Locations as marked on your visors—"*

The adjutant overrode Ned's visor display and those of the others. A schematic of the *Swift* and four points at some distance from the vessel appeared against a neutral background. The dot at the bow pulsed, indicating the location Ned would share with Tadziki.

"That's a hundred meters out, not a cordon and not an ambush, just listening posts. Remaining personnel form a reaction group under Lordling's tactical control. Out."

"Adjutant," Lissea said. *"I don't want you running out into the jungle like that. Choose somebody else for that slot. Over."*

"Captain," Tadziki said, *"you have full authority to remove me from my position and make any assignments you please. Adjutant over."*

One or both of the Warsons chuckled. Ned himself grinned.

"Assignments confirmed," Lissea said in a flat voice. *"Prepare for braking. Captain ou—"*

The final consonant was smothered by the roar of the engines dropping the *Swift* finally toward the planetary surface.

At the hatchway, Herne Lordling handed a man-pack sensor to the low man of each outpost team. Ned took his, paused while Tadziki lifted the unit onto him, and grunted as he trotted down the ramp.

Twenty kilos of electronics, plus the submachine gun, two bandoliers, helmet and body armor, equipment belt with tools and medical kit, ration pack, and two-liter condensing canteen. The ground at the base of the ramp smoked, and the leaf mold had burned to carbon dust in the exhaust.

The buttress roots of great trees were festooned with vines and epiphytes beyond the ellipse the *Swift* had cleared for itself to land. The debris rotting on the forest floor was dusted with fungus and pale-leafed saplings that would die soon unless something ripped a hole in the canopy so that light could reach them.

Ned's load made him waddle in the soft soil. He had outfitted himself this way even though they wouldn't be so far away that he couldn't hit the *Swift* with a thrown pebble, if it weren't for the trees in between.

Raff was on the *Swift*'s upper deck, carrying the tribarrel as well as his rocket launcher. Dewey and Hatton clambered up the external ladder with the weapon's base and two canisters of ammunition. Three steps beyond the edge of the exhaust-seared clearing, Ned couldn't see them or the ship. Voices were muted, and though metal clanged, the direction even of audible sounds was uncertain.

Tadziki led. Both men carried cutting bars, but they didn't need to hack their way. Ned stumbled twice on surface roots, and once the loop of a heavy vine rapped his helmet hard enough to stagger him, but there was no close-woven ground cover to turn travel into an exercise in carpentry.

There was no sign of Kazan's human colonists, either.

"Here," the adjutant said, dropping to one knee where the leaf mold humped above a long, linear mound. Trees, spaced so closely that their roots formed knotted handshakes on the ground, cut optical sightlines down to a few meters, but the electronic sensors wouldn't care.

Tadziki was breathing hard, though he didn't have the additional burden of the sensor pack. Instead of reporting verbally, he broke squelch twice with his helmet radio, indicating that Team Two was in position.

The adjutant must be nervous. Ned sure was. The sweat wicking through his utilities beneath his body armor was only partly the result of heavy work in a hot, saturated atmosphere. He hit his pack's cross-strap release buckle, then helped set the sensor unit up on its own short legs.

Ned eyed the green/green-brown/green-black/chartreuse surroundings with his submachine gun ready to fire. The pack's built-in screen defaulted to LIFE FORMS/50K+, but Tadziki shifted it through the alternative readouts one by one.

"Well, I'll be hanged!" Tadziki said. He sounded surprised, not concerned.

Ned grinned. "So it tells fortunes? What else d'ye see?"

He glanced down at the unit. The built-in screen wasn't strictly necessary since the data were transmitted to the base unit in the *Swift,* but people in an observation post like to know what's going on around them too.

Tadziki used the tip of his cutting bar as a trowel, curling plant debris off the mound where he'd been sitting. He didn't turn on the tool's vibrating blade.

The display, set to neutron-emission patterns, showed the ground plan of a built-up area. Nothing but trees and lesser vegetation appeared to Ned's naked eyes. He scraped at the mound with the edge of his boot.

Tadziki reached down, grunted, and came up with a squared stone which dripped dirt and pink worms. The upper surfaces of the stone were scorched, and the bits of remaining mortar were calcined from heat.

"There's a whole foundation down here," Tadziki said. He dropped the stone and worked out another. "Building burned and the foundation knocked over with hammers and prybars."

"The bomb blast," Ned suggested. "They were using nukes. The background radiation's still five times what it ought to be here."

"Negative," Tadziki said. "Wrecking bars." He pointed to the parallel chips from one edge of the ashlar; upward pressure had flaked the stone away.

Ned looked to where his boot had scored the leaf mold. A jagged spike of bone stuck up from between jumbled stones. Ned levered one of the blocks away with his heel and pulled the yellowish shaft free. The other joint was intact.

"Human arm," he said.

"Thigh bone," Tadziki corrected. "A child's."

Ned put the bone down gently in the hole from which he had drawn it. He switched the sensor display to the default setting again.

"Like Burr-Detlingen," he said. He tried to imagine what the city had looked like before men bombed it, burned it, and pulled down the very stones of its foundations. Not even an archaeologist could tell without first clearing the jungle which had recovered the site.

"Not like Burr-Detlingen," Tadziki said. "On Burr-Detlingen, they fought like cats, tearing each other's throats out."

"What would you call this place, then?" Ned asked. He watched the screen out of the corner of his eye. Its pink field would ripple with interference patterns if an animal entered its hundred, hundred-and-fifty-meter range. The sensor's shielded back prevented it from registering the outpost crew.

Tadziki brushed his hands together, then wiped the remainder of the clinging dirt off on his trousers. "This was a cancer," he said softly. "The people of Kazan were sheep, and their rulers were cancers that they wouldn't cut out. They obeyed until they'd destroyed everything. At the end, I suppose the oligarchs died too, but by then it was too late."

"Why in hell did they want to do *this?*" Ned demanded. "The rulers, I mean?"

"In Hell, yes," Tadziki said, "Because they were insane, I suppose. And because, instead of rebelling, people took their madmen's orders right down to the end, until there was nothing left. If people will take crazy orders, there's always somebody to give those orders."

His mouth quirked in something that could have been described as a smile. "Maybe the people were afraid to fight them, maybe they were just conditioned for too long to obey. Either way, they're all dead now."

A broad-bodied worm or caterpillar crawled over the leaf mold, oblivious to the humans. The creature was brilliantly scarlet and covered with fine hairs. It was as long as Ned's foot. He shifted cautiously to avoid coming in contact with something so obviously poisonous.

"What's the answer, then?" he asked. "Fight the crazies or knuckle under to them, you're saying it comes to the same thing in the end?"

"Sometimes there aren't any answers," the adjutant said. "No good ones, at any rate."

He braced his palms against a tree-truck and stretched until he'd bowed his back into a reverse curve. The muzzle of his slung submachine gun knocked against the pulpy bark. "I needed to get out of the ship," he said.

Ripples shimmered across the sensor screen, but the source that caused them didn't appear as a point on the display. Something of large or moderate size had walked through the jungle, roughly paralleling the edge of the coverage area.

Ned relaxed again. "What," he said, looking at the older man, "do you think about Lissea and Carron?"

Tadziki laughed. "I'm impressed by your subtlety," he said.

Ned gave him a hard grin. "I thought of saying, 'Lissea and the new fellow seem to work well together,' " he said. "But you're going to know what I mean, so instead of pretending to manipulate you, I just asked."

Tadziki nodded. "So you did," he said. "What I think is . . ."

He looked at Ned, assessing him, and resumed. "Lissea needs somebody. For 'release,' however you want to phrase it. Del Vore's an outsider. She can—deal with him without causing the problems there'd been if she chose anybody from the crew. The real crew."

"Sort of what I thought," Ned said, turning to face the jungle. Voices hooted in the near distance. He thought they might be birds, though he hadn't seen any flying creatures here, even at the invertebrate level.

"I don't think," Tadziki continued calmly, "that Del Vore would be Lissea's first choice under other circumstances. The situation could change when we get back to Telaria and Lissea takes her place on the board."

"Dream on!" Ned said.

"Umm?"

Ned looked at the adjutant. "They aren't going to give her a seat," Ned explained. "Tadziki, this sort of politics I know— I've *seen.* I saw it when my uncle Don came home to Tethys."

"What *will* happen, then?" Tadziki said. "Assuming we get back."

"Oh, yes, assuming that," Ned said. Politics were part of

the Academy's curriculum, because the politicians make the decision to hire and release the mercenaries who are the final arbiters of right.

"What I think," he continued, unconsciously aping the adjutant's delivery of moments before, "is that when Lissea returns with the capsule instead of dying conveniently out of sight as her relatives had intended . . . I think they'll give her a further runaround."

The muscles of his face set in planes that made him look wholly different, and not entirely human. "Then I think she'll stop playing the game by their rules. And play by ours."

"Outpost Two," warned the *Swift* in Lissea's voice. *"There's a group of creatures approaching your location. They may be the local inhabitants, over."*

He and Tadziki had forgotten the screen as they talked. Black ripples streamed back from eight—no, seven points advancing toward the outpost. The thickness of the ripple was related to the size of the creature being sensed, while the angle of the V indicated the speed at which it was moving. These were broad and shallow, suggesting creatures at the upper human parameter sauntering very slowly through the jungle . . . or creeping forward to attack.

Tadziki keyed his helmet. *"Roger, we're observing,"* he said. *"Two out."*

Ned heard the hooting again, coming from their front. He checked the loaded-chamber indicator on his submachine gun's receiver, switched the weapon off safe, and slipped three meters away from Tadziki to crouch in the gray folds of a buttress root. He silently adjusted his helmet to echo the sensor data as minute points in the upper left-hand quadrant of his visor. He needed to know where the intruders were, but not at the cost of degrading his ability to see and shoot.

Brush crackled. Voices hooted to one another. If this was a hunting or war party, the members had terrible noise discipline. That didn't mean they *weren't* hunting. The local prey might have dull senses by human standards.

The midmost of the seven dots was ahead of its companions. The creature it indicated must be very close to—

Hairy hands gripped a fan of leaves two meters from Ned and tore them away. The creature reached for a vermilion fruit swelling against the uncovered tree-trunk an instant before it saw Ned staring through his gunsight.

The creature weighed in the order of two hundred kilograms. It was covered with delicate blond fur, all but the face, which was bare and human. Its blue eyes flashed fully open as the creature leaped onto its hind legs and fluted a mellifluous challenge with its long arms spread wide.

Ned didn't move. His weapon was aimed between the creature's nipples. He wasn't sure that the submachine gun's 1-cm charges could stop an animal so large if it rushed him.

It was male. Its pubic triangle was marked by darker fur.

Wild crashing sounded in the forest beyond. The dots indicating the remainder of the pack, or family, rocked back the way they had come.

The creature facing Ned dropped to its knuckles and hooted angrily again. Ned didn't move. The creature turned suddenly and vanished into the forest. After a moment, Ned let out his breath and stood up.

He keyed his helmet. *"Two-two to base,"* he reported. *"All clear. Just local apes. Over."*

"Roger," Lissea said. *"Base out."*

He returned to sensor pack. Tadziki was still there, his submachine gun ready.

"You saw what it was?" Tadziki asked.

"Yeah."

"There aren't any indigenous apes on Kazan," Tadziki said quietly.

"There are now," Ned said. He thought of the radiation readings, at this site and the Lord knew what in other flattened cities.

The *Swift*'s drill whined, beginning to pierce the laterite in search of water for the vessel's tanks. The next layover—Celandine—was a highly developed planet. It would feel strange to resupply through normal commercial channels.

Tadziki keyed his helmet and said, *"Adjutant to outposts. Things seem pretty quiet. Each post can release one man at the senior's choice. The other fellow will be relieved in two hours. Out.''*

He looked at Ned. Ned shook his head. He didn't want to go back to the ship any more than the adjutant himself seemed to want to.

Ned squatted down. "Hey, Tadziki?" he said.

"Umm?"

"About Lissea and . . . and Carron, what you said?"

"Yeah."

"Sometimes there aren't any good answers," Ned said. His smile was as humorless as a knife blade.

Celandine

ÎLE DE RAMEAU on Celandine was the busiest spaceport in a trading cluster of twenty worlds. The sound of ships taking off and landing was a constant rumble through the roof and walls of the closed dock in which the Port Authority's tugs had lodged the *Swift*.

The dock could easily have held a freighter of one hundred thousand tonnes or a score of smaller vessels. The *Swift* was alone; the two robot tugs had returned to orbit before the clamshell roof closed again.

The members of the Pancahte Expediton watched the main forward display tautly. Six Celandine officials drove an open vehicle through a small side door and across the dock's scarred floor toward the *Swift*. The locals chatted to one another.

"They've got guns," Josie Paetz said.

"Two of them are cops, an escort," Ned answered loudly before anyone ratcheted the mercs' nervousness up another notch. "The pair in back have enough braid between them to sell brass for a sideline. That kind of rank doesn't show up if they're expecting a firefight.''

"Wish I had a gun," Deke Warson muttered in frustrated wistfulness.

"When I decide to declare war on a planet this size, Warson," Lissea snapped, "you'll be the first one I'll tell."

All the weapons aboard the *Swift* were in closed containers. Not concealed, not even locked away, most of them: there was no way the *Swift* could pretend here to be a peaceful freighter. Tadziki had insisted, however, that none of the crew be openly armed when they greeted the Celandine authorities.

The adjutant's belief that they had to tread lightly was supported by the way the authorities sequestered the *Swift* in a closed dock and ordered the crew to stay buttoned up until further instructions. None of the mercenaries argued the point, but nobody was happy about it either.

Everyone but the driver, one of the policemen, got out of the vehicle. An official in civilian clothes put the end of a contact transducer against the airlock and spoke into it. *"Inspection team coming aboard,"* the *Swift*'s hull announced. *"You may open your hatches now."*

Tadziki opened the main boarding ramp. As the hydraulics whined, Toll Warson said in a lilting voice, "We've come this far with no problems, boys. Let's get the rest of the way back, all right?"

Ned couldn't tell whether or not "with no problems" was meant to be ironic.

Echoes from other spacecraft made the huge hangar rumble like a seashore. The most richly decorated Celandine official raised his voice with familiar unconcern as he and his fellows walked up the ramp, roaring, "I'm Port Commander Flamond and I want you lot to understand two things right off!"

Flamond glared at Lissea and her crew, drawn up two abreast in the aisle on either side of the head of the ramp. Ned and Tadziki headed one rank. Ned hoped that none of the mercenaries behind him were going to catcall in response to Flamond's bluster.

"First," Flamond said. He seemed to have decided Tadziki rather than Lissea, who was on the other side of the aisle, was

captain. *"I'm* in charge of Île de Rameau Spaceport. I don't look kindly on anything or anybody who makes my life difficult."

Tadziki nodded. His expression was open, solemn—that of a responsible man agreeing with another responsible man. The lower-ranking Celandine officials looked around the *Swift* with interest, surprise, and—in the case of the armed policeman—obvious concern.

"Second," Flamond said, "there's three warships from Pancahte docked here since two tennights."

Carron stood beside Lissea. His mouth opened in horror. Ned's stomach dropped through the deck plates, and his hands began to tremble.

"They've put in a claim for return of this vessel and crew to answer charges on Pancahte," Flamond continued, "so you people are *already* causing me difficulties."

"Commander Flamond," Lissea said, "I'm Captain Doormann—"

The port commander turned to face her.

"—of the *Swift*. We're registered on Telaria and I'm on the board of Doormann Trading there. The Pancahtans have no right to detain my ship. If they believe they have a claim, they can prosecute it in our courts."

"Which," Tadziki interjected, "are a great deal more fair than the mixture of piracy and imbecility to which we were subjected on Pancahte."

Flamond looked from Lissea to the adjutant and back. He smiled, in a manner of speaking. "Are you telling me that I don't have the authority to hand you over to the Pancahtans, Captain?" he asked softly.

"No sir," Lissea said. "Celandine is a major commercial power, just as Telaria is. You have your law codes, and if they require you to . . . hand us over to murderous pirates, you most certainly have the authority. As well as the power. But I would be surprised to learn that Celandine's codes contained such a provision."

"What's she saying?" Josie Paetz whispered loudly to his uncle. Yazov, standing directly behind Lissea, put a stiff index finger to Paetz' lips. From his expression, he was willing for it to be a pistol.

Flamond guffawed. "Good, good, you understand the position, then," he said. "Which that Del Vore from Pancahte doesn't seem to. He keeps claiming that our laws don't hold for a prince of Pancahte."

He eyed the assembled mercenaries. "I told him that our guns held him, if it came to that. The same holds true for your lot, Doormann. Squashing you like a bug would solve my difficulties quite nicely. Give me half an excuse and that's just what I'll do. *Do* you understand?"

Somebody in a rank behind Ned started to speak. Somebody else had sense enough to elbow the troublemaker hard.

"Yes sir," Lissea said quietly. "We were hoping to water and resupply here for the last leg of our journey back to Telaria. If circumstances make that impossible, we of course understand."

She cleared her throat and lowered her eyes. "We only ask that you hold the Pancahtans here for a few days. To do otherwise would be to turn us over to pirates."

The two civilian officials behind Flamond whispered to one another. The subordinate military officer joined the conversation after a moment.

"That's what you request," Flamond said harshly. *"This* is what you'll get. First, your vessel can resupply here in normal fashion. I will add that although you'll be charged for the use of a bonded hangar—"

He moved his head in a quick upward jerk, indicating the structure which enclosed the *Swift*.

"—you're not being charged the additional costs you've imposed on my operations by the fact I can't permit other vessels to share Hangar Thirty-nine with you. Under the circumstances."

Lissea nodded contritely.

"Second," Flamond continued, "you have five days from now to leave Celandine. If you don't leave, you will be expelled. And I assure you, armed resistance would be most unwise."

The other military officer nodded grimly.

"Third," said Flamond, "no weapons will be taken out of or into this hangar. There will be a police detachment to enforce this prohibition at Entrance Five—"

He thumbed back toward the open doorway through which his vehicle had driven.

"—which will be the only entrance unsealed during the time you're here."

"We understand," Lissea said, nodding again.

"Fourth and finally," Flamond said, "all the same regulations apply to the Pancahtan contingent, who are *also* in a bonded hangar. The deadline for leaving Celandine is the same for both parties. And it *will* be enforced."

"What the hell's he expect us to do, then?" Coyne demanded. "Just shoot ourselfs?"

Lissea turned her head. "Herne," she called in a cold, deadly voice to Lordling, who stood at the end of the formation, directly behind Coyne. "The next time someone speaks out of turn, silence him."

Flamond raised an eyebrow at the tone. "As a matter of fact," he said to Lissea, "what I hope and expect you'll do is to negotiate a mutually acceptable compromise with this Del Vore."

Carron winced at the repeated name. Flamond ignored him to continue. "From discussions with the Pancahtans, I have reason to believe they might be satisfied with less than their stated demands. To that end—"

He beckoned forward one of the civilians, a squat man in his fifties who carried a briefcase of naturally striped leather.

"—since it will lessen my difficulties, I'm putting Master Nivelle at your mutual services. He's head of the commercial mediation staff here at the Port Authority."

Nivelle made a bow of middling depth. "Mistress Captain," he said without a trace of irony, "I'm looking forward to working with you. If you have a few minutes after Commander Flamond finishes, I can suggest some neutral venues for meetings with the Pancahtan parties."

The mediator stepped back. Flamond nodded crisply.

"Yes," he said, "well, I'm almost finished."

He looked hard at one half of the *Swift*'s complement, then the other. "I need hardly mention that in addition to regulations specific to the present situation, Celandine has normal civil and criminal codes, all provisions of which will be enforced by the proper authorities."

Deke Warson grinned at Flamond from over Carron's shoulder. Toll nudged his brother warily.

"Apart from that," the port commander continued, "Île de Rameau Spaceport averages a hundred and thirty-one movements per day. We get all kinds here, even your kind. So long as you keep your public behavior within reason, I think you'll find that our community can supply any kind of entertainment you're able to pay for. That's all."

Nivelle said, "I'll wait for you at the entrance, Mistress Doormann. I realize you may want to discuss matters among yourselves in private for a few minutes—but only a few minutes, I trust."

Flamond nodded curtly. He turned on his heel and marched back to his car, followed by his entourage. Tadziki raised the ramp behind them.

The mercenary ranks dissolved into babble. Over the ruck of voices Westerbeke said, "Well, that lets us know where *we* stand!"

By chance, Ned's eyes met those of Carron Del Vore as he looked away from Lissea. He realized from Carron's blank tenseness that the Pancahtan noble *didn't* know where *he* stood.

"No one leaves here until I release you or Tadziki does," Lissea said to the mercenaries standing formally at ease in one of the Hotel Massenet's three bars, rented for the afternoon. "Colonel Lordling is in charge."

"The drinks are on the expedition account," Tadziki interjected, "but I suggest you recall that we may be leaving very curst fast when we go."

Eyes flicked from captain to adjutant. The bartender

watched with his lips pursed and his hands spread on the bar's polished granite surface.

"Lissea, I ought to be upstairs with you," Herne Lordling said. There was more despair than bluster in his voice.

"This is where I need you, Herne," Lissea said crisply. "I can handle a negotiation, and I've got Tadziki and Slade to help with the technical presentation."

"And," Deke Warson cooed, "she's got the princey along for swank."

Men laughed. Herne Lordling flushed, and Lissea trained eyes as hard and gray as the bar-top on Warson.

Deke looked away. "Sorry, ma'am," Toll said.

Yazov and Paetz were on anchor watch. The rest of the complement had come with the negotiators to the Massenet. There wasn't any reason to keep specialists from the navigation and powerplant side on duty, since the *Swift* couldn't lift off until the authorities opened the hangar roof. Flamond *was* in charge, there were no two ways about it.

"I'll give you men a full report after the meeting," Lissea said. "I know you're nervous, but there's nothing here that I can't work through if you'll remain patient and keep the lid on. That's all for now."

She turned and strode from the closed bar. Tadziki was at her side, Ned behind them, and Carron Del Vore scrambled to join the movement that had caught him unawares.

"Why's she think we're nervous?" Ingried asked as the mercenaries surged toward the bar.

The Massenet was a dockside hotel, but it catered to ships' officers and wealthy transients. The lobby staff included a discreet security presence to prohibit roistering crewmen, and the internal decor was expensively florid. The capitals of the square stone pillars supporting the double staircase were flanged outward to form bases for lions holding coats of arms; crystal electroliers glittered down on the lobby.

Though the Massenet was decorated in classic fashion, there was nothing antique in its operations. The molded ceilings themselves glowed to supplement the electroliers with soft, shadowless illumination. Movement between floors was by means of modern demand-actuated lift- and drop-shafts rather than elevators (or the staircases, which were kept for show).

There were about a dozen non-uniformed people in the lobby. The couple checking out were probably civilians, but the rest were divided between hotel security and plainclothed governmental types.

Nivelle had known what he was doing when he chose the venue for negotiations. Seeing the security presence made Ned feel calmer. The *Swift*'s personnel weren't going to get into a bloody war with Pancahtans here in the hotel while the expedition's cooler members negotiated in the roof garden.

Delegation of tasks among expedition personnel was *ad hoc,* but by now areas of specialization were pretty obvious. Ned's job included worrying about possibilities that gunmen—better gunmen—would have laughed away.

Carron looked at the heavyset Celandine personnel with their good clothes and eyes like trip-hammers. He wrung his hands.

Lissea stepped to the liftshaft and reached for the call button. Ned blocked her hand and said, "Captain? Let me lead."

"He's correct," Tadziki said. "I'll bring up the rear."

"This isn't a combat patrol!" Lissea said, but she let Ned take her place on the lift disk.

"Not if we handle it right," Tadziki murmured.

Ned held the attaché case close to his chest and poked the R button. The lift mechanism judged its moment, then rotated the meter-diameter disk on which Ned stood into the shaft and raised him in a single smooth motion.

At the top of the shaft, the disk rotated outward again and deposited Ned in a kiosk in the roof garden. He stepped out, meeting the professional smile of another security man whose briefcase certainly did *not* contain electronic files and a hologram projector as Ned's did.

"They're waiting in the gazebo, sir," the Celandine said with a nod.

The gazebo was a substantial building, a heavy roof on tile-covered columns with couches to hold thirty-odd visitors in comfort. Several security men faced outward from beyond the low hedge encircling the structure. Nivelle and half a dozen brightly garbed Pancahtans led by Ayven Del Vore were seated at a round table in the center.

The liftshaft shunted Lissea onto the roof. Ned nodded acknowledgment and led the way toward the gazebo.

The walkways were tiled in a herringbone of green and white that *clock*ed beneath their boots. Ned glanced at the flowering shrubs bordering the path and said, ''A pretty blue, aren't they?''

''Slade, don't be an idiot!'' Lissea replied.

He grinned toward a fountain. Fish of an unfamiliar breed, almost as clear as the plashing water, curvetted among lilies and snapped insects out of the air.

Ned felt loose and positive. For a moment he didn't understand why. Then he realized that he knew he was physically safe in the midst of such tight security. It was the first time his unconscious had been sure of that since the *Swift* lifted from Telaria.

Of course, there wouldn't be any safety at all in four and a half days if they blew this meeting.

The liftshaft sighed open again. Ayven stood up and very deliberately spat onto the tiles at the gazebo's threshold. ''Good afternoon, brother!'' he called. ''*So* glad to meet you on Celandine. For a time I thought perhaps I'd miscalculated.''

''Good afternoon, Ayven,'' Carron answered calmly. ''I would just as soon have left you to your interests on Pancahte while I live my own life in the wider universe.''

Ned had been doubtful about bringing Carron to the meeting—not that anybody'd asked his opinion. Even if Carron kept his temper (and so far, so good), his presence was likely to have a bad effect on his brother. He suspected the reason Lissea brought Carron was that she didn't want to risk leaving him in the company of the mercenaries when she wasn't there to protect him.

Ned put his case down on the table and opened it. From what he could tell, the Pancahtans accompanying Ayven were simply muscle, soldiers who were uncomfortable without their powered armor. Their suits would be aboard the vessels—and completely useless to them here under Celeandine supervision or if the Pancahtan squadron ran down the *Swift* in space later.

The mediator rose and offered his hand to Lissea. "Glad to see you again, Captain Doormann," he said. He was a cultured man, but in his way just as tough as any of the security personnel standing quietly in the background. "And this would be Carron Del Vore, one of the bones of contention?"

"Master Nivelle," Lissea said, shaking hands. She nodded to Ayven. "Prince Ayven. But as for Carron here, he's a free citizen—of Pancahte, as it chances—and not an object to be bargained."

"He's a traitor," Ayven said flatly. "We want *him,* and we want the capsule you stole. When those two items have been turned over, we'll permit the rest of you to go where you please, *despite* the damage you did to Astragal."

"Succinctly put," Nivelle said. "But may we all sit down, please? There's less chance for actions being misunderstood if—"

"I'll stand!" Ayven said.

Lissea pulled her chair out and seated herself. Ned, Tadziki, and—a half-beat later—Carron followed her lead.

"Master Del Vore," the mediator replied, "I would be most appreciative if you would sit down as I requested you do."

It occurred to Ned that Nivelle considered his position here to be as much arbitrator as mediator, and that the Celandine certainly had the force to back up his will. Ayven must have realized that too, because he suddenly dropped back into his seat beside Nivelle.

The prince was an extraordinarily handsome man. The flush on his cheeks complemented his blond hair.

"Master Slade," Lissea said in the tense silence, "will you run the first set of clips, please?"

Ned switched on the hologram projector in his briefcase.

"This was assembled," Lissea explained to Nivelle and the

Pancahtans as the equipment warmed up, "from the helmet recorders we normally wear—and wore throughout our stay on Pancahte. The full texts from which the clips were taken are available, sir"—

She nodded to Nivelle—

"Should there be any question about the authenticity of the excerpts."

A view of the throne room in Astragal hung above the center of the table:

"The tanks—" Lon Del Vore's image boomed from his throne, while the image of Ayven stood beside him and nodded agreement.'"—they're an irritation. If you can destroy them, then I'll let you have the capsule you claim."

"Yes, I accept," said an image of Lissea in profile, viewed from the recording lenses in Ned's helmet.

The view cut quickly to a figure—Ned, though the view was from behind and the resolution wasn't very good—running toward one of the Old Race tanks. The figure patted at the concealed latchplate and the hatch opened to him.

From the recording, it looked as though Ned had known what he was doing. His guts knotted as he watched the scene, recalling how utterly lost and alone he'd been at that moment.

The view shifted again: Ned, helmetless, staggered toward the viewpoint against a landscape of magma and hellfire. In the background was the tank he had abandoned in the last seconds of its existence. Armor slumped, and the gun's long barrel hung askew because the mantlet could no longer support the weight.

The image panned too fast for good resolution. The recording viewpoint, Lissea, looked back over her shoulder. The tank she had crewed against the alien starship was dissolving in a pool of yellow-white rock.

The demonstration clip ended with a silent pop of light. Ned switched off the projector.

"Fulfillment of the agreement is the basis on which we removed the capsule," Lissea said. "Although the capsule is itself Telarian property. As a matter of fact, it was the coffin of my great-granduncle. We carried out the Pancahtan terms to the letter. *Despite* the fact that the Treasurer and his son here concealed the existence of—"

"We concealed nothing!" Ayven shouted as he jumped halfway from his seat.

A burly Celandine put a hand on the prince's shoulder and pushed him straight back down. Two soldiers started to rise and thought better of it when they noticed the guns pointed by other security men.

Nivelle's mouth curved in a smile that didn't reach his eyes.

"Thank you for your forbearance, Master Del Vore," he said softly. "Let me remind you all that my instructions from the port commander are to remove this problem by any means within the laws of Celandine. The force that will be used to suppress, for example, the felony of assault and battery would achieve Commander Flamond's desires."

He looked from the Pancahtans to Lissea. "*Will* be used," he repeated. "And as for you, Mistress Doormann . . . I would appreciate it if you avoided the use of loaded terms yourself. They won't advance the discussion."

Lissea nodded. "I'm sorry, sir," she said, sounding like a good actress pretending to be contrite. "I might better have said that disabling the tanks as requested brought my crew and myself into dangers that we had no reason to expect."

Ned's fingers moved, cuing another chip while he continued to watch the eyes of the Pancahtan contingent.

"That ship was your doing!" Ayven snapped. "You used it to cover your escape with what you'd stolen—and with my brother who helped you steal it."

Ned switched on the projector. The image began with the dumbbell-shaped starship, half-risen from the shaft in which it had laired for centuries or millennia. Tiny figures of men ran toward their vehicles. The gigantic ship continued to rise.

The notion that the starship was somehow a ruse of Lissea's was so ludicrous that even the careful Nivelle smiled. Aloud he said, "I think we can dismiss that, Prince Ayven, since you've already stated that you're willing to forego damages caused during the incident in question. And—"

His tone hardened, though the mediator hadn't raised his

voice at any point in the proceedings. Ned switched off the projected image.

"—it appears to me that Captain Doormann has made an unanswerably strong case for her continued possession of the capsule. That leaves the other point."

Nivelle eyed Carron with the expression of an inspector viewing a quarter of beef. "The request for extradition of your brother here."

"No doubt Celandine honors the principle of asylum?" Lissea said coolly.

"Celandine has enough problems of its own without our feeling the need to import troublemakers from outside the polity," Nivelle replied. "We certainly do *not* grant asylum."

He turned like a bullfighter between two animals to face Ayven again. "Nor, I might add, do we extradite to other states as a matter of right."

Ayven's face had remained set in anger during the exchange. The smiles of several of his subordinates wilted like frost-killed flowers.

"What Celandine *will* do," Nivelle continued, "is to view evidence presented by the state desiring extradition, and to make a binding decision whether or not to extradite. What evidence can you provide, Prince Ayven?"

"He stole a thing, a device, from our father," Ayven said, coldly precise. "I saw him give it to her."

He glared at Lissea. "That was why the tanks didn't kill her: that theft. Carron is a traitor and has been *convicted* as a traitor on Pancahte." He nodded, terminating his statement.

The trial Lon gave his younger son had probably taken all of thirty seconds, Ned thought.

Carron stared at Lissea. He reached sideways to take her hand. She twitched it away without looking at him.

"Yes, that could constitute a serious charge," Neville said. He tapped Ned's briefcase with the tip of his index finger. "But what *evidence* do you have, Prince Ayven?"

Tadziki drew Carron close to him and whispered into the younger man's ear. Lissea continued to watch Ayven and the mediator, as though no one else in the open room existed.

Ayven flushed again. "It didn't occur to me," he said, clipping his words in his cold rage, "that I would be treated with such disrespect by *bureaucrats.*"

Nivelle nodded calmly, protected from insult by consciousness of his absolute authority. From what Ned had seen of Celandine thus far, it was a place with common-sense rules and very good people enforcing them.

"However," Ayven continued, "we have recordings just like they do."

He flicked his chin in the direction of Ned and the hologram projector. "I watched Carron hand over the device, and my suit recorded it. The recording itself is on Pancahte, but you have my word of honor that it exists."

Nivelle nodded again. "Mistress," he said, "gentlemen, I'm going to propose a course of events. You'll have time to consider it, the remainder of the five days. And while I can't compel agreement—"

He smiled to underscore the patent lie.

"—if one party agrees and the other does not, it's likely to affect Commander Flamond's further actions. Is that understood?"

"Get on with it," Carron Del Vore rasped. His fingertips were pressed tightly together, and his eyes were on the center of the large table.

"First," Nivelle said, "the capsule in question remains the property of Captain Doormann."

He looked at Ayven. "If you wish to press your claim for it, you may do so through the judicial system of Telaria."

"Go on," Ayven said, his voice a near echo of his brother's.

"Second," Nivelle continued, facing Lissea. "Carron Del Vore will remain on Celandine at his own expense for five tennights to permit the Pancahtan authorities to provide evidence substantiating their demand for extradition."

"No!" said Carron. Tadziki dragged him back down into his seat before a Celandine security man did.

"If evidence isn't forthcoming within that period," Nivelle continued, "or I deem the evidence insufficient for the purpose offered, Master Del Vore will be free to go or stay as he desires. If, however, Pancahte meets its burden of proof—''

He smiled again. ''—in my sole estimation . . . then Master Del Vore will be handed over to the Pancahtan authorities.''

''Lissea,'' Carron cried, ''you can't let them *do* this to me! I—''

Lissea turned like a weasel striking. ''Carron,'' she said, ''if you can inform me on how your situation would be improved if the *Swift* and everyone aboard her were blasted to plasma, then do so. Otherwise, please *shut* your mouth!''

Carron swallowed.

Lissea stood up slowly and easily. The mediator wagged a finger to warn off his security men before one of them reacted. ''Master Nivelle,'' she said, ''I'll take your suggested procedure under advisement. I'll have a response for you shortly, certainly before the deadline.''

Nivelle nodded. ''I understand that you'll want to consider the matter privately, mistress,'' he said. ''But as you no doubt realize, the matter is absorbing Celandine state resources to very little state benefit, so a prompt response would be appreciated.''

Lissea walked out of the gazebo. The three men got up and followed. Tadziki gripped Carron's shoulder in what could have been a comforting gesture.

The Pancahtans scraped back their chairs. ''I'd appreciate it if you gentlemen stayed with me a few minutes,'' Nivelle said with his normal bland insistence.

Tadziki put Carron into the dropshaft, then took the next disk himself. As Ned waited with Lissea, he heard Ayven Del Vore snarl, ''I suppose you think you've got me over a barrel, don't you?''

Lissea stepped off.

''Yes, Prince Ayven, I do,'' the mediator agreed. ''But it doesn't affect my judgment on what would be a fair result.''

The mechanism swung Ned into the dropshaft. He didn't know that he'd want to live on Celandine. But he respected the people who did.

Lissea and Tadziki, with Carron between them, were already striding to the temporarily private bar. Mercenaries cheered as Lissea opened the door. The sound was so viciously bloodthirsty that several of the security men in the lobby reached beneath their tunics.

Ned smiled with cold reassurance. "Not a problem," he murmured to the nearest Celandine. "They're just happy."

He closed the door behind him.

Lissea waved a hand for silence, but the men had already quieted. They weren't tense, exactly, but none of them were so drunk that they didn't realize the importance of the meeting that had just concluded.

"Gentlemen," she said, "Tadziki has booked a corridor of rooms for you at the Sedan House a block west of here. Anybody who wants to stay at the Massenet is welcome to do so, but I believe the comfort range of the Sedan House is more in keeping with your requirements."

"They'll cater liquor and girls at the Sedan," Tadziki amplified. "Or you can bring your own."

"That's *my* requirement!" Deke Warson shouted.

"We'll continue with two-man anchor watches," Lissea said. "Westerbeke and Slade, you're on in an hour and a half. You'll be relieved in another eight hours, but if you've got anything urgent I suggest you take care of it fast."

Ned met her eyes without comment.

"I've got some decisions to make," Lissea continued, "and I'm going to make them alone. I don't want to be disturbed, and I *won't* be disturbed. Do you all understand?"

"I understand I'm going to be too busy to worry about anything but where my prick is in about three seconds flat," Westerbeke muttered, shaking his head with irritation at where his name appeared on the duty roster.

"Tadziki, do you have anything further?" Lissea asked.

"Toll and Deke, I need to speak with you," the adjutant said. "Nothing beyond that."

"Dismissed, then," Lissea said. She turned. Ned opened the door for her.

Carron Del Vore caught up with her in the lobby as the

mercenaries spilled out, heading for the street door. "Lissea—" he cried.

"Carron," she said as Ned and, from within the bar, Tadziki and the Warsons watched, "if you lay a hand on me, I'll turn you over to Nivelle right now. I doubt he's left the building yet. Is that what you want?"

"But—"

"Is that what you want?"

Carron walked toward the street door. He hunched as if he'd recently had an abdominal operation.

Ned left the Hotel Massenet through the door at the far side of the lobby. He thought he'd have a drink, but not here.

Part of Ned didn't like what he'd just seen done to Carron Del Vore. That same part didn't like the other part of Edward Slade's mind, grinning gleefully to have watched Carron's humiliation.

Josie Paetz waited with Yazov just inside the entrance to Hangar 39. They wore their commo helmets and there was no access to the *Swift* except past them, but it seemed to Ned that the two men were jumping the gun on their liberty a little.

Paetz regretfully unfastened the pistol belt with twin right-hand holsters and handed it to Ned. "See you, then," he said. He seemed keyed up—and happier than prospects for a drink and a woman would have made him. "Lay it on my bunk, okay?"

The heavy door was beginning to close. Paetz jumped out to avoid pushing the call button so that the police guards outside would open the hangar again. Yazov followed.

Ned opened his mouth to say that one of the pair ought to wait until Westerbeke arrived to fill the minimal anchor watch. He suppressed the words. There was no real risk and anyway, Paetz and Yazov weren't going to pay the least attention.

Westerbeke and Carron Del Vore leaped into the dock an instant before the door slammed.

Westerbeke looked at the gunbelt Ned held. He raised an

eyebrow. "Expecting trouble?" he asked.

Ned shrugged. "They're Paetz's," he explained. "In his terms, he's just thinking positively."

He thought about the attitude of the men he'd just relieved and added, "They were acting . . . as if they expected to land hot. Does that mean anything to you?"

Westerbeke looked in the direction Paetz and his uncle had gone, though there was a massive door panel between them by now. He shrugged in turn and said, "Tadziki called them after he'd grabbed Deke and Toll. Maybe they've got something up, but they haven't told me—"

He grinned brightly. "Which suits *me* just fine. I pilot spaceships. I always figured 'When bullets fly, I don't,' was a curst good rule to live by."

Ned didn't comment, but he remembered Westerbeke's flawless extraction from Buin and his landing at the same point an orbit later. Like many (though not all) other members of the *Swift*'s complement, the pilot chose to downplay his accomplishments rather than boasting.

"Westerbeke," Carron said, intruding with the air of a man committing to a high dive. "I'll take your watch. You can go back and . . . and—whatever you want to do. I need to talk to Slade."

"I don't think—" Ned began with a frown.

"You know, *that* suits me too," Westerbeke said. He reached for the call button.

Ned caught the pilot's hand. "I don't—" he repeated.

"Slade," Carron said, "I *need* to talk with you. It's critically important. All of our lives are at stake."

Westerbeke's eyes bounced from one man to the other. The pilot looked more entertained than concerned.

Ned scowled, then came to terms with his own jumpiness. There was no way into Hangar 39 except at the will of Celandine spaceport police; and if he couldn't handle Carron Del Vore by himself, then he deserved whatever happened to him.

"All right," he said, pushing the call button for Westerbeke. It was mildly amusing to note that he'd assumed control, and that neither of the other men had attempted to argue with the assumption.

He looked Carron over without affection. "You're here for the full eight hours, *Prince,*" he said. "You don't get another chance to change your mind."

The door rumbled open. Outside, artificial lights supplemented the rosy sunset. A policeman stood beside the weapons detector with his pistol drawn. Westerbeke gave Ned a three-fingered salute and sauntered out for renewed liberty.

An armored conduit snaked across the concrete between the *Swift* and a junction box near the door. The walls were thick enough to swallow radio and microwave signals. The vessel had to be patched into the planetary system in order to communicate beyond Hangar 39.

Ned waved the Pancahtan toward the *Swift* ahead of him. "What is it, then?" he demanded. "That you need to say to me?"

"You know that my brother can't be trusted, don't you?" Carron said.

"I think that a number of people in your family," Ned said, "feel they have a right to do anything they bloody well please." Until he heard the venom with which he spoke, he hadn't realized how much he hated Carron.

Ned's tone didn't seem to concern or even affect the Pancahtan. "If you turn me over to Ayven," Carron said as they walked up the boarding ramp together, "he'll still hunt down your ship and destroy it. You made fools of him and my father. We made fools of them. They'll never forgive us."

"I don't make those decisions," Ned said, being deliberately obtuse.

The interior of the *Swift* looked even more like an animal's lair now that Ned had spent the past eight hours in civilized surroundings. It was filthy, it stank, and the disorder was more akin to a heap of rotting vegetation than it was to living quarters. It would take days to clean and disinfect the ship when they returned to Telaria, if and when . . .

"I've come to you," Carron said, "because you're intelligent enough to understand what I'm saying."

He stood in the central aisle, staring aft toward the capsule.

Half the external panels had been removed, exposing circuitry.

Carron's back was to Ned. "Also," he continued, "because you will keep your word to me. The others, any of them—"

He turned to face Ned. His expression was cold and imperious, that of a king greeting his conqueror.

"—would promise but would betray me; though it will be all your lives unless you accept my plan."

"Do you think I wouldn't lie to you?" Ned wondered aloud.

"You will do what you think is necessary," Carron said flatly. "I accept that. But I trust your honor as well as your capacity to see where necessity lies. Even Tadziki—"

He shook his head angrily, the sort of motion a man with his hands full makes to shoo a fly.

Josie Paetz slept in the top bunk, now vacant, forward on the port side. The cellular blanket was twisted in a heap, and the replaceable sheet which covered the acceleration cushion was gray with dirt. Ned put the gunbelt on the integral pillow and sat down at one of the navigational consoles.

"What about Lissea?" he said to the forward bulkhead.

"I've come to you, Slade," Carron said.

In sudden anger, the Pancahtan continued, "Doesn't it mean anything to you, all I've sacrificed? You'd have failed, *died,* on Pancahte a dozen different times if it weren't for me! And what I'm doing now, it's the only way for you to survive again! Do you *want* to die?"

Ned rotated the console, facing it aft toward Carron. "Not a lot, no," he said. "Tell me your plan, then."

Carron nodded. "Yes," he said. "The only way the *Swift* will be able to reach your home—be able to leave Celandine's space, even—is if my brother is aboard. My father's ships won't destroy us if Ayven is our hostage."

"Go on," Ned said, resisting the impulse to sneer. Carron had been consistently right in his assumptions, particularly those involving the behavior of his father and brother.

"He'll come to you," Carron said. "Here, to the ship,

where you can capture him. If you offer him what he wants.''

Ned looked at Carron coldly. The Pancahtan stood in the aisle with his arms akimbo, smiling slightly.

"You," Ned said. "You as his prisoner."

Carron nodded. "That's correct," he said. "Me as his prisoner."

There was fear in the young Pancahtan's eyes, but the smile didn't leave his lips.

Herne Lordling hadn't been too drunk to function since a three-day family celebration when he turned twelve, but he was nonetheless carrying a load as he walked up to the sidewalk from a sub-level bar. He didn't remember that there'd been steps when he entered, but he negotiated them in a satisfactory fashion anyway.

The bar faced the high berm surrounding Île de Rameau Spaceport. A starship rose on a plume of plasma, shaking the night sky with a familiar thunder. Lordling had been in a lot of ports, on a lot of planets. Now he wished he were on another one—and in a universe in which Lissea Doormann had never existed.

The sidewalk was busy. Vehicles ranging from monocycles to a forty-roller containerized-cargo flat snarled slowly along the circumferential road which girdled the port. Lordling swayed. He was considering the alternate possibilities of going upstairs in one of the buildings behind him to find a woman or throwing himself out in front of traffic.

A bright blue bus marked Spaceport Shuttle pulled in on its programmed circuit. The spiked barriers that kept ordinary traffic from parking in the shuttle stops withdrew before the nose of the bus. Sailors jostled past Lordling to board. The bus attendant watched from his cage in the center of the vehicle.

Lordling squeezed in with the others and presented his credit chip to the reader beside the attendant. One thing about a major port: your money was always good, though they might discount it forty percent from face value depending on how difficult they expected clearance to be.

Lordling didn't care what things cost. All he really wanted was someone to kill. Several choice candidates shuttled back and forth through his mind. It took all the remains of his self-control to keep from grabbing the unknown sailor next to him and squeezing until the man's eyeballs popped out.

He punched two-three-seven-one into the destination panel. It was only after he'd done so that he realized it wasn't the location of the closed hangar which held the *Swift*.

He stepped to one of the benches. It barely had room for a child remaining. Lordling seated himself with a double thrust of his elbows. A fat sailor cursed and stood up. The attendant watched but didn't interfere. Lordling stared at the sailor's face, his puffy neck . . .

The sailor turned his back.

The bus pulled away from the stop. Because the vehicle was full, it left the curb lane and shunted across the circumferential to the next spaceport entrance. The whine of the turbine and the high-frequency clacking of the shuttle's spun-metal tires buzzed Lordling into a haze of alcohol and bloody dreams.

The bus drove a route it chose for itself based on the destination codes loaded by its passengers. The attendant was aboard to summon emergency services if there was a problem among the human cargo, and to report if the vehicle was involved in an accident. Breakdown codes were, like the actual driving, the responsibility of the shuttle itself.

Ten passengers got off at the first stop, the hiring office in the port's administrative complex. The shuttle moved down the line of docks on an elevated roadway, occasionally pulling into a kiosk to drop or to load passengers. There was little other traffic.

Beneath the roadway were huge conveyors shunting goods unloaded from starships into warehouses or vehicles for ground transportation. When the bus passed over an operating conveyor, the low-pitched rumble jarred Lordling temporarily alert again.

The lights of work crews dotted the landing field. At regular intervals a ship landed or lifted off in overwhelming glare and thunder.

"It's yours, buddy," the attendant said. "Hey! It's yours!"

He reached through the cage and shook Lordling's shoulder. Lordling came alert with a reflex that brought both hands toward the man's throat. The attendant lunged against the back of his tubular cage to get clear.

"*Hey!*" the attendant shouted again, fumbling for the handset of his red emergency phone.

Lordling lurched to his feet. "You shouldn't grab a guy like that," he muttered as he stepped toward the door. It started to close at the end of its programmed cycle, then caught and reopened as the attendant pushed the override button.

Lordling stepped from the shuttle. He was the last of the passengers who'd boarded outside the spaceport, but the vehicle was half-full of sailors headed into the city.

The attendant watched, holding the handset to his mouth until the door closed behind Lordling.

The location sign in the kiosk had been defaced by names and numbers scratched on its surface, but the huge building the stop served had BONDED HANGAR 17 in letters a meter high across the front wall. Lordling walked down the zigzag flight of steps to ground level and started toward the hangar entrance.

He hadn't had a drink for half an hour. That didn't make him sober, but he had enough judgment back to know what he was doing wasn't a good idea. Not enough judgment to prevent him from doing it, though. Anyway, the sort of decisions a professional soldier regularly makes aren't those a civilian would consider sane.

To either side of Hangar 17 were open docks, discharging the cargo of twenty-kiloton freighters along conveyor belts. The stereophonic racket dimmed only when a large vessel took off or landed. Cargo handlers wore helmet lamps to supplement the pole-mounted light banks along the rollerway.

Two men in the green-and-black uniform of Port Authority police watched from their air-cushion van as Lordling approached. One of them got up, yawned, and drew his bell-mouthed pistol. He gestured the mercenary to the detector frame set a meter in front of the closed doorway.

"Through here, buddy," the policeman ordered. He didn't look or sound concerned by the fact Lordling wore stone-pattern utilities rather than the orange-slashed yellow uniform of the Pancahtan naval personnel.

Lordling hesitated. He wasn't stupid, and he'd survived decades in a business where often you get only one mistake.

"Look, pal," the policeman still in the van said, "if you're not going in, piss off! I don't want you hanging around, you understand?"

Anger—at the cop, at life, at a woman who fucked boys but wouldn't give Colonel Herne Lordling the time of day—jolted the mercenary. He stepped through the frame and grasped the latch of the sliding door.

Neither the latch nor the door moved.

"Don't get your bowels in an uproar," the first policeman ordered. "This don't open till we tell it to open."

He turned to his partner. "Is he okay?"

"What the hell's wrong with your back, buddy?" the man at the detector readout within the van demanded. "You got bits of metal all through it!"

Lordling stared through the van's windshield. "Shell fragments," he said. "If it's any of your business."

"Bloody well told it's our business," the policeman said, but he touched a switch anyway.

Servos slid the vehicle-width door slowly sideways against its inertia. The panel was fifteen centimeters thick and far too massive for an unaided man to move. Lordling walked inside.

Though the three Pancahtan vessels within Hangar 17 were individually much larger than the *Swift* in Hangar 39, they were still dwarfed by the vast cavity in which they rested. Inlaid letters on the bow of the nearest announced that it was the *Courageous.* The next over read *Furious,* and Lordling couldn't be sure of the third.

Lordling walked along the side of the closed dock, staying at a considerable distance from the *Courageous.* The vessel had two flat turrets, offset forward to port and aft to starboard.

They were faired into the hull and shuttered for the moment. Lordling judged that each could mount a pair of 20-cm power-guns, weapons as heavy as the main gun of the largest armored vehicles.

A team of Pancahtan sailors had removed access plates from the stern of the *Furious*. They were working on the attitude-control motors. There was a man at the foot of each open hatchway. Other yellow-and-orange personnel moved between vessels on their errands, but no one paid any attention to Lordling.

The complements were probably in the order of a hundred men per ship, counting crewmen and soldiers together. As with the *Swift*'s personnel, most of them would be billeted in portside hostelries while the ships were on Celandine.

A belt of linked plates circled the vessel's midpoint. Alternate sections slid sideways so that missles could be launched from the openings. There was a variety of other hatches and blisters as well, some of which housed defensive batteries of rapid-fire powerguns to protect against hostile missiles.

The *Swift* mounted no external armament whatever. If the Pancahtans ran her down in space, as they surely would unless Ayven Del Vore was mollified, the Telarian vessel would provide only target practice—and that not for long. Lissea had to surrender her . . . her *boy*. There was no other survivable choice.

Perhaps Herne Lordling could himself arrange for Carron to wind up in the hands of his brother.

Lordling turned with decision toward the door in the enclosure wall. He was steady on his legs again, and his vision had sharpened through the earlier haze.

The door rumbled open while Lordling was still fifty meters away. He paused, standing close to the grease-speckled wall. A party of Pancahtan sailors entered the hangar, laughing and calling to one another. There were seven of them. When he was sure the last man was inside, Lordling broke into a run. He had to get to the doorway before the servos closed it.

A Pancahtan caught the motion out of the corner of his eye

and turned around. "Hey?" he called. "Hey there! Who the hell is that?"

The last of the sailors shifted to put himself in Lordling's path.

"Hey, it's one of—" the Pancahtan shouted. Lordling kicked his knee out from under him and dived through the door an instant before it slammed against the jamb.

"Freeze, you!" shouted a policeman as he leveled his gun at Lordling. *"Freeze!"*

An orange light winked within the van, the call signal indicating that someone within the hangar wanted to get out. The second policeman aimed a similar weapon from the van's open window.

"Keep them in there!" Lordling cried as he got to his feet. "There's six of them—they'll kill me if you let them out!"

"Stand in the fucking frame, you bastard!" the first policeman cried. "If you're packing anything now, you're cold meat!"

Lordling backed into the detector frame again. The plasma exhaust of a landing starship reflected from Hangar 17's facade, throwing the mercenary's tortured shadow toward the waiting policeman.

"He's clean!" reported the man in the vehicle. "But you know, I figure if he's one of them Telarians nosing around here, then anything he gets is what he's got coming to him."

He touched a switch. The servos whined, beginning to open the door again.

Lordling ran toward the conveyor serving Dock 18. Pallets supporting huge fusion bottles rumbled down the belt at intervals of five or six minutes. They moved very slowly because of the enormous momentum which would have to be braked before the cranes at the far end could lift the merchandise.

A few cargo handlers stood on catwalks along the conveyor, watching for signs of trouble. There was little they could do if a pallet began to drift. Stopping the belt abruptly would more probably precipitate a crisis than prevent one.

The trestles supporting the conveyor were enclosed in sheet metal to form a long shed. There were doors at fifty-meter intervals, but the first one Lordling came to was closed with a hasp and padlock.

He jogged on to the next. He was breathing through his open mouth. He'd never been a runner, and though adrenaline had burned the alcohol out of his system, it hadn't given him a younger man's wind. The second door was padlocked also.

Lordling glanced over his shoulder. Men in yellow-and-orange uniforms were grouped at the entrance to Hangar 17. Lordling was in the hard shadow cast by light banks on the conveyorway above, but one of the Celandine policemen pointed in the direction he'd run.

Bastard!

The Pancahtans started toward the conveyor. Lordling knew he couldn't outrun them. He stepped back and brought his right foot around in a well-judged crescent kick. The edge of his boot sheared the hasp and sent it whizzing off into darkness with the lock.

Lordling opened the sheet-metal door, slipped in, and tried to pull the panel closed behind him. It swung ajar, and anyway he couldn't expect to fool the Pancahtans as to where he'd gone.

The interior of the shed was echoing bedlam. Stark, flickering light leaked in through seams between the conveyor and the support structure as the belt material flexed. Flat loops of power cables feeding the rollers' internal motors quivered in the vibration. The piers and trestles were fifty-centimeter I-beams, useless for concealment if any of the sailors pursuing carried lights.

Lordling ran across to the other side of the shed. He'd break out through one of the doors there, wedge it shut from the outside, and climb up to the catwalk while the Pancahtans searched the shed. From there he would go outward, to the ship that was unloading, rather than directly back to pick up the shuttle.

He ought to be able to find a weapon before he next saw a yellow—

There were no doors on the other side of the shed. Access was from one side only.

The door by which Lordling had entered swung back. A handlight swept him and jiggled as the Pancahtan waved his comrades over. . . .

Lordling kicked at the metal siding, trying to find a seam he could break. The sheet belled and fluttered violently. It was too flexible to crack the way he needed it to do if he was going to get out.

All six Pancahtans entered the shed. They were illuminated from above and by side-scatter from the lights two of them held.

The sailors carried crowbars and spanners with shafts a meter long. They'd broken into a toolshed for the conveyor maintenance crews. Lordling wondered if the bastard cop had told them about the shed, also.

He shifted so that he stood a meter in front of one of the support pillars. That would cover his back but still give him room to maneuver.

When a bottle moved down the conveyor overhead the noise in the shed was palpable, and even when the rollers turned without load there was too much noise for voice communication. The Pancahtans fanned out and advanced in the harshly broken light. They stayed in an arc, close enough for mutual support but not so tight that they'd foul one another when they struck. They knew their business.

Lordling braced himself mentally. He could take one down with a spearpoint of stiffened fingers, but the others would be on him before he broke through to the door. Even if he got to the door, he couldn't outrun the sailors; he'd—

The door opened. The Pancahtans, three meters from their prey and preparing for the final rush, didn't notice the men who entered the shed behind them.

Light as white and intense as a stellar corona blasted from the doorway. It threw shadows sharp enough to cut stencils against the metal of the wall behind Lordling. Pancahtans turned.

The shots were silent in the background thunder. Orange muzzle flashes and the bright blue glare of a powergun flickered from the fringes of main light source. Pancahtans thrashed in their death throes. A fid of hot brains slapped Lordling in the face, hard enough to stagger him.

All the Pancahtans were down. The light switched off. Its absence was as shocking as silence would have been. Lordling was blind, and his ears were numb with thunder.

A shadowy figure stepped close and handed Lordling a commo helmet. He slipped it on. The positive-noise damping was a relief greater than he could have guessed before it occurred.

The unit was set to intercom. *"Hey Paetz,"* Deke Warson crowed. *"You fucked up. This guy's tunic's all over blood. We can't use it."*

"Fuck you, Warson! I shot him in the fucking head, didn't I? How'm I supposed to keep him from bleeding?"

"We've got five, that's enough," said Tadziki. Lordling's retinas had recovered enough for him to recognize his companions: Tadziki, carrying a 30-cm floodlight and its powerpack, Paetz and Yazov, and the Warson brothers. *"Lordling, are you all right?"*

Toll Warson stood in the open doorway with his pistol concealed as he watched for possible intruders. The other four were stripping the dead Pancahtan sailors. Paetz had set his powergun on the concrete beside him. The glowing barrel would have ignited his clothing had he dropped it back in his pocket.

"Yeah, I'm okay," Lordling said. *"That was curst good timing, though. Where'd you get the guns?"*

"I've never been in a port where you couldn't find just about anything you were willing to pay for," the adjutant said. He grunted and straightened his torso so that he could unstrap the heavy lightpack. *"Île de Rameau is no different."*

"Hey, Cun'l?" Deke Warson said. He'd taken off his own tunic, mottled in shades of gray, and was pulling on the orange-and-yellow jacket of the headless corpse before him. *"You did just fine. I was going to be the bait, but we saw you and thought we'd use the Big Cheese instead."*

One of the Pancahtans had taken ten or a dozen high-velocity projectiles through the face. The mercenary shooter hadn't trusted an unfamiliar weapon—but it'd worked just fine, and there was a tight pattern of holes in the bloody sheet metal beyond. The Lord only knew where the bullets had wound up.

"*You saw them come after me?*" Lordling demanded. "*You could've stopped them before?*"

Tadziki was putting on a Pancahtan tunic that was too long for his torso but still tight across the shoulders. "*We couldn't have done anything without the police seeing it until we had some cover,*" he said. "*Herne, since you're here, you can watch our gear. We shouldn't be too long. Don't do anything to attract attention and there shouldn't be a problem.*"

"*What we did, Cun'l buddy—*" said Deke Warson as he stepped to the doorway to take his brother's place—"*is watch you get off the bus and trot right into the hangar. So we thought we'd wait and see.*"

He wore Pancahtan trousers and jacket. A very careful observer might notice that his boots were nonstandard for the uniform.

"*You—*" Lordling said. He didn't know how to complete the sentence. Instead, he turned and kicked the sheet metal. This time a seam split, letting in a quiver of light from Dock 19's rollerway.

"*Look, you can't get into the hangar with those guns!*" Lordling said loudly. "*Or do you plan to shoot the cops? Via, that'd send us all for the high jump!*"

Tadziki's trousers didn't fit well either, but at least the jacket's overlap covered the way he'd folded the waistband over his belt rather than cuff the pants' legs. "*Herne,*" he said, "*this one's in the hands of the proper parties. When we're done, you can get back to the* Swift *and sleep it off. Chances are we'll be leaving Celandine very shortly.*"

"*But what are you going to do?*" Lordling demanded.

Tadziki looked over the men he'd brought. All of them wore Pancahtan uniforms. Yazov had slung the jacket over his shoulder to conceal the blood that had speckled the front of it. He wouldn't be the first sailor wearing an undershirt in public while on liberty.

The men laid their bootlegged guns beside the corpses. Tadziki took his helmet off and handed it to Lordling. Lordling took it blindly as the others followed suit.

More cargo rumbled its way cacophonously down the conveyor belt. Tadziki gestured and moved toward the door with three of his disguised men.

Deke Warson cupped his hands between his mouth and Lordling's ear and shouted, "What we're doing is our job, Cun'l. Now, you be a good boy while we're gone."

And then Deke too was gone.

The door stayed open as the five men in orange-slashed yellow uniforms entered Hangar 17 one by one, processed through the detector frame by the policemen outside. Deke Warson did a little dance, circling while his feet picked out a surprisingly complicated step. He tried to grab young Josie Paetz, who angrily pushed him away.

The party made for the *Furious,* the midmost of the three Pancahtan vessels, with more deliberation than speed. Deke linked arms with his brother Toll. They did a shuffling two-step across the concrete until they were hushed by Tadziki. The stocky man looked older and perhaps more nearly sober than his companions.

The boarding stairs of the *Furious* were wide enough for two men abreast, but both brothers tried to cram themselves in beside their leader. He turned and growled an order while the two sailors on access duty watched from the top of the stairs.

The Warsons subsided. Tadziki climbed the last two steps. He threw a salute that started crisply and broke off with him staggering against the rail.

"You got the wrong ship, Compeer," one of the on-duty pair observed, reading the name tapes on Tadziki's right breast and around his left sleeve. "The *Glorious* is the next berth over."

He nodded toward the vessel farther from the hangar's entrance.

"Good stuff, boys?" the other on-duty sailor asked with amusement.

"The best fucking stuff I've drunk since the last fucking stuff I've drunk!" Deke Warson said forcefully. He pulled a square-faced bottle of green liquor from a side pocket. The seal was broken, but only a few swigs were gone. He thrust the bottle toward the men on watch. "Here, try some."

As he spoke, Yazov lifted a similar bottle, nearly empty, and raised it to his lips.

"Hey!" Josie Paetz bleated. "Save some for me!"

One of the sailors looked quickly over his shoulder to see if an officer was watching. The ship was almost empty, and the duty officer was probably drunk in his cabin. Ships' crews on Pancahtan vessels were definitely inferior compared to the soldiers of Prince Ayven's entourage. Morale among sailors suffered as a result.

"Naw, we don't—" his partner said.

"The hell we don't!" insisted the first sailor as he took the bottle and opened it. He drank deeply and passed it to his fellow. "Whoo! Where'd you get that stuff, boys?"

"We are here," Tadziki said with a gravity that suggested drunkenness better than if he had staggered, "to pay a debt of honor. Honor! To Charl-charl . . . Charlie!"

"Who the hell is that?" the first sailor said. He reached for the bottle again. Yazov handed his bottle to Paetz and pulled a fresh one out of the opposite pocket.

"Charlie," Toll Warson said. "Charlie is our dear friend. *He* told us that Dolores, the headliner at the Supper Club, made it onstage with a Kephnian Ichneumon."

"We doubted him," Deke said. "Our friend, our friend . . ."

There was a full bottle in the right-side pocket of his jacket. He fumbled at great and confused length in the empty left pocket instead.

"An Ichneumon?" the second sailor repeated. "They're female, though. I mean, the ones that're a meter long, they're female. That's not really a dong."

Josie Paetz spluttered liquor out his nose. Yazov clapped

him on the back. "She's queer, then?" Josie giggled. "Dolores is queer?"

"Our good friend Charlie is on duty," Tadziki said. "In our wicked doubt, we bet him that Dolores did *not* make it with a Kephnian Ichneumon, and we were wrong. We are here to pay our debt of honor to Charlie."

He lifted yet another bottle into the air.

The on-duty sailors looked at one another. "Look, you mean Spec One Charolois?" the first one asked. "About fifty, half-bald, and looks like a high wind'd blow him away?"

"That's the very man!" Deke cried. "Our friend Charlie!"

Toll Warson watched the hangar entrance out of the corner of his eye as he waited with a glazed expression on his face. He and his brother were the only ones necessary to this operation, but the others had insisted on coming . . . and Toll was just as glad to have them along. Not that they'd be able to do any real good if it dropped in the pot.

"What would he know about the Supper Club?" the second sailor said, shaking his head. "Charolois's as queer as a three-cornered wheel!"

"Just like Dolores!" Josie Paetz chortled. "Charlie and Dolores, my dearest, dearest . . ."

He looked up. "Hey! Gimme another drink, will you?"

Tadziki pointed to the bottle in the first sailor's hands. "That's yours," he said, "if you let us go see Charlie. Right?"

The sailors exchanged glances again. The second one shrugged. "Yeah, well, keep it down, okay? If he's on board, Charolois ought to be in his cabin forward."

The five men wearing *Glorious* tallies slipped into the *Furious*. Despite the concerns of the men on watch, the strangers were amazingly quiet once they were aboard.

Ayven Del Vore wasn't with the two Pancahtans who entered Hangar 39. The men rolled between them a portable sensor pack, similar to those the *Swift* carried, but even bulkier.

Before the door slammed, Ned glimpsed two more men

waiting at the police outpost. They wore the lace and bright fabrics of Pancahte's military nobility. Though the lighting was from behind and above, Ayven's trim figure and ash-blond hair were identification enough.

The Pancahtans approaching with the sensor were tough as well as being big men. Ned waited for them at the top of the boarding ramp.

"I told Prince Ayven to bring only one companion!" he called. "I'm here alone with the prisoner."

One of the soldiers mimed *"Fuck you"* with the index and little fingers of his right hand. "Four's the minimum to drive and control a prisoner, dickhead," he said. *"If* it's you alone, then the prince and Toomey come aboard to collect the dirt. If you don't like the terms, you can stick them up your ass."

The sensor's small wheels balked at the lip of the boarding ramp. The men lifted the unit by the side handles and carried it to the hatchway. From the way they grimaced, the pack must weigh closer to a hundred kilos than fifty, though Ned doubted it was as capable as the Telarian man-packs.

Still, it was as well that Ned had decided not to try concealing additional mercs aboard the *Swift.* The sensor would easily sniff them out.

Ned backed away to let the Pancahtans set up their unit. He wore a 1-cm powergun in a belt holster. "You know if you spend a lot of time dicking around, somebody's going to come back aboard, don't you?" he said harshly.

"Come *here* when there's all Île de Rameau out there?" a soldier sneered. "Sure, buddy. I'm really worried."

"Don't matter if they do," his partner said as he closed a chamber in the side of the sensor to get a baseline reading. "They don't like the deal they're offered, well, I'd just as soon fry the lot of you in orbit."

He grinned at Ned. "You see?"

The hatch through the bulkhead astern of the main bay was open. One of the soldiers stalked down the aisle, climbed around the capsule, and entered the engine compartment.

"It's clear," he announced to his partner. "No sealed containers, not unless they're hiding in the expansion chambers."

"I guess we can risk that," the man at the sensor said. The radiation levels inside a well-used expansion chamber were in the fatal-within-minutes range.

He switched the sensor pack to area sweep, watching the readouts intently. The unit clicked to itself as it analyzed temperature, carbon dioxide levels, and vibrations down to and including pulse rates.

"Looks good," he said as he straightened to his returning partner. "Nothing but the chump and the package."

He looked at Ned. "Call the gate now, and I'll tell the prince it's clear."

The navigation consoles were rotated to face aft. Carron Del Vore, bound and gagged in the portside acceleration couch, stared wide-eyed as Ned picked up the land-line telephone from between the consoles and handed it to the soldier.

"Boy, you high-class foreigners," the other soldier said, looking around the vessel's interior. "You really know how to live—like pigs!"

Ned sat at the open console. "Do your business and get out," he said. "Then you won't have to worry about how we live."

His voice trembled slightly. That didn't bother him. He was ready to go—good jumpy. His subconscious thought it would be very soon now, and his subconscious was right.

The entrance door opened. The walls of the enclosed hangar damped the spaceport racket, particularly at the higher frequencies. Though the door itself wasn't particularly noisy, it slid open to the accompaniment of metallic cacophony from the wider world.

Ned got up and reached beneath Carron to lift him. "Give me a hand!" he ordered the nearer soldier. "The quicker this is done, the better I like it."

"You're doing fine, dickhead," the soldier said. He squeezed back to let Ned and his burden pass in the aisle.

Ned set Carron down in a sitting posture on the lower bunk facing the hatchway. Ayven and a third Pancahtan soldier strode up the ramp. The outside door slammed closed behind them, returning Hangar 39 to relative silence again. The soldier who'd operated the sensor pack removed a panel on the back of the unit.

Ned nodded toward Carron. "You've got what you came for," he said.

"So we shall," Ayven said. He stepped to his brother and pulled off the gag.

"Ayven!" Carron cried. "They kidnapped me! Thank the Lord you're here to rescue—"

Ayven reached a hand behind him. The soldier at the sensor pack pointed a projectile pistol of Celandine manufacture at Ned. He gave the prince a similar weapon, then held out a third pistol so that the partner who'd helped with the sensor could reach around Ned and take it.

The sensor's necessary shielding provided concealment from the detector frame. The police had either missed one of the compartments in the large unit, or they had simply checked to be sure the sensor functioned—as, of course, it did, whether or not a baseline chamber contained three pistols as well as air.

"Ayven—"

Ayven smacked his brother across the forehead with the butt of his pistol. Carron went glassy-eyed, bounced off the bunk support, and fell backward. There was a bloody streak at the base of his scalp.

"You two," Ayven said. "Get the capsule out. The curst fools have it all in pieces."

"The capsule wasn't part of the deal, Del Vore!" Ned said in a trembling voice.

The soldier behind Ned stepped up close behind and stuck the muzzle of his pistol in Ned's ear. Toomey, who'd arrived with Ayven, leaned forward and drew the powergun from Ned's holster.

"The deal," said Ayven, "is whatever I—"

He raised his arm to swing the pistol again, this time at Ned. He was smiling, but his face was white with rage.

"—*say* the—"

Ned ducked, kicked Ayven in the crotch, and slammed his left elbow into the stomach of the soldier behind him. The motions weren't quite simultaneous, but they overlapped enough. The Celandine pistol's *whack!whack!whack!* slapped the back of Ned's neck, but the high-velocity bullets ripped trenches in the lining of the ceiling aft.

Ned grabbed the shooter's wrist. Ayven tried to level his gun while his left hand gripped the numb ache in his lower belly. Ned yanked the soldier over his shoulder and knocked the prince down.

Toomey pulled the trigger of Ned's pistol repeatedly. Nothing happened—the weapon wasn't loaded. He thumbed the safety in the opposite direction and tried again. His body blocked the third soldier behind him.

Carron's false bonds draped him loosely. He'd risen to one arm, but his eyes were unfocused. Blood dripped down his right cheek. When he raised his hand to dab at it, he slid off the bunk into the crowded aisle. A needle stunner dropped out of his sleeve.

Ned snatched the pistol he'd clipped beneath the bottom bunk facing the hatchway. Toomey smashed the butt of the unloaded powergun into the left side of Ned's neck.

White pain blasted in concentric circles across Ned's vision. He fired three times into the man who'd struck him, dazzling cyan spikes flaring across the waves of pain. The Pancahtan slumped sideways, gouting blood.

Ned's trigger finger stabbed two bolts more into the man still standing. The soldier's face exploded, ripped apart by flash-heated fluids. The unfired Celandine pistol flew out of his hand.

Ayven and the remaining soldier had gotten untangled. Ned aimed, squeezed, and nothing happened. Jets of liquid nitrogen cooled a powergun's bore after every bolt. Ned had fired so quickly that the plastic matrix of the last round was still fluid when the gas tried to eject it from the chamber. Instead of flying free, the spent matrix formed a stinking goo that jammed the pistol.

Ned threw the powergun at Ayven. Ayven ducked sideways. The other Pancahtan rose to a kneeling position and aimed at Ned. The pistol's smoking muzzle was a meter away as Ned scrabbled for another weapon.

A burst of cyan bolts hit the soldier between the shoulder blades. Exploding steam flung the body forward.

Ned found the needle stunner with which Carron was supposed to surprise his would-be captors. Ayven turned in a half-crouch, aiming back over his shoulder.

The front of the capsule was open. Lissea Doormann stood in it, aiming through the holographic sights of a submachine gun. Heat waves danced around the weapon. The muzzle glowed white from the first long burst.

Ned put needles into Ayven's midback and right shoulder. Lissea fired simultaneously, ripping six or seven rounds all the way up the prince's breastbone. Ayven's chest blew open in a mush of ruptured internal organs.

Carron lay across his brother's feet, pinning them. His eyes were open. What remained of Ayven slumped down on Carron like a scarlet blanket.

Ned tried to pull himself to his feet. His left arm wouldn't obey him. It flopped loose, and that whole side of his torso pulsed with hammerblows of pain. He braced his right shoulder against a bunk support and used his legs to thrust himself upright.

The temperature of the vessel's interior had shot up five degrees Celsius from the released energy. Matrix residues, ozone, and propellant smoke mixed with the stench of men disemboweled and cooked in their own juices.

Lissea put her boot against the side of a dead Pancahtan and tried to push him out of the hatch. The body was freshly dead, as limp as a blood sausage. She held the submachine gun out to her side. The barrel shimmered, cooling slowly in the heated air.

"Carron?" she croaked. She knelt down. "Carron, are you all right?"

He moaned and raised a hand to his head.

Lissea looked at Ned. "Sound recall," she said. The gunshots had half-deafened Ned, giving the words a rasping, tinny sound. "Get everybody back on board soonest. We'll lift in an hour if terminal control will clear us."

"Yeah," Ned said. "Yeah."

He dropped the needle stunner and stuck a projectile pistol through his waistband. He and Carron had put the loose weapons aboard the *Swift* in lockers so that they wouldn't be to hand for the Pancahtans they intended to take hostage. He should have known Ayven wouldn't have come unless he'd figured out how to bring weapons with him.

"Oh, Lord," Ned wheezed. He found the land-line phone and flipped open the protective case.

"The capsule was shielded," Lissea said. She wasn't talking to him, just reviewing the steps that had led to the unacceptable present moment. "I heard you and Carron talking as you came aboard. I didn't trust any of . . . of—with the *Swift* and the capsule. So I waited."

Ned keyed the outside line, keyed a separate code for a commercial paging system that would access the commo helmets of the *Swift*'s personnel, and then typed the recall code: six-six-six.

"I didn't have any choice!" Lissea shouted. Her voice broke with the strain and foul air. She was gripping Carron's left hand. "I *had* to turn him over, didn't I?"

Carron groaned and tried to get up. He didn't seem to be aware of his surroundings.

"There was a choice," Ned said. "We took it, the three of us."

He had a little feeling again in his left arm. He didn't think the collarbone was broken—or his neck, but there'd be time enough for the medicomp to check him later, if there was any time at all.

"We'd better not dispose of the bodies until we're in space," Lissea thought aloud. She stood up abruptly. "It was probably a crime, wasn't it?" She laughed, cackled. "That's a joke! Shooting somebody, a crime."

Ned fumbled the handset. "Lissea," he said, "you'll have to call terminal control. With one hand, I can't manage the phone and access the necessary codes from the data bank."

Carron moaned.

Noise hammered within the enclosed dock as the entrance

opened again. Lissea turned, pointing the submachine gun. Ned stumbled to the hatchway over Pancahtan bodies.

The men of the *Swift*'s complement were pouring into the hangar. They couldn't possibly have reacted to the summons so quickly.

The whole crew was present and accounted for, though a few of them were drunk enough to lean on the shoulders of their fellows. Moiseyev and Hatton, the two junior engine-room personnel, carried Petit, their senior.

There were two Pancahtan uniforms in the midst of the loose grouping. The Warson brothers wore them. They did a shuffling dance, arm in arm.

Josie Paetz was the first man up the ramp. "Hey," he said. *"Hey,* not bad!"

Yazov gripped Ayven Del Vore's short hair and tilted the undamaged face to the light. "And I thought *we'd* done something!" he said, shifting an appreciative glance from Lissea to Ned and back.

"Lissea, we've got to get out of here fast," Tadziki said. Westerbeke, looking squeamish, hesitated at the top of the ramp. The adjutant tugged him forward and gave him a push toward the navigation consoles.

Lissea had returned to the phone when she saw the new arrivals were her men rather than Pancahtan reinforcements. She put it down again. "Yes," she said. "They're processing the clearance now. It'll take—"

She shook her head as if to clear it of cobwebs. "I don't know. Half an hour? An hour?"

Herne Lordling tried to put his arms around her. "No!" she screamed. *"No!"* She twisted away hard, her boots slipping in blood.

Ned looked at the Celandine pistol he'd drawn without being conscious of the movement. Tadziki stepped close to him with a concerned expression.

Ned tossed the gun on a bunk. He began to tremble. In a loud voice he said, "We need to get away fast, before the Pancahtans sort out a new leader. They won't dare go home without catching us, but just for the moment they'll be disorganized.''

"Everybody get in your couches," Toll Warson boomed. "Don't worry about the mess, we've all smelled worse, haven't we?"

" 'Specially Harlow has," Coyne shouted. "Did you see what he was doing to that pig in the Double Star?"

Harlow hurled his helmet at Coyne, but it was a good-natured gesture.

"And you're right about the Pancahtans being disorganized," Toll continued with a broad, beaming smile. "When the *Furious* engages the liftoff sequence in her navigational computer, there's going to be a little software glitch."

He waved his hand to the adjutant, as if presenting him to an audience.

"Her fusion bottle," Tadziki said with a smile as cruel as a hyena's, "is going to vent. I don't think *any* of the three ships in Hangar 17 are going to be functional for a very long time."

Dell

———✦———

THE SHIP LANDED on Dell as the last sunlight touched the tops of the tall evergreens surrounding Doorman Trading Company Post No. 103. The plasma exhaust threw iridescent highlights across the clearing. Livestock in the corral bellowed.

The factor waited a few moments for the ground to cool, then sauntered out to meet the strangers. The vessel wasn't one of the familiar tramps that shuttled back and forth in the Telaria-Dell trade.

This one had radioed that it was the *Homer,* operating under a Celandine registry, a first for Post No. 103 in the thirty-seven years Jirtle had been factor here. He looked forward to seeing some new faces.

The vessel's boarding ramp lowered smoothly. The *Homer* was quite small, which wasn't unusual; in fact, a large vessel would have been hard put to land in the clearing in front of the post. There wasn't a real spaceport at Post No. 103—or virtually anywhere else on Dell.

Lone entrepreneurs ranged the forests of Dell, culling the

products that were worth transporting between stars and bringing them to the nearest Doormann Trading outpost. It was small-scale commerce, but it appealed to those who found cities and governmental restrictions too trammeling.

It appealed to Jirtle and his wife.

Four men stood at the head of the boarding ramp. They wore body armor and carried stocked powerguns. They looked as stark and terrible as demons.

Jirtle gasped and turned to run. There was no reason for pirates to come *here,* there was nothing worth the time of those engaged in criminal endeavors on an interstellar scale. But they were here. . . .

"Jirtle!" a woman's voice called. "Jirtle, it's me!"

The leaf mat slipped beneath the factor's slippers and threw him down. He fell heavily. He was an old man anyway, gasping with terror and exertion after only a few steps. He couldn't have outrun the pirates, and nobody could outrun a bolt from a powergun. . . .

"Jirtle, it's *me!* Lissea!"

The factor looked over his shoulder. "Lissea?" he said. *"You're* back? Oh, thank the Lord! They'd said you were dead!"

Pots clanged from the summer kitchen behind the post, where Mistress Jirtle was cooking dinner for twenty with the somewhat bemused help of her husband.

Lissea glanced in the direction of the noise. "They were more parents to me than Grey and Duenna, you know," she said affectionately. "I only saw my mother and father one month a year when they were allowed to come to Dell on vacation. The rest of the time, Karel kept my parents on the Doormann estate."

The *Swift*'s personnel were gathered in the factory's public room. There was plenty of space on the near side of the counter. In treacle-wax season, as many as a hundred forest scouts might crowd into the post demanding that the Jirtles weigh their gleanings *"now, before these other bastards!"*

"Yes, fine, it's nice you've had this reunion," Herne Lordling said curtly. "But we landed here for information before we made the last leg to Telaria, and *I* don't like the information we got."

Lissea sat on the factor's counter with her legs dangling down. Carron stood beside her. The rest of the personnel spread in an arc around the walls, bales, and barrels in the public room.

"If the Doormanns believe the story of Lissea's death," Ned said, "then we've got the advantage of surprise. Of course, Karel may have spread the story himself."

Tadziki shook his head and raised his hand to quiet the half dozen men who began talking at once. "I think we can take that as real," he said when he'd gotten silence. "It's too circumstantial to have been entirely invented—all of us dying on Alliance when the Dreadnought landed and the plague broke out there."

He looked at Lissea and added grimly, "Besides, that was the point at which Grey and Duenya Doormann were taken into close custody."

"And we can assume they'll take me in charge also, just as soon as I reappear," Lissea agreed calmly.

"They may *try!*" said Herne Lordling.

"Yes," said Lissea. "Well, I don't think fighting all Telaria is the way to proceed."

"We could do that, you know, ma'am," Toll Warson said quietly.

Everyone looked at him. Half the men present started to speak, mostly protests. Toll, sitting on a bale of lustrous gray furs, waited with a faint smile.

Ned frowned. The Warsons were jokers, but they weren't stupid and they didn't bluster in the least. Toll (and Deke even more so) had the trick of stating something so calmly that nobody would believe him—

And then ramming the statement home to the hilt.

"Wait!" Lissea ordered with her hand raised. "Toll, go on."

"Everybody here's worked in the business," Toll said.

"We know folks. Some of us have had rank, some haven't . . ."

He grinned at Herne Lordling.

"But we've all got reputations that'll get us listened to by the folks who've worked with us before."

Toll glanced around the room, then back to Lissea. "We can raise you an army on tick, ma'am," he said, his voice as thin and harsh as the song of a blade on a whetstone. "We can bring you twenty brigades on your promise to pay when the fighting's over. *I* can, Herne can. If Slade can't bring in the Slammers, then his uncle curst well can!"

He slid off the bale to stand up. The crash of his boots on the puncheon floor drove a period to his words.

"Blood and martyrs, he's right!" Lordling said. "Doormann Trading's enough of a prize to cover the cost, and it *will* cost, but—"

"No," said Lissea, her voice lost in the general babble.

"—it's worth it in the mid- and long-term," Lordling continued enthusiastically.

"Hell, short-term is that we all get chopped when we land on Telaria," Deke Warson said, "Fuck *that* for a lark if you ask me!"

"No," repeated Lissea. "No!"

As the room quieted, she went on, "I didn't come back to wreck Telaria forever. I'll—I'll deal with those who lied to me, who mistreated my parents. But all-out war on Telaria will leave . . ."

She grimaced and didn't finish the sentence. *Burr-Detlingen. Kazan. A hundred other worlds where men had settled.*

"Look, Lissea," Herne Lordling said in the tone of an adult addressing a child, "all of a broken dish is better than no plate at all. And Warson had a point about what's going to happen to us if we land openly on Telaria—"

"I don't think we need be concerned about our safety," Tadziki interjected. "The professionals, that is. As Toll pointed out, we are individually, ah, men of some reputation and authority. I don't believe Karel Doormann will go out of his way to antagonize the sort of persons—''

He smiled coldly.

''—who might be offended by our needless murders.''

''What do we do then, ma'am?'' Deke Warson demanded. As he'd listened to the discussion thus far, he stroked the barrel of his slung powergun. His fingertips had a rainbow sheen from iridium rubbed off onto his skin. ''Do you want Karel dead? I can do that, any of us can do that. But that alone won't give you what you want.''

He thumbed toward his brother. ''Toll's right. You've got to smash the whole system so there's nothing left to argue with you. You need an army behind you if you're going to force your kin to your way of thinking . . . and even then, it'd be better if they were dead. All of them.''

He spoke with the persuasive rationality of a specialist advising a professional client. That's what he was. That's what they all were.

''No,'' Carron said, speaking for the first time since they entered the trading post. ''There is a way.''

''All right,'' Toll Warson said. ''I'll bite, kid.''

Carron stepped forward, so that he stood between Lissea and the men present. She frowned slightly from her perch above him.

''I have been studying Lendell Doormann's device,'' Carron said, ''as you know. I think at this point I understand the principles on which it operates.''

Lordling guffawed.

''I can land us on Telaria, kid,'' Westerbeke said huffily. ''With or without tower guidance. *That's* no problem.''

Carron shook his head fiercely. ''No,'' he said. ''No, the device is necessary, but not as transport, of course.''

He glared imperiously at the mercenaries, in control, and well aware of it. ''We will land openly,'' he said, ''on Telaria . . .''

Telaria

—⁂—

TWO MORE TRUCKLOADS of Doormann Trading security personnel pulled up before the *Swift*'s landing site. About half the guards wore body armor over their blue uniforms and carried submachine guns in addition to their sidearms. They looked wide-eyed, and the faces of their officers were set and white.

The scores of city police and Doorman personnel already present were swamped by the civilian crowd including newspeople which had gathered within minutes of the *Swift*'s arrival. Westerbeke had come in under automated control, letting the ship's AI handshake with that of the terminal. No humans were involved in the process until the slim, scarred vessel dropped into view and spectators realized that *"Movement Delta five-five-niner, Telarian registry,"* was the returning Pancahte Expedition.

Ned, Tadziki, and Carron Del Vore stood at the base of the boarding ramp. They wore their "best" static-cleaned clothes; in Ned's case, the uniform that had the fewest tears. Nothing available from clothing stocks on Dell would have been more suitable for present purposes.

Ned's dress clothes were in storage in Landfall City, but he wasn't about to send for them now. His feet were thirty centimeters apart and his arms crossed behind his back as he waited for someone with rank to arrive.

An official car pulled through the crowd, the driver hooting his two-note horn. A man Ned remembered was named Kardon, an assistant port director, got out. He was accompanied by a woman who was probably his superior. A police lieutenant tried to get instructions from the pair as they strode toward Ned. The woman waved him away without bothering to look.

"Everyone move back-k-k," crackled a bullhorn. *"This is a closed area. Everyone moo-*urk!*"*

Toll Warson led the six-man team opening the *Swift*'s external storage bays and undoing the lashings within. More armed mercenaries stood or squatted in the hatchway, grinning out at the Telarians.

There were three meters of cracked concrete between Ned and the edge of the crowd. Media personnel shouted questions across it, but no one stepped closer. Harlow, at the spade grips of the tribarrel mounted on the upper plating, grinned through his sights as he traversed the weapon slowly across that invisible line on the ground.

"I'm Director Longley," the woman said. "This vessel is quarantined. Take me to Captain Doormann at once."

The director was in her thirties, younger than her male assistant. She radiated an inner intensity. Her voice and manner didn't so much overpower the confusion as much as they rode over it.

"I'm in charge now," Ned said harshly. Out of the corner of his eye he noticed a squad of blue uniforms deploying on the terminal's observation deck. "Captain Doormann's dead, a lot of people are dead. But we brought back the capsule—"

Ned was rigidly focused on the step-by-step accomplishment of his mission. It was a series of hurdles, and it couldn't matter that some of the obstacles might be blood and fire. Part of him wondered, though, what his expression must be to cause Kardon to flinch that way.

"—and we brought Lendell Doormann besides."

"*Got* the fucker!" Deke Warson cried. The crew gave a collective grunt and tipped the large sealed casket out. The plastic box was a clumsy piece of work, but it was as sturdy as befitted the skill of men whose training was in starship repairs rather than cabinetry.

The clear top the crew had added on Dell didn't improve the casket's appearance. Lendell Doormann grinned out at the crowd. He looked like the personification of Death by Plague.

Ned gestured. "As you see. Now, one of you take me at once to the board of Doormann Trading. I need to speak to the board immediately."

There was movement inside the *Swift* as another team carefully walked the capsule up the aisle to the hatchway. Lendell Doormann's device had been returned to its original status, with all the internal and external panels in place. The front of the capsule was open, displaying the empty interior.

"Keep your shirt on, Master . . . Slade," Longley said, reading the faded name tape on Ned's breast. "You've landed without proper authorization, and—"

"Excuse me, Director," Tadziki said, "but we landed normally—as the navigation records will prove."

"You're Tadziki, aren't you?" Longley said, turning her attention to the adjutant. "I've dealt with you before. Well, Master Tadziki, I can tell you right now I don't appreciate you sneaking in on the regular landing pattern this way. *Look* at this chaos!"

She waved her hand at the crowd. "Somebody's likely to be killed in a mess like this!"

As if that triggered a memory, Longley pointed up at Harlow. "And put that cursed cannon away or I'll have you arrested right now! I'll have you all arrested!"

Harlow grinned.

Kardon looked over his shoulder toward the mixture of police, security guards, and civilians. He thrust his way past Carron and started to climb the ladder extended from the *Swift*'s side to access the gun position.

Deke Warson muttered something. Raff slung his rocket

gun and grabbed the assistant director by the wrists, plucking him easily from the ladder.

"Kardon, what are you playing at?!" Longley demanded.

The Racontid swung Kardon around, holding him well off the ground. Kardon bleated with rage. Several of the police and guards had drawn their weapons, but their officers were angrily ordering, *"Don't shoot! Don't anybody shoot!"*

"That's enough!" said Tadziki.

Deke Warson slit Kardon's waistband with a knife sharp enough for shaving, then pulled the man's trousers down over his ankles.

"That," Deke said, "is enough."

He nodded to Raff. The Racontid let his victim down. Kardon bent over to grab his pants and tripped. There was laughter, but it was all from mercenaries and civilians.

"Director," Ned said, "you're not a fool, so stop acting like one. If you want real problems, for yourself and for Doormann Trading, then indeed go ahead and arrest these men who have risked their *lives* for Doormann Trading. We are *not* a rabble, mistress! I'm nephew to Slade of Tethys, and my companions are men of rank and power in their individual right!"

"We are here to report, mistress," Tadziki said forcefully. "To report, and to be paid under contract. We've suffered enough for Doorman Trading. We don't choose to be chivied by bureaucrats who can't control traffic in their own port!"

A pair of three-wheelers bulled through the crowd, carving a path for the limousine behind them. A video cameraman didn't move out of the way. His bellow of anger turned to fear as an escort vehicle knocked him down from behind.

The trike drove over the man's ankle and crushed part of the tracery of lenses which provided three-dimensionality for the holographic images. The cameraman's producer managed to drag him out of the way of the limousine that was following.

Lucas Doormann opened the door of the limousine and got out. Time constraints and the crush of the crowd prevented the driver from waiting on his master in normal fashion.

"Where's Lissea?" Lucas demanded. His gaze traveled

over the *Swift* and those around it.

"Via!" he added with a moue of distaste. "Are all these guns necessary? Put them away, all of you."

He gestured imperiously to a captain wearing a Doormann Trading uniform. "You! There's no need for guns! Put your weapons up at once."

"Captain Doormann is dead, Master Doormann," Ned said as Lucas' eyes returned to him.

"Dead?" Lucas repeated.

Kardon, holding his trousers up with one hand, looked as though he was about to interrupt. Longley shushed him with a curt chop of her hand.

"On Pancahte," Ned said grimly. "We retrieved the capsule, though, and I *must* speak to your board immediately."

"The capsule is an amazing advance over Transit," Carron Del Vore said. "Your ancestor was right, *but,* for two-way traffic the device must—"

"Who is this?" Lucas demanded. Before anyone could answer, he spun on his heel. "Clear the crowd back, can't you?" he shouted toward the red-faced officer who'd been bawling orders to the security personnel. "Blood and martyrs, what *is* this? A circus?"

Longley made a quick decision and stepped away from the discussion. She took a communications wand from her shoulder wallet and began speaking crisp orders. There were by now several hundred blue- and green-uniformed security personnel present. What was lacking was central direction, and Longley could supply that.

"Prince Carron," Tadziki said, "is the heir and emissary of Treasurer Lon Del Vore of Pancahte. He is in addition a respected scientist, who believes it will now be possible to set up instantaneous communications between Telaria and Pancahte."

Lucas' eyes narrowed in surprise. "The lost colony really exists?" he said. He shook his head. "I suppose it must; I . . ."

"I must speak to the board of Doormann Trading," Ned repeated again. "And the capsule should be returned to its original location in Lendell's laboratory.''

Ned knew that Lucas was swamped by the situation. The Telarian noble's mind was on a knife-edge, tilting one way and the next without real composure. If nudged successfully, Lucas had the rank and ability to do all the things necessary for the operation to succeed.

"Lendell?" Lucas said. He looked, perhaps for the first time, at the crude casket. "That's Lendell. Good Lord, that *is* Lendell! What happened to him?''

"He never really left Telaria," Carrion said, though "explained" would give too much effect to his words. "Though he couldn't be seen here and he *appeared* to be present on Pancahte. That's why the device must be returned to its original location, as precisely as possible, to permit two-way communication.''

"Good *Lord,*" Lucas repeated. "And Lissea . . . I didn't think anything would really, would—''

He made a fist and broke off. He stared at his clenched fingers for a moment, then relaxed them and looked up at Ned again.

More police and guards were arriving, but the haste and panic of the early moments were over. The security personnel worked in unison, guided through their in-ear speakers by Longley and her assistant.

The crowd continued to grow as word of the *Swift*'s arrival spread beyond the spaceport boundaries, but nothing was happening to raise the emotional temperature. Harlow tilted the muzzles of the tribarrel skyward, though all the mercs kept watch from beneath easy smiles and gibes to one another.

"I very much regret all of this," Lucas said. "The— Lissea.''

He looked at Ned. "Yes," he continued. "An emergency board meeting was called as soon as my father heard of the *Swift*'s arrival. I will take you to the meeting, Master Slade. If you're worried about your claims for payment, don't be. I will personally guarantee them.''

"Thank you, sir," Ned said, "but it's necessary I report in person to . . . those who sent us to Pancahte.''

"And the device?" Carron put in. "This is an advance beyond conception!"

Lucas glanced at the Pancahtan, then back to Ned. "Should he be present at the board meeting?" he asked.

"No," Ned said. "But Prince Carron *should* supervise the placement of the capsule back in the laboratory. That isn't the first thing on your mind or on mine, sir, but I have no doubt that he's correct in his valuation of the device."

"All right, then," Lucas muttered. He turned his head. "Director Longley? Director!"

Longley stepped quickly back to Lucas. "Yes sir?" she said. Kardon, still holding his trousers up, continued to oversee the security details.

"How quickly can you get two separate vans here?" Lucas demanded. "I want this object—"

He gestured to the capsule.

"—taken to the laboratory in the basement of the Main Spire in the Doormann estate. And I want my . . . my great-granduncle's body taken to the family chapel. That will require cargo handlers as well."

Lucas looked at the mercenaries standing in falsely relaxed postures. "None of these gentlemen," he added, "will be involved in the work."

Longley spoke into her communications wand, then met the young noble's eyes again. "The vehicles and crews will be here within ninety seconds, sir," she said, "or I'll remove a department head. They'll need clearances to enter your family's estate, of course."

Lucas nodded brusquely. "Yes, of course; I'll clear them through. Just get it done and done quickly. It's not seemly to have—"

He looked at the casket and grimaced. "Was it really necessary to use a clear top?" he muttered, half under his breath.

"I'll accompany the device," Carron said to the port director. Longley glanced at Lucas.

"Yes, yes!" Lucas said with an irritated wave of his hand. Doormann looked at Ned again, and his eyes hardened.

"You won't be allowed in the meeting room armed, Master Slade," he said.

"Of course," Ned with a sniff of surprise. He unlatched his pistol belt and handed the rig, powergun and all, to Tadziki. "On Tethys, it would be an insult to appear armed in public."

The first of two spaceport service vehicles pulled through the gap the police had made in the spectators. Lucas turned and strode toward his limousine.

"Come along, then," he muttered. "They'll be expecting *my* report. Father didn't want me to come."

As he got into the big car, Lucas added, "I just can't believe someone so alive as Lissea . . ."

"Hey, Tadziki," Deke Warson called from the hatchway. "Master Customs-Agent here says he's maybe going to quit hassling us so we can get our asses out of here."

Tadziki spun his navigation console to face aft. He gestured toward Warson to indicate that he'd heard but continued talking earnestly to someone on the other end of the *Swift*'s external communications link.

The vessel's bay looked more of a wreck than it had at any time since initial liftoff from Buin. Men had sorted their gear, but most of it remained on top of their bunks, and spilling into the aisle. In truth, most personal items had been reduced to trash during the voyage, but the bald willingness to walk away from objects that had been companions for so long was alien to civilian sensibilities.

The men of the *Swift* weren't civilians.

Tadziki finished his conversation and stood up. "There," he said as he picked his way down the aisle to the hatch. "I've got lodging arranged for all who want it at the Clarion House, admission on ID or an expedition patch. And I've got a mobile crane rented. Coordinates to both are downloaded. You say the rigmarole here's taken care of?"

The gray-suited customs supervisor with Warson bridled. "Master Tadziki," he said, "I realize you men have gone through a great deal, but Telaria is civilized and civilization requires rules. I assure you my people and I have made quite extraordinary efforts to clear you immediately.''

He looked around with unintended distaste.

''Are we 'go,' then, Tadziki?'' Deke Warson asked in a voice that surprised the customs official for its gentleness.

''That's right,'' the adjutant said.

He stepped to the hatchway and looked out. The security presence had shrunk to about thirty green-uniformed police, but the media were gone and the tension had left the remaining crowd.

The *Swift*'s personnel were drawn up in two lines at the base of the ramp. Three vans rented from a spaceport delivery service waited nearby. The crates in the back of two of the vans were full of weapons and ammunition. Customs officers nearby eyed the vehicles and the mercenaries with disquiet.

''All right, boys,'' Tadziki called. ''Have fun, and if there's a problem you'll find me here.''

He gave the troops a palm-out salute. The men returned it in a dozen different styles. None of them were very good at the gesture. In the field, the only purpose of a salute was to target a hated officer for an enemy sniper . . . and these men were more likely to use self-help for even that purpose.

''Dismissed!'' called Herne Lordling. The ranks broke up. Men scrambled to the vans. Dewey and Bonilla from navigation, and Petit and Moiseyev from the engine room, boarded the empty vehicle. The rest split among the vans carrying crated weapons.

Deke turned and shook the adjutant's hand. ''Hey, good luck,'' he said. ''Sure you wouldn't like a little company?''

Tadziki smiled wanly. ''We've gotten this far, haven't we?'' he said. ''What can happen now?''

Motors revved. Deke ran down the ramp and jumped in through the open back of a van as his brother drove it away.

''I, ah . . .'' the customs supervisor said. ''Where are they going with all those weapons? I realize that it's technically beyond my competence, but . . .''

Tadziki watched the vehicles until they disappeared around a maintenance building. The mobile crane he'd rented was in a lot on the north edge of the spaceport, convenient to their destination.

"They're going to take them back to the warehouse," Tadziki said at last. "They're Doormann Trading Company property, you realize?"

"Yes, of course," the supervisor said. "Most of them. I'm familiar with the manifest, of course. Some of the serial numbers weren't—but that's not a serious matter. As I said, we had no intention of delaying you gentlemen needlessly. And the individuals' data were in order from your initial entry to Telaria."

He paused. The inspectors under his direction waited on the concrete, murmuring among themselves and glancing at the battered black hull of the *Swift*.

Tadziki stared northward, toward Landfall City and the Doormann family estate beyond it. He blinked and looked at the supervisor again. "Eh?" Tadziki said. "Sorry, did you say something?"

"I notice," the supervisor said, "that your men are still wearing their uniforms?"

"Well, what else do you expect them to wear?" the adjutant snapped. "This wasn't exactly a pleasure cruise, you know, with twelve trunks for every passenger."

He waved toward the rumpled disaster area which the vessel's interior had become.

"Anyway," he continued in a milder voice, "they aren't uniform. Not here. They're battledress from as many different units as there were men aboard. And if you mean the commo helmets—"

Tadziki gave the supervisor a wry grin.

"—we're used to using them, you know. I've downloaded routes and locations into the helmet files."

The supervisor nodded. It was all perfectly reasonable, but he felt uncomfortable. This wasn't a standard task. The pilot who was in charge while Tadziki made calls said that one of the Doormann family had cleared through a number of passengers without even registering them. Well, what could you do when your superiors wouldn't let you do your job?

He shook himself back to the present. "I'm sorry, Master Tadziki," he said. "We both have business to attend, I'm sure. I shouldn't be wasting your time."

"All I have to do," Tadziki said, staring out of the hatch, "is to wait. But I'm not in a mood for company right now, that's a fact."

The supervisor stepped down the ramp. "Come on, all of you," he ordered as his subordinates stiffened at his notice. "The *Puritan* landed half an hour ago with seven hundred passengers on board!"

The *Swift*'s adjutant had gone back inside. The supervisor didn't know how the man stood it. The vessel made *him* extremely nervous.

"Look, I don't know if I ought to be doing this," Platt whined at the door to the basement laboratory.

"Will somebody *please* make a fucking decision?" grated the foreman of the cargo handlers carrying the capsule. The load wasn't exceptionally heavy for the four-man team, but the seedy-looking attendant was obviously capable of dithering for hours.

Carron Del Vore snapped his fingers. "What do you mean you don't *know*, dog?" he demanded. "You've got orders from the chamberlain, haven't you?"

"*All* I got," the attendant said, "is somebody called and said she was the chamberlain. Look, I think you better bring me something in hard copy. I don't know you from Adam and these guys, they don't belong in the spire at *all*."

Platt straightened. He fumblingly tried to return the electronic key to the belt case from which he'd taken it a moment before.

Carron looked at the cargo handlers. "Set that down," he ordered. "On its base, and *carefully*. Then beat this creature unconscious and open the door."

"No!" Platt bleated.

"Suits me," said the foreman. The crew tilted the empty capsule to set it down as Carron ordered.

Though Platt spilled most of the contents of his case onto the floor, he managed to hold on to the key. He pressed it against the lockplate. The cargo handlers started for him an instant before the heavy door began to open.

"No!" Platt said, squeezing himself against the doorjamb and raising thin arms against the threatened blows.

"That's enough," Carron said to the foreman. "Carry the device to the platform at the other end of the room. I'll show you exactly where it goes."

The men sighed and lifted the capsule again. One of them spat on the attendant as they passed him.

"We're going to be on overtime before we get back," the foreman muttered. "And *won't* Kardon tear a strip off me? As if I could do anything about the estate staff getting its finger out of its bum *every* curst door we had to get through."

"Hey, did you see Kardon having to hold his pants up?" another handler said. "Whoo-*ee,* I'd have liked to see when that happened!"

The carefully positioned lights flooded the lab and every-one in it with their radiance. Carron watched nervously as the crew wound its way between benches and free-standing equipment. For all their nonchalance, the men didn't bang the capsule into anything. Platt peered from the doorway, scowl-ing and rubbing his shoulder as if he'd been punched.

"What is this place, anyway?" a man asked querulously.

"Don't move the mirrors out of alignment!" Carron warned. The crew was edging its way to the dais. It wasn't clear that it would be possible to put the capsule back *without* moving one of the pentagonal black mirrors that ringed the location.

"Don't have kittens!" the foreman snapped. He paused, judging the relative shapes and sizes. "All right, Hoch, let go now."

The man at the base of the capsule with the foreman obedi-ently stepped away. The foreman eased forward, ducking his shoulder. By keeping the device low, he managed to dip it under the narrowest point and then raise it to clear the dais.

"There!" he announced with justifiable pride. He lowered

the ring base, and his men lifted together to set the capsule upright.

"We're not done yet," Carron said sharply.

He switched on a measuring device from the kit he'd brought with him from Pancahte. It projected a hologram of the capsule taken at the moment Lendell Doormann vanished from Telaria for the next seventy years and compared the recording with present reality.

"There, you see?" Carron said. "The orange points are out of synchrony. Turn it clockwise ten degrees and move it a centimeter closer to the wall."

Two of the cargo handlers moved to obey. The foreman waved them back. He viewed the image, then spread his arms around the capsule and himself began the minute adjustments.

Carron watched his measurement device tensely. The areas of orange slipped into the cooler end of the spectrum. "That's far enough!" he cried as the foreman's boot scraped the capsule the necessary distance toward the wall. "But keep turning, another degree."

The foreman's face was set. His mouth was open, and he watched the holographic display out of the corner of his eyes. The display wavered into the violet range then back toward indigo. He released the last pressure and stepped away, breathing hard. The main image was violet again.

"There!" he said.

The door of the capsule showed red to orange on the display. It had been closed when Lendell Doormann vanished. The foreman put his hand on the curved panel to swing it shut.

"No!" Carron cried, grabbing the man's arm. "No, don't do that! This is fine, this is perfect the way it is."

The foreman shrugged. "Whatever," he said. He stepped out between two mirrors. "You know," he added, "this is a spooky place."

"It is?" said Carron in puzzlement. "I wouldn't have said so."

The cargo handlers were sauntering back toward the door. "No, I don't guess you would," one of them muttered loud enough to be heard.

Carron walked out of the laboratory behind the crew. The lights cut off automatically. Platt shut the door, avoiding the eyes of the visitors.

Carron paused and looked at the attendant. "I have the phone number of your station," he said. "You or someone else will be present at all times, is that not so?"

"Yeah, it's fucking so," Platt muttered. "Unless somebody gets me up to dick around in the lab again, at least."

"I may be calling soon," Carron said. "You will regret it if you do not carry out to the letter any instructions I may give you."

But the despicable little man would regret it even more if he *did* do as he was told. . . .

The boardroom of Doormann Trading Company was on the top level of the crystal spire in the center of the family estate. It was nearly an hour before the board readmitted Lucas to its presence. Ned had waited a further hour alone. He paced slowly around the broad walkway which served as an observation deck.

Two guards with submachine guns stood at the ornate bronze doors giving access to the boardroom. There were two more guards at the single elevator which opened onto the observation deck on the opposite side of the circuit. As a further security precaution, before entering the armored boardroom one had to walk all the way around it.

The two guards who'd come up with Lucas Doormann and Ned kept pace behind Ned now. They were bored, but not too bored to remain watchful.

The exterior of the spire was optically pure and had the same refractive index as Telaria's atmosphere. Though the curved, fluted walls were at no point flat, they did not distort the view.

The view was breathtaking. The Doormann estate spread over hectares of rolling hills in every direction. Ned knew from his view out of the limousine that the surface in the frequent glades and bowers was as carefully manicured as that of the surrounding grassy areas.

Buildings in a mix of styles, mostly those of Terra's classical and medieval eras, nestled in swales or sat on hillsides. None of the structures had more than two above-ground stories, though from the traffic in and out, some had extensive basements. The aggregate floorspace of the outbuildings probably totalled as much as that of the central spire, but the careful planners had succeeded in preserving the illusion of agrestic emptiness.

Machines and humans in drab uniforms worked like a stirred-up anthill to keep the grounds pristine. Ned noticed that when people in civilian clothes walked near or paused to view the formal gardens, maintenance personnel moved out of the area so as not to disturb them. Most of those who lived within the estate were the Doormanns' servants and office staff, but even they had the status of minor nobility on Telaria.

One of the buildings on the grounds was the Doormann family chapel. Ned would learn where it was when he needed to; which would be very soon, unless his interview with Karel Doormann proceeded in an unexpectedly reasonable fashion.

The door to the boardroom opened with only the sigh of air and the faint trembling from the electromagnets which supported and moved the massive panel. Ned turned. Lucas Doormann walked out. "Master Slade," he said, "the board is prepared to see you now."

"Yes," said Ned as he stepped forward. The entranceway was constructed on the model of an airlock. An iridium-sheathed panel closed the inner end whenever the main door was open. The designers had taken no chances with a guard going berserk and spraying the boardroom with his submachine gun.

The outer panel slid shut behind Ned and Lucas. Ned felt as if he were riding a monocycle at high speed across glare ice. At any moment he could lose his balance and go flying, and he had no control at all. . . .

The inner door snicked upward with the speed of a microtome blade. It was time.

Eight men and three women faced Ned from around the

oval central table. There was an empty place for Lucas, who remained at Ned's side.

Karel Doormann was neither the oldest nor the most expensively dressed of the board members, but his dominance would have been obvious even had he not been seated at the head of the table. He watched Ned with the smile of a cat preparing to spring.

"Mesdames and sirs," Ned said, taking off his commo helmet. His voice was clear and cool. He spoke as the peer of any of these folk. "I am here to tell you of a necessary deception. Lissea Doormann is alive on Dell, awaiting the outcome of this meeting."

Karel Doormann's smile broadened. His son made a startled sound. A heavyset man leaned close to the woman beside him to whisper, but both of them kept their eyes on Ned.

"I say 'necessary,'" Ned continued, "because Lissea and yourselves have the same basic desire: to avoid trouble. Had she returned with the *Swift,* an underling might have taken actions that were not in the best interests of Doormann Trading, and which might have prejudiced chances of a beneficial outcome."

"Go on, Master Slade," Karel Doormann said. There was a catch in his voice between words, like the sound of a whisk on stone. "Explain what you consider a beneficial outcome."

"Lissea," Ned said, "Mistress Doormann. Has completed a task that we all know was thought to be impossible. The capsule which she has returned to Telaria has the potential of revolutionizing star travel—and with it the profits of Doormann Trading."

The board members were silent, facing Ned like a pack of dogs about to move in. The table was black and shiny and slightly distorted on top. It had been made from a single slab of volcanic glass—useless as a working surface, but richly evocative of the power of the men and women who sat around it.

"I understand business, mesdames and sirs," Ned said. "I understand politics. I don't ask you to grant Lissea the place she demands out of justice or fairness or any of those other things which are quite properly excluded by the walls of this room."

Lucas Doormann backed a step away. His father, still smiling, nodded to Ned. "Go on," he said.

"What I put to you is this," Ned continued. "Lissea Doormann has displayed the resourcefulness that will make her an invaluable member of this board, and at some future point a worthy leader of it."

He waited, looking down the table at the board members.

" 'At some future point,' " Karel Doormann repeated. "I believe our relative's demand was for immediate chairmanship."

He raised an eyebrow.

Ned nodded. "I said I understood politics," he said. "I can't sell what I wouldn't buy, Master Doormann. In your place, I certainly wouldn't buy that."

Karel nodded approvingly. "You know, young man," he said, "there could be a place for you in this organization if you cared to accept one. However."

To this point, the president's tone had been playful, cruelly humorous. Now it became as hard and dry as a windblown steppe.

"First," he said, "this board has no confidence in the willingness of your principal to accept the terms you're offering on her behalf. Your Lissea made it clear from the beginning that she wants *everything*. Her ability to control a band of murderous cutthroats does nothing to dispel our concerns about her future behavior."

Some of the board members glanced at Karel in concern. The president was obviously no more interested in their opinions than he was in the opinions of the obsidian table.

"Second and, I'm afraid, finally, Master Slade," Karel continued, "we expected some such trick as this. As soon as I learned the *Swift* had arrived via Dell, I sent—this board sent—a shipload of company security personnel to that planet. They will . . ."

He shrugged, then resumed, "I hate to say this, sir, but your public assertion that Lissea was dead was a bit of good fortune. It will help greatly to avoid future difficulties."

"Father!" Lucas Doormann cried. He started around the table. "Father, you can't *think* of this, of *murder!*"

Karel pointed a warning finger. "Lucas," he said, "stop where you are. Otherwise I'll face the embarrassment of seeing the automatic restraint system act on my offspring."

Father and son glared at one another. Lucas turned and covered his face in his hands.

Karel looked at Ned and raised an eyebrow in prompting.

"Yes," said Ned. "Master Doormann, I very much regret this."

He reverted to at-ease posture with his hands behind him and went on. "Now, sir, what does the board intend for the rest of the crew and myself?"

"Your due," Karel said calmly. "You've accomplished a difficult task for Doormann Trading. You'll be paid according to your contracts, and there'll be an added bonus for success."

Karel pursed his lips as he chose his next words. "I can't imagine that many of your fellows would care to remain on Telaria, nor will they be permitted to do so. Their passage will be paid to their planets of residence and, if they claim no residence, to their planets of origin. Deported, if you will, but certainly not wronged."

He paused. "I will make an exception for you, Master Slade, if you choose."

"No," Ned replied curtly. Braced as he was, his eyes were focused on the wall above the president's head. "I do not so choose."

"I thought as much," Karel said, "though you would have been welcome."

The dry chill returned to his voice. "Let me make the matter very clear to you, Master Slade. This is a Telarian problem. We have no desire to offend you or the other members of your company, but you will *not* interfere in our affairs."

He smiled again. "I know you're intelligent enough to realize that without Lissea's presence as a rallying point, there is no possibility of gathering a coalition to redress what—"

He paused.

"—for the sake of argument we may describe as the 'wrong' done her. Some of your fellows may not be as sophisticated. I trust that you'll be able to convince them not to . . . do themselves harm."

Ned nodded. "I'll do what I can," he said tonelessly. He raised his commo helmet and settled it back on his head. "I believe we've said everything that needs to be said," he went on. "With your leave, I'll return to the *Swift* and gather my personal belongings."

"As you choose," said Karel, gesturing toward the doorway behind Ned.

"Lucas," Ned said, "I would appreciate a few words with you outside."

"Did you think I'd stay here?" Lucas snarled. He strode into the anteroom ahead of the mercenary. The stroke of the inner panel closing cut off sight of his father's frown.

"I can't believe this!" Lucas said as the main door opened.

"I can," Ned said. *For my sins, I can.*

The commo helmet was set to the channel linking it with the *Swift*, and locked against all other parties. As Ned stepped out of the shielded boardroom, he faced south and broke squelch twice.

The alarm clanged through the *Swift*'s internal PA system.

Carron Del Vore was straightening the bunks on one side of the aisle. Unlike playing solitaire or staring at the ceiling, it gave him the illusion of accomplishment. He'd worked his way to the third pair, pulling the sheets tight and arranging the jumble of gear and tattered clothing in neat piles at the foot and head respectively. He jumped as if he'd been stabbed in the kidneys.

Tadziki sat at the backup navigational console, facing aft. He was as still as a leopard in ambush. Occasionally in the past twenty minutes he'd blinked his eyes; when the alarm sounded, he blinked them again.

"It's time, then," he said to Carron. "Make the call."

"I think . . ." Carron said. He tried to lick his lips, but his tongue was dry also. ". . . that we ought to wait a, a few minutes."

"No," said Tadziki as he rose to his feet. "We shouldn't. You can either use the console, or the handset—"

He indicated the unit flexed to his console. Its keypad permitted handier access to some planetary communications nets than the voice-driven AIs built into commo helmets did.

"—or a helmet, if you'd be comfortable with that. But it has to be done at once. Preset five."

"Yes, I know it's preset five," Carron said. He flipped up the handset's cover, held the unit to his ear to be sure of the connection, and pressed SYSTEM/FIVE.

The *Swift*'s main hatch was open. Sounds of the spaceport rumbled through. At the graving dock nearby, polishing heads howled and paused, then howled again as they cleaned the hull of a freighter.

"I don't like having to do this," Carron said to Tadziki as circuits clicked in his ear. "I know it was my idea. But I don't like it."

"We aren't required to like it," the adjutant said, looking through the Pancahtan and into his own past life. "People depend on us, so we'll do our jobs. Lissea depends on us."

"I know . . ." Carron said.

The paired chimes of the ringing signal rattled silent. *"Yeah?"* a voice croaked. *"Two-two-one, ah . . . Fuck. Two-two-one-four."*

"Platt," Carron said imperiously, "this is Prince Carron Del Vore. You are to go into the laboratory at once and close the door of the device we brought in this afternoon."

"What?" the attendant said. *"What?"*

"Close the door of the device so that it latches, but don't slam it," Carron said. "Otherwise the atmosphere will degrade the interior and cause irreparable harm. And don't touch the mirrors surrounding the installation."

"Look, this isn't my job!" Platt cried. *"I'm not even supposed to go into the lab—I'm just here to watch the door!"*

"Platt," Carron said, as implacable as a priest of the Inquisition, "I will arrive in a few minutes with mercenaries from

the Pancahte Expedition. If you have not carried out my instructions to the letter, they will kill you. Hunt you down and
kill you, if necessary. Do you understand?''

"Yeah, yeah, I understand," the attendant whined. *"Look,
I'm doing it, I'm doing it right now. But I shouldn't have to,
you see?"*

Platt broke the connection.

Carron sighed and closed the handset. "The man's scum,"
he said to Tadziki. "But there must be thousands of people in
the building now. We don't have anything so large on Pancahte. So tall, at least. Because of the earthquakes."

Tadziki eased past the younger man and stood in the hatch,
looking outward.

"What happens now?" Carron asked. He hadn't been part
of the tactical planning from this point on.

"We wait," Tadziki said. "I wait, at least. You might want
to get out of the way, hide somewhere in Landfall City. I can
arrange credit for you if you don't have any of your own."

Carron stood beside the adjutant. An articulated three-
section roadtrain clanked slowly by on steel treads, carrying
heavy cargo. Tadziki was looking beyond it, and beyond anything visible.

"You think there's going to be trouble here, then?" Carron
asked.

"There's going to be a great deal of confusion," Tadziki
said. "If the state organization is good enough, there will certainly be police sent to arrest everyone aboard the *Swift*. I
don't expect that. There's a far greater chance of rioters attacking, however."

He smiled wanly at Carron. "Some of the men—men from
the ship's crew—didn't choose to be involved further. They'll
stay low in their hotel room until the business is done. The
combat personnel are where they need to be also. And I'm
here, because the potential need for a command post is greater
than the risk."

Tadziki's hand gripped the hatch coaming so hard that the
veins stood out. His skin blotched white and red because the
tense muscles cut off their own blood supply.

"I wouldn't be much good to Herne and the others," he said harshly toward Landfall City. "I'm a fat old man, and I could never hit anybody far enough away that his blood didn't splash me."

Carron looked at Tadziki and swallowed. "Yes," he said. "Well, I think I'll stay here too."

Dockyard machinery screamed like lost souls.

The limousine was parked in front of the building. It was unattended because both the security personnel from the vehicle were escorting Ned.

There were two similar cars whose driver/bodyguards were still present. Most of the board members would have come to the meeting via underground tramlines from their private residences within the estate rather than being driven.

The guards opened both doors of the limo's passenger compartment deferentially. The Telarian noble paused and said to Ned, "Did you really want to speak to me, or . . ."

Ned nodded. "Could we drive slowly around the estate for a moment?" he asked. "Back trails?"

"Yes, of course," Lucas said. He gestured to the man holding his door, the driver. "Go on, then."

Lucas looked drawn. People on the stone-flagged patio fronting the spire watched the tableau sidelong. The armed, uniformed attendants in front of the building were the only ones who felt they could openly stare at the folk who rode in limousines; and that only while Lucas and Ned stepped through the weapons detector that covered the entranceway.

Ned and Lucas got into the car from opposite sides. As soon as the doors *thunk*ed closed, Ned retrieved the needle stunner he'd hidden between the seat cushions during the ride from the spaceport. His body concealed what he was doing from his companion.

"Master Lucas," he said, "I don't like what's going to happen now—"

"You know this is none of my doing!" Lucas burst out. "I—I'll leave home, I won't stay on Telaria even, not after this. But it's already done, Slade. There's nothing I can do now!''

The guards closed themselves into the front with the same solid shocks as those the rear doors had made. Ned's view forward ignored the guards. The limousine pulled away silently, heading down a curving drive.

"I know that, Lucas," Ned said. "That's why I wanted you out of the building. You're not the only innocent person, I realize, but you're the only one I know personally."

"I don't understand," the Telarian said. He frowned as he tried to fit the mercenary's statement into a knowledge base which had no category for it.

Secondary trails within the estate were only wide enough for one car at a time, so there were pull-overs every half kilometer or so. The limo approached one of them. A bank of red and white flowers grew on the left side, with a bower of trees with long flexible tendrils in place of leaves on the right. There were no other persons or vehicles in sight.

"Just a moment," said Ned. He reached forward with his left index finger and touched the switch controlling the armored window between the front and rear compartments.

The driver started slightly at the sound. The guard broke off a comment about the soccer final and twisted to face the men in back. "Yes sir?" he said to Lucas.

"Would you please park here a moment?" Ned said.

Lucas nodded. "Yes, do that," he said. He looked disconcerted. "There's an intercom, you know," he added as the limousine pulled beneath the trees.

Ned shot the guard, then the driver, in the back of the neck with his stunner. The weapon clicked as its barrel coil snapped tiny needles out by electromagnetic repulsion.

The guard went into spastic convulsions while the fluctuating current passed between the opposite poles of the needle in his spine. The driver arched his back and became comatose. His foot slipped off the brake, but the limousine's mass held the vehicle steady against the idling motors.

Lucas screamed and slapped the door latch. Ned grabbed Lucas around the neck left-handed but didn't squeeze.

"Wait!" Ned shouted. "They'll be all right! *Don't* make me hurt you."

The door was ajar. Ned slid sideways, pushing Lucas ahead of him from the vehicle. He continued to hold the Telarian for fear the fool would try to run and he'd have to shoot him down. Needle stunners could do permanent nerve damage or even cause death through syncope. If Ned had wanted *that*, he'd have left the boy in the boardroom with his relatives.

"What are you doing?" Lucas gasped. "You can't get out of here, you know that! Am I a hostage?"

Ned opened the driver's door with the little finger of his right hand. The driver fell to the pavement in catatonic rigidity. His submachine gun and that of his fellow still stood muzzle-up in their boots on the central console.

"You're not a hostage," Ned said. At any moment, somebody might drive up and he'd have to kill them. "Look, this car has an autopilot, doesn't it? Program it to drive to the family chapel."

"But—"

"*Now,* curse you, now!" Ned said. He thrust Lucas' head and torso within the driver's compartment. He was bigger than the Telarian and stronger for his size, but it was the sheer violence of Ned's will that dominated Lucas utterly. The presence of the submachine guns within millimeters of Lucas' hands was no danger.

The Telarian called up a map on the dashboard screen. He touched a point on it without bothering to check the index of coordinates. The mechanism chimed obediently.

The guard thrashed again, then subsided. He'd lost control of his sphincter muscles, voiding his bladder and bowels. Lucas stared at the man in obvious terror.

Lucas withdrew from the car. "You can't get off-planet in your ship," he said to Ned. "The port defenses will destroy it before you're a thousand meters high. And even if you got to Dell, it's too late for Lissea—you *heard* my father!"

"Listen to me," Ned said. "If you're smart, you'll just lie low here for the next while. I don't care what you do, I don't care if you raise an alarm—it won't change anything now. But for your own sake, *don't* go back to the spire.''

Ned got into the limo. He dropped the stunner into his pocket—waste not, want not—and charged one of the submachine guns. He looked again at Lucas, still standing frozen above the uniformed driver. ''You've been as decent as you know how, Doormann,'' Ned said. ''I wish it didn't have to happen this way.''

He engaged the autopilot. The dash beeped at him chidingly: the rear door was open.

Ned crushed his boot down on the throttle pedal. The limousine's metal tires sang, chewing divots from the rubberized road material as they accelerated the heavy vehicle. Inertia slammed the door shut.

Ned lifted his foot and let the car drive itself as he checked the other submachine gun. Lucas stood in the center of the road, staring after the limousine until a curve took the vehicle out of sight.

Platt muttered to himself as he opened the laboratory door. He forgot to squint as he stepped inside, so the sudden harsh illumination slapped his eyes. The fog of fortified wine in his brain ignited in a fireball that made him curse desperately.

After a time, Platt regained enough composure to pick his way through the ranks of equipment with his eyes slitted. There was an unfamiliar humming in the big room, but he couldn't identify the source. Anyway, it might have been the wine.

The capsule squatted on the platform at the end of the lab, as ugly as an egg after hatching. Pareto, the night man, claimed there was a corpse in the thing when they found it, but Platt didn't watch the news himself much.

He didn't trust that bastard Pareto, either. Pareto kept asking for the lousy ten thalers he'd loaned Platt last . . . last— whenever it was.

Platt lurched into one of the mirror stands. It was anchored to the floor. Instead of toppling over, the stand threw the attendant back with the start of a bad bruise. He cursed again, rubbing himself and thinking about the unfairness of life.

The black concave mirror whined shrilly, then slowly returned to synchrony with the others.

Platt touched the door of the capsule, then leaped away. He thought he'd received an electric shock. When he rubbed his fingertips together, he realized that the feeling was simply high-frequency vibration.

Gingerly, he gripped the edge of the door and slammed it with all his strength. Air compressing within the ovoid prevented the *clang!* from being as violent as Platt would have liked.

The humming was louder. It appeared to be coming from around the capsule, rather than from the capsule itself. The attendant turned away and started for the door.

Red light bathed the room. Platt glanced over his shoulder, suddenly afraid to face fully around.

The capsule was glowing. Atoms within its structure were coming into sequence with their selves of seventy years before. The meld was not absolute, but as more and more points achieved unity, they dragged neighboring atoms into self-alignment also. Closing the front of the ovoid started the mass down a one-way road to critical perfection.

The capsule was fire-orange, then yellow. As the blaze verged into white, all trace of physical structure was lost within the radiance.

Platt tried to run. His uniform seared brown and the hair on the back of his head burst into flame. The hum was a roar and the fires of Hell were loose.

All the lights in the laboratory shattered, but their absence was unnoticeable. Platt threw himself behind a massive computer console, unable to hear his own screams. The soundproofing cones in the walls and ceiling sublimed and drifted as black cobwebs in fierce air currents.

Matter attempting to fill the same space as its own earlier/later self became the energy that alone could escape from the catastrophic paradox. Laboratory equipment shattered. Metals and plastics began to burn in temperatures beyond those achieved in the carbon-iron cycle of a dying sun.

Devouring radiance ionized the whole contents of the laboratory into plasma. A spear of light sprang up the long axis of what had been the capsule, piercing the armored ceiling above like an oxygen lance through tissue.

The humans on the floor above didn't have time to scream, nor did those on the floor above them; but the fire screamed like a god of destruction.

A switch on the dashboard could lock the tracks of the mobile crane into linked plates fifty centimeters long to lower the equipment's ground pressure on yielding surfaces. For this concrete roadway Westerbeke, who was driving, left the tracks at maximum flexibility. They sang at high frequency, giving the impression that the 80-tonne crane was moving much faster than its actual forty kilometers per hour.

A car that had been trapped behind the crane for some time managed to get into the center lane. It passed with its horn hooting angrily. Josie Paetz leaned out of the crane operator's cab and screamed, "Fuck you! Just fuck you!" to the vehicle.

Yazov drew him back. The boy had kept his guns hidden, so there was no harm done. "Let him be, Jose," Yazov said. "We'll have something real to do soon enough."

"Amen to that," Deke Warson said. His fingertips caressed a submachine gun beneath the tarp beside him on the crane's back deck. The big construction vehicle was taller than the other traffic, but guards on the wall surrounding the Doormann Estate could still look down on it. For the moment, the guards had nothing better to do.

Raff and Herne Lordling were in the driver's cab with Westerbeke. The rest of the mercenary crew rode on the back of the vehicle. They wore ponchos to conceal their battledress, body armor, and slung weapons.

The team was in position: the crane had been driving along the innermost lane of the highway paralleling the walled estate for the past five kilometers. Until the signal, the mercenaries could only gaze at the wall and the twenty-meter band of wired and mined wasteland protecting the Doormann family's privacy. Occasionally a blue-uniformed guard watched idly from the wall.

Every half kilometer stood another tower mounting a huge anti-starship weapon.

"When are we—" Josie Paetz said.

Something within the estate flashed brightly enough to be seen in the full sunlight.

"Got it!" Josie Paetz screamed, ripping off his poncho. Yazov clutched him. A moment later, Lordling ordered through the commo helmets, *"Don't anybody move! We've got to get closer to the gun tower before we move!"*

"Then get fucking moving," Deke Warson whispered through clenched teeth. Toll looked at him, but Deke was just letting off a touch of the pressure building in the instants before insertion.

When the column of light bloomed within the estate, the crane was nearly midway between a pair of the towers mounting 25-cm weapons. As the treads whined forward, the tower behind the mercenaries dropped out of sight because of the wall's curvature.

A pair of company guards, visible from the waist up, stood on the firing step of the wall outside the approaching tower. They were four meters above the road surface and across the buffer strip. The light from within the estate had broadened into a ball of iridescent rose-petals. The guards, a man and a woman, must have heard a sound inaudible over the singing chatter of the crane's treads, because they turned.

Westerbeke slipped the right-hand set of steering clutches but kept full power to the left track. The crane squealed and executed a right turn, heading directly toward the gun tower.

Westerbeke locked the track plates when he felt soil shift under the crane's weight. A series of antipersonnel mines went off harmlessly beneath the treads, whacking like a string of firecrackers. Dirt and black smoke flew out.

The guards on the wall spun back at the sound of the mines and the clanging treads. At least six of the mercenaries fired simultaneously, blowing the guards' heads and torsos apart in cyan fury.

An antivehicle mine containing at least ten kilos of high explosive went off under the left-hand tread. The track broke and the forward road wheel flew skyward. The men on the rear deck had to grab for handholds when the cab lifted, but Westerbeke kept the crane grinding onward.

The drive sprockets were at the rear. The vehicle held a nearly straight line, though one broken end of the track remained where it was on the ground. The wheels rode off it. Festoons of razor ribbon and vines streamed back from the running gear.

The huge powergun started to depress. The weapon couldn't be aimed low enough to bear on a vehicle already at the base of the tower, and the next gun position in either direction was out of sight. A guard ran from the building, tugging at his holster. Both Warson and Josie Paetz shot the fellow before his hand was fully around the butt of his pistol. The body, headless and eviscerated by the bolts, spun off the firing step like the others.

The crane hit two more big mines, both on the right. The vehicle tilted sideways, then settled back upright on its shattered road-wheels. Westerbeke disengaged the drive train.

Yazov clutched in the crane itself. The vehicle had come close enough that the end of its boom already projected above the wall. Yazov lowered the boom until it—a massive square-section girder—rested on the masonry. He shouted after his nephew, but Paetz was already racing up the boom ahead of the rest of the mercenaries.

The armored hatch in the side of the gun tower was open. A woman in blue was trying to tug it closed. Paetz fired toward the gap as he ran along the girder. His submachine gun put two bolts of the three-round burst into her head.

Paetz jumped to the parapet, then caromed within the tower structure as part of the same motion. A man crouched at a console with a microphone in one hand and a pistol in the other. Paetz fired, and Toll Warson fired his 2-cm weapon from the boom. The Telarian guard's right arm flew from his torso.

Warson's shot singed the hair from the back of Paetz' neck, but it probably saved the younger man's life as well. Even head shots with the submachine gun's lighter bolts might not have been instantly fatal.

A circular metal staircase with an open railing of tubes led up to the gunhouse. A guard hesitated on it, halfway through the opening to the upper chamber.

Paetz emptied the rest of the submachine gun's magazine into the man, igniting his clothing and blowing chunks of the stairway into dazzling sparks. The Telarian slipped down the treads, howling mindlessly and dragging a pink trail of intestine.

The room stank of ozone and burned meat. Paetz ejected the empty magazine and slapped a fresh one home in the well. Toll Warson swept past, aiming his powergun upward but letting his brother lead. Deke carried a submachine gun, and the lighter weapon would be quicker to swing onto targets from uncertain directions. They leaped the dying guard and pounded up the stairs.

There was no one in the gun chamber. Identical chairs and consoles sat right and left of the gun's breech and loading mechanism. They and the weapon rotated together with the floor of the chamber.

Screens above either console provided a three-hundred-and-sixty-degree panorama from the gun tower. Fine orange crosshatching covered the portion of the display showing the estate proper. Lockouts within the control system prevented the gun crew from accidentally aiming their weapon toward the area they were defending.

"We're clear here!" Toll Warson shouted down into the lower chamber. "We'll take care of the rest!"

Deke's miniature toolkit lay on the barbette floor beside him. He'd already removed the plate covering the front of one console.

The screen above Deke showed the spouting geyser of plasma which was devouring the estate's central tower, but he ignored it. He had work to do.

* * *

"Look at that!" Westerbeke said as he—last of the mercenaries to leave the mobile crane—jumped down to the wall's firing step. *"Look* at it!"

The clear exterior sheath of the office spire crumbled away, dropping in bits like snowflakes toward the mist of charged ions at the base of the building. The floors and the central support column containing the elevator and utility conduits looked like the remains of a fish after filleting.

The remnant was beginning to waver. Distance silenced the screams of humans who shook from the edges of the structure. Bits of furnishings and partition walls fell with them.

Cars on the six-lane highway slowed and pulled off on the median. Civilians were stopping to watch what they thought was a major accident. Harlow and Coyne eyed the scene. Together they raised their 2-cm weapons and opened fire, raking the soft-skinned vehicles.

Most Telarian cars used ion-transfer membranes to power hub-center electric motors. The fuel cells ruptured in balls of pale hydrogen flame which quickly involved upholstery and plastic body panels.

Survivors ran screaming, some into the path of oncoming vehicles. A tanker of petroleum-based sealant exploded into a huge orange mushroom, raining fire across the entire highway.

Coyne and Harlow crouched on the firing step to reload, then dropped to the mown sward within the estate to join their fellows.

"What the hell do you think you're playing at?" Herne Lordling grumbled.

Harlow grinned. "Just giving the cops something to worry about besides us," he said. "And having a little fun."

A one-lane road ran parallel to the boundary wall, separated by a few meters of grass. At one end it dipped over a hill in a profusion of pink and blue flowers. The moan of a loud klaxon swelled from that direction.

Ten of the mercenaries poised. Lordling gave Paetz and Yazov a two-fingered gesture to watch the wall behind them:

guards might approach along the firing step from the neighboring towers.

Westerbeke remained kneeling as he scrolled through the map display on the inner surface of his visor. The team had known neither its destination nor the point at which it would enter the estate, since the latter depended on when the spire's destruction gave them the signal to come over the wall. Westerbeke carried a pistol and a submachine gun, but his prime value in *this* company wasn't his marksmanship.

A three-wheeler carrying two guards and a tribarrel came over the rise at ninety kilometers per hour. Cyan bolts blew the Telarians out of their saddles before they had an inkling of the emergency they'd been summoned to deal with.

The trike lifted and was fully airborne when Raff put a rocket into the center of it. The little vehicle disintegrated in black smoke and bits of metal. Its klaxon cut off with a startled croak.

"Why'd you do that?!" Josie Paetz screamed at Raff. "D'ye want to fucking walk?"

"Paetz, watch your—" Herne Lordling began.

A second trike, running silent twenty meters behind the first, squealed and fishtailed as its driver broke the single rear tire loose in trying to stop. The gunner was desperately swinging his tribarrel toward the wall, but he didn't have a target when Paetz' one-handed burst killed him and his partner.

The three-wheeler twisted broadside and flipped at least a dozen times before it came to rest a hundred and fifty meters down the road. The riders, two of the three wheels, and shards of the instrument console lay scattered at angles to the main track.

"Blood *and* martyrs!" Ingried said in amazement.

"Shall we ride yours, then?" Raff said to Josie Paetz. "But good shooting, very good."

A half-tracked water tanker, marked FIRE and painted red with white stripes, rumbled into sight behind the wrecked three-wheelers. The four-man crew wore fire-retardant suits and helmets with neck flares as protection from falling debris.

The driver and one crewman baled out on the far side of the vehicle.

The truck coasted to a halt. The other man in the cab crawled out the driver's door, but one of the firefighters on the tailboard actually started paying out a hand-line toward the burning wreckage of a trike. When he saw eleven mercenaries in motley battledress running toward him, jingling with weapons, he froze.

None of the mercenaries fired. They jumped aboard the truck, clinging to the handholds above the tailboard and climbing on top of the four-kiloliter watertank.

Westerbeke got behind the wheel and drove the vehicle off. Paetz fired another one-hand burst at the pair of people he glimpsed at the edge of a grove two hundred meters away. They were grounds-maintenance personnel. He killed them both.

The firefighter standing by the road watched his hand-line jounce behind the disappearing truck like a thin white tail.

The limousine brought itself to a perfectly calibrated stop before a gray stone building, Gothic in styling but only seven meters high to its peak over the rose window. A black van, built on the body of a luxury car and polished to a soft gleam, was parked around to the side.

A number of civilians stood in front of the chapel, looking in the direction of what had been the central spire. They were all well dressed—not menials. One of them, a woman, wore clerical robes and collar. They stared in amazement as Ned, in tattered battledress and carrying a pair of submachine guns— one slung, the other in his hands—got out on the driver's side.

Ned's legs were shaky. "Where's Lendell's body?" he demanded in a high-pitched shout. "Where's the coffin?"

Klaxons rose and fell from several places within the Doormann estate. The unsynchronized moans were further distorted by Doppler effect as emergency vehicles sped through the growing chaos.

"Sir?" said the woman in clerical dress. "Sir? Who are you?"

A terrible sound drew Ned's head around despite his focus on the task at hand. The spire had begun to collapse. Because of the building's size, the process went on for more than thirty seconds. It seemed to take minutes.

The release of energy in the sub-basement laboratory had finally dissolved the concrete spine from which the upper floors were cantilevered. A cloud of plasma enveloped the lower hundred meters of the building. Now the upper portion of the structure sank slightly and began to tilt like a top at the end of its rotary motion.

Figures jumped or fell from the visible floors. They disappeared in the boiling ions beneath.

The spine plunged downward at an angle. Stress broke the upper levels apart while the lower portion of the huge structure simply crumbled in a disintegrating bath. The building dropped out of sight a moment before it hit the ground.

Seconds after the impact, dust and smoke sprang skyward in a great, flat-topped pillar that hid and smothered the sea of ions. The crash took ten seconds to arrive at the chapel. It went on for at least that long.

A man in the quiet black garb of an undertaker stared at the destruction. His legs folded beneath him. He knelt and began to pray, moving his lips, as tears rolled down his cheeks.

"The coffin!" Ned snarled. No one looked at him. He ran into the chapel. The swinging butt of one weapon knocked a splinter from the dark wood of the door panel.

The chapel was quiet. There were three closed pews in front for members of the Doormann family and six open rows behind for their retainers. Light streamed through stained-glass windows illustrating Old Testament scenes. The building was bowered in trees. The light—equal to north, south, and through the east-facing rose window over the door—was artificial.

A pair of folding trestles waited before the altar, but the coffin wasn't on them yet. The small door to the side behind the pulpit was open. Ned pushed through it.

He was in what would normally be a changing and storage room for the chapel staff. To the right was a staircase leading up to the choir loft. On the floor, Lendell Doormann grinned from the clear-topped casket the *Swift*'s crew had built on Wasatch 1029 and rebuilt on Dell. Beside the plastic box was a traditional coffin of dark, lustrously rubbed hardwood.

Ned stepped to the casket, looking around for a tool. The female cleric walked into the room. "Sir!" she cried. "You must leave at once!" Two of the undertaker's assistants stood in the doorway behind her, looking doubtful.

The woman grabbed Ned's arm. He pushed her away. A heavy screwdriver lay on the floor beside the coffin. He bent to pick it up.

"Sir!" the woman shouted. "I'm the Dean of Chapel! What are you doing?"

One of the assistants stepped forward with a set expression on his face.

Ned dropped the screwdriver to point his submachine gun. "Get out, you fuckheads!" he screamed. "Do I have to kill you? Get out!"

The dean got to her feet. "Sir," she said in a trembling voice, "this is sacrilege. You must leave here—"

She extended her hand. Ned took up the slack with his trigger-finger, then raised the muzzle and put a single bolt into the ceiling.

Shattered plaster exploded across the room. The undertaker's assistant grabbed the dean from behind. He dragged her back into the nave as the other assistant jumped out of the way. The three of them were gabbling unintelligibly.

Ned tried to sling the weapon he'd just fired. It clanked against the other submachine gun. He swore and dropped the gun beside him on the floor.

The plastic casket was welded smoothly all around the top. Ned set the screwdriver blade against the seam and slammed the butt of the tool with the heel of his right hand. The blade scrunched in, but only a few centimeters of the weld on either side broke.

A klaxon howled to a halt in front of the chapel. Voices

shouted to one another. Ned stretched out his foot and kicked the door shut as he levered the lid upward. More of the weld broke, but the transparent sheet Tadziki had used for the lid was too flexible either to lift away or shatter the way Ned wanted it to do.

He stepped back and brought his boot up hard, smashing his heel into the juncture just beyond where he'd managed to crack the bead. The gray sidepanel broke apart, tags of it still clinging to the clear top.

Ned grabbed the slung submachine gun and aimed toward the doorway. The door flew open. Two security guards burst in, one of them rolling in some desperate vision of how to enter a room safely against an armed man.

Their pistols were drawn. The rolling man fired into the wooden coffin as his partner shot a robe hanging on a peg in the far corner.

Ned hit the standing man twice in the upper chest. The guard's pistol flew out of his hand. His body fell, its legs tangled with those of the man on the floor. Ned fired a long burst into both guards.

Somebody in the nave screamed.

The guards' uniforms only smoldered, but the hanging robe managed to sustain a low, acrid flame. Smoke and ozone made Ned's eyes water. He stepped over the casket and laid the gun he'd just fired across its top.

The broken sidepanel permitted a two-hand grip on the lid. Ned pulled upward and back with all his strength, ripping the seam apart and flinging the submachine gun against the wall behind him.

Lendell Doormann lay now on his side, disturbed by the violence with which Ned had opened the casket. Ned rolled the body out. It was as light as a foam mannequin. He pulled up the layer of red baize from the stock of trade goods on Dell.

Lissea lay beneath the baize. Her eyes were closed, and her chest did not move.

Ned fumbled an injector out of his belt wallet. Klaxons outside the building were suddenly much louder: the chapel's outer door had opened. He reached over the casket for the gun with which he'd fired the shot into the ceiling. The limo's driver and guard had carried only four spare magazines between them, so he had to watch his ammo expenditure.

Ned aimed the submachine gun at the door with his right hand. Holding the injector against his left palm, he let his fingertips trail along Lissea's shoulder to the skin at the base of her throat. He squeezed down with his thumb, breaking the seal and triggering the injector.

Three Doormann security personnel rushed the door. They wore back-and-breast armor and helmets with faceshields.

Ned knelt behind the casket and blazed the twenty-nine rounds remaining in his magazine into the trio. The tightly grouped bolts chopped the guards apart in thunder and blue glare despite their armor. The Telarians were firing their submachine guns also, but wildly. The third guard shot the woman in front of him several times in the back before Ned killed him.

Ned groped behind him for the other gun he'd brought from the limo. The air was gray and his lungs burned. He supposed that was because of the flames and powergun residues, but maybe the security people had thrown tear gas at him.

Perhaps they hadn't used frag grenades because the body of a Doormann was in the room, but it was equally likely that such equipment wasn't an item of issue for security personnel. They were guards, after all, not combat troops.

Lissea groped at the edge of the casket.

Ned reached beneath Lissea's shoulders with his left arm and lifted her upright. Like her great-granduncle, she seemed almost weightless to Ned's adrenaline-fueled muscles.

"Oh Lord!" Ned gasped. "You're all right! Are you all right?"

Lissea clutched him. "I think you're supposed to kiss me, aren't you, prince?" she murmured.

Effects of the drug and its antidote suddenly washed her face saffron. She leaned out of the coffin and vomited the bile which was the sole content of her stomach.

Pews scraped in the nave. The door between the rooms was ajar. Ned took a chance. He got to his feet and stepped to the hinge side of the inward-opening door.

A whistle blew. Ned reached around the door left-handed and fired a short burst into the nave. Then he put his shoulder and full strength against the panel to slam it shut. A dead guard's foot was in the way. Ned kicked it free, then banged the panel against the jamb.

Bolts from the nave hit the panel, but the wood was heavy and the chapel's architect had added metal straps for the look of it. The security forces carried 1-cm pistols and submachine guns. If a few of them had been issued projectile weapons or even 2-cm powerguns, they'd have blasted through the door and the man behind it; but they weren't expected to fight a full-scale war.

They shouldn't have fucked with Lissea Doormann, then. . . .

"Ned!" Lissea screamed.

Smoke and haze swirled as security personnel outside the building jerked open a door that Ned hadn't noticed because the burning clerical robe hung beside it. The man lunging in hosed the room with his submachine gun, firing blind because his eyes weren't adapted to the smudgy atmosphere.

Ned tried to swing his weapon, but the target was on his left and the submachine gun was still in his left hand. The guard's line of bolts snapped toward him across the partition wall, chest-high.

Two cyan flashes lit the Telarian's faceshield, spraying a mist of vaporized plastic into the man's eyes. His hands flew upward.

Ned shot the guard in the throat and, as the Telarian toppled backward, sprayed the doorway and the further guards clustered there. They fell or scattered. He knelt and replaced his magazine, though there were still a few rounds in the one he dropped into his pocket.

Lissea climbed out of the casket, holding the pistol she'd scooped from the floor where a dying guard flung it. "Stairs!" she cried. "There's stairs behind you!"

"Go!" said Ned. He saw movement through the open doorway and shot, aiming crotch-high in case the guard was in body armor. Return fire chewed the door panel and jamb, but none of the security people outside were willing to rush the scene of sudden carnage again.

Lissea ran to the stairs, bending over as if she were in driving rain. She hesitated once, to tug a submachine gun out of the hands of a fallen guard. His fingers twitched mindlessly for the missing weapon.

Ned backed after her. The hiss*crack!* of bolts wove fiery nets across the changing room. Bits of stone exploded from the walls like shrapnel, stinging and even drawing blood. The door to the nave exploded in a welter of splinters and cyan as a dozen Telarians opened fire on it together.

More klaxons sounded outside the chapel. Many more klaxons.

The firetruck slowed. *"Hold your fire,"* Herne Lordling ordered. *"I'm not going to commit till I know what we're getting into."*

"Who died and made him God?" Josie Paetz muttered, but the three tense veterans on the tailboard with him were nodding grim agreement to Lordling's words.

There was heavy firing to the front of them, small arms and at least one tribarrel; no high explosive. Rushing into a doubtful situation was a good way to get killed. It wasn't a good way to accomplish anything useful, either, and staying alive was a higher priority of most of the *Swift*'s complement than a grand gesture was. They'd lived to become veterans, after all.

The truck plowed through a bed of white-flowering bushes. The bluff cab crushed the shrubs down, and the tracks supporting the rear of the vehicle chewed up foliage and spat it out behind.

The firetruck hadn't attracted dangerous attention in the midst of so much violence and confusion. Westerbeke was driving a straight vector to the rendezvous point. He didn't want to take chances with a road net designed for scenic vistas rather than high-speed communication.

As a sensible security precaution, there were no openly

available maps of the Doormann estate. The team didn't have time or the proper equipment to break into the estate's data base now.

Besides, the data base had probably been housed in the central spire.

In the cab, Lordling called up a chart of recent powergun discharges onto his visor display. The weapons' bursts of ionized copper atoms threw high spikes into the radio-frequency bands. The energy of each discharge was closely uniform within classes of weapon, permitting easy correlation between signal strength and range. Though the sensors built into a commo helmet were rudimentary in comparison to those of dedicated packs, they gave Lordling a fair schematic of the fighting half a klick ahead of the firetruck.

Shots had been fired from thirty-one points during the past five minutes, though some of the locations might have been alternate firing positions for a single weapon. Most of the points formed a pair of inwardly concave arcs a hundred meters apart. A gun or guns were also being fired frequently from the point squarely at the center of the common radii.

"*Set your helmets to receive,*" Lordling ordered. "*Now!*"

Copies of the display Lordling had summoned echoed on the visors of his team, then vanished. The men could recall it from their helmets' data storage if needed.

"*Yazov,*" Lordling continued, "*take four men and jump off in thirty seconds. Leg it into position. Don't start shooting until I give the signal from the other side. And don't forget, they may be getting reinforcements so you need to watch your back. Clear?*"

"*Worry about your end, Herne,*" Yazov said. "*I'll take care of mine. Harlow, Coyne . . . Hatton, I suppose.*" He didn't bother naming his nephew to the team he would lead. "*Execute—now!*"

The five men stepped off the truck's tailboard at the edge of a glade. The trees were forty meters high and waved brilliant streamers into the air to attract winged pollinators. The team quickly melted into the manicured shadows among the trunks.

The firetruck made a sharp turn in order to curve around the firefight. It growled out of sight.

Using hand signals, Yazov sent Harlow and Coyne out on the flanks. He didn't especially trust Hatton, an engine-room crewman, but he supposed the fellow would be all right if they kept an eye on him.

The fire team moved through the glade in line abreast, with a five-meter interval between troopers. Birds twittered invisibly, but the only sign of human beings was a woman's shoe caught in a branch high overhead. It looked badly weathered.

The estate was enormous, and the people working in it were concentrated in a relatively few nodes. With all that was going on, there shouldn't be many strollers out, either.

On the far side of the glade was a narrow path. It appeared to be made of brick laid in a herringbone pattern, but it had a rubbery resilience underfoot. They trotted across it.

The path was bordered by waist-high clumps of pink and magenta flowers, interspersed with saw-edged grasses that shot tufts up six or seven meters tall. Yazov had fought in vegetation like that before. He couldn't imagine anybody having the stuff around if he employed gardeners—or owned a flame-thrower.

"Yase, the shooting's died down," Josie called. "What do you think that's because?"

Yazov signaled his nephew angrily to shut up. The kid was good, no question; but he hadn't lived long enough to have good *sense*. Well, that was why Josh Paetz had sent his bastard brother Yazov along with Josie.

They'd come to a two-meter hedge growing along a low stone curb. Yazov signaled Josie to watch their backs: they didn't need a squad of locals jumping them from behind. The rest of the team flattened behind the curb and peered through the scaly lower branches of the hedge.

They were looking into a rectangular garden, fifty meters by one hundred. Walkways from corner to corner and down the long axis met at a stone fountain of four stacked bowls in the middle. Each quadrant had at its center a tree sculpted into a slim green spindle. The trees and stone benches scattered among artistically ragged plantings made it impossible to see everything within the garden from one point, and perhaps even from four points.

Yazov's team was arrayed on a long side of the garden. Within the rectangle and facing in the same direction along the parallel hedge on the far side were eighteen or twenty Doormann security personnel.

The guards had a three-wheeler. They'd parked the vehicle so that a large marble urn gave it a modicum of protection, but no one was crewing the pintle-mounted tribarrel at the moment. Instead, several Telarians crouched behind the trike, muttering over a casualty sprawled in a bed of variegated flowers.

The hedge had sere yellow scars where powergun bolts had pocked it. Portions of the foliage still smoldered. The large scallop which outgoing bolts from the tribarrel had cut was twenty meters from the trike's present position.

Other guards lay tensely prone, well back from the hedge so as not to draw fire. The fighting certainly wasn't over, but no one was shooting at the moment.

The hedge was thorny and impenetrable, at least to anything short of a bulldozer or some minutes' work with a cutting bar. There were arched bowers at each corner, however, giving access to the garden. The terrain on Yazov's side of the barrier was flat, with regular beds of knee-high flowers. They didn't provide any cover, but they were decent concealment.

Yazov keyed his commo helmet. *"Harlow and Coyne, opposite corners,"* he ordered. *"Wait for it. Paetz and I'll drive them to you. Hatton, watch our back. Paetz, take the crew around the tribarrel when you get the signal. Nobody get early or we'll get somebody killed. Move out."*

The end men scuttled into position. Both of them carried 2-cm weapons. At this range and these conditions, Yazov would as soon they had submachine guns, but they were pros. They'd manage.

Hatton faced around with an obvious air of relief. Josie thrust his left hand into the hedge to broaden his viewpoint. Yazov was ready to snap an order, but the younger man was merely eager, not rabid.

Nothing to do now but wait for the signal.

"Yase, why aren't they shooting?" Josie said over the spread-band radio net. *"Why're they just sitting there?"*

"They're waiting for something," Yazov explained. *"And don't ask me what it is because I don't know."*

What Yazov did know was that *"it,"* whatever it was, was nothing he wanted to be around to see. He took four fresh magazines out of their pouches and set them by his left hand, behind the stone curb.

"It would be nice if you got your thumbs out of your ass, Herne," he mouthed, but the thought wasn't even a whisper.

"Go," said the command channel, and Yazov's trigger finger had blasted the head off a Telarian security man before his ears caught the *whop!whop!whop!* of powerguns firing from Lordling's side of the double ambush.

Yazov swung to the next target, a guard lying prone who lifted her head to look at the comrade who'd died a few meters from her. Yazov's bolt converted her startled expression into a cyan flash.

One of the Telarians ministering to the casualty leaped to his feet; his two fellows tried to flatten when the shooting started. All three of them were down now, their limbs thrashing in their death throes. Josie had taken them out in three aimed bursts, though the separation between trigger-pulls was scarcely more than the normal cyclic delay of his submachine gun.

Coyne and Harlow both fired, but Yazov couldn't see their targets through his narrow niche in the hedge. A guard scrambled toward the tribarrel. Josie shot him in the cheek, ear, and temple. The victim's cap flew off and he plowed a furrow through ankle-high flowers with his face.

Yazov dropped his weapon, braced his left hand on the curb, and tugged a fragmentation cluster from its belt carrier. Simultaneous pressure from thumb and fingertips released and armed the weapon. Yazov gave the thumb-switch another poke to change the setting from TIME to AIR BURST, then lofted the bomb high over the hedge. A third squeeze on the thumb toggle would have set the fuse to CONTACT.

A guard, either wild with terror or trusting in his body armor, jumped up in a crouch behind the fountain. He held his submachine gun at waist height.

Harlow and Coyne shot him simultaneously in the torso. The ceramic breastplate shattered like a bomb under the paired 2-cm bolts. The guard's body did a back-flip, flinging his unfired weapon through the spray of the fountain.

The fragmentation cluster popped into three separate bomblets. They burst in red flashes two or three meters above the soil of the garden. Guards leaped up like a covey of birds rising. Five of them died in instantaneous gunfire from the waiting mercenaries.

A surviving guard waved his pistol from a clump of low-growing evergreens. Yazov shot the arm off and, as the screaming Telarian lurched upright, finished the job and the 2-cm weapon's five-round magazine.

Yazov stripped in a fresh clip. Coyne and Harlow stood in plain sight in the archways, raking the guards who cowered among the low plantings. Most of the Telarians were dead already, but the muscle spasms of a beheaded corpse were enough to draw a bolt for insurance.

Josie Paetz got to his feet, wild-eyed with enthusiasm. His submachine gun's iridium barrel glowed white.

"Wait!" Yazov ordered. He was still kneeling. He aimed his powergun at the gnarled base of the hedge plant. Six or eight stems twisted from the sprawling roots.

Yazov fired twice. The plant lifted on a blast of cyan plasma. The soil was moist enough to erupt into a cavity also. Splinters and microshards of terra cotta sprayed out in a circle.

The shrub's fragments fell into the garden, still tangled by thorns and interwoven branches. Josie Paetz leaped through the gap without hesitation, dragging branches with him further into the killing zone.

Yazov reloaded and followed more circumspectly, brushing grit off his faceshield. His mouth smiled, but the expression had nothing to do with what was going on in his mind. "Hatton, you can come on through," he said, "but keep your eyes on the back-trail."

The whole team was in the garden. Coyne stood at the tribarrel; Harlow checked the mechanism of the Telarian submachine gun in his left hand while he held the shimmering barrel of his 2-cm weapon safely off to the side.

Insects buzzed among the flowers. The firefight had done surprisingly little damage to the plantings, though the stench of the shooting and its results weighted the air worse than the miasma of any swamp.

A guard with no obvious injuries lay spread-eagled near the line Yazov followed across the garden. Blue flowers lapped her cheeks and neck.

Yazov swung his weapon one-handed, like a huge pistol. He fired into her back as he passed. Vaporized fluids turned bit of rib bone into shrapnel. The guard's head and heels lifted waist-high, then flopped again. The point-blank charge had virtually severed the body at its thickest point.

Better safe than sorry.

Yazov knelt at the far hedge. "Coming through!" he bellowed at the top of his lungs. There hadn't been any radio communication with Slade. "Coming through! Coming through!"

His own team was in position. Yazov held the powergun out at arm's length and fired into the root-stem juncture of a plant beyond the one he crouched behind. Powergun bolts had little penetration; the twisted branches and foliage of the hedge provided almost as much protection as a steel wall could have done.

The shrubbery blew apart as before. Splinters blazed, but the raggedly severed ends of the stems themselves were too green to do more than smolder.

There were still occasional shots in the near distance. With luck, that meant Lordling's team was policing up its area too.

"Coming through!" Yazov shouted again. Coyne seemed to think the tribarrel was operable, because he now crouched in the sidecar saddle with his hands on the weapon's double grips.

"Come on then, curse you!" cried a voice too cracked for

Yazov to identify the speaker. "And we're bloody glad to see you!"

Yazov risked a glance outward. This side of the garden faced a gray stone building. The facade was shattered by powergun bolts. A limousine and half a dozen emergency vehicles burned in front of the structure, a van of some sort burned around to the right side, and the lower floor of the building itself burned like the box of a wood stove.

The flames had driven Doormann security personnel out of the building. The bodies of at least a dozen guards lay in a straggling windrow where submachine-gun fire had laid them.

Ned Slade dangled Lissea Doormann from the cavity that had been a window on the second floor. She pushed off from the wall so that she landed in the drive, well clear of the black smoke gushing from the doorway. Slade jumped after her. It took him a moment to rise again to a crouch.

Yazov led his men through the hedge. Lordling's team appeared from the woods behind the shattered structure. The firetruck snorted along behind them as Westerbeke steered it between the well-spaced boles.

Lissea helped Slade stand. His commo helmet was skewed sideways. A powergun bolt had grazed it, melting the outer sheathing and shattering the ceramic core.

Slade reached down to grab the ammo pouch of a fallen guard. Lissea pulled him upright again. As the rescue team closed in on the couple from both directions, she kissed Slade full on the lips.

"Water!" Ned croaked. "Gimme—"

Three mercenaries thrust their condensing canteens at him. Herne Lordling tried to push the nipple of his canteen between Lissea's lips, like a clumsy father feeding a newborn. She snatched the canteen out of his hands and drank greedily on her own.

"Hey, Harlow," Coyne called. He was astride the driver's saddle of the captured trike, which he'd maneuvered out through the hedge despite the curb. "Come drive this thing and I'll work the tribarrel.''

"Have you got transportation?" Lissea asked Yazov.

The skin was peeling over her right cheekbone, and the brows and eyelashes were scorched away. Ned didn't remember how that had happened. It might have been a hostile bolt striking almost too close, but Lissea's own weapon could have done it when a guard lunged unexpectedly up the blazing staircase. The Telarian had grappled Ned from behind and was pushing him toward the window. Lissea leaned close to be sure of her target and fired one round.

"Like hell you'll get me on that!" Harlow said. "If I wanted to die, I'd eat my gun.''

"We've got a truck," Lordling said. "Westerbeke's coming in it." He looked drawn. Three of the two-magazine pouches of his bandolier were empty, and the submachine gun he carried now wasn't the weapon he'd had when he left the *Swift*.

"Chicken!" Coyne gibed. "Okay Hatton, *you* drive. And don't give me any lip!''

Hatton looked uncomfortable, but in the midst of a firefight, the big gunman was too high on the pecking order for a ship's crewman to object. Hatton took over the trike's steering chores as Coyne settled behind the tribarrel on the sidecar.

The firetruck pulled up beside the burning building. The troops climbed aboard. Men moved deliberately, as though they had walked forty klicks and knew that the day's work was not yet over.

"Here's a helmet, ma'am," Raff said to Lissea. "It was Ingried's. He bought it back there.''

The Racontid had four mutually opposable fingers on each hand. He gestured toward the woods with two of them while the other pair gripped the commo helmet he was offering to Lissea.

"He have any kin?" Ned wondered aloud.

"Get aboard *now* or we'll be telling yours that we left you behind," Herne Lordling snapped.

"We've been lucky," said Yazov. "We've been *bloody* lucky.''

The firetruck pulled out. Lissea and Herne were in the cab; Westerbeke drove. Ned hugged his chest close to the chromed vertical rail at the side of the tailboard. If he let himself dangle at arm's length, the first serious turn would send him flying from the vehicle.

Hatton started off leading the firetruck in normal escort fashion, then realized that Westerbeke would be choosing the course. The three-wheeler pulled onto the grassed shoulder to let the bigger vehicle accelerate past.

Coyne waved cheerfully. Ned wasn't sure the trike would even be able to follow on its small wheels if Westerbeke headed through soft terrain, but he didn't have enough energy to worry about that now.

Ned felt cold. His stomach was threatening to vomit up the water he'd drunk moments before. If his commo helmet worked, he could have listened to the chatter among the rest of the team, but he didn't have even that.

Raff, Yazov, and Paetz were on the tailboard with him. The Racontid looked at Ned's submachine gun, then lifted the weapon between paired fingers to stare at it muzzle-on.

Ned looked also. The iridium barrel had sublimed under heavy use until the bore was almost twice its normal diameter.

Ned grimaced and reached for the equipment pouch that should have carried two spare barrels and a barrel spanner. He wasn't wearing the pouch. His present gear was what he'd taken from the limousine's crew. Doormann Trading Company had never dreamed its guards would shoot a barrel out.

Raff grinned with a mouthful of square vegetarian teeth. He offered Ned the 2-cm weapon and bandolier which he wore slung beside his own rocket gun. "Better, yes?" he said.

"Better," Ned agreed. "Ingried's?"

He dropped the burned-out submachine gun onto the tailboard beside him.

"Ingried's," the Racontid confirmed.

The weight of the 2-cm weapon reassured Ned. When he draped the bandolier over his shoulder, it clacked against the pair of submachine gun magazines in the left side-pocket of his tunic. He thought the magazines must be empty or nearly so, but he didn't guess they were doing any harm where they were.

When the terrain rolled, Ned caught glimpses of the gun towers on the perimeter wall. The team was nearing its goal. Westerbeke had been keeping to the roads, perhaps in consideration of the men on the three-wheeler.

The firetruck approached a replica of a Greek temple on the crest of a barely perceptible knoll. The reliefs on the triangular pediment were painted in primary colors, with red and blue predominating. The stone of the structure itself was stained a creamy off-white.

Civilians stood on the temple porch, staring at the vehicles and the gang aboard them. The Telarians didn't appreciate that the mercenaries were really exactly what they looked like, a band of heavily armed pirates, murderous and as deadly as so many live grenades.

Coyne stood on his footboards and doffed his helmet to the watching civilians. Ned looked back sourly at him, wondering how the fellow could have the mental or physical energy left to clown.

A civilian shouted to the man next to her and pointed. She was looking at something in the distance.

The trike exploded in a jet of cyan brighter than the sun. The thunderclap of a 20-cm bolt from a tank's main gun shook even the heavy firetruck.

Ned raised his eyes. A tank, streaming stripped branches and pushing a mound of loam ahead of its bow skirts, shuddered its way through a belt of flowering dogwoods a kilometer away.

Ned reached to key his helmet, remembered that the radio didn't work, and checked the load of the 2-cm powergun that he'd ignored since Raff handed it to him. Ned was alive again, fully functional.

"Behind the building, fast!" Yazov shouted through the integral mike. *"Tank coming!"*

The firetruck fishtailed wildly. Westerbeke had failed to react quickly enough, and one of the others in the cab forced the steering wheel over against the driver's grip.

The second 20-cm bolt clipped the nearest of the four free-standing columns across the temple facade. If Westerbeke had made the hard left turn as ordered, at least half the bolt's energy would have centerpunched the vehicle instead of blasting a cavity in a wall of brick and climbing vines nearly a kilometer beyond the intended target.

The column, concrete beneath a marble finish, exploded violently. Head-sized fragments broke the shaft of the next pillar over and hammered the building's front wall. Concussion and flying stone knocked down all those standing on the porch. Calcium in the concrete blazed with a fierce white light.

The pediment lifted with the initial shock. It settled back, cracked, and fell on the twitching bodies beneath. Seeing Telarians killing their own people didn't make Ned feel better about the things he'd done; but it reminded him that this was war, and war had its own logic.

The firetruck pulled down the back of knoll on which the temple stood—at least a temple in appearance, whatever the Doormanns were using the structure for in present reality. Westerbeke had slowed to sixty kilometers per hour to maneuver: the full tank of water made the vehicle top-heavy as well as sluggish.

Ned bailed off the tailboard, reflexively executing a landing fall, and rolled upright again. Heartbeats after Ned left the firetruck, Raff, Paetz, and Yazov jumped away from it also.

The vehicle continued on, accelerating slowly out of its S-curve. Westerbeke kept the temple and the knoll itself between him and the hunting tank. The truck climbed a triple terrace of flowering shrubs and disappeared for the moment through an arched gateway.

An air-cushion tank was capable of twice the firetruck's best speed empty, and the half-track's path cross-country was unmistakable. The tank would destroy the truck and everyone aboard it—Lissea included—if somebody didn't stop the tank first.

That was what Ned Slade was here for. Somewhat to his surprise he found he was heading a team. He'd jumped at the side of the building, out of the tankers' line of sight only if he stayed low. The other three mercs scrambled toward him from the rear of the temple.

Ned waved them down. He stood, presenting his powergun and screened only by the mass of the temple beside him.

The tank had covered half the intervening distance. The driver didn't have enough field experience to handle the huge vehicle properly off-road, where the surface was less resistant than paving to highly pressurized air. He should have tilted his fan nacelles closer to vertical to keep a finger's breadth between the ground and the lower edge of his skirts. As it was, the tank plowed a shallow trench across the carefully tended soil.

The tank wasn't alone. Four air-cushion Jeeps, similar to those the *Swift* carried, flanked the bigger vehicle. Each Jeep mounted a tribarrel on a central pintle.

One of the gunners saw Ned and opened fire. His 2-cm bolts formed a quivering rope that smashed the side of the building like a wrecker's ball, several meters above their intended target.

Ned shot the gunner, shot his driver, and shot the driver of the other near-side Jeep. Then he ducked and ran as though he'd just lighted the fuse of a demolition charge.

Which, in a manner of speaking, he had. The tank turret rotated as the two Jeeps described complementary arcs and collided in a spray of plastic and bodies. The gunner of the second vehicle, the only crewman Ned hadn't killed, landed like a sack of flour thirty meters from the wreck.

The tank fired. Tribarrel bolts had punched holes in the temple wall, even though the weapon was firing at a slant. The charge of the 20-cm main gun blew the whole side of the building in. Because the concrete had no resilience, the enormous heat-shock shattered it. Refractory materiels sublimed instantly to gas. The concussion threw Ned flat and sprayed him with gravel-sized bits of wall.

Either the tank gunner was uncertain about what lurked in the eruption of dust and blazing lime, or he was rapt in a sudden orgy of destruction. The tank fired twice more into the temple, blasting inner partition walls and the furnishings into self-immolating fireballs. Trusses slipped because their support pillars were broken. The main roof tumbled in as the porch had done moments before. A jet of flame-shot smoke spurted from the wreckage.

Ned crawled blindly on his hands and knees, wheezing and trying to blink away the grit covering his eyeballs. His damaged helmet was gone, and the nose filters probably wouldn't have worked anyway.

Hands grabbed and held him as other hands expertly tied a moistened kerchief across his nose and mouth. "I had to get us better cover," Ned gasped when thought he could speak.

Raff held him; Yazov had provided the field-expedient filter. The dust cloud spread as it settled onto the rubble, covering an increasing area with its white pall. "Paetz," Ned ordered, "take out the Jeeps. The rest of you aim low, punch holes in the skirts. It can't move if the plenum chamber can't hold air."

He clambered onto a slab of concrete, looking for a firing position in the shifting wreckage. "Come on, out of sight! And don't shoot at the tank till I give the signal—they'll pull off if they figure what we're doing. Come on!"

Josie Paetz ran out at an angle from the collapsed building. A tribarrel chased the motion. Suspended dust flashed and scattered the concentrated packets of plasma well above the mercenary.

Paetz chose his point, ducked, and then rose again, firing when the two maneuvering Jeeps crossed in line with him, three hundred meters away. Both vehicles spun out of control.

The Jeep crews were in body armor. The burst of submachine-gun fire—it was only eight or nine rounds all told—wasn't enough to guarantee lethality with hits on armored torsos, so Josie aimed at faceshields. Although the haze of dust combed the bolts and reduced their effect, all four of the targets were dead before the careening vehicles flung them out.

Paetz ran back, hurling himself toward cover. The tank began to swing wide of the crumpled building, keeping two hundred meters clear. The main gun fired again, shocking the ruins like a boot kicking an ash pile.

Larger fragments sprayed outward; finely divided dust *whoomp*ed up into another mushroom. Ned fell sideways. Broken concrete slid, pinning his right boot. He couldn't breathe, couldn't see.

He flipped the sling over his head so his weapon hung crosswise on his chest, clearing both hands to tug at the weight holding his foot. The individual chunks were small enough, head-sized or thereabouts; but the jagged corners caught at one another like puzzle pieces. Some of them were still joined by twists of finger-thick reinforcing rod.

The main gun fired. The impact lifted Ned free and flung him in a stunning somersault down again on the bed of rubble.

By accident or design, the tank gunner was doing precisely the correct thing. So long as he continued to fire into the wrecked building, there was no chance that the mercenaries lairing there would be able to disable the tank. Disruption from the 20-cm bolts kept the team from aiming accurately, and there was a high likelihood that the huge impacts would kill them all despite the excellent cover the concrete provided.

The tank cruised parallel with what had been the long side of the temple. The turret was rotated ninety degrees from its midline carriage position, so the fat, stubby muzzle overhung the swell of the plenum chamber.

A line of cyan flashes licked across the tank's bow slope. Someone was shooting at the vehicle from straight ahead.

Ned unslung his weapon and leaned against a tilted slab to steady his aim. His vision danced cyan and its orange reciprocal, and his lungs felt as though he was trying to breathe the contents of a heated sandbag.

Herne Lordling stood in the track of the firetruck across the topmost of the three terraces. He turned his submachine gun sideways, loaded a fresh magazine, and emptied the weapon again in a single dazzling burst toward the Telarian tank.

There was absolutely nothing useful the light charges could do to the massively armored tank—

But they could draw the attention of the tank's crew, and they did so. The turret gimballed around to bear on the new target. Ned fired, Raff and Yazov fired, Josie Paetz fired—his submachine gun wasn't going to help any more than Herne's but it didn't matter; this was no time to save ammo.

The skirts surrounding the tank's plenum chamber were steel—thick but not as resistant to powergun bolts as the iridium armor of the hull. Ned and Yazov planted five bolts each along the swelling curve, blowing divots of white blazing steel and leaving holes you could stick your fist through.

The main gun fired. Everything within a meter of where Herne Lordling stood dissolved in a flash of blue so saturated it could have cut diamond.

Raff's first magazine of rockets had HE warheads. They left sooty black scars across the skirts, denting but not piercing the steel. The Racontid reloaded faster than Ned or Yazov. The next four rockets were tungsten penetrators that sparkled through the skirts, with at least a chance of clipping fan nacelles within the plenum chamber, besides.

The cushion of air which should have floated the tank's weight roared out through the holes in the skirts. The tank dug its port side still deeper in the soil and skidded to a halt. Its turret rotated toward the ruins again with the deliberation its great mass demanded.

Ned got up and ran, bandolier flapping and his heavy shoulder weapon held out at arm's length like an acrobat's balance bar. The team had disabled the tank, but they couldn't destroy it. There was nothing to stay around for except certain death from the battering the tank gun would give the ruined temple.

The building had been eight or nine meters across, though in collapse the fragments slumped over a wider area. Paetz and Yazov dodged around the rear of the pile and threw themselves down.

Raff had chosen a firing position on the far side of the ruin to begin with. The Racontid vanished to safety in a clumsy jump. His arms and legs flailed like those of a cat flung from a high window.

Ned stepped to a heap on the fractured roof from which to push off in a similar leap. He might break something when he landed six or eight meters away, might even knock himself silly, but the turret was turning and—

The mound was powder over a grid of reinforcing rods. Ned's right leg shot through a rectangular gap. The rods clamped him just above the knee. If they'd caught him just a little lower, inertia would have torn all the ligaments away from the joint. As it was, the pain was agonizing—and the thumb-thick rods held him as firmly as a bear trap.

Ned looked over his shoulder. The tank's 20-cm gun steadied in perfect line with his torso. In the far distance, motion in the corner of Ned's eye marked a second Telarian tank following the furrow dragged by the first. Cyan light so bright it was palpable engulfed the disabled tank.

The massively armored bow slope burst inward from the jet of plasma. Everything within the fighting compartment ionized instantly; ready charges for the main gun and the cupola tribarrel added their portion to the ravening destruction. The fusion bottle ruptured and the turret, a 60-tonne iridium casting, spun into the air like a flipped coin.

For a moment, Ned could neither see nor hear because of the blast. He had closed his eyes instinctively when the muzzle yawned to spew his own death, but eyelids could only filter, not bar, the cyan intensity. The shockwave of metal subliming in the energy flux made the air ring like a god's struck anvil. It lifted the turf in a series of ripples spreading from the point of impact on the tank's bow.

The anti-starship weapon from the gun tower on the eastern horizon fired again. The second Telarian tank exploded. This time the hull shattered. The vehicle's dense iridium flanks flew outward, crumpling like foil in a flame.

Deke and Toll Warson had removed the lockouts from the fire-control computers, thus turning the captured gun tower into a support base for the teams within the Doormann estate. They'd taken their bloody time about it, but close only counts in horseshoes—

And hand grenades.

Ned began to laugh, humor or hysteria, he really didn't care. "Hey!" he croaked, "somebody get me out of here! Hey, can anybody hear—"

Yazov's boots thumped on the rubble. Raff had flung the big man halfway up the pile as if he were a sandbag. Yazov scrambled closer, detaching the cutting bar from his belt. His nephew followed him in a similar high-angle trajectory.

Yazov thumbed the bar's trigger to test the tool. The blade hummed eagerly. "Some of them laughed when they saw all the gear I was carrying," he remarked smugly. " 'He'll need a Jeep, he can't walk with all that cop,' they said."

"*I'm* glad you've got it," Ned remarked. The veteran sounded perfectly normal: too normal. He wondered just how well Yazov was doing inside.

He wondered how well *he* was doing inside. He'd be all right so long as he kept everything on the surface, though.

"You bet you're glad," Yazov said. He chose a point, set the bar against it, and cut through the mild steel rods with a shriek and a shower of red sparks. "You can't have too much gear when it drops in the pot. You know that, don't you, Slade?"

"You bet," Ned agreed. When the powered blade howled through a second joint, he felt some of the pressure release. He still wasn't free.

Josie Paetz stood beside his uncle, changing the barrel of his submachine gun. He was smiling, all the way through. His face was more terrifying than the bore of a 20-cm powergun.

Yazov made a third careful cut. "There," he said, offering Ned his shoulder for a brace.

"I'll lift him," said Raff, who had climbed the ruin normally. The left side of the Racontid's body was blackened where a nearby bolt had singed the normally golden pelt.

The stench of burned hair clung to Raff, but he seemed to be in good shape regardless. His gentle strength raised Ned like a chain hoist, vertically, with none of the torquing that could shear and tear.

Ned checked his powergun. It had a full magazine. He must have reloaded after firing the second clip into the tank's skirts, but he couldn't imagine when or how he'd done it. "Let's get going," he said aloud.

His right leg hurt like hell, but it supported him. Raff nonetheless kept an unobtrusive grip on Ned's equipment belt as they descended the pile of debris.

"Cutting bars are great when you have to get in close, too," Yazov said conversationally. "You ever do that, Slade?"

"Yeah," Ned said. "Once. Lissea shot him off me."

They headed along the path the firetruck had torn across the grounds. The swale at the base of the terraces would have been boggy, but the landscape architects had run perforated tiles under the turf to a catch basin disguised in the base of a sundial.

"Well, keep it in mind," Yazov said. "Beats hell out of a gun butt. Though a sharp entrenching tool, that can work pretty well too."

Yazov sounded nonchalant, but he looked to the other side as the team skirted the crater of vitrified soil the main gun bolt had punched where Herne Lordling briefly stood. "You know," he added, "I never liked that bastard. I still don't. It's a hell of a thing. I still don't like him."

"I don't think it had much to do with liking," Ned said, wishing that his eyes didn't blur like this. "It was a matter of doing his job. Like we all did."

A smoothly resilient path led through the brick archway. The truck must have followed it, though they couldn't see the tread marks. For the moment, the gun tower that was their destination was out of sight also.

A klaxon moaned. The precise location was lost in the bordering shrubs, but it was close and getting closer.

The team melted into ambush position: Paetz and Yazov beneath flowering branches to the left, Raff in a similar position on the right, and Ned behind the end support of a stone bench set along the path for strollers. It wasn't good concealment, but it would protect his torso against even a 2-cm bolt. . . .

Yazov jumped up and ran into the center of the pathway. "Wait!" he cried, waving back to Ned who didn't have a commo helmet. "Wait! She's coming through!"

A three-wheeler skidded around the hedge-hidden corner twenty meters beyond the team. The metal tires chirped as

Lissea braked hard to keep from hitting Yazov. She brought the little vehicle to a chattering halt just short of the veteran and raised her faceshield.

Ned stumbled as he ran to the three-wheeler because he couldn't see for tears. "You're all right?" he said.

"You're all right?" Lissea echoed. "You're all all right?"

"Ma'am, you're out on this alone?" Yazov said doubtfully, checking the vehicle's tribarrel, still locked in its traveling position.

"It's what I could find after the truck bogged," Lissea said. "The fighting's over. Lucas is in charge. He's called a cease-fire with a general amnesty, and I've accepted."

"That's good," Ned said. "He's smart, Lucas is, but that's *good* too."

Then he added, "I'm glad I didn't kill him."

"Come on," Lissea said. "Everybody climb on. This will hold us if we're careful."

"It's an overload," Raff said doubtfully.

"Worse things have happened today," Ned said as he settled himself on the pillion. He put his left arm around Lissea's waist; the arm that didn't hold his well-used powergun.

Ned stood with his hands on his hip bones, staring north from the roof-level banquet hall of the Acme. At the large table placed in the center of the room for the discussions, Lissea and Lucas Doormann worked out the final wording of their agreement with a civilian lawyer each in support. Both lawyers were female.

If you knew where to look and you used moderate magnification, you could see that one of the anti-starship weapons on the Doormann estate's perimeter wall was trained on the hotel. The precaution was probably unnecessary, but nobody thought it was a bluff.

Nobody in his right mind thought it was a bluff.

There had been street traffic all night. Now that dawn had washed away the patterns of head- and tail-lights, the number of vehicles visible through the clear walls of the room increased exponentially. It seemed to be business as usual in Landfall City.

There had been virtually no damage in the city and rural areas outside the estate boundary. Within that perimeter, well—the Doormann Estate had been an enclave on the world it ruled. It would be some time before Telaria as a whole appreciated just what had happened on the previous day.

Ned made a sound in his throat.

"Sir?" said Deye, the Telarian in his late fifties standing at the window a few meters away. Deye was a military man by his carriage, though at the moment he wore ruffed civilian clothes. Lucas had made the Acme his temporary headquarters, but in this room, by agreement, the principals were supported by only two aides apiece.

"I was thinking," Ned said. "About what they're going to say. About us."

Deye nodded seriously. "I lost some friends today, Ensign Slade," he said.

The voices of the lawyers chirped at a high rate like gears meshing. They spoke and gestured simultaneously at the holographic display in the center of the table. The words fell into unison, as if the pair were giving a choral reading.

"But I want to say," Deye continued, "I'm proud to have faced you. I wouldn't have believed anybody could fight at the odds you faced. Fight and win, I'll give you that; you *won!*"

Ned looked at him. *Are you insane? We killed hundreds of people and most of them were civilians. We killed thousands of people, and we were ready to raze Landfall City to the ground if you hadn't capitulated!*

Aloud he said, "That isn't quite what I had in mind. And I . . . haven't quite processed everything that's gone on."

Deye's arm twitched. With a convulsive gesture, the Telarian extended his hand for Ned to shake or reject. He had the air of a man reaching into a furnace.

More embarrassed than he could have imagined ever being, Ned shook Deye's hand. Ned had bathed as soon as they reached the hotel, but he still felt as though his skin was sticky with blood.

"Agreed?" Lucas said on a rising inflexion.

Ned and Deye faced around.

"Agreed!" Lissea said, standing to extend her hand across the table to her cousin. The lawyers bent their heads together for a further whispered conversation as their principals shook on the deal.

Lissea stepped back from the table. "We can have the other parties in now," she said. "I think it will be best for me to present the terms so that they can be quite clear that I *am* in agreement."

"Yes, a good idea," Lucas said. He raised the multifunction stylus he'd been using as a light pen and spoke into the opposite end.

The door to the hall opened. "Yes sir?" said the attendant, a solid-looking woman named Joyner. She had been chief of Lucas Doormann's personal staff before yesterday's disaster wiped out Telaria's governmental bureaucracy.

"Send in the . . ." Lucas said. He paused, groping for a word other than "survivors." His attorney whispered to him.

"Send in the successors in interest, Joyner," Lucas said.

No one in the Acme wore a uniform, much less battledress, today. Ned wore ultramarine trousers and a teal jacket. The fabric was processed from the tendrils of a colonial invertebrate which floated in hectare-wide mats across the seas of Tethys. Ned looked more like somebody's date than a— whatever he was.

But when Joyner's eyes fell across him, her face congealed in a mixture of awe and terror.

Thirty-odd chairs had been arranged in a single row set forward from the room's flat partition wall. Ushers guided a file of men, women, and children from the doorway to their places. The principals sat; guardians, a mixture of attorneys and spouses out of the Doormann bloodline, stood behind the chairs of their underage principals. Some of the children were infants in the arms of mothers or nurses, but the range extended through adults in their fifties.

Grey and Duenya Doormann, Lissea's parents, sat in the two end-seats. They watched their daughter with as much suppressed nervousness as the others in their company did.

Lissea eyed the gathering. "Mesdames and sirs," she said. "Master Lucas, acting in his own behalf and for yourselves as agent, has come to an agreement with me regarding my claims against the Doormann Trading Company."

One of the infants began to cry. Its mother offered a bottle.

"The shares of my branch of the family, previously voted by the late Karel Doormann, have been transferred to my control," Lissea continued. "I have voted those shares in favor of Lucas Doormann to fill the position of President of Doormann Trading left vacant at his father's death."

There was a collective sigh of wonder and relief from the assembly. Two of the guardians began to whisper, then broke off when they noticed Ned watching them.

The infant cried louder. Its bottle bounced down onto the hand-loomed carpet brought in for the occasion. The mother lifted the child close to her face and began to croon under her breath.

"I myself," Lissea said, "will proceed to Alliance to set up an office there for Doormann Trading. I'll be traveling with my consort, Carron Del Vore, who has interests and expertise in the Twin Worlds. The recent opening of the Sole Solution to free trade will cause massive structural adjustments on the Twin Worlds. There are huge profits to be made by the companies which are first on the ground. We—"

The infant began to wail. Its mother rocked and stroked her child. Tears were running down the woman's cheeks. The man standing behind a neighboring chair bent over with a disapproving look to say something.

"The baby is all right," Ned said.

Everyone stared at him. The leaning man looked like a beast caught in the headlights.

"Babies cry," Ned said. His face muscles were as stiff as a gunstock. "It's all *right*."

Lissea glanced over her shoulder. She nodded, turned again, and said, "Master Slade is correct."

Clearing her throat she went on. "Doormann Trading Company will be in the forefront of the new expansion beyond the Sole Solution. I expect we'll be able to double our gross trade figures within the decade. Even with the higher margins due to long Transit distances, net increases should be in the order of twenty percent."

The mother took a soft block from her bag. The infant chewed it and gurgled.

"I would expect to be absent from Telaria for the foreseeable future," Lissea said in a cool, dry voice. "My father Grey will act as my agent when required, though all decisions regarding the normal running of Doormann Trading will be made by the president as before."

She looked across the row of her relatives and their representatives. Only a few of them would meet her eyes.

"Are there any questions?"

A seated woman of thirty or so, overweight and overjeweled, looked at Lissea, opened her mouth—

—caught Ned's expression from the corner of her eye—

I wasn't even thinking about her!

—and closed her mouth without speaking.

"Lissea and I," Lucas Doormann said, "have discussed yesterday's events and the situation that gave rise to them. Lest there be any question, let me say that everything that happened before today is a closed book. Doormann Trading Company is starting fresh, with a solid structure and bright prospects."

He looked at Lissea and added, "I appreciate the confidence Lissea has shown by supporting me for the position of president. I intend to show myself worthy of that confidence by focusing on the company's future. *No* one will be permitted to undermine that future by word or action."

The sitting and standing lines of representatives faced Lucas Doormann, but many of them watched Ned out of the corners of their eyes.

No one in his right mind thought it was a bluff.

"Very good," Lissea said, verbally gaveling the meeting closed. "I'm informed that the president will call an organizational meeting for the new board within the next few days. I may still be on Telaria at that time, but I won't be at the meeting. Therefore I'll take leave of all of you now.''

She bowed stiffly to the representatives, then glanced over her shoulder. "Ned," she said, "I need to see you for a few minutes in my suite.''

Lissea started for the door. Her lawyer got up and reached toward Lissea's shoulder for attention. Lissea batted the hand away. "Not now!" she said. Joyner opened the door as Lissea swept toward it with Ned silent at her heels.

The hallway was packed with aides, attendants, and Door-mann guards identifiable by the blue collar flashings on their civilian clothes. The security personnel broadened the corridor they already held open between the banquet hall and the bank of elevators.

Lissea got in with Ned and touched 12. The whole twelfth story had been converted into a suite for her and her burgeoning household. Ned waited till the elevator had dropped to midfloor and touched EMERGENCY STOP. A chime sounded three times before he got the access plate open with a tool from his wallet and switched off the alarm.

"We can talk in my suite," Lissea said. She licked her lips and added, "Carron isn't there.''

"That's all right," Ned said. He had to force himself to meet her eyes. "I wanted you to know that I'm going back to the *Swift* to pick up my pay from Tadziki. I'll ship out then. I'm not sure where to.''

Lissea backed against the side of the cage with a thump. "Ned, I want you to come to Alliance with me. I'll *need* you on Alliance. S-s-somebody I can trust.''

"No, I'm going to travel for a while," Ned said. "I . . . have some things to think about.''

He was staring at his own haunted eyes in the polished brass wall of the elevator cage. He'd looked away without realizing it.

Lissea took his hands. "Listen to me," she said. "Carron understands. But I made a promise to him, Ned. I can't . . . I shouldn't . . . break a promise like that. He put his life on the line.''

Ned grinned wryly. "Yeah, he did," he said. "Carron's a decent guy, and he's got a lot of guts. I wish you both well.''

"Ned!"

He looked at her again. Embarrassment forced his grin into a rictus.

"Don't you *care?*" she demanded. "I'm offering you everything I can. You know I am!''

"Lissea," he said, "I fought for you, I did things for you that I'd never have done for myself. I'd partner you anywhere in the universe. But I'm not anybody's consort. And I'm not *anybody's* puppy!''

He reached past her and touched EMERGENCY STOP again, releasing the cage.

Lissea's face was white. "Things can change, you know," she said harshly. "It might take time, a few years even, but I waited longer than that to get justice here on Telaria. You've got to take the long view sometimes, Ned!''

The cage stopped. The door opened onto a foyer full of servants and recently hired bodyguards nervously awaiting the arrival of the stalled elevator.

"I do take the long view," Ned said. "I want to be able to live with myself. Good-bye, Lissea.''

She stepped out of the cage with her back straight and her face composed. Ned touched LOBBY.

As the door closed, he thought of calling, "Lissea, I love you!''

But that would just have complicated matters.

Ned walked up the ramp of the *Swift*. Part of the engine-room hull plating was off. A mobile crane prepared to lift out one of the drive motors.

A rehab crew from the dockyard had made a pass over the main bay already. The bunks and lockers had been removed, the spray insulation stripped and replaced, and a fresh coat of robin's-egg-blue paint applied.

All that was fast work, but the *Swift* had become the private yacht of Mistress Lissea Doormann, the controlling stock-holder of Doormann Trading Company. The vessel would carry her and her immediate entourage to Alliance as soon as its reconditioning was complete.

Tadziki sat at the portable data unit placed before the aft bulkhead. Carron Del Vore was with him. Carron gave Ned a plaster smile.

"Hey, trooper!" the adjutant called. "The Warsons were just in, asking about you. How did the business go?"

Ned grinned back, slipping unconsciously from one persona to another because of Carron's presence. "Slicker 'n snot," he said, watching the prince blink in disgust. "Full amnesty, full pay and bonuses. The only thing Lucas would have called a deal-breaker was if Lissea had insisted on staying on Telaria. She already knew that was impossible after all the people we'd killed."

Carron nodded twice as though priming a pump to bring up his words. "Our new duties on Alliance should be very interesting, shouldn't they, Slade?" he said in a voice resembling that of a hanging man's.

"*Your* duties," Ned said nonchalantly. "I'm going to—I don't know, knock around a while. I've got no apologies for anything we did to get through the Sole Solution, but—"

His mouth quirked. "There's more widows and orphans on the Twin Worlds just now than I want to look at."

Tadziki watched Ned with a raised eyebrow, but he didn't enter the conversation.

"Ah . . ." said Carron. "Ah. I'd understood you'd be accompanying Lissea as her personal aide?"

"I regretted turning the offer down," Ned said evenly. "But I thought it was better that I do so."

Carron swallowed. "I see," he said with obvious relief. "Ah. Do you chance to know where Lissea is now?"

"Back in her suite in the Acme," Ned said. "At any rate, that's where she was going when I left her after the negotiations were complete."

"Master Slade, Master Tadziki," Carron said, nodding to

either man, "I'll leave you then. Good day."

Tadziki waited for the Pancahtan to stride down the ramp before saying, "A better day for *him* than he expected to be having a few minutes ago, anyway." Then he added, "You all right, Ned?"

"Via, I don't know," Ned said honestly. "I *will* be all right."

He looked around for someplace to sit. Apart from Tadziki's chair and the navigational consoles forward, there was nothing.

Tadziki slid a software file sideways and offered a corner of the portable data unit.

"No, that's all right," Ned said. "Look, I just came to draw my pay. I—"

His vision blurred for a moment. "I'd kind of like to get off Telaria without seeing the rest of the crew, do you know? I—"

He was choking. He swallowed. "Tadziki," he said, "they're the best there ever was. If I have grandchildren, I'll tell them *I* served with the Pancahte Expedition, with all of you. But when I see your faces, I think about things that I'm not ready to handle just now. Do you understand? Do *you* understand?"

"As it happens . . ." the adjutant said. His fingers called up a file. He loaded a credit-transfer chip. "I do."

He hit EXECUTE; the data unit chuckled to itself. He looked up at Ned. "You'll get over it," he added. "I don't say that as consolation—it isn't consolation. But everybody gets over it in time, you and me . . . and your uncle did, I'm sure."

The unit spat the loaded chip halfway out of the top slot. Tadziki pulled the chip the rest of the way and handed it to Ned.

Ned looked at the value imprinted on the face of the chip. He shook his head. "It's a lot of money, isn't it? For a soldier."

"It's never the money," Tadziki said. "Nobody does it for the money."

He smiled sadly at Ned. "Do you think you've proved

you're a man, then?'' he asked.

Ned blinked. "Is that how you see it?" he said.

"How do *you* see it, Ned?"

Ned looked toward the bulkhead and through as much time as he could remember. "I think . . ." he said, "that there's a guy named Ned Slade, a person. And I learned that there's a big universe out there, and that he hasn't seen much of it yet."

His face broke into an honest grin. He reached across the data unit. "It's been good to know you, Tadziki," he said. "With luck, we may meet again in a while."

"I'd like that," Tadziki said as they shook hands. To Ned's back, as the younger man walked out of the *Swift*'s hatch for the last time, Tadziki added, "When you're ready."

Ned watched through the fence surrounding Berth 41 as the integral cargo-handling machinery of the *Ajax* finished stowing within the vessel's hold the contents of a lowboy. The emptied lowboy whined away on its multitude of full-width rollers. The waiting line of eight similar vehicles jerked forward by fits and starts.

The *Ajax* was a mixed passenger/freight vessel displacing some four kilotonnes. She was configured for operations on less-developed worlds, where the port facilities might be limited to human stevedores and animal transport. On full-function ports like that serving Landfall City, the *Ajax* docked at outlying quays and still loaded as quickly as the port's own systems could manage at the more expensive berths.

The load that had just gone aboard the *Ajax* was small arms and ammunition.

Whistling "You Wonder Why I'm a Trooper" under his breath, Ned walked to the berth office, an extruded-plastic building set into the fence. Three sides were bleached white, but there were still traces of the original pink dye around the north-facing window- and door-jambs. A balding man in his mid-thirties stretched at the desk within. He covered his yawn when he saw Ned.

"Can I help you, sir?" he asked, politely but with a slight

wariness. "I'm Wilson, the purser."

"I was wondering where the *Ajax* was loading for," Ned said.

The walls of the small office were covered with holovision pinups of both men and women. The images ranged in tone from cheesecake to pornography that would be extreme on nine worlds out of ten. Apparently it was a tradition that the purser or supercargo of every ship using Berth 41 tacked up his or her taste.

"Looking for a job?" Wilson asked, eyeing Ned carefully.

Ned wore a casual tunic and slacks, brought from Tethys and stored on Telaria. The garments were pastel green and yellow respectively, with no military connotations.

Wilson gestured to the rickety chair before his desk. "Go on, have a seat."

"I'm not certificated," Ned said, sitting down. "I was just noticing your cargo."

Wilson frowned. "Look," he said defensively, "I know what you're thinking, but you're wrong. This isn't anything to do with that business yesterday. And we're not gunrunning; we've got all our licenses."

Ned laughed. "In broad daylight, out of Landfall City?" he said. "I know you're straight. I just want to know straight *what?*"

Wilson relaxed again. It was a hot day. His jacket and saucer hat hung on a peg behind the open door. "Well, it's like this," he explained. "A pharmaceuticals firm from Magellan, they tried to set up a base on an unidentified planet they'd found. It doesn't have a name and *I* don't have the coordinates—that's a trade secret. All I know is it's a jungle."

Ned nodded. When his head moved, the image of one of the pinups—a woman with Oriental features—performed an act that Ned would have thought was impossible for a human to achieve.

"Well," Wilson continued, "the folks from Magellan went in, and they got handed their heads. Literally. There weren't enough of them left alive to lift ship, and half the rescue force got killed besides. After that, they knew the size of the operation it was going to take.''

The pinups were tacked one over another in multiple layers. The image that had caught Ned's attention was stuck directly against the wall, but later-comers had carefully avoided covering the woman's amazing abilities.

"Magellan couldn't fund anything like that alone," Wilson said, "so they did a deal with Doormann Trading. Doormann supplies hardware and the capital to hire a support force. Magellan provides the science staff. And the coordinates, that's the big one.''

He tapped his electronic desk. "We're carrying the Doormann Trading share to Magellan. I don't know if they'll hire us to take part of the expedition from Magellan to the new site or not.''

"They'll be hiring on Magellan, then?" Ned said. "Guards, I mean.''

Wilson shrugged. "I can't imagine they wouldn't be," he said. "Curst good rates, too, I shouldn't be surprised. But if you're thinking we might give you passage on tick against your hiring bonus . . .''

The purser's voice trailed off. Ned noticed that Wilson didn't flatly bar the possibility.

"No, nothing like that," Ned said as he fished from his pocket the credit chip Tadziki had paid him a few hours earlier. He put the chip on the desk before Wilson. "If you've got a cabin open, you've got a passenger.''

Wilson's eyebrows rose when he saw the amount printed on the chip's exterior. "We've got cabins," he said, poising the chip at the edge of his desk's processing slot. "Only thing is—''

He looked up. "We're going to lift as soon as we've got the cargo loaded. Midnight, I'd guess, maybe an hour or two later. Is that a problem?''

Ned shook his head. "Suits me fine," he said. "I'll have my baggage sent over immediately.''

Wilson pushed the chip in far enough for the transport mechanism to take over. He entered the class and destination codes onto his keyboard. "We're getting a bonus for fast delivery,'' he explained as he typed. "That's why we're in a hurry to lift. With all that brouhaha yesterday, I thought it was going to hold us up. But the new bosses, they say the deal's still on.''

The desk chuckled to itself as it processed the data. Wilson smiled and stretched again. "Hey, wasn't that something yesterday? I've been talking to a couple of the port police. Via, what a hell of a business!''

Ned nodded. "That's the word, all right,'' he said. "Hell.''

A new chip, imprinted with the lower amount of the first chip less cost of passage, sprang from the output slot.

Wilson slid it over. "Here you go,'' he said. "Just show up an hour before liftoff or take your chances. We've got your identification from the credit transfer.''

The personal data from Ned's credit chip appeared on a small screen inset at an angle into the desktop. The purser glanced down as he referred to it, then blinked in astonishment. "Slade?'' he said. "*Edward* Slade of Tethys?''

Ned dropped the credit chip into his pocket again and stood up. "That's me,'' he said.

"But blood and martyrs, Master Slade!'' Wilson cried. "You're the guy? You're the one who took out two tanks with a submachine gun yesterday?''

"Me?'' said Ned as he walked out the door. "No, but that sounds like something my uncle Don might have done.''

The Berth 41 office was closed when Ned returned. Wilson lounged at the wicket of the fence with an armed crewman. Beyond, the *Ajax* gleamed in the beams of the positioning lights set in pits in the concrete.

The purser waved cheerfully at Ned's approach and called, "You're in plenty of time, Master Slade. We've stowed your baggage—four pieces, that was?''

"Four,'' Ned agreed, stepping through the wicket. Much of Ned's own gear was dress clothing, which he couldn't imagine needing on Magellan or thereafter. He was keeping the clothes, though. They were a link to . . . to home, to civilization; to life.

The lowboys had discharged their cargo, but the vessel's three holds were still open. A pair of service vehicles in Doormann Trading blue were parked before the hatches, and several figures there gestured conversationally.

The sailor with Wilson stared at Ned. Ned wondered what the purser had been telling the man.

"Also," Wilson said with a smirk, "your friend just came aboard. She'll be waiting in your cabin."

"Partner?" Ned said.

Wilson and the sailor exchanged quick glances. "Ah, yessir," Wilson said carefully. "A Mistress Schmidt from Dell. She said she was going to give you a sendoff to Magellan. Ah—is there a problem, sir?"

Ned grinned. He felt light enough to float into the starry sky. "No problem at all," he said as he walked down the light-taped path to the *Ajax,* to the future—

And to Lissea Doormann.

AUTHOR'S NOTE

The earliest form of the legend of Jason and the Argonauts can be reconstructed only from literary fragments and vase paintings. In this version, Jason appears to have sailed west, into the Adriatic, rather than east to the ends of the Black Sea. Readers with an interest in Greek myth will notice that I've adapted portions of this *Urmythus* in the plot of *The Voyage*. Most significantly, the original Jason doesn't sow the dragon's teeth. Rather, he yokes the bronze bulls to battle the water monster which guards the Golden Fleece.

I don't mean to imply that I ignored the *Argonautica* of the third century B.C. poet Apollonius Rhodius. On the contrary, Apollonius was my inspiration and main source.

The problem facing Apollonius is similar to that of a modern writer who intends to rework ancient myths. Apollonius was a cultured man working in a period of high civilization. His material, however, was that of the Heroic Age and would inevitably be compared to the use made of the Heroic Age by Dark Age writers like Homer (the two Homers, in my opinion).

The result is oddly disquieting. Apollonius was a very skillful writer. His characters are well drawn and their motivations are perfectly understandable to a modern reader. The problem is that the events and activities Apollonius describes are generally those of a much harsher period; a period that *wasn't* civilized, by his standards or by ours. The result reads like a saga about sensitive Vikings or the autobiography of a self-effacing quattrocentro duke.

The partial failure of an excellent craftsman like Apollonius was a warning to me. To achieve what I believe is a more suitable tone for my adaptation, I reread the *Iliad*. Frankly, Homer's stark vision of reality is closer to that of my own mind anyway.

Apollonius wasn't merely a negative model for me, either. Many of the classical authors had a remarkable talent for sketching minor characters with a line or two. Apollonius was near the forefront of that group.

The members of the *Swift*'s crew are generally the characters whom capsule descriptions in the *Argonautica* evoked in my mind. Thus Apollonius' Idas became my Herne Lordling; Telamon and Peleus became the Warson brothers; Calais and Zetes became the Boxalls (though here I mined Propertius as well); the young Meleager became Josie Paetz, while his two uncles were combined into the character of Yazov; Periclymenus became Raff—and so on.

Most (though not all) of the *Swift*'s layovers are from points Apollonius describes in the course of the *Argo,* though I've significantly reduced the number as well as changing their sequence. I've tried to maintain Apollonius' rough balance of events on the outward voyage, in Colchis, and on the return.

Because some readers will want to know the originals from which I built my fictions, and because (based on my past experience) most reviewers commenting on the sources will get them wrong, the equivalents are as follows:

Telaria/Iolcos;
Ajax Four/Mt Dindymon;
Mirandola/Lemnos;
Paixhans' Node/Salmydessos in Thrace;
Burr-Detlingen/the Isle of Thynni;
the Sole Solution/the Planctae (the Clashing Rocks);
Buin/the Island of Ares;
Pancahte/Colchis;
Wasatch 1029/Trinacria (which isn't really Sicily; but then, I don't suppose Colchis was much the way Apollonius describes the place either);
Kazan/a combination of Crete (which Talos guards) and the Po Valley;
Celandine/a combination of the Brygaean Islands and Drepane (Homer's Phaeacia);
Dell/Mt Pelion

Apollonius ends his poem just as the *Argo* comes back home to harbor. There's reason for his decision—the same reason that Eisenstein halts the action of the *The Battleship Potemkin* where he does: what comes next is pretty horrifying. I went on and described the return as well; partly because it is a major part of the myth, but primarily because I find it morally necessary—for me—to show precisely where certain courses of conduct and tricks of thought lead.

The use of force is *always* an answer to problems. Whether or not it's a satisfactory answer depends on a number of things, not least the personality of the person making the determination.

Force isn't an attractive answer, though. I would not be true to myself or to the people I served with in 1970 if I did not make that realization clear.

Dave Drake
Chatham County, NC

DAVID DRAKE

☐	51356-8	BIRDS OF PREY	$3.95 Canada $4.95
☐	51168-9	BRIDGEHEAD	$3.95 Canada $4.95
☐	50999-4	CROSS THE STARS	$3.95 Canada $4.95
☐	53605-3	DRAGON LORD	$3.95 Canada $4.50
☐	51332-0	FORLORN HOPE	$3.95 Canada $4.95
☐	53620-7	FORTRESS	$3.95 Canada $4.95
☐	50198-5	THE JUNGLE	$4.99 Canada $5.99
☐	52004-1	SKYRIPPER	$3.99 Canada $4.99
☐	51989-2	THE SQUARE DEAL: Car Warriors #1	$3.50 Canada $4.50

Buy them at your local bookstore or use this handy coupon:
Clip and mail this page with your order.

Publishers Book and Audio Mailing Service
P.O. Box 120159, Staten Island, NY 10312-0004

Please send me the book(s) I have checked above. I am enclosing $ _____
(Please add $1.50 for the first book, and $.50 for each additional book to cover postage and handling. Send check or money order only— no CODs.)

Name _____

Address _____

City _____ State / Zip _____

Please allow six weeks for delivery. Prices subject to change without notice.

MORE OF THE BEST IN SCIENCE FICTION

☐	50892-0	CHINA MOUNTAIN ZHANG
		Maureen F. McHugh
☐	51383-5	THE DARK BEYOND THE STARS
		Frank M. Robinson
☐	50180-2	DAYS OF ATONEMENT
		Walter Jon Williams
☐	55701-8	ECCE AND OLD EARTH
		Jack Vance
☐	52427-6	THE FORGE OF GOD
		Greg Bear
☐	51918-3	GLASS HOUSES
		Laura J. Mixon
☐	51096-8	HALO
		Tom Maddox
☐	50042-3	IVORY
		Mike Resnick
☐	50198-5	THE JUNGLE
		David Drake
☐	51623-0	ORBITAL RESONANCE
		John Barnes
☐	53014-4	THE RING OF CHARON
		Roger MacBride Allen

Prices:

- CHINA MOUNTAIN ZHANG — $3.99 / Canada $4.99
- THE DARK BEYOND THE STARS — $4.99 / Canada $5.99
- DAYS OF ATONEMENT — $4.99 / Canada $5.99
- ECCE AND OLD EARTH — $5.99 / Canada $6.99
- THE FORGE OF GOD — $5.99 / Canada $6.99
- GLASS HOUSES — $3.99 / Canada $4.99
- HALO — $3.99 / Canada $4.99
- IVORY — $4.95 / Canada $5.95
- THE JUNGLE — $4.99 / Canada $5.99
- ORBITAL RESONANCE — $3.99 / Canada $4.99
- THE RING OF CHARON — $4.95 / Canada $5.95

Buy them at your local bookstore or use this handy coupon:
Clip and mail this page with your order.

Publishers Book and Audio Mailing Service
P.O. Box 120159, Staten Island, NY 10312-0004

Please send me the book(s) I have checked above. I am enclosing $ _____ .
(Please add $1.50 for the first book, and $.50 for each additional book to cover postage and handling. Send check or money order only — no CODs.)

Name _____

Address _____

City _____ State / Zip _____

Please allow six weeks for delivery. Prices subject to change without notice.